Also by Michelle Spring

THE NIGHT
LAWYER

THE NIGHT LAWYER

A NOVEL
OF SUSPENSE

Michelle Spring

BALLANTINE BOOKS

NEW YORK

The Night Lawyer is a work of fiction. Names, characters, places, and
incidents are the products of the author's imagination
or are used fictitiously. Any resemblance to actual events,
locales, or persons, living or dead, is entirely coincidental.

Published in the United States by Ballantine Books,
an imprint of The Random House Publishing Group, a division
of Random House, Inc., New York.

BALLANTINE and colophon are registered trademarks
of Random House, Inc.

LIBRARY OF CONGRESS CATALOGING-IN-PUBLICATION DATA
Spring, Michelle.
The night lawyer : a novel of suspense / Michelle Spring.—1st ed.
p.   cm.
ISBN   0-345-43746-2 (HC) — ISBN   0-345-43748-9 (MM)
1. Women lawyers—Fiction. 2. Newspapers—Fiction.
3. London (England)—Fiction. I. Title.
PR6069.P725N54 2006
823'.914—dc22   2005058512

Printed in the United States of America on acid-free paper

www.ballantinebooks.com

2 4 6 8 9 7 5 3 1

First Edition

Book design by Victoria Wong

*This book is dedicated to Ashley Moffett
and to the other special friends
who saw me through the storm*

ACKNOWLEDGMENTS

My thanks to a number of people who were generous with help and advice during the preparation of this book, and especially to: Araminta Whitley and Peta Nightingale of Lucas Alexander Whitley, Jane Chelius of the Jane Chelius Literary Agency, Anna Moffat and Gay Harrington of Women in Docklands, Derrik Ferney, Black Belt in traditional Shotokan karate, Nick Hutchins of the Met Office, Gerry O'Donovan and Marsha Dunstan of the *Telegraph,* Harvey Kass and Mary Russell of the *Daily Mail,* Bob Black, Steve Livings, Ben Amey, and Steve Rawlings of Newham Emergency Security Services, Joe Blades of Ballantine/Random House, copyeditor Cecilia Hunt, as well as to Janet Parks, Cllr. Denise Jones, Mark Gelf, Josh Held, Broo Doherty, Selina Walker, Sheila Crowley, Kate Pullinger, Lesley Grant-Adamson, Sandy Mitchell, Dr. Natasha Maunther, Synnove Frydenlund, Dr. Ashley Moffett, Kathryn Skoyles, Daphne Wright, Lucy McCullagh, Rosa Held, Dr. Janet Reibstein, and the Unusual Suspects—Natasha Cooper, Manda Scott, Andrew Taylor, and Laura Wilson.

THE NIGHT
LAWYER

CHAPTER 1

Eleanor Porter doesn't look one little bit like a woman with murder on her conscience. She's not beautiful, but she has two outstanding assets that make her more conspicuous than she'd like. There's her reddish gold hair; it's long and full and curly, and, on damp days—of which there have been precious few this spring—it frizzes out and forms a halo round her face. There's also, on occasion, her cleavage. Though Ellie's scarcely aware of it, heads turn and grown men weaken when she shrugs off a shawl to reveal a well-cut black dress and a décolletage to die for.

Ellie's mother insists that it's crucial that girls should look good, and generally Ellie disagrees. Ellie would like to be judged not on her appearance, but on who she is and what she does. This morning, however, is different. It's Ellie's first day in her new job as night lawyer. She is a bag of nerves; because of that, she has spared nothing in her effort to look the part. No décolletage today. No little black dress. Instead, she has eased herself into a tailored suit with a narrow skirt, and tamed her hair into a prosaic plait. She made up her delicate features as artfully as she could. Before she left the house, she stood for minutes before the mirror, practicing a Gioconda smile. Ellie may be quaking in her court shoes, but she won't let it show on her face.

"You can do this," she whispers fiercely to herself, as she clicks shut her document case and steps out the door of her house. "They wouldn't have appointed you as night lawyer if they weren't confident you've got what it takes."

Night lawyer. She rolls the title around on her tongue as she covers the short distance to the Docklands Light Railway. Night lawyers are people possessed of nerve and impeccable judgment; that's what Harriet said. *Pompous or what?* Ellie thinks, as she smoothes her skirt and takes her seat on the train.

But Harriet hasn't been the only one to put an alarming slant on this night lawyer business. Ellie uses the short journey north to Canary Wharf to run through the things that the head of the legal department stressed during the interview. Clive was a short man, with a brisk, cheerful manner, and a tendency to pepper his conversation with random words in French. Just before he'd offered her the job, he had cleared his throat. "The night lawyer is responsible on his *or her* own," Clive had said—nodding pointedly at Eleanor, as if she might need to be reminded of her gender—"for the version of the paper that is finally sent to press. He *or she* is expected to approve the front page, or not, as the case may be. To ensure that, after the day lawyers have gone home, nothing creeps onto the page that could land the paper in court. If you're lax," said Clive, looking very serious indeed, "and if you wave everything through, there'll be damages to pay."

"And if I err on the side of caution?" Ellie asked.

"Even worse," Clive shot back. "Cut the good stories, and there'll be no news to sell. Editor will be down on you like a ton of bricks."

Eleanor alights from the train and hurries across the open space toward a sleek building with a stainless steel surface that reflects back the darkening sky. One Canada Square is where the *Chronicle* has its offices and it's a good address. It's the centerpiece of the Canary Wharf development and, some would say, the first skyscraper in Britain. It's a symbol of British confidence and prosperity. Wharfers call it simply "the tower."

Her smile resolutely in place, Ellie passes into the tower's vast luxurious lobby. She scrambles for her new identity card and flourishes it at the barrier. She locates the lift to the twenty-third floor.

Her shift begins at 5:45. Ellie arrives early, and wishes she hadn't. The day team aren't ready for her yet. She stands awkwardly in the narrow corridor waiting for Clive. As soon as he is free, he introduces her to the other members of the legal team. They are slipping into mackintoshes, snapping shut their briefcases, preparing to depart. Hands slide forward and clasp hers quickly. There are a few questions—Still no sign of rain? Did you used to work for Rogers & Quilter?—and one or two mildly curious glances. It's a courteous encounter, and a brief one. The day lawyers are there, all dark suits and gold wedding bands and practiced smiles, and then they are gone.

Clive beams as they depart. The day staff are a tightly knit team, he tells her. They swap stories, share ideas, and help one another out. They operate very much *ensemble*. But on the night shift, Eleanor's shift, it's different. Eleanor will work alone.

"Toute seule," Clive says, with an impish grin. "You're not a Night Lawyer, Miss Porter. You're *the* Night Lawyer. Singular, that's you."

CHAPTER 2

"A tour?" Clive asks, flourishing his hand in the direction of the newsroom.

"Oh, yes. Yes, please." Ellie is eager to take stock of her new domain.

Clive insists on starting with the library, where anything from magazine cuttings to a Serbo-Croat dictionary can be supplied. "A dictionary of Serbo-Croat, if you please," Clive says to the librarian, as if this is a particular point on which Ellie must be convinced, and they wait while someone goes to fetch one.

Clive parades her up and down thinly carpeted corridors. Past the mainframe computer, sealed in glass. Through the pre-press area, where pictures and advertisements are electronically manipulated before they're inserted into the finished page.

"Electronically manipulated?" Ellie says. "Sounds rather sinister, don't you think?"

"Just don't get caught in there yourself," Clive says, with a twinkle. He shuffles her past the goods lift, squeezing his way around tall metal trolleys. Ellie notices that they're stuffed with a bizarre assortment of objects: a birdhouse, a trio of rag dolls, a lamp. On a newspaper? "Home and Leisure section," Clive explains.

And everywhere she looks, there are clocks. Round-faced and metal-rimmed, they appear on every wall and in every alcove. Ellie spins on her heel and counts five.

"So you've noticed!" Clive says. "My dear, when you work for a newspaper, time is everything."

Clive is perhaps forty to Ellie's thirty, and the "my dear" sounds to Ellie's ears like an affectation designed to lend him an air of authority. But she doesn't want to hurt his feelings, so she smiles and lets it pass.

It is clear from the spring in his step that Clive enjoys showing Ellie around. He takes her elbow as if they were on promenade and steers her past the glass-paneled offices belonging to the design editor, the chief of layout, the managing editor, that line the outer walls. It's going-home time. Empty desk chairs point in the direction of office doors, as if the occupants had raced off in a hurry.

At last Clive escorts her into the muted light of the newsroom. Ellie can't help but catch her breath. This enormous room with its quiet gray carpet is not at all what she'd expected. Large oval tables are set out across the carpet like a string of islands in a vast ocean, their surfaces picked out by pools of cool light. People are positioned at intervals along their curved perimeters. They work steadily and unsensationally, their heads tilted toward computer screens like flowers to the sun.

Apart from the air conditioner's hum, the vast room is unexpectedly quiet; voices are subdued and words indistinct. There's an atmosphere of purposeful calm. Ellie can feel her own pulse starting to slow.

"Something wrong?" Clive asks.

"It's only—" Ellie stops abruptly. What she'd expected was Watergate, Deep Throat, Enron: the excitement of big stories breaking, the thrill of corruption exposed. A frenetic pace. An atmosphere vibrant with righteous reportage. "No, no. It's nothing." The hustle-bustle newsrooms of her mind echo to shouts of "Hold the front page!", a consequence, almost certainly, of too many Saturday afternoons spent snuggled down with Will watching films from the thirties and forties. Yet another way in which Will had led her astray.

"Come," Clive says. He is gentle now, sensing Ellie's shyness. "Come and meet the rest of your colleagues."

Clive trots her around the room, pointing out editors, sub-editors, and journalists, pausing here and there to make introductions. *Arts:* a friendly man with a delicate frame and a Glaswegian accent. *Current Affairs:* a woman whose spectacles, and even her jacket, resemble those of Elton John. A chap underneath a checked starter's flag in the motoring section who calls Ellie "love" in a calculating tone. The sheer quantity of information is overwhelming. Ellie's Gioconda smile is fading fast and she longs to be alone.

The assistant sports editor comes as a relief. She's the kind of girl with looks that seem made for television. A luminous complexion. Lustrous hair in subtle shades of blond. Long, lazy legs. But she has a name that Ellie will remember—Ariana Raine—and such compelling charm that when the journalist is called away, Ellie feels as if she's stepped into a draft.

"I'm so pleased to see another girl," Ariana says. "There are altogether too many men here. I've been hopelessly outnumbered." And, as they part, she adds, with a wink at Clive, "It's a *very* friendly place to work." Ellie hopes so.

At last the time has come to do some work. Clive briefs Ellie on the stories that have occupied the legals during the day. "If I were you," he says, "I'd watch that Tory Filbert case."

Ellie struggles to recall the story. She has been too concerned about preparing for the job to read the paper, and when it comes to dredging things up from earlier in the week, her memory—overloaded with Ella from Advertising and Lennie from Arts—doesn't cooperate.

"That fifteen-year-old, you know," Clive says with a trace of impatience. "The one who was stabbed by his classmates in Hackney?" He finds the reference on the screen. "Here. Watch it, my dear. The judge is out to hammer the media on this one. Other than that," he says, "it's pure routine."

"Routine?" Ellie echoes. *Not for me. None of it is routine for me.*

"Shouldn't give you any trouble," Clive says. He is watching her face.

Ellie can't resist the question. "What kind of trouble?"

Clive smiles broadly as if she's made a joke. He doesn't reply, but his eyes twinkle like those of a clean-shaven Father Christmas.

Ellie watches intently over Clive's shoulder as he opens the story on-screen and shows her how to mark it up. "You suggest an alternative phrasing like so," he says. He glances at Ellie. "Of course, you know all this?"

For a fraction of a second—a fraction that seems like hours—Ellie's mind empties of everything she learned at her retraining seminars. A knot of fear lodges in her stomach. Then she puts her chin in the air and looks straight at Clive, making him blink from the power of her pale gray gaze.

"Know it? Of course I know it. I'm *the* night lawyer. Aren't I?"

"*Toute seule,* Miss Porter," Clive says with a chuckle.

CHAPTER 3

Ellie Porter is nothing if not disciplined. Every spare minute, while the men from the Millwall Fire Brigade have held themselves in readiness for strike action, while the United States and Britain have prepared to launch attacks on Baghdad, while crocuses scattered beneath the trees in Island Gardens have blossomed and died, Ellie has struggled with Tekki Shodan. She has pegged away at her moves, and the effort has paid off. Her stance is firm. Her blocks are hard. Her kicks are swift and high.

Perfection, Ellie tells herself, but the corner of her mouth lifts in a giveaway smile. She may have mastered the individual steps, but to produce an impeccable kata—over fifty perfect movements in an unvarying sequence—is quite another matter.

"*Gankaku.*" Lawrence Striker spits out the name of another kata in a commanding tone. He begins to demonstrate the key position. It's known as Crane Leg Stance in English, but Ellie prefers the Japanese title: Tsuru Ashi Dachi. And again, because she likes the sound of it, she whispers to herself, "Tsuru Ashi Dachi." She keeps her lips more or less motionless and her eyes fixed on Striker.

Striker's feet are bare. He wears the gi, the loose white karate uniform, and he approaches Crane Leg Stance like a man doing under-water ballet. His movements are big and slow and assured. He settles his weight onto his right leg and flexes the knee and sinks toward the floor. He holds the crouch. He raises his left foot and hooks it behind his right knee.

Then, still in a cool and unhurried way, he folds his fists against his solar plexus and stares quietly off to the left. *Gankaku:* crane on a rock. Lawrence Striker, the crane, is poised to pounce on his prey.

Ellie corrects herself. He is not Lawrence Striker, strictly speaking, not even Mr. Striker or sir. According to karate etiquette, he's Sensei. Teacher. Master. Striker has the physical presence to match his title. He is a head taller than the tallest in the class. The bones in his hand, his foot, his jaw, are chiseled and unyielding. His skeleton exudes author-ity. Ellie doesn't much care for Sensei as a person; his coldness, his machinelike quality, his absolute humorlessness, repels her. But she respects his skill and she admires his courage; other black belts may justify their status by technical prowess, but Striker insists on defend-ing his rank by fighting.

Sensei continues to crouch, as unmoving as a mountain, in his po-sition of perpetual readiness. He is still, but he's not passive. Lawrence Striker, a black belt fourth dan, can shift into Tsuru Ashi Dachi in the blink of an eye. He can crouch one-legged for minutes on end, his bal-ance immaculate and his muscles firm. And from that stance, in less than a blink, he can deliver a snap kick that's high enough to hit a man's temple and ferocious enough to shatter his skull.

Sensei uncoils and draws himself upright. He addresses Ellie and her purple belt colleagues, while all around the room the other karate-ka listen and watch intently. "You've worked on Tekki Shodan in sections," he says. "The time has come to put it all together."

When, as now, Striker uses his everyday speaking voice, he has a barely discernible lisp. But when he barks out the harsh Japanese syl-lables, his tone is abrasive. "Tekki Shodan! Medium speed, no count."

The trio who stand shoulder to shoulder now are the only purple belts with white stripes in the Isle of Dogs Karate Club. On Ellie's left is Vikesh Patel, whose dedicated involvement with karate is marked by grace and consistency rather than by technique. He is screwing up his eyes in a desperate effort to recall the movements for Tekki Shodan.

"You can do it, Vik." She whispers it out of the corner of her mouth in a small act of rebellion. First names are forbidden in the dojo. Talking, unless Sensei invites it, is forbidden.

"You, too," Vik whispers back.

On Ellie's other side, Tony Mannix is shifting his weight from foot to foot, radiating nervous energy like a three-bar fire. In their last training session, Ellie screwed up a series of moves and Sensei tore a strip off her. Tony Mannix won't let it rest.

"Psssst. Porter! If you get lost, you can always follow me."

She just manages to whisper, "Up yours, Tony," before Sensei gives the order and they're off.

Tony opens fast and clear. His first block is as sharp and flat as a knife.

Vik begins late.

Ellie struggles with the opening movements—cross legs, dropping onto ball of foot, bottom extended. Her movements are jerky, like those of a dancer under strobe light.

It's only as they sink into the Horse-Riding Stance, Kiba Dachi, that the rhythm takes hold. The punches and blocks begin to flow like links in a chain, each movement calling forth the next. Ellie kicks and turns, and finally, at last, her muscles take over so she's no longer consciously thinking about the kata at all.

It's not over yet. There is a brief lull as the three of them look to the side before Nami Ashi. Harsh breathing, like the panting of a monster, bounces back at them from the walls. Ellie is distracted. Only by managing to track Tony's movements can she locate herself in the kata once again.

For a few exhilarating seconds, the trio move crablike across the dojo, shifting and turning in synchrony. Ellie's confidence leaps. The kata has taken on its own momentum now. As if a switch has been flicked, she finds herself performing at greater speed. She can feel the triumph in the final quarter of her kata: it is swift and fluent and fierce.

And when she completes the sequence—with a block to the left and a double punch to the right—Ellie feels a surge of triumph. She feels as if she has just climbed a mountain, swum a river, slain a dragon. As if she has raised her sling and brought the giant thundering to the ground.

I did it! Ellie feels a sweep of joy as she stands at attention between Vik and Tony in the absolute silence of the gym. There's no coughing at the completion of the kata. No fidgeting. Even the juniors are still. The heat begins to rise off Ellie's body in waves.

"Miss Porter." Sensei summons her out of line.

Ellie steps forward, struggling to ignore that incongruous lisp. She is suddenly aware that her uniform clings to her shoulder blades and that there is sweat trickling down between her breasts. A cramp settles into her right calf. She tries unobtrusively to stretch her leg, but she keeps her eyes firmly fixed on Sensei's face. He's going to tell her off for that hesitant opening, she's sure of it, but she won't let him bring her down. Her ending was terrific, and that's what she intends to remember. She tips her head back to meet Sensei's gaze. *"Uss,"* she says. Which means, in karate-speak: yes. I hear you. I'm paying attention. You're the boss.

"You know about the grading? In June?"

Karate works to a strict hierarchy: teacher versus pupil; senior versus junior; higher grades versus lower. At each of the quarterly gradings, members of the class are selected to try for promotion. To perform their katas in front of examiners. To demonstrate rigor in the tough kumite exercises. If they're advanced enough, to fight. Novices who perform well in their first grading are entitled to wear a belt of royal blue. Blue belts who are successful move up to red. Red belts climb to orange, and orange to yellow, and so on, through a hierarchy as intricate as embroidery.

"Uss, Sensei." Of course she knows. The grading, announced weeks ago, is specifically for candidates aiming for brown belt, the rank of experts-in-waiting, of seniors whose technique, self-control, and confidence in action are outstanding enough to mark them out as the potential black belts of the future. No one from their club has been put forward, but Ellie plans to attend just to see what it's like.

"I'm putting you forward for third Kyu."

"I—I beg your pardon?" A fresh flush of crimson rushes up to her cheeks. Third Kyu—brown belt! Can this be true?

"You have work to do. You must make yourself ready."

Everyone knows that Sensei is not one for praise. No superlatives, not even to encourage the juniors. *Not bad,* Sensei will say, after an excellent performance, or *Better than before,* as if the balm of approval might corrupt their souls.

And now he has given her the highest praise of all. He has singled her out—her, Ellie Porter; not Tony Mannix, not Vikesh Patel—for promotion. One part of her kata today was bloody good, she knows that, but still . . . After astonishment comes exhilaration. *Me. Ellie Porter. Brown belt!*

And then the alarm. *June? Oh, my God.* Ellie calculates quickly. The seventh of June is just around the corner. It can't be done. Her katas are far from perfect. And more worrying still—

She glances at her closest colleagues. There's an expression of surprise on Vik's face, but he lowers one eyelid in the most subtle of winks. Tony Mannix looks rigidly ahead, avoiding her glance. His fists are clenched and the veins stand up on the backs of his hands.

Sensei waits. His blue eyes, cold and apparently indifferent, have settled on hers.

"Sensei, if I may speak, please." Ellie knows that he despises excuses, but she finds herself unable to pull back. "Part of the grading, Sensei—the sparring. I'm not ready to . . ."

He holds up a hand for silence. The juniors fall silent and so does Ellie.

"I've made my decision, Miss Porter." He scans the rest of the class as if searching for any reckless soul who might dare to object. Seeing no sign of resistance, he shrugs with an elaborate shifting of the shoulders. "You will compete. Whether or not you pass will depend on how hard you work. It's up to you." In the years that Ellie has been training in karate, she has rarely seen Sensei smile. He does so now, an uncertain grimace that signals an end to the discussion.

Ellie bows. "*Uss,* Sensei."

Whether or not you pass . . . ? Well, if Ellie goes in for the grading, one thing is certain. She's going to give it her all. She has the best part of twelve weeks. She'll practice, she'll work out, she'll raise her fitness, she'll go over and over the syllabus until she can practically teach it. She's fit, she's stronger than she's ever been, and she is very, very determined. Why shouldn't she pass?

"Sensei?"

Striker swings around in surprise. He thought the conversation had ended. But etiquette or not, Ellie has to tell him, and she can't hold back a smile as she does so.

"Sensei," she says, "I promise you: even if it kills me, I'll be ready."

CHAPTER 4

Ellie had once, over their second bottle of wine, in a rare moment of indiscretion, told a friend that karate had saved her life. The friend laughed and changed the subject. *Saved my life.* That conversation, we say, that coin for the loo, that cup of coffee: saved my life. It's a hyperbole, a throwaway line, a cliché. Everyone knows it's not to be taken seriously. But Ellie means it seriously. She means it literally. *Karate saved my life.*

Three years ago, Ellie had what people euphemistically refer to as a breakdown. *My daughter can no longer function on her own,* that's what Ellie's mother had told the authorities, in her irritating imitation of a genteel accent. Unable to function: Ellie did not even bother to deny it. She had not had the slightest desire to *function.* Eating, sleeping, working, washing—all the mundane activities that make up a functioning life—had ceased to be of interest when William De-Quoyne had abandoned her.

Ellie was admitted to a psychiatric unit, where her alienation from the world was heightened by humdrum hospital days and drawn-out desperate nights. It was only through the discovery of the restorative value of Terry's Chocolate Orange—a chance gift from her friend Harriet—that she began to rebuild a sense of purpose. From that moment on, Ellie used slices of Terry's to give meaning to her day. She turned it into an art form. Each successive segment was admired for its smoothness, its crescent shape, its uncompromising color of sooty brown. When the nurse wasn't watching, Ellie would insert a segment between her lips and press it onto her upper palate like a dental plate. She would hold it in place with the tip of her tongue while the sleek surface softened and yielded. She would draw out liquid strands of chocolate and send them trickling down her throat. In a supreme act of focus, she learned to make a single segment last the full fifteen minutes until time came around for the next.

She came out of her weeks in the psychiatric unit with an addiction to chocolate and a stomach the size of a basketball. Gone was her hard-earned job in a criminal practice. Gone was the only man who'd ever really mattered. Gone was her last shred of self-confidence. She was a wreck—another cliché, of course, but just one glance at the unkempt hair and the dirt under her fingernails and you'd know that it was true.

From the moment Ellie arrived home—forced to live temporarily with her mother again—Annabel harped on endlessly about Ellie's weight.

"Honestly, Eleanor, to let yourself go like this. It's such a waste," her mother said.

When this tactic didn't work, Annabel tried another. "Weight Watchers, Eleanor, have you thought of that? For the support."

Ellie shuddered at the idea of Weight Watchers. It sounded like a club. It sounded like torture. "All together now" has never been a phrase to gladden Ellie's heart.

"Exercise, then. What about aerobics?"

Ellie fixed her with a stony stare, but Annabel wouldn't be silenced. She glanced pointedly at the antidepressant tablets on Ellie's bedside table. "Anyway," she said with a shrug, "you'll never feel truly better, Eleanor, until you look like a woman again."

Annabel's ring-studded fingers smoothed the flat front of her own trousers as she spoke. She had told Ellie often enough—had told anyone who would listen—that she hadn't put an inch on her waist since the day she'd married Ellie's father. "And, Eleanor?" The ultimate warning: "If you ever want to attract another man, you'd better lose some weight."

It was a threat that cut no ice with Ellie. Another man? No way.

Will had been man enough. She'd loved him, she'd lost him, and that was decisively that.

But Annabel kept up the campaign, and in the end, too tired to field any more excuses, Ellie shuffled into a long narrow studio with a sprung wooden floor in search of Fab Abs, Tums, and Bums. She got the day wrong. The door was firmly closed before it registered on her that this wasn't aerobics at all.

In the room, there were two dozen people, all wearing loose white trousers rolled up around their ankles. Twenty-four bare chests showed through the V of white cotton jackets. Forty-eight feet, all bare and vulnerable-looking, paced the wooden floor.

The athletes stood shoulder to shoulder in two lines along the length of the room. There was the kind of tautness in the air that radiates from members of a chorus line just before they burst into song. But when at last, in response to a command, the karate-ka moved, there was none of the razzmatazz of a musical chorus. There was, instead, a muscular intensity, sinew on sinew, bone on bone, that meshed with some matching rhythm in Ellie's soul.

Ichi! Ni! San! Shi! Go! . . . One! Two! Three! Four! Five!

On command, the athletes broke into movement, straining up and down the room, still in line. They twirled with fists clenched above their heads and shouted in unison. They jumped and landed on the balls of their feet. The gymnasium pulsated with the thump of feet on floor, the swish of fabric, and the beat of breaths.

If Ellie was required to identify the one thing that thrilled her most about karate in that first stolen glimpse, she would say it was the absence of speech. Since Will's departure, she'd become impatient with a world that was cluttered with language. Speech—that so often said less than was wanted, or more than intended—made her bone weary. But in the dojo—as she quickly learned to call the training area—all speech was honed down to guttural commands.

Ellie stood spellbound on the sidelines. When she tired of standing, she braced her back against the cool wall and slid down to rest her bottom on the floor. She had, as always, a chocolate orange in her pocket, but she forgot to eat a single segment.

No one seemed to notice her. All eyes were on the instructor, who was tall and dark and moved with a ferocious grace.

After the class had disbanded, when only a solitary student remained, Ellie gathered her courage and approached the instructor. He was demonstrating a side snap kick from the hip: out and up, slow and powerful. Ellie stood quietly by his elbow, waiting. When he finally acknowledged her, she cleared her throat and spoke as firmly as she could.

"I'd like to join," she said. "I want to learn karate."

Lawrence Striker looked mildly astonished at the sight of this plump young woman, pale and ill-kempt, with long flaming hair. Ellie was surprised too. For the first time in months, here was something she actually wanted.

It's quite, quite simple, Ellie thought to herself that night, lying in bed at her mother's house.

Some people's longings are fierce and sharp and sour.

To live in luxury. The gated compound, the car lined with leather, the legroom on a plane.

To have power. To lord it over others. To make them cringe and cower. To make them take the blame.

To be at the center of things. To be so important, so indispensable, that one never, ever has to be alone.

Ellie cares for none of these things. Not anymore. There was something she'd wanted fiercely for a time, but it was taken from her, and her longings now are simpler and more practical.

She wants to be independent: financially, physically, and emotionally. She wants to be calm and strong and secure.

Ellie Porter took to karate like a duck to water.

Determined to become fit and robust.

Determined to be forceful.

And then—impregnable? She considered, her chest swelling. But she rejected the word as too sexualized.

Impermeable. Impenetrable. That's it. That's what she'd become.

Invulnerable. Invincible. Inviolable.

Safe.

And, for the first time in twenty-two years, free from fear.

CHAPTER 5

The week has been so packed full of incident that Ellie's head is spinning. She has spent hours pondering the best way to prepare for her grading. She's drawn up a plan. She pulls a clipboard out of her document case and takes a quick peek. It's comprehensive and clear. Twelve weeks in total. During weeks one to four she'll learn in detail the four quarters of her kata, from weeks five to eight she'll refine her technique one quarter at a time, and from week nine onward she'll put the whole thing together; speed and fluency will be her aim. In addition, she'll step up her fitness training. Three runs a week, increasing speed with each run; two sessions in the gym, one working on her upper body and the other on her legs and hips and back. It will be tough, but she will do it even if everything else—her garden, shopping, socializing, reading—has to go to hell in a handbag. She ticks off the boxes for week one—two runs, two workouts with weights, two training sessions, and attention to her kata. Tick. Tick. Tick. Tick. The sight of all those little ticks in all those little boxes fills her with satisfaction. She slides the clipboard back into its place at just the moment that Clive enters the newsroom. He pads around the foreign desk and heads straight toward her workstation.

"There you are," he says, "bright and early as usual. And looking very well, if I may say so. It's your second week, little Elle. Any thoughts on how it's going?"

"The work, you mean? I'm enjoying it, Clive. It's fun not knowing what stories will come up. There's something different every day. The only thing—"

"Yes?"

"I feel as if I haven't really been tested yet. The day team are so efficient; they've vetted most of the copy before I come on shift. I haven't had a difficult story to deal with yet. It feels a bit as if I'm waiting for the ax to fall."

"Ho, I shouldn't worry too much about that, my dear. You'll get your chance soon enough to show what you can do. Now," Clive says, with a quick glance at the clock, "we'd better get on with the briefing." No more small talk. Clive is twinkle-free and in a hurry. He flings his hands about for emphasis as he marches briskly from point to point. His mind is on his exit.

But then, after taking his leave and snapping shut the latches on his briefcase, Clive turns back and gazes at her intently. He taps a pudgy finger twice against his upper lip, and presents her with a warning.

"The front page, Eleanor. The headline?" He waits for her nod before he continues. "Be two hundred percent certain before you ever sign it off."

Panic surfaces in Ellie's eyes. "Have you got a reason for saying this, Clive? I mean, have I—?"

"No, no, no. Just a thought. Nothing like that." He checks his watch. "Be a terrier. Nip away at the headline writers' heels until you're perfectly satisfied."

Then with a quick *cheerio,* Clive slopes off, and Eleanor is alone.

Ellie surveys her workstation: a beige computer and a beige printer; a telephone and a typist's chair. Bog-standard equipment, but all the same, she feels a swell of proprietorial pride.

She likes the fact that she is seated on the foreign desk, just inside the entrance to the newsroom. That puts her in the thick of the action. The desk is long and curved—like an island, Ellie thinks—and journalists and editors cluster in shallow coves along its shoreline. They're within hailing distance of one another; in the course of their work, they often pass pieces of paper back and forth or exchange quick remarks. Ellie wishes she were closer to them, but her own mooring is a secluded one on the island's tip. Clive said she'd work alone, and it turns out to be true in more ways than one.

Ellie sighs and settles herself into her chair and flips open the first story on her screen. It's a piece intended for the financial section, about proposed changes to a company's pension arrangements. She skims first to get the general idea. In the second sentence, "Donald MacIntyre, Executive Director" juggles awkwardly with "non-contributory final-salary deferred benefits pension scheme." Ellie has to rein in the urge to edit. She's paid to produce legal opinions, not perfect prose. She puts her virtual pencil firmly away.

Ellie scrutinizes the piece once again with legal questions firmly to the fore. She reads slowly and carefully, word by word, like someone who is out of the habit.

Ding! The e-mail messenger interrupts. Ellie clicks the message open hoping for another story but finds only the briefest of greetings. *Hi.* Nothing more. Not another word.

The name at the top is *jroberts@chronicle.co.uk.* A colleague, then. But she can't recall the names of any of her coworkers except for Clive. Oh, and that sports journalist, Ariana Raine. It's obviously not either of them.

She tiptoes her chair around in a circle and scans for anyone who might be looking her way. The few staff who are still in the newsroom are working furiously, or surfing, or they are talking as they type with mobiles tucked beneath their chins. There's no one who appears to be focusing on Ellie.

Two paragraphs into the next piece, another message comes whizzing in. *Hi again!* Ellie swings around quickly, but the other people in the newsroom are still absorbed in their own affairs. Ellie feels a prickle of irritation. Anonymous messages are *so* not cool.

She is just getting stuck into the article again when a sound from the other side of the foreign desk itself catches her attention. She tries to block it out.

There it is again. Like Morse code. *Click click click. Clack clack.* The insistent tapping of a fingernail on the hard gray surface of the desk. Ellie looks up from her keyboard, but she can't see beyond the stack of paper trays that mark out the boundary of her workstation. She leans forward and shifts the stack to the right. Through the gap, Ellie sees a square, tanned face and a close-cropped head of hair that would be wavy if it weren't so short. She sees a hand resting on the table and a massive grin. He's looking straight at her. As she gazes back in surprise, he lifts one finger and taps sharply three times.

Ellie mouths a greeting. *Mr. Roberts, I assume?*

He spreads his hands in acknowledgment and mouths something back. She shakes her head. He tries again and this time she picks it up. *At your service, ma'am.*

He pushes back his chair and stands and stretches, and Ellie can't help but watch. He is a tallish man, solid-looking, at ease with his own body. He saunters round to her side of the desk.

Ellie swings to face him. Now the name comes flooding back. Jonathan, she remembers. The foreign editor. Of course.

He stops a few feet away and grins down at her. "Took you long enough to respond to my message," he says. "I'd almost decided you were downright unfriendly."

"Sorry. I couldn't see you over the paper trays."

"I could see you, Eleanor Porter. In fact, I've been watching you for days."

"There hasn't been a lot to see. Girl sits in front of computer. Girl reads. Girl types. Girl goes home."

"Watching the night lawyer is always fun. Especially when she's . . ."

"When she's what? A nervous newcomer?"

"You? Nervous?" Jonathan steps back and looks her up and down. "You give the impression of being as cool as a cucumber. In complete control, I would've said."

"So you decided, did you, that anonymous messages would be the way to rattle me?"

"I'm sorry." Jonathan hangs his head in mock humility, but the edge of a grin gives him away. "Let me show that I'm a harmless creature, really. Will you join me for a drink?"

Ellie hesitates. "I wish I could, but I've only just started my shift."

"Well, let get you something, then. A cappuccino? A juice? Or," he says, "why not reward yourself for all this hard work with a slice of chocolate cake?"

"All right then, cake it is. And a cup of tea. White, no sugar." With a courtly bow, Jonathan rejects the coins she offers. Ellie, on an impulse, holds out her hand. His lips are soft as he presses them to her fingers. They grin at each other for the briefest of moments and then he is gone.

Ellie starts back at the beginning with the pensions piece again. Halfway through, she comes to a sudden stop. My God, she thinks, flirting. I was actually flirting. And then, fuelled with fresh confidence, she finds herself reading at twice the pace.

CHAPTER 6

It is gone nine-thirty that night when Ellie passes among the twin-kling lights of Canada Square and boards the Docklands Light Rail-way. Her favorite seat at the front is free. From here she has an unhampered view as the Isle of Dogs rolls past: the half-domed en-trance to the Jubilee Line, like a miniature Sydney Opera House; the spectacular new buildings at Heron Quays; at West India Docks, a glittering expanse of water.

Farther south, the buildings decline in size and opulence, and the traditional island is in evidence, but even here, tendrils of gentrifica-tion have twined down from Canary Wharf. Riverside walkways and private estates are slowly filling the empty land left by German bomb-ing; they are beginning to outflank the seedy 1960s blocks of council flats. Here, at Mudchute Station, before the railway burrows down beneath the Thames, Ellie alights. She climbs to the top of the station mound, and pauses there. There's been a shower of rain while she was at work, the first in days, and the air smells fresh and new.

Ellie likes new things. New and fresh. Unsullied by the past. Her mother, Annabel, spends hours in antiques shops rooting out art deco furnishings and accessories. *Collectibles,* Annabel calls them. *Detest-ables* is Ellie's unspoken assessment; she finds them heavy and self-conscious and ornate.

Ellie doesn't want to be surrounded by things that are secondhand. Give her fresh furnishings and new buildings and a clean sweep any day. That's why, after she left the hospital and with her grandmother's legacy burning a hole in her pocket, she gravitated to the Isle of Dogs. Ellie fancied a smart little flat with big windows and granite work-tops and perhaps, if she struck it lucky, with a view of the river. She couldn't afford Canary Wharf, so she aimed instead for the southern tip of the island.

The agent, with a discreet cough, designated the area as a "neigh-borhood in transition." Derelict factories and chain-link fencing stood side by side with new terraced homes, and the billboards that fronted the show flats—with their images of men and women who were necessarily affluent and invariably young—had a slightly desperate air.

Ellie, tape measure in hand, trudged from one display flat to another. The agent urged her to envisage the swimming pools, the gyms, the saunas that would eventually arise from the rubble. Ellie fretted about the mean proportions of the rooms. For the first time, she couldn't be certain that new was what she wanted. When she spotted a FOR SALE board outside a corner house on an older terrace of flat-fronted cottages, she insisted on a closer look. And when she noted that the road was called Hesperus Street, she absolutely had to look inside.

The estate agent didn't know, and Ellie didn't tell him, that *Hesperus* was special to her. Ellie had been an inconspicuous sort of school-girl. She didn't have the legs for athletics, or the eye for netball, or the shins for hockey. She lacked the voice for choir or the lips for flute. When it came to art with a capital *A*, her flair never made up for lack of technique. She was well-behaved, conscientious, and bright, but on public occasions, she would pass unnoticed. Only once, did Ellie shine. At a Christmas pageant, with tears springing to her eyes, she recited a Victorian ballad about a tiny child who drowned during a storm at sea; the ship's captain, her own papa, had lashed her to the mast. There was spontaneous applause. Told with such feeling, parents said—as if "The Wreck of the *Hesperus*" could have been recited in any other way.

So Ellie didn't buy a modern flat after all. The estate agent was no fool; when he realized that Ellie fancied the two-up, two-down terraced house, he took her through to the garden straightaway. The minute Ellie saw the lustrous veronica that flourished near the wall, and the silver birch that swooned in the corner, she knew this was a home that could help her forget. Even before the surveyor's report declared it sound, Ellie knew that she would have it, and have it she did.

And now that she owns the house, she's made it her own. The traditional exterior gives little clue to the minimalist interior that Ellie has created. The ground floor consists now of one substantial room, longer than it is wide, which Ellie has stripped of anything that isn't strictly needed. The fireplace she has kept, with its graceful black grate and the shelves in the alcoves on either side. She has added a small cream-colored sofa, a standing lamp, a rug with an abstract design, and a rolltop desk that once was her father's. She has painted the floorboards white, and when she flicks a switch, the long sidewall is washed in a soft light.

A few units in an L-shape and a glass-topped table serve as a kitchen. Beyond that, the patio doors open wide onto her precious garden, and the pendant lamp that hangs above her table throws an oblong of light across the darkened lawn. Ellie sighs with contentment and tunes in to the familiar sounds of home.

The hum of the refrigerator.

The tick of a fragment of soot settling in the chimney.

The clunk of the clock.

Finally, the sound she's been waiting for: metallic, rhythmic, close by, and perfectly clear.

Whirrrrr-clunk.

Whirrrrrrr-clunk.

Whirrrrr-clunk.

Getting louder. Over and over.

Whirrrr-clunk.

Ellie smiles and heads for the refrigerator. She finds a celery stalk in the salad drawer, takes a hearty bite out of it, and clamps what remains between her teeth like a cigar. The noise stops. She remains perfectly still until it starts up again.

Ellie stands next to the glass-topped table and lowers herself until she can maneuver the celery into a narrow opening in what looks like a stack of plastic cylinders. There's a scrabbling sound. Ellie loosens her grip and the stalk of celery is snatched into the cage.

When the sound of gnawing ceases, Ellie lifts a flap and gropes inside until her fingers close around a small warm bundle of muscle and fur. She lifts the hamster out of the cage.

"Odysseus." He has bright black eyes and a coat the color of walnuts. She cups her hands together and brings the tiny face up so that his whiskers brush against her nose. "It was a good day," she murmurs, "since you ask. I shaved a minute off my running time. Work went smoothly. And a man named Jonathan Roberts bought me a piece of cake."

Odysseus begins to move in a circle around her hand.

"What do you think of that, little one?"

Odysseus curls up in her palm and goes to sleep.

CHAPTER 7

"Hey, Eleanor. How's it going?"

"Hey, Jonathan."

How's it going? Ellie overdid her training this morning and her knee is sending off twinges; but she's not about to say so. She looks up at Jonathan, who has a smudge of newsprint on his tanned cheek. "Going fine. But I feel like it's time for a break. D'you want to come with me? Why don't you call me Ellie?" she says as they move together toward the lift and up to the next floor.

"Only if you call me Jon."

At the entrance to the slick, modern cafeteria, they both hesitate; Jon steps back and Ellie enters first. Ellie has a handful of coins; she pays for her hot chocolate and his caffe latte.

"You're not a feminist?" he asks. His smile is amused.

"Nope. Just a woman who values her independence."

"Me, too. Well, not the woman, obviously, but the independence. Next time, it's my turn to buy."

In the caf, unlike the newsroom, the windows are bare, and the view is breathtaking. In the distance, the dark streak of the river, the sleek surface of the Millennium Dome, and the silver pods of the Thames Barriers. Nearer in, the cluster of towers in Canary Wharf and Heron Quays. The north of the island is stubbled with construction; between the high-rises, new buildings are springing up like saplings in a forest. Jon and Ellie stand at the window with polystyrene cups in hand as dusk approaches, watching the lights of London pop on one by one, watching as the night spreads its wings over the Isle of Dogs.

"Look," Ellie says, pointing south to where a green laser beam marks the Greenwich Meridian. "I use that as a marker to locate my house. It's right down there, just this side of the river."

Jonathan turns and looks her up and down. "You're an islander, then?"

"A resident, yes. But not an old-timer. Until I was twenty or so, I don't think I even knew the island existed."

"Seriously?"

"Uh-huh. It just wasn't part of my world. I grew up in north London. Crouch End. I spent evenings out in the West End. I shopped in Camden Town and Oxford Street." She shrugs. "Apart from occasional forays to the Festival Hall, I hardly ever ventured south of the Thames or east of London Bridge."

"I was a Twickenham boy myself. And to us, the Isle of Dogs was nothing more than a bomb site, the one-time stomping ground of Millwall supporters, and a place to be avoided."

"I daresay that's how lots of people from other parts of London think about the East End. Nothing but stereotypes."

They'd finished their drinks. He takes her cup, drops both cups into the bin, and steers Ellie to a table. "Stereotypes?" he prompts.

"You know the sort of thing, Jon. Smoke-grimed terraces and working-class warmth. Close-knit families and organized crime."

"Whenever the East End was mentioned, my wife—ex-wife, rather; we've been divorced for three years now—used to go on about sturdy folk standing firm against German bombs. Is that the sort of thing you mean?"

Divorced, huh? "Yes, exactly. Fact and fiction—the stuff we picked up from novels and television—all mixed up together." Ellie pauses, not wanting to expose the full extent of her ignorance. Not wanting to say that, until she moved to the island, she knew east London only as Albert Square, where villainy and the salt of the earth live cheek by jowl. As Limehouse, where Sherlock Holmes repaired to smoke opium. As the sordid alleys of Whitechapel, through which Jack the Ripper made his murderous way. "The East End seemed a place of nostalgia and at the same time—"

"Dangerous? Like Fagin? Or Jack the Ripper?"

"You're a mind reader, Jon Roberts!"

"And now?"

"Now west London, east London—it's all of a piece." She dances her arm in a smooth curve to suggest the broad blue ribbon of the Thames. How it snakes through Richmond and Barnes, Battersea and Lambeth, and finally under London Bridge, on its course toward the North Sea. How it coils south toward Greenwich and north toward Blackwall in a horseshoe bend, and how the river stamps the Isle of Dogs—a peninsula, really, rather than an island—with a shape so strong that it might be a part of a giant's jigsaw.

"And the *Chronicle*? Do you feel at home here?"

Ellie shivers and lowers her arm to the table. "Not quite. Not yet. You see . . ." Ellie searches his eyes. "You see, I still feel terribly much like the new girl. Afraid that I'll mess it up. That I'll get it all wrong." Oh, she could kick herself! Why, oh why, has she said that? Jonathan will think she's pathetic.

But Jonathan breaks into a big indulgent grin. "Ellie?" Lightly he touches his finger to her chin. "Why on earth should you mess up? You're bright, conscientious, and hardworking. And for what it's worth, you're drop-dead gorgeous, too. What could possibly go wrong?"

CHAPTER 8

Carl Hewitt knows the Isle of Dogs like the back of his hand. Knows every inch of it—from the West India Docks, where bonded warehouses once housed mahogany and coffee and sugar from all over the world, to the Blue Bridge that lifted so that ships could pass into the Blackwall Basin. When he was a boy, his granddad used to meet him after school with a bag of ginger biscuits and they'd walk and they'd talk. They would trace the north-south route of the horse-drawn buses that used to travel up and down the Isle of Dogs. They would relive the industrial heyday, when firms like Badger's and Le Bas Tubes were the community's lifeblood. They'd walk the length of

East Ferry Road as it swept down the island, C
side, Millwall on the other.

Granddad Rory was a docker, but he should h
neer. He knew everything about the island's industr
on humps of rubble left by German bombing, mu
while his grandfather detailed the making of sacks   ,
pipes and propellers, chains and tubes and tanks. Granddad Rory
brought back to life the landscape that existed before the war, using
words to rebuild a row of terraced houses here and a shipyard there.
Carl Hewitt learned to see the island through the eyes of a much older
man.

Carl now walks the island on his own. He is coming to the end of
one of his mammoth hikes, following the brick-paved walkway that
cuts through Millwall Park. He is kitted out with a pair of trainers
that are the spitting image of Nikes. Bought them yesterday at the
market, at only a third of the price you'd pay in one of those posh
sports shops in Canary Wharf. But he wouldn't try them on, not right
there in the open air, and now a seam is clawing at his heel.

As Carl draws near to East Ferry Road, a jogger in a rugby shirt
hurdles over the cycle barriers and almost crashes into him.

"Fucking well watch yourself!" It's out before Carl has a chance to
think. Come on now, Carl, he tells himself, don't lose the plot. Not
now. He picks up the pace in spite of his blister.

"Sorry, mate," the jogger calls, his voice fading as he races into the
distance.

Carl glances north toward the Wharf, where the tower blocks
stand shoulder to shoulder like bodyguards. He spins on his blistered
heel and heads south toward the river. He cuts along Westferry and
goes into the Ship for a drink. "Pint of pale ale, mate," he says, and
the bartender pulls him a cool glass of beer. There's a man standing at
the counter next to him. Nods his head and raises his glass in a greeting. Obviously in a mood to talk. A tourist, Carl decides. Bound to be
with that pricey-looking video camera. Though what a tourist's doing
here, he can't imagine. This isn't Trafalgar bloody Square.

The man speaks. "You live in Docklands?" he asks.

Carl swirls his beer around in his mouth and then shakes his head.
"No," he says.

He leaves his beer on the counter and saunters to the loo. He pisses slowly and zips himself up, thinking the while, then sluices his hands under the cold-water tap and dries them on the towel that hangs on a nail. He pushes open the window for a breath of fresh air. Even in here, the crowds can get to him.

When he returns to the bar, the tourist starts in once more. "Where you from, then?"

"I grew up on the island," Carl says. "Lived with my granddad just around the corner." Carl's thumb jerks in the direction of the Chapel House estate.

"What? Well, then, you are from Docklands." The tourist is starting to feel uneasy. Maybe he's having his leg pulled. The pub is small and bare and rough-looking, like a kid's clubhouse furnished with bits and pieces from a skip. The handful of customers don't look any too friendly. Maybe he should be getting back to his B and B.

He picks up his rucksack and starts to shrug himself into the straps.

The other man at the bar has just completed a day's shift on a dust-cart. At the rasp in Carl's voice, he digs into his pocket, pulls out some change, and clunks it down on the counter. He waves a hand to the barman and heads for the door.

"Look," says Carl. He can feel his throat begin to tighten, as it always does when he is annoyed. His head feels funny, too. Sort of spacey. "Just tell me one thing. What the bloody hell do you mean by Docklands?"

The tourist takes a step back. "Docklands?" he squeaks. "Well, it's—" He looks around the room for help. An elderly man seated at a table exposes toothless gums in a vacant grin. The barman busies himself wiping glasses with a dingy-looking towel. The only other customer, a girl with a face as thin as a wafer, stares fixedly at the fruit machine. The lights from the machine flash green and orange in the gloom of the pub.

"Get on with it," urges Carl.

The tourist takes a deep breath, and begins, carefully. "Well, Docklands, I read about it. It's the land either side of the Thames where docks were built—we're talking a long time ago, maybe 1800—to load and unload the ships that were too tall to slip under Tower

Bridge." Warming to his topic now. "That's right," he affirms. "St. Katharine's Dock, West India Docks, Millwall, and—Look, I can't remember all the names, but they're all in here." He taps a guidebook with his forefinger. He's wearing a neat gold wedding band. "The docks helped to fuel industrial expansion. Made London—that's what I read—the commercial center of the world."

"And?" says Carl. The word is buried in a kind of cough, as if he's about to spit across the room, and his face is crumpled like a fist. But the tourist is busy recalling the contents of his guidebook and doesn't take the warning.

"And? Well, Docklands became the industrial heartland of London, that's what they say. Chemicals. Brewing. Timber mills. You name it. It all happened here. But it couldn't last forever. Container ships were too big, so new docks had to be built farther down the coast. This area fell to pieces. That's progress," he says.

The tourist has settled on an argument that he feels will be decisive. "And that's why," he says, looking around for support, "the Docklands Development Corporation was set up." Wafer woman thumps the machine. "To give Docklands—" He emphasizes the word *Docklands,* and there is a hint of mockery now in his voice. "To give Docklands, which was practically derelict by that time, new roads, new architecture, new railway, new employment. Regeneration, that's what it is. Good old progress."

He stops, pleased with his lecture. His thumb plays with the corner of the guidebook that has served him so well. He looks at Carl expectantly and raises his glass.

"Bollocks," says Carl.

The tourist is stunned. He pushes the guidebook in front of Carl's face. "Look!" he says, one finger tapping the word DOCKLANDS in the title. "Look at this."

Carl clears his throat noisily and this time he uses a spittoon in the corner near the bar. "Double bollocks," he croaks again. "With an arsehole thrown in."

The tourist has forgotten to feel uneasy now. He has forgotten that he is on alien territory, that he's an interloper, that he doesn't know the local ways. He comes close to shouting. "Bollocks? What the heck do you mean by that?"

Carl is glad to have got a rise. He is right and he knows it. And when you have right on your side, Granddad Rory used to say, stand firm and you'll prevail. His grandfather was a strict Presbyterian. When the dockers gathered before the shift at six AM to drink a glass of rum, Rory stuck to cocoa. He had an unswerving belief in right and wrong.

"What do I mean by 'bollocks'?" Carl asks. "You really don't know?" His rasping voice is difficult to hear over the incessant slam of the fruit machine. The tourist is forced to lean closer. "Bollocks is a coarse term for testicles," Carl says. "Used as an exclamation, it means *rubbish*. And that's exactly what you're spouting. Bollocks about Docklands. Bollocks about regeneration. Bollocks about bloody progress." He shifts his weight so that he is a little closer to the tourist, who moves a step or two away. "You can't tell me about the docks," Carl says. "My father worked in the docks until they made him redundant. My granddad and my uncle, too."

Carl downs the last three inches of his pint, and sets the glass decisively on the counter. "The docks were real, all right," Carl says. "But 'Docklands'? No such thing. It's a name invented by bureaucrats, nothing more. Before the developers came in with their cash and their lies, no Londoner would say"—Carl puts on a mincing voice—" 'Me, I'm from Docklands.' " Back to his familiar rasp: " 'I'm from Newham,' " that's what a Londoner would say. Or Wapping. Or Limehouse." With the name of each borough, Carl makes sharp wet slaps on the wooden counter with the palm of his hand. "And me? I'm not from bloody 'Docklands.' I'm an islander, you hear me? Like him"—he points to the barman "—and him"—the toothless old geezer—"and her." Wafer woman favors Carl with a wan smile.

Carl remembers slamming his fist on the counter and how his glass and the tourist's glass jumped. He remembers shouting the last few phrases, or trying to do so. His voice had withered away until his shout was little more than the scrape of a shoe on pavement. Not much louder than a whisper, he thinks with disgust.

After that, Carl remembers nothing. He must have walked throughout the night. Lucky he didn't freeze to death. He wakes up on a bench near the embankment, with his jacket dirty and damp from dew, and the trail of a snail across the knee of his trousers. A mist in the air blurs the streetlamps. A tugboat cuts a sharp path on the far side of the river and something large and almost human bobs in the chevron that trails behind.

CHAPTER 9

Mrs. Jessop is eighty-eight and definitely mobile. "What do you mean, 'getting old'? As long as I can get around, we're staying put." That's what she tells Ted and Eileen, her children, when they broach the subject of a care home. They think she can't look after Stanley anymore, but they're wrong. She can still make it down to the grocery and back. She can still cook a shepherd's pie, his favorite, or an omelette for his tea. And she can still take her little walk down to Saunders Ness every day to see to her chickies.

Here she is. Minnie Jessop reaches the riverside and leans against the railings. She is out of breath, just a little, and her back is bent. She saw her reflection in a shopwindow yesterday and it gave her such a shock. Who's that old woman all hunched over like that, she thought. It didn't make her happy at all, not at all, when she realized it was her. She clutches onto the lamppost and tries to ease her back, just a little, but it's as stiff as a board. She waits to catch her breath.

It's dusk and the sky has turned a deep luminous blue. The Old Royal Naval College on the other side of the river is already illuminated. Its pale stone gleams in the light. The river itself is pulling back, the tide rapidly retreating. The water, black as midnight, is fringed with pale froth.

"Here, chicky. Chicky chicky chicky."

The tiny waterbirds cluster at the point where the tide exposes the oily mud of the riverbank. They dart in and out of the water, chasing the foam. They peck at the mud aggressively, then patter along the shoreline to peck at a different patch.

Minnie is fascinated by the waders. She loves the way they drift together along the shoreline, never straying far from their fellows. She loves their quick, sure movements; like little lizards, they are. She is intrigued by the way they come with the receding tide, and disappear shortly after. Tonight they are pecking away at something that juts up out of the shallow water. They're standing on it. They appear as if they're walking on the surface of the water.

"Over here, chicky." She reaches into her vinyl shopper, below the bacon she has bought for Stanley's tea, and pulls out a bag of nuts and seeds. Sesame seeds, mainly. "Here's your treat."

Minnie tosses a handful. There is a spitting noise as they hit the mud. A curlew detaches himself from his perch and scurries to where the seeds are sinking slowly into the sludge.

The water has pulled back a fraction farther, and now Minnie can see that the object the birds are standing on is spherical in shape. No, not a ball; there are holes in the surface and—Minnie can make it out more clearly now—there are something like handles attached to either side. Her eyes aren't so good anymore, especially at night, and it is dark now outside the circle of the lamplight. She can hardly see.

Minnie should get back to Stanley, but for some reason she is desperate to know what's in the water. Fifty meters away, toward the opposite bank, a tugboat chugs its way downriver. A door opens in the Trafalgar Tavern and there's a raucous exchange of laughter. Minnie shakes the sound away. She maneuvers one size-four tennis shoe onto the concrete wall, and, gripping the railings with both hands, pulls herself up. She cranes her neck and leans forward as far as she can just as the wash from the tugboat reaches the shore. It picks up the object and sets it down again—gently, almost reverently—within the circle of light cast by the lamp.

Minnie's vision isn't what it once was, but still she recognizes it right away. Even with only two gaping holes where the eyes should be, even with slimy weed lodged in the mouth, there's no room for error.

"Oh, my God," she whimpers. "Oh, my God."

Another wave slaps onto the shore and the body slides into view.

Trembling now, her knees unruly, Minnie hauls herself down off the wall and picks up her shopper. She is exhausted. But even if it takes her longer than usual to get home, she'll still have time to call Ted and Eileen. She'll ask them to take her tomorrow to see the care home. Then she'll ring the police, just as soon as she's put the bacon on the grill for Stanley's tea.

CHAPTER 10

"I know I put it in here," Harriet says.

There's a screeching noise in Wagamama as Harriet Firestone scrapes her bench away from the communal table. Other diners turn to look as she plonks her briefcase open on her lap and, with the deliberation of a bargain hunter, plucks objects from its depths. Onto the table drops a set of keys, then a highlighter pen, a leather glove, some baby wipes. Ellie extends an arm and catches a folded copy of the *Times* just as it is about to slam into a vase of anemones.

"I know I put it in here," Harriet says, oblivious of the chaos. She unzips a cosmetic case and paws around inside. "Anyway, Eleanor, what I want to hear about is the new job. Are you on top of things?"

It was in this very same restaurant just a few weeks ago that Harriet broke the news to Ellie about the new post. "They're looking for a night lawyer," she said. "You know, the person who checks the paper before they send it beddy-byes. It's evening work and, of course, I thought of you."

"We're talking about the *Chronicle*?" Ellie did her best to suppress the squeak in her voice. The last thing she wanted to do was to appear desperate.

Harriet sat up ramrod straight. "You've no objections to working for a tabloid, I trust?" Harriet had gone to some trouble to recommend Eleanor for the new post, and she didn't expect to be sneered at for her efforts. Besides, Harriet had worked at the *Chronicle* herself before she moved on to the *Mail*, and she cared a great deal how it was seen by others.

"No, no, Harry, not in the least. I'm not a 'tabloids bad, broadsheets good' sort of person. As far as I'm concerned, you'll find serious journalism and sensationalism on both sides of that great divide." In fact, at the prospect of working for the *Chronicle*—one of the more respectable tabloids, with a claim to the best and most provocative writers in the business—she'd felt a small shock of excitement.

So how's it gone? "Well, I was nervous at first, Harry—who wouldn't be?—but they've all been so nice to me." She thinks of Jonathan. "And—well, you'd have to ask Clive for a fuller report, but my impression is that he's satisfied with what I've done."

Harriet breaks off from her search to cast an appraising glance at the friend sitting opposite. She has to admit, the change is quite remarkable. Eleanor Porter came out of hospital two or three years ago resembling the back end of a bus, but now look at her. Her shoulders are straight, her eyes are bright, and her copper hair gleams. She's slim and perfectly groomed. Too pretty by half, Harriet concludes, with a sigh. But then, it's easy to keep up appearances when you have only yourself to care for. Eleanor doesn't have to get up—it was twice last night—to see to a crying baby.

The twitch of resentment passes in an instant. Harriet is, fundamentally, a good-hearted soul. She prides herself on looking after people. Ellie is hunched forward now over the menu. Harriet swirls a swig of sake around in her mouth and takes the opportunity to check her out again. Not perfectly groomed, she amends. Look at those hands. The stubby nails, the torn skin around the cuticle. Could it be that Eleanor's confidence is only skin-deep?

"An honest answer, if you please, Eleanor."

Ellie looks up and her eyes are wary.

Harriet takes another sip of rice wine and presses her point. "Are you absolutely positive you're ready for this return to full-time work?"

"For Christ's sake, Harriet. Do we have to go over this again?"

It's not just the question that gets to Ellie, it's Harry herself. The way she assumes an air of authority on every topic; the way she walks as if she might be the only person on the pavement; the way she flings her things about. Whenever she's with Harriet, Ellie finds herself constantly giving way. Picking up after her. Offering placating smiles to people whom Harriet has bumped into or cut across or interrupted. And as if that weren't enough, there's always a subterranean stream of meaning rippling beneath the surface of what Harriet actually says. Night lawyer for the *Chronicle* group. *Of course, Eleanor, I thought of you.*

Well, it is the case that, even before her breakdown, Eleanor had come to dislike criminal law—no, to be honest, to despise it. She had taken it up in the first place only because of the foolish fantasy of rescuing an innocent accused. She retrained for work in the world of publishing, and the job at the *Chronicle* is just the sort of entrée that she needed. Of course.

But—and here's the rub—Harriet's casual remark, of course, is also a reminder that there is no man in Eleanor's life. Harriet has a husband named Greg; he's a developer who is as affable over aperitifs as he is ruthless in business. She has a clever young daughter by the name of Alexis. She has a baby son with a bald head. Harriet has reason to be home in the evenings, whereas Eleanor—poor, dear, Eleanor—has nothing to look forward to but her karate (which, for Harriet, doesn't count) and her work.

And yet, and yet.

Ellie examines her friend's soft face, the purple shadows beneath her eyes, and knows how much it costs Harriet to maintain that ferocious focus on work and family and friends. Harriet might patronize Eleanor, might boss her around, but it was Harriet who came to the hospital again and again, bustling through those bleak corridors, the smells of Starbucks coffee and hope clinging to her cashmere coat. Most of Ellie's other friends maintained an uneasy distance. It was Harriet who took her shopping for a celebration dress when she lost her excess weight, and Harriet who engineered an occasion when Ellie could wear it. Harriet might be overbearing and complacent, but she was also, no question about it, Ellie's friend.

"Aha!" A shout from Harriet. She dives into the depths of the briefcase, and emerges clutching a pale gray business card. She holds it aloft like a pearl for all the restaurant to admire.

"You've got a pen? Oliver Nesbit," she says. "It was the most surprising thing, bumping into him there, at the Almeida. I recognized him instantly. Still those bedroom eyes," she drawls, rolling her own in appreciation. "He asked after you, Eleanor. I told him all about you, that you were working for the *Chronicle* and so forth, and he said do please give her my number and ask her to call."

Harriet reads each digit of the mobile number aloud at great volume as if Ellie were hard of hearing. A couple at the far end of their shared table nudge each other and giggle.

"You will call him, Eleanor? He seemed very keen to talk to you, and you never know . . ."

"The last I heard, Harriet, Oliver Nesbit was married and doing the suburban thing in Wimbledon. But if I have time, I'll call."

The food arrives and Harriet frowns at her plate for a moment, forking the prawns with an air of dissatisfaction. She looks as if she is about to send them back. But instead, she clears her throat and leans across the table.

"Eleanor, the job. Attention to detail. The crucial front page. All of that. You do understand what's involved?" Harriet points her fork along a line level with Ellie's nose, as if to skewer her to the question.

Eleanor maneuvers a morsel of chicken to her mouth. She closes her eyes and chews and swallows. Calmly, calmly now. "What's to understand, Harriet? There's nothing particularly difficult about it, is there? I'm a night lawyer. I work at night."

Harriet signals to the waitress to bring more napkins, but she doesn't let up. "Look, Eleanor," she says, in clipped tones, "you can't afford to screw up. You've got to be one hundred percent alert in this job, and don't you forget it."

A fat noodle slides from Ellie's spoon into her soup and the broth sprays her shirt. "Damn," she mutters. She wets her napkin in her water glass and dabs at her cuff. It's not the words but Harriet's vexed tone that shoots prickles of alarm up Ellie's spine. Harriet is teetering on the edge of anger, and Ellie's not good at anger. "I don't do anger," she said to the therapist at the hospital and on the whole, it's true. Ellie prefers to conciliate or to ignore, pretending that this is a strategy, but knowing in her heart of hearts that she's simply scared.

Had anger always frightened her? Perhaps not. Ellie likes to believe that as a child she might have lashed out in the face of attack. That she'd wailed *It's not fair,* and railed against injustice, as other children do. But certainly, by the time she was nine or ten, in the place of whatever anger she'd once possessed, Ellie had perfected a technique for deflecting adult rage. She recognized, as many children didn't, that the more readily she complied with adult demands, the sooner any unpleasantness, any discipline, any torment, would be ended.

"You're right, of course, Harriet," Ellie says. Any hint of sarcasm has been banished.

For a moment, Harriet toys with disbelief. Then she nibbles a slice of pickled ginger, pushes her plate away, and continues. The hurt fades out of her tone as she speaks. "This is not just a job, Eleanor, this is your whole career we're talking about here. Your future. It takes nerve to be a night lawyer, believe you me. Nerve and impeccable judgment." Harriet, who spent years as a night lawyer, is never too modest to pay herself a compliment. "If you manage to impress the management at the *Chronicle,* you're on target for better things. But if you mess up, well . . ."

Harriet fixes Ellie with a searching stare. "Look, Eleanor, are you absolutely certain you're up to it?"

"Up to it?"

Ellie knows perfectly well what lies behind the question. There's her breakdown, for a start; admission to a psychiatric hospital leaves a gap in a curriculum vitae and questions in the minds of friends. There's the fact that, between leaving hospital and winning the night lawyer post, Ellie had worked only as a locum. There's the fact that Ellie's legal experience is in the criminal courts.

No wonder Harriet has doubts. But surely Harriet—Ellie's oldest, dearest, most intimate friend—should know Ellie well enough to realize that this time she's really going to make it work. She has risen to the challenge. She has overcome her demons. The girl who went into meltdown when Will abandoned her is not the same girl who sits in front of Harry now.

"Eleanor!"

Ellie shakes off the thought and looks straight at Harriet, challengingly. "Up to the job?" she says. She puts her chin high in the air and, like a good lawyer, meets a question with a question.

"Up to the job? Why shouldn't I be?"

CHAPTER 11

Ellie's just settling down to work when the story wings its way in: BODY IN THE THAMES.

> Last evening, police officers from Limehouse Station were called to the Isle of Dogs, where they found the body of a man that had been exposed by the receding tide. The elderly woman who spotted the body while feeding birds is said to be seriously distressed. Police have cordoned off sections of the embankment, and divers have been called in to search the river. The body, believed to be that of a man in his thirties, has yet to be identified.

A shiver passes through Ellie at the thought. Alive one moment; dead the next, and buffeted by the cold, dark waters of the Thames. On one of her running routes, less than half a mile from her home. She ponders on the vagaries of life as she threads her way to the loo.

At least the story is uncontroversial, she decides. Nothing to alarm a legal there. Doesn't sound as if much news will be available until the Tower Hamlets police call a press conference tomorrow morning, by which time they might have some idea who the man is and how he died.

So when Ellie returns to her desk, she is surprised to find another story waiting that is ostensibly about the body. MORE TROUBLE ON THE ISLAND is how it's billed, and it's attributed to an editor named Blocombe. The first paragraph describes with a degree of artistic license the horror of a corpse pulled dripping from the Thames. From there on, the piece is increasingly speculative. Even though the cause of death has not yet been determined, recurring references to "danger" and to "the difficulties of walking at night unmolested on the island," strongly imply that there's been foul play. Then the writer mentions two incidents of violence nearby in the past couple of months, and includes interviews with shopkeepers about local children who've given them trouble. Blocombe doesn't come right out and say that these children should come under suspicion for the death of the floater, but the hints couldn't be broader and the implication is clear.

Ellie is aware of Jonathan coming into the newsroom and taking his seat on the other side of the desk, but she is too absorbed in the piece to give him anything other than a quick wave. Obviously, the writer, Blocombe, has a point to make about local yobs. She searches for a reformulation that will keep the gist of the story intact, while ensuring that the *Chronicle* isn't censured for pointing a finger of suspicion at innocent children. She marks up the piece with her recommendations, takes a deep breath, and taps *Return to Sender*.

The second it's gone, she longs to call it back. To check the story over once again. But her comments are already winging their way to Blocombe. Did Ellie meet "T. Blocombe" on her first evening in the office? The name draws a perfect blank. She doesn't even know if this *T.* refers to a man or a woman, and somehow the uncertainty hikes up her unease.

Skin taut with tension, Ellie can't resist tracking down her message in the Sent folder. Her proposed amendments still seem reasonable when she reads them through again, but then what does she know? T. Blocombe—Terence Blocombe? Tommy? Tilda, perhaps?—might view her comments as crap. Worse still, impertinent. Worst of all, incompetent. Tilda Blocombe might be on her way this very moment to lodge a complaint about the new night lawyer and her impertinent, incompetent crap.

Ellie opens a fresh file and sits for a couple of minutes in fidgety silence. A mechanical growl from the printer makes her jump. She watches astonished as the printer pushes out a sheet of paper. She snatches it up and, anxiously, she reads: *Spot-on, Miss Porter. Thanks for yr swift response and welcome to the club. Tristan. T* for Tristan. Tristan Blocombe. Who would have guessed it?

As far as Ellie can recall from her tour of the newsroom, the home desk is toward the north wall, way off to the right. Ellie tiptoes her chair around to face it. She leans back and lets her gaze meander across the ceiling, as if she were daydreaming. Eventually, she slides her glance down toward the desk where she supposes Tristan works. An Anglepoise lamp comes into view. Then a letter tray. Then a slack-faced, shock-haired man who seems to be staring directly into her eyes. Slowly, still holding Ellie's gaze, he raises his arms in the air and awards her a flamboyant two-thumbs-up salute. His smile says *welcome* even more fulsomely than his printed message did.

Ellie waves a hand at him. She barely manages to keep her delight in check until she's turned back to her workstation.

Then she slips off her shoes and sets to work in earnest. She keeps her head lowered so that anyone passing by won't remark on the grin that lights up her delicate features.

CHAPTER 12

One of the advantages of the position of night lawyer is that evenings are much quieter than days. When Ellie leaves work at ten PM or later, there are rarely more than a couple of people still tucked away in corners of the *Chronicle* office. She doesn't have to join the rush-hour throng. She doesn't have to field awkward questions about her plans for the evening. She doesn't have to wedge herself into an overcrowded lift and struggle there to avoid the one (there is always one) who is too large or too damp or who emits a faint unpleasant smell.

When Ellie leaves the office, she steps into empty corridors. Into a lift in which she touches no one because there's no one there to touch. Into solitude.

She glides down twenty-three flights to the ground floor, timing the descent. One elephant, two elephants, three elephants . . . A reassuring bump, the doors slide open, and Ellie steps into the lobby. Alone. *Toute seule.* Gloriously so.

The first time Ellie visited One Canada Square, the sheer size of the lobby made her blink; it is as massive as an aircraft hangar, with prodigious pillars of rose-colored marble and marble facings and marble floors. At rush hour, when daylight streams in through glass walls, the lobby seems like a pedestrian precinct in some impossibly prosperous city. Men and women in a black-bottoms-white-shirts uniform flow like human lava out of the offices, through the corridors, and down the lifts. They cascade into the lobby. They tumble out into effortless lines, moving purposefully toward the car park, the DLR, or the Jubilee Line. There is little unnecessary noise, and no signs of drunkenness or passion, but the restrained murmurings from thousands of throats and the soft scuff of leather on the marbled floor together fill the foyer with a chorus of sound.

But when Ellie leaves the *Chronicle,* rush hour is long over and the murmurs are those of ghosts. The glass walls disclose only a black night beyond. The click of Ellie's heels strikes like a spear against the silence. Alone in the lobby, acutely aware of the sculptures that line the walls and the lilies and the soft shining lights, Ellie—shot through with a sense of privilege—feels like Beauty, wandering through a palace provided solely for her pleasure by the Beast.

Still thrilling to Tristan Blocombe's endorsement and her own sense of relief, Ellie listens to the music in her head. It's a rhythm smooth and soaring; she sways from side to side. She sets her document case gently on a leather stool and rises up on the balls of her feet. She is Catherine Zeta-Jones in *Chicago.* No, that's not it. She reaches back into her memory. She's Ginger Rogers in *Top Hat.*

Ellie twirls, her arms outstretched, and twirls again. She steps onto an open expanse of marble flooring, and begins to dance. She dances on, and on again, until a rush of air from a closing door shakes her to her senses. She opens her eyes to the latest commodity prices that flash up onto a wall-mounted screen. She sees a sleepy security guard as he lowers his eyes and looks away.

Ellie quickly exits the tower. She refuses to think about the security guard. All the way home she focuses instead on Tristan Blocombe's salute.

That night in bed she goes over and over it. *Spot-on, Miss Porter. Welcome to the club.* It was, all in all, a pretty terrific day.

You see? Ellie tells herself as she drifts off to sleep. *No one wants to punish you. You did a good job today—a fine job—and there is such a thing as a fresh start.*

CHAPTER 13

Carl Hewitt has been watching Canary Wharf from the beginning, even before he took his current job. From the closure of the West India Docks in 1980 to the arrival of the first of the bulldozers, Carl has been on the case. He's even studied the statistics. He knows that One Canada Square is the highest tower in Britain, with fifty floors running to eight hundred feet in height. That the tower has two freight lifts, two firemen's lifts, and thirty-two passenger lifts, and that they soar from the lobby almost to the roof in forty seconds. Carl knows that the aircraft-warning light on the top flashes 57,600 times a day.

Carl knows only too well the resources that have been swallowed up in its construction. Half a million bolts, for a start. Twenty-seven thousand metric tons of British steel. Ninety-thousand square feet of marble brought all the way from Italy and Guatemala for the lobby alone.

And still, knowing all he does about the tower, Carl despises it.

He turns his attention to the cameras that cover the lobby. It is just after ten PM. Except for the maintenance staff who keep the hours nobody else wants, most of the seven thousand people who work in the tower have gone home. Most, but not all.

Carl zooms in on the girl who steps out of the lift and snorts with disdain. She walks ramrod straight, like one of those Miss Universe birds, with her head held high. Then suddenly, with her back to the camera, she comes to a halt. Fifteen meters away, one of the security guards at the reception desk looks up and watches as the girl's head begins to move from side to side, like maybe she's ill. Then her shoulders move, too, and soon her whole body starts to sway like one of those bloody Hare Krishnas who used to prance around London in the 1970s. She is carrying a kind of case under her arm. She sets it down and swings into a dance. Carl laughs out loud. Dancing in the lobby! Doesn't she know how ridiculous she looks? Doesn't she care?

It's clear the silly cow doesn't have the faintest idea that Carl is watching.

She whirls then, and waves her arms in the air, and her tiny feet do a three-step thingy on the marble floor. She looks, Carl thinks, like she's just thrown off the weight of the world. Carl is astonished to find within himself a small, hard cube of envy.

The name comes to him as they always do. The Dancing Queen. That's what he'll call her.

And then, she twirls again, and straightens, with her arms stretched toward the ceiling and a smile on her lips. And suddenly . . . The eyes. The flaming-red hair. The gap between her two front teeth. A lump of recognition lodges in the back of his brain. The Dancing Queen. My Dancing Queen. After years of searching, could he finally have found her?

CHAPTER 14

Carl Hewitt is one-third of the way through the twelve-hour shift before he finally manages to wrench his mind away from the Dancing Queen. Before something else catches his attention, has him reaching for his unofficial log. The man on the screen is twenty-four. Twenty-five tops. He is walking through Cabot Hall with a slow, confident stride. Walking, not loitering, or lurking; not stealthy in the way that would catch the eye of a security guard. He wears black jeans and cowboy boots and his long coat flicks around his ankles with every pace. This guy is different. He's not a trader, not one of the big-bucks men, and he's not a service worker like Carl. This guy is different, but difference alone doesn't cut it for Carl. What Carl responds to is something much more subtle. He senses evil.

To be up front about it—Carl believes in being up front—Carl Hewitt may be only a security technician, but he's a man with a nose for evil. The word is out of fashion; he recognizes that. It's too uncompromising, too committed, for today's taste. It's not at all what Denise would call postmodern. But Carl doesn't apologize for using the word. He hasn't got a degree like some of Denise's friends, but that hasn't stopped him thinking. About nature versus nurture. About genes versus the environment. About free will versus compulsion. Carl's decided that in the end, whatever fancy theory you dress it up in, sometimes *evil* is the only word that fits.

Carl can spot evil a mile away. He can watch a man who oozes respectability—soft voice, expensive suit, moisturized skin—and know within minutes that he's up to no good. He's done it, many times.

There was a terrible occasion, many years ago—seeing the Queen has brought it back to him—when Carl didn't follow up on his intuition. When he had an inkling of evil but let himself be silenced. He'd swallowed his suspicion. He'd let evil slip away. But that was then and this is now. Carl is tougher now. He won't allow himself to be silenced again.

Carl leans forward in his plastic chair as the young man with the long coat changes course. As he swings around and strides toward the escalator. As he feels in his pocket, takes out something. Carl zooms in for a close-up. Sees the man tap out a Gauloise, lift it to his lips. His fingers continue to grip the cigarette for a couple of strides, and then, like an executioner's blade, they snap it in two.

A sharp sense of longing plonks itself down in the pit of Carl's stomach. He remembers only too well the feel of a cigarette in his fingers, his hand dangling over the arm of the chair, and the smoke curling up reassuringly beside him. He remembers exactly what it's like, that first drag in the morning. Sit up in bed, reach blindly for the packet, put the fag in your mouth—your mouth so dry the paper sticks to your lips—and grab the lighter. Pause long enough to anticipate the rush of nicotine, and then: click. The flame is hot on your skin. Your nostrils flare. Your heartbeat accelerates. You give an involuntary cough, and then you draw the smoke in and hold it deep inside your lungs. Your body starts to tingle. Hello, morning.

Well, no more cigarettes, not anymore. The doctor read Carl the riot act. Not that laying down the law would have done any good if Carl hadn't already decided to quit. But has quitting helped? Bloody hell it has! Carl's voice is as scratchy as before.

The man in the overcoat is swinging down the stairs into Canada Square. As he passes by, he flicks the two halves of the cigarette onto the statue of a reclining youth. The litter lands, as far as Carl can tell, in the cleft of the upturned chin.

Carl won't be making a note about this man on his clipboard, no way. That's the official record and it is reserved for what Richard, his supervisor, calls trouble. "Trouble," Richard always says, "with a capital *T*." And what does Richard mean by trouble? He means an intruder with a banning order, maybe, or a shoplifter, or a brawl, and it has to be happening now. Richard isn't in the least interested in preventive security. He all but forbids it. Carl pauses over *forbid*, savoring the rage that flows when he thinks of it. Richard forbids Carl to record other information. "Keep it simple," Richard says. "Keep it brief. Ever heard of information overload?" Richard has skin that is pitted with acne scars, and when he talks like this, he makes Carl want to puke.

The main problem with Richard, in Carl's humble opinion, is that he doesn't like to read. Richard is twenty years younger than Carl, younger than most of the other operatives, too, but just because he has a bloody degree, he's been put in charge. As supervisor, he has to scrutinize (that's Richard's word) the official record every twenty-four hours. The less information in the record, the less pressure on Richard's feeble brain.

What does Carl do when Richard forbids something? Carl nods— he rarely argues—but he does exactly as he pleases. He doesn't care what Richard says, he keeps an unofficial log of his own. He has a hardcover notebook and he carries it with him everywhere. He might whip it out in Starbucks, say. He might use it on the train. He makes notes right here in the control room, when Richard's not around.

Carl grasps the notebook in large blunt hands and bends it backward to loosen the spine. At the top of a brand-new page, he writes the date. With a plastic ruler, and one eye still on the screens, he draws a pencil line from top to bottom. To the left of the line, he writes the time and lists the cameras involved. On the right, he sets out a description: Caucasian male, mid-twenties, five foot eleven, circa fourteen stone. Hair: black. Distinguishing features: Ray-Bans.

Carl checks the cameras. Two men arguing in the lobby; body language says that the quarrel won't go any further. A group of youths with skateboards; they'll be seen off by security soon enough. A woman carrying bags of groceries; a cleaner, no doubt, coming off shift and heading home to Deptford.

With one eye on the screen, Carl flicks through the entries for the previous week. Information, that's the thing. When it comes to law enforcement, information is the most important weapon. Oh, there are times when hardware comes in handy. Carl wouldn't deny that. That standoff between the police and anti-globalization protesters in the City of London is a case in point; anyone could see that body armor was essential there. But on the whole, information takes you further than truncheons or Tasers. You can hold off rioters with truncheons; with quality information, you prevent the riot from arising in the first place.

The cleaner struggles to lift her shopping and hobbles onto the train. She must be fifty-eight, sixty. Too old, Carl decides, to be dragging industrial hoovers around.

The thought of being old and infirm makes Carl wriggle in his seat. He's only in his forties, not old by a long chalk. But all the same . . . If only he could feel confident of getting this promotion, of becoming a supervisor on the day shift. Carl's applied, of course. Why not? He's got more experience and—let's face it—more sense about security than most of the others. Sure, he doesn't have formal qualifications. But in security you don't need theory, you need to be able to see, and to understand what you see. You have to know that something that looks as innocent as ice cream or as spontaneous as road rage may be part of a cold and calculating act of violence. Looking is only half the battle; the hardest part is getting to the meaning of things.

Take that man on camera 43. The one who got out the Gauloise. Smoking is forbidden in lots of areas of the Wharf, but the geezer in the long coat didn't look like someone who follows rules on principle. No, he looked like a man who was anxious not to draw attention to himself. Carl opens the notebook and adds a final comment next to his description: *Something to hide.*

Then with one eye on the cameras, he thumbs back through the entries for the past few days.

All his favorites are in there. All his regulars. Tarzan, with the bull neck and the shock of long hair. Betty Boop and her big gold hoops. The Forecloser—expensive jacket, mean mouth, mobile phone glued to his ear.

Carl doesn't need to think up a name; it just comes to him as they always do. Billy the Kid. Because there is something about the man, that long coat maybe, that reminds Carl of a gunslinger he saw in a DVD. In fact, now that you get right down to it, there is a whiff about him of sudden death.

Carl sets his notebook down, taking care to slide it under his lunch box in case his boss comes in. Not that Richard would notice, Carl thinks. The prick wouldn't notice a Sherman tank cruising along Fisherman's Walk. But still.

Carl unzips his coolbag and lifts out a Dr Pepper.

Only seven hours to go.

CHAPTER 15

Carl rose early this morning, his thoughts in turmoil, and walked the entire perimeter of the Isle of Dogs while the rest of the island slept. Denise had been dead to the world when he'd left. Usually, she knocks herself out with a sleeping pill round about eleven, but last night she'd sat up into the wee small hours, poring over that new Andrew Taylor novel. Carl had longed to talk to her about the job, to hear her reassurances, but all she'd said was *"Sssh."* Once he had stirred, and there she was, with a cardigan buttoned up, engrossed in her book. Carl turned his back and closed his eyes and tried to block out the gentle sound of her lips moving as she followed the words on the page.

When Denise stays up late like that with a novel, Carl knows that her book club will be meeting the following day. Sure enough, he returns from his shift to find three or four cars piled onto the grass verge in front of his house. Carl stands for a moment just inside the front door, listening. They're crowded into the sitting room, and the discussion appears to be well under way.

"A historical novel? That makes it sound like a swashbuckler or something, and it's not at all like that."

"Has anyone read his Lydmouth series?"

"I stayed up all night reading. Couldn't put it down." That's Denise.

The women talk across each other, not aggressively, but as if they are bursting with things to say, and there is a chink of spoons in mugs and the sound of footsteps on carpet as someone enters from the kitchen. There are sudden bursts of laughter.

Carl leaves his outdoor shoes in the tray by the door. He pads down the hallway and stops at the arched entrance to the sitting room. The room is overflowing with women. Four of them are crowded up together on the sofa like children in a hammock, and others are perched on kitchen chairs around the edges of the room. Two of the younger women sit cross-legged on cushions on the floor.

Denise stands by the sideboard, pouring coffee from an insulated jug. She opens her mouth as if she is about to speak. Then someone notices Carl standing in the doorway and a hush settles over the room.

The silence lasts only a second or two, but it seems longer.

"Hello, Carl." Denise's friend Kris waves a slice of flapjack in his direction. "Would you like to join us?" Several of the others laugh as if this is an outrageous suggestion. Denise sets the coffee jug down and comes toward him.

"Sorry to disturb," Carl mutters. He backs off and heads for his room. Before he reaches the stairs, the hubbub starts up again, and above the other voices, he hears Denise's giggle.

Denise's giggle: soft and clear like water trickling over pebbles. During the months after they married, he could get a hard-on just thinking about that laugh. They lived then in a flat on the Chapel House estate. They'd prepare supper together in the tiny kitchen, and Denise would talk to him, her words spilling out in a good-natured stream. She'd gesture as she spoke and punctuate her story by waving the wooden spatula or a dishcloth in the air. Carl loved the fact that she shared with him all the gossip and the details of her day.

"Oh, and, Carl," she'd say, "Lindsey is still seeing that bloke, the one with the tattoo. After what happened on Saturday night, can you believe?"

And the plans. Denise always had plans. It was, "Carl, there's a vacancy coming up for an assistant manager, should I apply? Could I handle all the paperwork, what do you think?" Mostly Denise used to answer her own questions. Just putting them to Carl helped her to see her way clear, that's what she said. Her breezy observations, her ideas, her laughter, washed over him like a healing wave.

That was fifteen years ago.

Carl unlocks the door of the little room he calls his study. It's nine feet by six, just barely qualifying theirs as a three-bedroom house. Other families might have used it for a nursery, but Denise and Carl never had children. They'd thought about it for a while—what married couple doesn't?—but it didn't happen. As time went on, Denise minded less and less.

Carl keeps a lot of special things in this little room. Things that inspire him. He doesn't worry that Denise will come across them. Denise never comes in here. Not even to clean. She finds his hobby macabre. *Macabre.* That's a word she learned at her book club. Like *forensic,* and *facetious,* and *disingenuous.* He used to admire the way she could talk, and all the amazing words that used to pepper her conversations. That was when they were courting, and in the early years of their marriage. But now he suspects that Denise puts on these words like body armor to keep him at a distance.

The room is cheaply furnished with an IKEA bookshelf, and a small tub-shaped armchair that Carl dug out of a skip. Carl plumps the cushions in the armchair and settles himself down. He picks up his files, but he manages only a few pages before he nods off.

After a while, he hears movement down below. Voices calling. Car engines starting up outside. The front door closes. He looks up expectantly as he hears a footstep on the stairs, but no, it's just an echo from below.

CHAPTER 16

Ellie sleeps soundly for the first time in weeks. When she burrows her way out from under the bedclothes and slips downstairs, clear spring sunshine is flooding in through the patio doors. She pulls on a pair of jeans and a T-shirt, downs a cup of coffee, and heads for the river. At Island Gardens, the gates stand wide open. There are seats outside the café and there are benches on which old men hunch against the breeze, but Ellie heads straight for the embankment. She nudges up against the iron railings. The rising wind off the river tongues the water into silver pleats that dazzle when they catch the sun and whips Ellie's curls around her face.

Ellie leans on the railings and gazes ahead, enchanted, as always, by the view. To her left, the river rolls away past the cranes of Newcastle Draw Dock. To her right, it flows past the masts of the *Cutty Sark* and then snakes out of sight along the western perimeter of the island. Directly opposite where Ellie is standing, the Old Royal Naval College is splayed along the riverfront, its columns standing in stately pairs and the gilt weather vanes that cap its domes glistening in the sun. The sparkle of the river throws up flashes onto the pale stone. On the brow of the hill behind stands the Royal Observatory and the prime meridian, where east meets west. And halfway between the brow of the hill and the bank of the river, standing alone on a lawn that's bright with April growth, is a white stone house with nearly perfect proportions. Ellie has never been one for historical detail; she is vaguely aware that King Henry VIII was born on this site, and Queen Elizabeth I, and Bloody Mary, too, but her pleasure comes purely from the view.

Ellie leans for long minutes on the rail, while a motor launch rumbles its way downstream. Then she retreats to a bench and lets the sunshine warm her upturned face. It's the sound of a dog's bark that brings her back to the here and now and makes her look up eagerly. Ellie always notices dogs. When she was a child, she longed for a spaniel—an English springer—that would trot out to meet her as she came home from school. Too messy, Mother said. Too much trouble. Too much noise.

Ellie might have acquired a dog for herself after leaving law school, once she had a real job and a flat with access to a garden. But then William DeQuoyne came into her life, and Will, it turned out, had an aversion to dogs. "Not if you want me," he'd said, and Ellie had buried the idea of a spaniel then and there.

The creature that lopes along the embankment now is not a spaniel, but an aristocratic dog, an elegant creature with silky hair that swings with every step. The young woman who clutches its lead and skips behind it is tall and voluptuously pretty, with pale hair that bounces on her shoulders as she moves. Ellie is so entranced by the pair of them that they are only yards away before she recognizes her colleague from the sports desk, Ariana Raine.

Ellie raises a hand in greeting, but at that very moment, the dog begins to pull, and Ariana, straining at the lead, has to run to keep pace. Laughing, she glides past Ellie without even a glance.

On impulse, Ellie reaches after her. Perhaps she is emboldened still by Tristan Blocombe's endorsement. "Ariana," she calls.

And then she notices, tucked into the shadow of the foot tunnel on the path just ahead, the stocky figure of a man.

"Ariana," Ellie calls again, urgently now, but the name comes out in a croak and echoes back across the river like the bark of a carrion crow.

The man steps into Ariana's path. The dog strains toward him, barking and tugging his mistress along. Laughing still, and shushing the dog, Ariana lets the man sweep her into his arms. She fusses over the dog and the man fusses over her. A brief moment of mutual petting and then all three of them are gone.

Ellie sits back again, and disappointment settles like a lump of bread in her throat. She'd wanted to catch Ariana's attention. Had wanted that wide, wry smile to include her in its warmth.

But it didn't happen. Ariana had a rendezvous with a man, and Ellie was once again unnoticed. Once again, part of the background. Unnoticed, unsought, a kind of wallpaper person.

Unnoticed? Ellie glances nervously around, feeling the beginnings of a blush of embarrassment. Were there witnesses to the snub?

There's a hunched-over pensioner near the railings throwing bread to the gulls, and a boy in a hoodie doing wheelies on the grass; both seem oblivious of anything but their own activities. There's also a man on the bench next to Ellie's. As her glance searches him out, he looks away and buries his chin in the collar of his fleece.

He is probably in his mid-forties, and the hair that's pulled back in a ponytail has faded to a dull sandy color. Ellie notices deep lines that run from nose to mouth, pulling his expression downward and making him appear despondent. His clothing is a blend of the banal and the flashy: polyester slacks that don't meet the tops of his trainers, a fleece with an autumnal scene sketched across the front, and a bomber jacket with some sort of badge on the arm.

But there's something else. Something curiously familiar. Ellie sneaks another glance. His hands: they are unexpectedly large, as if they might belong to a much taller man. And there is something about the curious way he rests them—on his knees, as if he's holding his legs together—that rings a bell.

Don't be silly, Ellie tells herself. He's no different from hordes of other middle-aged men. She takes one more swift glance, and turns decisively away. Let's face it, you don't even know anyone that age. Oh, except for Clive. And Clive has nothing in common with this man. Nothing at all.

The man's head swivels slowly. The whole of his upper torso shifts too, in a strange twisting movement, until he is looking straight at her.

With a rush, Ellie stands and starts toward the embankment, and then halts in confusion. What if she bumps into Ariana and her boyfriend? Ellie doesn't want to appear to be following them.

Abruptly, she changes course and stumbles across the grass. She senses the man with the big hands staring at her. Her scarf falls to the ground. As she stoops to retrieve it and it slips through her fingers again in her haste, she hears him speak.

"Eleanor," he says.

His voice is dry and crackling, a voice stripped of goodness. It gives her the shivers. It reminds her of straw, Ellie decides. A voice of straw.

And again, more urgently this time: "Eleanor?"

Don't be silly, Ellie, she tells herself. You don't know that man from Adam. Where would he get your name? It's just the wind. But all the same, Ellie gives his bench a wide berth. And as she stumbles on toward the exit, behind her she fancies she hears a voice like straw that is calling her, again. And again.

CHAPTER 17

Carl Hewitt stands and dusts the crumbs from his cherry danish off the bench, but he's actually intent on tracking the bird out of the corner of his eye. Dancing Queen looks better in the flesh, he decides. Her hair is bright like untarnished copper. The resemblance is uncanny.

Carl follows with his usual rolling gait as she approaches the exit. He deliberately keeps his pace slow. Wants to watch her; doesn't want to catch up. When he arrives at the gates, about a minute after the Queen, he gets a weird, shivery, feeling. The area still seems—well—inhabited. Think of it: a mere sixty seconds ago, Dancing Queen's trainers touched this very patch of pavement. She brushed her fingers along the bars of this iron fence. She listened for the sound of traffic on Westferry Road, as he does now.

He pauses, straining in the direction that she went. He lifts his face and sniffs as if her scent might be carried on the breeze. Finally, he draws a deep breath, shoots a gob of spit into the grass verge, and, reluctantly, sets off the other way.

Moments later, Carl enters the scruffy interior of the newsagent's shop. The angled shelves with the Sunday newspapers come into view. Carl intends to buy a *Daily Mirror,* but he sees the front page of the *Chronicle* and stops short.

Behind the counter, a powerfully built Pakistani man with a balding head and a gleaming black mustache slouches on a stool. He's concentrating on the wall-mounted television, where an old movie is playing on the flickery screen.

Carl shakes off the excitement of the morning and pulls his mournful features up into a smile. "Morning, Al."

Al has developed a sophisticated repertoire of grunts for the benefit of his customers. The grunt he offers Carl has a distinctly grudging tone.

Carl rests his hip against the counter and leans across. "Here's one for you, Al. What did the lady gnu say to her husband after she gave birth?"

"Dunno," Al says, eyes still on the telly.

Carl taps Al's muscular forearm. Al glances over.

Carl delivers the punch line with a smile as broad as the M25. "I've got gnus for you!"

"Gnus," muses Al, turning back to the telly. "Hmmmnnn." He doesn't catch the angry look that Carl throws his way.

To hell with him, Carl concludes. Anyway, how can you trust a man with a mustache like that? Carl smooths the *Chronicle* out on the counter and begins to read about the body in the Thames. The results of the autopsy are in. The man was murdered. He's an American, it turns out, an electrician, in England for two weeks with his wife and daughter. Holiday of a lifetime. He took one day out to tour Docklands and some bugger went and throttled him. Jesus! Daughter had been looking forward to going to the Tower of London with her dad, and now the only place she'll go is to the funeral.

Al holds out his hand for the money, but his gaze remains fixed to the screen where a petite redhead is doing a courtly dance with Vincent Price. Carl recognizes *The Masque of the Red Death*.

"That's Jane Asher," he says, for Al's benefit, nodding at the screen. "She used to go out with McCartney, you know. Sir Paul, as is."

He can picture them, clear as day, her in a short pink A-line coat, and him in one of those collarless jackets, standing on a sidewalk holding hands. It was the very first time Carl had ever been out of the East End, when his granddad had taken him to the Natural History Museum for a birthday treat. They'd had supper afterward, and as they came out of the chippie, there was the Beatle and his glamorous girlfriend standing on the other side of the street, just like real people.

Al is shaking his head in disagreement. "Uh-uh," he says. As grudging as the grunt. "Girlfriend's Heather Mills. Blond. One with the leg."

"You're wrong there, Al my lad. Heather Mills is Sir Paul's wife. Second wife, as is. I'm talking girlfriend here, before he married Linda."

Al, who wasn't even born until 1973, is losing interest. "How long ago was that, then?"

"Oh, must be—" When exactly was it? 1968? Carl does a quick mental calculation. "Thirty, thirty-five years ago. Before your time, my lad."

As Carl tucks his copy of the *Chronicle* under his arm and leaves the shop, a black cloud settles over his head. Thirty-five years! He never thought he'd live to see the day when he could say, like his granddad used to: *Yes, that was thirty-five years ago.* Almost as if it were normal to be so damned old.

What has he got to show for his decades on this planet? A wife who prefers her reading group to him. A crap job. No prospects. That bastard, Richard, never even bothered to tell Carl that the supervisor's job had gone to someone else. Carl had to winkle it out of him last night. *Richard,* he'd said. *Richard?* Richard had been readying some out-of-date tapes for disposal—exactly the kind of mindless task that Richard liked. At first, he tried to ignore Carl. Carl waited thirty seconds and then he called again. Richard heaved an exaggerated sigh. *What is it, Carl? I'm busy.* Carl could happily have smacked the kid across his chops. But he couldn't afford to alienate him. *Richard, has a decision been made yet about that job? They said Friday.* Richard looked back at the bank of tapes longingly, as if he'd rather do anything other than answer Carl's question. When he spoke, his voice was ever so offhand: *Oh, yeah. Didn't they tell you? They've decided to give it to that Sergeant whatever her name is. The one who's just left the police force.* For the first time he looked directly at Carl as if he were expecting Carl to say something. Carl was silent. He knew that if he tried to speak whatever came out would lose him his job and he couldn't afford that.

So here's Carl now. In a crap job with no prospects. With a mortgage he can hardly manage. With nothing—nothing—to look forward to with pride.

The girl with copper hair. Dancing Queen. She looks as if she might take pride in herself. It's a new idea and one that Carl finds dis-

turbing. But then the shock is chased away by a new and more encouraging thought. Maybe, Carl thinks, just maybe a time is coming
when he can put right some of the failures of the past. When he can
do something to show what kind of man he is. Something to make
people sit up and take notice. All he has to do is settle once and for all
that Dancing Queen is the one he's been looking for, and then the real
challenge will begin.

CHAPTER 18

Ellie has trained hard today, and she's feeling virtuous and rather
self-satisfied as she finishes the briefing with Clive and slips into
her work. She is scrolling through her stories, deciding where to
start, when she senses that there is someone standing at her shoulder.
Something—probably the undertone of cigarette smoke—brings Will
instantly to mind.

"Eleanor Porter? Is that really you?"

For three years, Ellie has fretted on and off about this moment of
meeting. Confronted by the man who'd rejected her, would she break
down? Would she be able to maintain some shred of composure?

Now the moment has come and Ellie is astonished at how serene
she feels. She swings her chair around to face him. There he is, slouching as only very tall people can slouch, and managing, in spite of it, to
look self-assured and offhand and urbane. His expression is quizzical.
"Ellie?"

"Will." Ellie acknowledges him in that one word. Despite her
fears, her tone is cool and untroubled. "Of course it's me. I've recently taken over as the night lawyer at the *Chronicle*. What's your
excuse for being here?"

Will sweeps a hand in the air like someone waving smoke away.
"Oh, some features on twenty-first-century design. You know the sort
of thing: the new urban quarters—luxury and simplicity combined.

What's what in the design world, and who's who." A careless shrug. "I'm the consultant. A favor to someone on the supplement."

So very William DeQuoyne, Ellie thinks. Any other architect who'd been invited to oversee a series at the *Chronicle* would be bursting with swagger. Only Will would present it as something into which he'd been thumbscrewed.

Will fumbles in his pocket, an automatic gesture that is as much a part of him as the slouch. Checking his cigarettes. He withdraws his hand and rests it on the back of Ellie's chair. She can almost feel the warmth of his fingers on the nape of her neck.

There is a longish pause. Ellie hears, in the distance, the swish of a skirt as Ariana makes her way along the corridor.

"You know, Eleanor," he says, with a trace of surprise, "you look marvelous."

Will has always been one for the casual compliment, but Ellie is almost certain that on this occasion that he means it. And why ever not? The last time he'd seen her—in the hospital, after he'd abandoned her—Ellie had been at a very low ebb. Will had heard from a mutual friend that she'd been hospitalized, and had shown up one afternoon while Ellie was off at a therapy session. When Ellie trudged back into the ward, Will was draped over the reception desk, flirting with the sister. Ellie had been overwhelmed by a rush of longing. Of loss. Of, above all, shame that he should see her as she was, with her grubby sweat suit and her face raw from tears.

Will had stayed with Ellie for a quarter of an hour. He had told her in a kindly voice that she needn't be ashamed about the onset of depression. He was so vehement on this point that Ellie could sense his relief. His logic was transparent and self-serving. Ellie is depressed; depression is an illness; ergo, no blame attaches to Will. If Ellie has been paralyzed by panic attacks, unable to think, unable to sleep, it isn't Will's fault. If judgment deserted her, and she had to give up work, it was because of the depression, and not because of him.

And no way could it be Will's fault that in the weeks since he'd dumped her Ellie had ballooned from voluptuous to fat.

None of this could be blamed on Will.

"It's the illness," he'd assured her with an expression as solemn as funeral music. And then he had left.

Six weeks later, Ellie discharged herself from the hospital. She had Will to thank for that. Will and her mother. Annabel had swept into the hospital, her presence announced by a swirl of perfume, and immediately after she'd learned of Will's visit, she'd launched into an attack.

"Well, Ellie, you've blown it now. He's seen you like this? You'll never get him back."

And for once, instead of retreating into sullen misery, Ellie had exploded. Her rageful words shot out like shrapnel, piercing Annabel in the most vulnerable of places: in her fear of aging, her concern for propriety, her vanity. The outburst felt magnificent.

It wasn't long after that that she drew aside the hospital curtains, looked out across a pigeon-stained roof, and realized with a sense of triumph that she was fiercely unhappy. To be unhappy was to be alive, emotionally speaking. It was enough.

What a transformation, people marveled a few months later. Ellie thought of it as a resurrection.

She tries to put some of this into words for Will's benefit. He seems both dazzled and discomfited by the changes in her.

"But you even look different," Will protests.

"I do," she agrees. Lighter, by two and a half stone. Fitter. Better dressed. Better groomed.

It had taken months of karate. Months of disciplined dieting; Ellie couldn't count the number of green vegetables she had eaten in the interest of weight loss, or the number of pastries she'd forgone. She had a wardrobe overhaul, adding dashes of vivid color—cerise and acid green and cerulean blue—to her basic blacks and navies, so that her appearance shifted from droopy to dramatic. She instituted a beauty regime that included a once-a-month facial, a two-monthly hair trim, and routine appointments to have legs waxed and eyebrows plucked. Ellie should look good. She's done everything short of surgery to pull herself into shape.

Ellie leans back in her chair and smiles tentatively at Will, warming to the admiration in his eyes. She has a sudden rush of confidence.

Small and perfectly formed, Tony Mannix had quipped during one karate session, his eyes resting frankly on her bosom. Ellie adored the phrase. For the first time in her thirty years of life, Eleanor Porter isn't a *shorty* anymore. She isn't even (that mincing word, that sop to the diminutive) *petite*. She is small and perfectly formed. And that means, among other things, that Will can no longer hurt her.

Not that he looks as if he wants to.

"So I've changed, have I? You seem not to have altered at all, Will." The same world-weary expression. The same sophistication leavened with a dash of sweetness. And the same attentive half smile, that flash of instant intimacy that is all the more winning because it comes from a man who makes a point of being supercool.

Footsteps from the corridor. Ariana approaches carrying a carton marked MANCHESTER UNITED. A new team strip, perhaps? Ellie gestures at Will to make way, but Ariana has to clear her throat before he takes any notice.

"Introduce me, Eleanor," Ariana says.

Will spares Ellie the trouble. Languidly, with scarcely a glance at the new arrival, he extends his hand. "William DeQuoyne," he says.

"William." Ariana rolls the name out as if there's something exotic about it. "William DeQuoyne, how do you do."

Ellie does her bit. "This is Ariana Raine, from the sports desk."

Ellie can see how this would usually go. Mention the sports desk in connection with a babe like Ariana and the conversation flows. They ask: *What's a girl like you . . . ?* and on they go from there. But not Will. His disdain for sport is dogged, particularly where teams are involved. Trying too hard, he drawls. Football is for people whose brains are in their feet. Ariana receives only the briefest of nods, before Will focuses once again on Ellie.

There is another pause. Will looks Ellie up and down again and then treats her to that rare, lopsided smile. "Well, it's been good meeting up with you, little one. I'll be lurking around the *Chronicle* over the next few weeks. We'll see each other again, you can be sure of it."

Ellie smiles uncertainly and smoothes her hair away from her face. It has been a long time since anyone called her "little one." Does Will remember that that was the term her father used? She can't decide which reaction is greater, her pleasure at hearing the once-familiar phrase, or her vexation.

"See you," she says, and is disconcerted when the words come out in a whisper.

CHAPTER 19

William DeQuoyne and Eleanor Porter met near Oxford Street, in a shop with exotic balls of wool in the window and racks and racks of yarn. He had popped in to collect a parcel. Ellie's passion at that time was weaving and she was merely looking—drinking in the richness of ochre and umber and teal. She showed him how unexpected colors might set each other off, and when she spoke of it, she ceased to be self-conscious and her eyes shone and Will was enchanted. They found themselves leaving the shop together, and when it began to rain, they went for a coffee in a Viennese deli and he admired the way she tucked into her pastry and on it went from there.

Ellie had been twenty-four. There'd been one or two lovers before. She had even, for a few months, formed a couple with a travel writer who did stand-up comedy in his spare time. They split up when she finally admitted to herself that their nights together were driven by duty more than desire.

Will was another story. Will was the first man—the only man, if it came to that—for whom Ellie had ever felt a longing. He made her feel voluptuous. He gloried in her hills and mounds—her magnificent landscape, he called it. On long afternoons in her flat, with the sun slicing sideways round the edges of the blinds, he would set out on expedition, trekking across her belly, gliding above her hinterlands, burrowing into her hills. He made her feel as beautiful and as nurturing as the sky.

Their attraction was immediate. On their fifth meeting, he declared his love for her, and he meant it. She had no doubt he meant it. She could see how greedily he looked at her. There'd been men who'd admired her breasts before. There'd even been one chap who was inspired by the sheer expanse of her arse. Will, on the other hand, adored every inch of her. He lavished care on her collarbone, on the curve of her armpit, on the ripples where her toes flexed against the soles of her feet. And Ellie came to feel a desire that was equally intense. Came to long to caress the muscle at the hem of his shorts, to stroke the soft skin on his inner elbow, to trace the lines of his rib cage with her tongue.

Ellie's mother usually didn't approve of the men Ellie dated, but she did approve of William DeQuoyne. She never quizzed Ellie about his intentions, as she had with previous boyfriends, or pressed for details of his background. "He's charming," she said in a ruminative way that made it clear that Annabel had never expected her daughter to come up with such a catch.

Ellie had always dreaded introducing men to her mother. She never knew how Annabel would react. She might be cold and off-putting, dismissing the man with a swish of distaste. She might be warm and gushing, might sidle up and offer the poor boy a deep and unexpected intimacy. She might confuse him by inviting him to collude in a put-down of her daughter. *Ellie is a lovely girl, isn't she, Simon? Or she would be, don't you think, if she would only eat a little less?* The men felt sorry for Eleanor, but it was a cruelty that frightened them off.

Ellie certainly never meant to loose Annabel on Will. It didn't seem appropriate, in the circumstances. It didn't seem wise. But then one spring day, she and Will were sitting at an outdoor table near Covent Garden, holding hands and waiting to pay so they could dash back to her place, when her mother came sailing toward them with her high heels clattering on the cobbles. Annabel was upon them before Ellie even realized. She insinuated herself between Ellie and Will. She fluttered at the waiter until he lifted a chair over the heads of the other diners and slid it under her. Annabel introduced herself with a smile she reserved for men. *You must be the boyfriend. How do you do?* She remained with them for half an hour, flirting with Will throughout, engaging him in guessing games, and making personal remarks. *Not many men would have the courage to wear a lavender shirt. Or, I might add, the looks.*

The odd thing was that this flirting didn't faze Ellie one little bit. She watched her mother's attempts to assert control—the machinations suddenly as transparent to Ellie as the workings of a clear plastic water pump—and, for the first time in her adult life, found them more pathetic than infuriating. Ellie scarcely even minded Annabel's presence and nor, it seemed, did Will. He joked to Ellie as they climbed into a taxicab afterward, "A good-looking woman, your mother. I expect she takes after you."

What Ellie remembers most is how, throughout the meeting with Annabel, his eyes, languid as ever, roamed the pavement area half-heartedly, appearing to notice little, but when they did stop, resting full-square on Ellie's face. And how, the minute they were seated in the taxicab, while he was still giving directions to the driver, his hand had slid up under her jumper and caressed her belly before moving on.

He loved her. She knows he did.

CHAPTER 20

It is gone eleven-fifteen when Ellie climbs the stairs from the underground platform into the open air. She sets off at a brisk pace along Spindrift Avenue, walking on the pavement nearest the shrubs and immature trees that cloak the avenue from the houses nearer the river. Anyone watching would notice how every few paces, she takes a little step sideways, or rotates to the left or the right. She's running through a kata in her head.

About a quarter of a mile along the avenue, Ellie takes a sharp left and disappears into a footpath that takes a dogleg through the trees. The path is strewn with fast-food cartons and used condoms, hedged about with blackberry runners and ground ivy, and it's unnervingly invisible from the houses at either end, but it's also the shortest way home. Ellie negotiates the bend without seeing another soul and emerges onto the top end of Hesperus Street. Behind her, a man who appears to be expecting a downpour—not only is he wearing a full-length mac and a wide-brimmed hat, but he's clutching an umbrella—staggers into the footpath and promptly steps into a cluster of blackberry canes. Must be drunk as a lord, Ellie concludes. She hears his yelps of pain and considers giving him a hand, but decides to let him recover on his own, and he does so, stumbling out of the foot-path as she approaches her house, crooning "Danny Boy" in a dread-ful parody of a Scottish accent.

Ellie inserts her key into the lock and as she does, the door next to hers flies open and a figure in a cloak rushes out.

"Jessica! You startled me," Ellie says.

Jessica Barnes lives in the house next door to Ellie's. She's a student—reading drama, perhaps, or theater studies, Ellie thought when they first met. That might explain the long lace dress. The swooping cloak. The maroon lipstick that makes her face look like that of a child who has raided her mother's makeup bag. But no, it turns out that Jessica—at her parents' insistence—is doing a founda-tion course in accountancy after disappointing results in her A-levels.

To Ellie's surprise, Jessica stops and edges her painted lips into a smile. Ellie casts around for something to say. "How was college today?"

Jessica expels a stream of air between pursed lips as if this is a question she dreads. "Oh, you know," she whispers, in an offhand tone. She clears her throat. Her eyes fix on Ellie's for a moment and then wander away.

As it happens, Ellie doesn't. She herself found college exhilarating. Loved being introduced to new ideas. Loved receiving essays back with favorable comments in the margins. In college, for the first time in her life, Ellie felt as if someone was really listening. As if she, Ellie, might have something to say.

Ellie gropes for understanding. "What, the course is difficult?"

Jessica fingers her leather collar, easing it away from her throat. "No. Not difficult," she says, in a sudden rush of confidence. "It's just not me, Ellie. You know? I feel like a fish out of water." Ellie watches fascinated as Jessica takes a ball of tissue from her pocket and slowly separates the layers. Two swollen-looking objects nestle in her palm. Jessica looks directly at Ellie and offers her a fig. Ellie isn't in the mood.

"Suit yourself." Jessica's dark-stained mouth forms an expression that hovers between a smile and a sneer. It's her way of dealing with rejection. She doesn't know what to say to someone like Ellie, but Jess thinks she's kind of cool. She likes the tentative way Ellie speaks, with a kind of question in her voice. She is intrigued by the fact that Ellie has taken to coming home late, and always alone. She suspects her of meeting a married lover in the evenings.

Jessica uses a pointed thumbnail to pierce the fig, ripping it in two, and then shears the fruit from the peel with her teeth. "I'm going down the river," she says. "Gotta find someone." Jessica turns, her cloak swirling behind her, and heads toward the river, and Ellie steps inside and rouses the hamster from his sleep.

Ellie doesn't notice that the drunken man who was singing "Danny Boy" has stopped outside her house. He stumbles and rests his shoulder against her door as if for support. It's amazing how much a man can hear through half an inch of wooden door. He hears her calling Odysseus. Hears the high-pitched chatter of the television. Hears her run a bath. And then, hoarding what he's learned, he strips off the mac and hat and, with a rolling gait, heads back across the island toward home.

CHAPTER 21

It's one of those enigmatic April days. The trees are giving off only the faintest hint of green at the tips, but the sun holds the promise of summer. Ellie makes a brisk start. Though she recoils from the phrase "to kill two birds with one stone," that is precisely what she has in mind. A long run through the foot tunnel to Greenwich, around the park, and up the hill. Then an hour with her mother (who complained only yesterday of neglect) and a brisk walk home. Filial duty and training session in one clean swoop.

She should have known better. Visits to Annabel are seldom clean. Ellie is doubled over, stretching her hamstrings, when Annabel opens the door.

"Ellie, honestly! Must you put your bottom in the air like that? Right here on the doorstep, where everyone can see? And look at you, you're sweating like a—" Annabel stops in midsentence.

"I believe the word you're looking for is *pig*."

"I didn't mean that, dear, I just—" Annabel heaves a sigh. "Well, never mind, do come in."

Annabel has an unbecoming scarf wrapped around her hair and she's wearing a Laura Ashley apron. She leads Ellie through to the kitchen, in the center of which, on a mat of old newspapers, stands a newly acquired side table.

"I've just laid the first coat of wax," Annabel says. The lavender scent permeates the room.

Ellie runs a finger over the surface. "It's lovely, Mum. Beautiful marquetry."

Annabel beams as if the table were her most talented child. "Now, lamb," she says, as she fills the kettle and collects up the things for tea, "tell me about the job. What are the people like? What about your boss?"

Ellie arranges the biscuits the way her mother expects, though neither Ellie nor Annabel will have any, and as she does so she describes in highly edited form what it's like to be the night lawyer at the *Chronicle*. She plays up the excitement of stories that come winging in, the pressure of time, the intensity in the newsroom at the end of the day. She describes Clive's good humor, Ariana's glamour, and Tristan Blocombe's endorsement. She doesn't mention Jonathan. She doesn't mention Will.

When the tea is ready, Annabel carries the tray through into the sitting room, and Ellie follows. Just inside the doorway, she suddenly pulls up short. Something's different.

"What's happened to the chest of drawers?"

"Sold," Annabel says, "to make room for my new table." She unloads the tea things onto the coffee table, slips off her shoes, and seats herself on the sofa, swinging her legs up beneath her. "I got rid of it, yesterday, through an ad in the free paper. A hunched old man— ninety if he was a day, I swear, darling—came in his SUV and hauled it away."

Ellie runs her hands along the back of the sofa where the chest of drawers used to stand. The empty space looks awkward. It looks wrong.

"What about the contents, Mother? The things you used to keep in there? You didn't get rid of those?"

"Sid, he said his name was. Sid! Can you believe it? Like someone out of an Ealing comedy. I was asking ninety-five pounds—it was a nice piece, all the drawers slid in and out as easily as pie—but he got me down to eighty. You've never seen anyone so persistent. In the end, I didn't have the energy to argue." She lifts the lid of the teapot and gives the contents a quick stir. "A minute more, I think. What were you asking, lamb?"

"The chest of drawers, Mummy."

"Oh, the chest. You didn't want it, did you? It really wouldn't go, you know. Your house is so modern. That chest would look quite out of place."

"I'm talking about the contents, Mother. Those photos and things. That old stuff."

Annabel unwinds her legs and sits up sharply. She pours a cup of tea and hands it to Ellie. "Stuff to do with your father, is that what you mean?"

"Yes. Yes, Mother, that's precisely what I mean. Where've you put it all?"

"Don't you think, Eleanor, that it's time we cleared that lot out? It's nothing short of morbid, the way you always want to come back to Tom and his death. For goodness' sake, dear, it's twenty-two years since your father died."

"Was murdered, you mean."

"Eleanor! What are you saying?"

"You know perfectly well, Mummy. We've never talked about that day, but we both know the truth about what happened. We know that I killed him." There's the faint noise of a key turning in a lock. Eleanor's hands are shaking so much that she is forced to set the teacup down. Annabel's voice lowers to a hiss.

"An accident, Eleanor. Your father was killed in a dreadful accident. The police—"

"Accident, my foot." Ellie slams her hands down hard on the back of the sofa, and there's a movement in the doorway.

"Hello, girls." Andrew, Annabel's husband, has an innocent-looking face on which is clearly etched every current of emotion. "Something wrong?" he says, his features drawing tighter with concern. "What's this about an accident?" Annabel goes to him and helps him out of his leather jacket. He wraps his arm around her waist. "You all right?" he asks.

"Perfectly," Annabel answers, for both of them, and gives him a peck on the cheek.

CHAPTER 22

Don't overdo the exercise; that was Ellie's plan. But when she sets out for home after seeing her mother, it's at a furious walking pace and before she reaches the *Cutty Sark*, she's running again.

Twenty-two years since your father died. As if Ellie doesn't know that. As if she doesn't every single year mark the anniversary of his death. Ellie was eight, going on nine, when *it* happened, his death, and even when she touched the body, she couldn't believe he was dead. She kept expecting him to stand. To speak to her. To lift her onto his shoulders and carry her away from the crowds, the flashing lights, the sirens. It wasn't until the funeral service, where her mother's hysteria punctured Ellie's awareness—wasn't until she found her own cardigan, covered in blood, where she had stuffed it under her bed—that Ellie could truly accept that her father was gone.

The tall masts of the *Cutty Sark* remind Ellie that she's supposed to be in training. She checks her watch. She'll see if she can shave a half a minute off her time. She eases her pace as she approaches the foot tunnel that leads under the Thames, back to the island. The descent down the curving staircase takes her from bright day into curious artificial lighting that resembles gaslight in its effect, into walls lined with ivory tiles that give off a creamy glow. Ellie's downward movement is fluid, her fingers trailing lightly on the handrail—eleven shallow steps, and a platform, and eleven shallow steps again. She doesn't need to count. This is as familiar as the feel of her fingers on the keyboard.

At the bottom, the tunnel is shaped like a tube: a flattened floor paved with brick, a concrete skirting, and curving tiled walls that meet overhead. Every ten feet or so, a light mounted on the ceiling casts hoops of shadow around the walls. Like the ribs of the whale in a children's version of the story of Jonah, Ellie thinks, as she hits the floor and gets into her stride. The tunnel could be the belly of the beast, rounded and gutless and pale, with warm light coming always from somewhere just ahead.

After a minute or two, the floor dips sharply, ramping Ellie lower and lower below the level of the river. She picks up the pace, bobbing and weaving around other pedestrians. Shadows slide along in front of her. She fights off the memory of other unhappy exchanges with her mother as the length of the tunnel unfolds in the distance.

After Tom Porter's death, Ellie had desperately wanted to talk to her mother about what had happened and how it had happened—about what she, Ellie, had done. She wanted to confess; she wanted to have her mother hold her and tell her it was all right, that she wasn't a wicked, wicked girl. But the longed-for conversation never took place. At first, Annabel was too bound up in her own grief. Later, she was too busy inhabiting the new status of widow. Each time Ellie tried to bring the subject up, Annabel kissed her, not ungently, and said, "Hush, lambie, they are such painful memories. Best not to talk about it. Silence helps forgetting."

Well, Annabel was right about that, in a way. Over the years, Ellie's memory of that day has become nothing more than a series of disconnected events. She couldn't piece it all together now if she tried. And she doesn't try. It's too terrifying. Annabel is right: Silence helps forgetting.

But Ellie hates the fact that she has almost forgotten her father. He exists now only in wisps and tendrils of image and feeling—the thrill when he held the back of her cycle, running, and then released her to wobble off on her own; the phone calls from overseas; the Sooty glove puppet that he used to make her laugh. She can never conjure up her father's face; an impression of size and warmth and strength is all she can muster, however hard she tries.

Ellie often pesters Annabel for photos and mementos of her father. She knows Annabel's kept some. She's certain of that. But Annabel is resolutely unhelpful: "I can't remember where they are," she always says, as if she were speaking about something as inconsequential as paper clips. When last year Annabel let slip about the chest of drawers, she immediately forbade Ellie access. I won't have you raking it all up again, Annabel shouted. Let sleeping dogs lie. But Ellie can't let sleeping dogs lie. Even if she'd killed him, he was her father. She'd loved him and she needs to know.

Mother didn't actually say she'd thrown out the contents of the chest of drawers. Did she?

Ellie has passed the central point in the tunnel. She has been jogging on an upward slope for almost a minute. She reaches the bottom of the staircase at the Island Gardens end of the tunnel as loud voices boom down from above. The noise crashes against the tiled walls. Voices harden into a giant wave of sound. Ellie stiffens—she can't help it—and presses her back against the wall as three boys, half her age and a foot taller, clatter into view. They shift halfheartedly to the side, but Ellie is still pinned to the wall.

"Excuse you," she mutters.

A lad with a backward-facing baseball cap directs a threatening glance over his shoulder. Ellie makes a sour face back and the others tug him on.

Suddenly, unaccountably, she is overwhelmed by tiredness. Her knees refuse to carry her up the stairs. Ellie presses the button for the old-fashioned lift and treads on the spot while she waits.

CHAPTER 23

Carl is sitting on a bench near the Thames with his legs stretched out in front of him. He has swapped his fleece for a T-shirt—it's another mild afternoon—and applied fresh plasters to his blisters. The second lot in two days, goddamn it. The chemist recommended some special kind with healing properties, but they cost a king's ransom. They'd have to stay on until Christmas to be worth the price.

His eyes are tracking a barge as it makes its way upriver, but his thoughts are on the Dancing Queen. It's twenty-four hours since the last time he saw her. Twenty-four hours, and Carl can't get her out of his head. Like Kylie, he chuckles to himself. How's it go? Oh, yeah. Carl mumbles his way through "Can't Get You Out of My Head." Two women who are taking snapshots of the Royal Naval College glance in his direction and gather their bags and make for the exit.

Carl continues humming as he heads for the kiosk. The man behind the counter holds out a Mars bar at his approach.

"You're the clever one, then, aren't you?" Carl says by way of a thank-you. He accepts the chocolate and hands over the exact change.

"Nope." The wire-haired man inside the kiosk—all the years Carl has been coming here, he's never learned his name—gives a lopsided grin and shakes his head. "The clever one, that's my brother. Retired eleven years ago, he did. Takes it easy, strolls by the river, sits in the sun. Me, I still get up five in the morning, every day of the week, come down here to work. Nope. I wouldn't call that clever at all. You off to the market?"

Carl nods and heads for the tunnel, worrying his way into the Mars bar as he goes. He presses the button and waits for the lift. Carl hardly ever takes the lift. Stairs, that's the thing. He's a strong believer in exercise. When he was a teenager, he had a series of epileptic seizures. Fits, they called them then. One, all alone, in his bedroom. He doesn't remember anything about it, except for the strange disconnected sensation that came before. One on a bus. The conductor threatened to throw him off for being drunk until another passenger intervened. And the worst one at school in the middle of a hockey game. Three only, and after that the seizures stopped. But these three were enough to end his career with the Metropolitan Police before it even started. Medically unfit, they said, and it still rankles.

The need to prove them wrong has got him out of bed early every single morning for the past twenty years. Every morning, without fail, he has followed a program of exercises designed for the Canadian Air Force, and there's nothing unfit about those geezers. He has worked up the levels until his performance is close to the peak. The recruiters for the Met were dead wrong; Carl Hewitt is primed and ready for action.

So when Carl takes the lift, it's only because he's forced into it by his blisters. But in fact, if he chose to take any lift in the world, it would be this ancient one. It's not a bit like those stainless-steel death traps in the tower. This lift is (to use one of Denise's big words that Carl actually likes) *capacious*. It's like a chapel, with an oval interior that's paneled in dark-stained wood and a bench that resembles a pew fixed to one wall. A CCTV monitor at eye height shows flickering images of the inside of the tunnel as if to keep your mind fixed on your destination.

Only the sound is wrong. If there has to be music, it should consist, in Carl's view, of cheerful, bawdy songs, the kind that Edwardian workers might have tossed over their shoulders as—dusty with cement, slicked with grease, scratchy with sugar, or shiny with metal shavings—they crowded into the lift after a day's work in the island's warehouses and processing plants. But, oh no. The bloke who operates this lift, the bloke who ruins the atmosphere by importing a blow heater and a cheap plastic chair, insists on a portable radio. Today it is blaring out a Robbie Williams track. *Let me entertain you*, Robbie bawls. Not bloody likely, Carl thinks. He shows his disapproval by remaining standing and keeping his eye on the screen.

In the far distance, he can make out a group of teenaged boys shuffling away down the tunnel. At the door of the lift, a girl swings her arms like someone treading water. Cooling down after a run, Carl decides. The island is full of them now. Joggers. They even have a Canary Wharf run for charity, can you believe? Richard asked Carl if he wanted to form a team. "A team? A Canary Wharf team? You gotta be joking," Carl said.

When the door opens, she's there, bent over double, with her fingertips grazing the floor. She jumps up and scoots inside. She stands as far away from Carl as she can.

The lift operator gives Carl a questioning look. Carl shakes his head. Change of plan. He isn't getting off. Not now that the Dancing Queen has come on board.

Carl shifts to the right so that he is directly behind her. He has made quite a lot of progress in the last few days. He knows where she lives. He knows she works for the *Chronicle,* though he's not yet established what she does. Above all, thanks to the electoral register—isn't democracy marvelous?—he has confirmed her name. Eleanor Porter. But these facts are just the surface. Carl means to go deeper. He means to know everything about her: how she thinks, what she feels, where she goes, whom she sees. To know her inside out. He wants to take stock of her life, to know what she amounts to. The need inside of him is inescapable and it's a need he means to satisfy.

In the seconds while the lift chugs toward the surface, he takes advantage of their closeness. No detail escapes him. He observes the strands of titian hair curling damply on the back of her neck. He listens to the way her breath catches in her throat; to the squeak as her trainers catch on the floor. He sniffs the enticing odor of perspiration on her clean body.

She is fumbling with a pouch at her waist. She grasps something—a small suede-bound book—and pulls it out. She fumbles, and the notebook flies from her grasp and flips over and falls to the floor.

Carl pitches forward. His fingers and hers close around the book. In that instant, he sees her thin wrist and her long fingers and he feels—he's certain he didn't imagine this—the heat from her hand. It is so, so warm. Not like before.

Her smile as she acknowledges his attempt to help is neat and unrevealing. She nods to the lift operator—small, delicate features, the pores of her nose glistening from the run—and steps out of the lift. For an instant, in the white light from the glass panels overhead, she is bleached of color. Then she is gone.

Carl remains like a statue, too stunned to move. The operator gestures impatiently. "You getting off?"

Getting off? No, she's already got off. She's gone.

The operator shrugs and closes the doors.

Carl goes down-down-down-down into the tunnel again. He has lost all sense of his surroundings. He could be in Leicester Square for all he knows. As the lift sinks deeper into the earth he is thinking only about the girl.

About her silhouette. The narrow nose, the slight build, the tightly curled coppery hair. All of that sits lightly but insistently in his memory.

About the smell, the acrid smell of her sweat. About the faint hiss of fabric as her thin fingers tap against her thigh. She is anxious, even after a run.

He sees it in his mind's eye, as if it were a video. And he names it. Naming, Carl knows, helps to fix the memory.

Names the arms, toned and lithe, and the small but discernible biceps. The crease of skin on the elbow. The hands; the thin fingers that twitch at her side. The round breasts in the pink sleeveless T-shirt and the stains under the arms.

The contours of her head. The hairline at the back, one side dipping lower than the other, with tendrils of hair lying in damp curlicues on her neck. The ears, ever so slightly protuberant, that give her a vulnerable air. The earrings, small ivory hoops strung with gold, that are too dressy for jogging; unchanged, perhaps, from an outfit earlier in the day.

He is racing through the list now, scrolling it through his mind, eager to fix every detail before it flies away. Her nails are short and ragged and without polish. Her arms have a soft reddish gold down. Her legs are smooth and behind the left knee—shaped like a teardrop, dusty rose against her pale skin—there is a tiny birthmark.

"Eleanor Porter," Carl whispers. "Eleanor Porter. Eleanor. Lenor. Ellie."

All his life, Carl has been plagued with doubts. Doubts about his adequacy, about his judgment, about his view of the world. But suddenly, in a shift as clean and decisive as a guillotine blade, the doubts abandon him, and absolute certainty steps up into their place.

Eleanor Porter. Eleanor Porter. Little Ellie.

Carl is absolutely certain.

She's the one.

CHAPTER 24

Clive is on his own in the office when Ellie comes on shift. "Yo, little Elle. How's my posse today?" He pushes his glasses up and looks at her with his beaming smile.

Ellie is so delighted by this easy acceptance that she doesn't even think to object to "little Elle." She returns the smile. "Gangsta talk? Gosh, Clive, aren't Lily and Rose a little young for"—she dredges up the only name she knows—"Tupac Shakur?"

"It's my nephew. We had Tupac's posthumous albums nonstop during his last visit." He waggles his eyebrows and assumes a pleading look. "Be gentle with me, Elle. Think of my suffering."

They run through the day's stories. A few court reports; a celebrity breakup. Nothing very challenging, Clive says. The briefing is over in a flash. Before Ellie has a chance to ask any questions, Clive has touched his fingertips to her cheek, buttoned up his waistcoat, and bolted for the lift.

Ellie takes a peek around the newsroom. Sees, in the far corner, a cluster of journalists exclaiming over a set of photographs. Ariana in tête-à-tête with another journalist, walking a finger along his arm as she speaks. She glances up and catches Ellie watching her, and winks.

Ellie digs her notebook—her good luck charm, really—out of her handbag and places it on the desk. Everything—her entire life—is in this book: addresses and phone numbers, things to do, notes about her training program (*Monday, 3.2 miles*). Tiny silver letters on the cover spell out her name; it's the only one of Will's presents that she kept. Ellie reaches over and squares the paper in the printer. She touches the mouse and the screen leaps into life.

Ellie is deep inside the celebrity divorce piece when a brand-new story pops up: BARRISTER QUESTIONED BY POLICE. Oliver Nesbit! Well, what do you know. She hadn't given Oliver a thought in years until Harriet mentioned him at Wagamama, and now suddenly here he is, smack-dab in front of her.

Ellie focuses in on the screen.

A man is being questioned today by police after photographs of a naked child were found among a batch of negatives sent to Boots for developing. Oliver Nesbit, aged thirty, the high-flying young barrister who hosts the ITV program *Day in Court,* told our reporter as he was leaving home this morning that "it was all a misunderstanding." He said he was confident that no charges would be laid. Since the police began to work with American investigators on operations designed to limit the use of child pornography on the Internet, photographic processing centers have become more and more alert to unacceptable images. A Boots spokeswoman says that this is the third such case in recent months.

Ellie experiences a surge of outrage. To be called in for questioning is bad enough, but to have one's name publicly linked with a scandal—it's appalling. The link the journalist makes to the larger police operation against pornography is nothing more than innuendo. Ellie is drafting a firm note to the editor who'd submitted the story when someone sweeps past the desk with a clip-clap of high-heeled mules. Suddenly there's a question hanging in the air. Ellie looks up, startled, into Ariana's beguiling smile.

"I've heard that Hal's dug up a story about a naughty barrister, Eleanor. Have you seen it yet?"

Ellie looks at the effortlessly attractive young woman in front of her. The thick, pliable hair, swept up today into a roll. The toasty complexion. The skirt that fits as if it grew on her. How does Ariana do it?

"Actually, I'm working on it right now."

Ariana saunters around so she's peering over Ellie's shoulder and skims through the piece eagerly, her lips moving as she reads. "Crikey," she says. "Sounds like this Oliver has been a ba-a-a-d boy."

"Don't you think it's a bit too early to say that?" Ellie shoots back.

"I smell a rat. Why would Nesbit take indecent photos to a commercial developer? Why would he take the pictures in the first place? For heaven's sake, the man is a barrister and a television presenter. He has a reputation to protect. And anyway"—it's out before Ellie can stop herself—"I know him. I used to date him."

"Oooh." Ariana squeezes her bum onto the edge of Ellie's desk, forcing Ellie to push her chair back. "Tell me!" Ariana says.

Ellie tries to backtrack. "It wasn't that big a deal. Only a few weeks, a couple of months, maybe, at university. We didn't have a lot in common, to tell you the truth. But—well, I always thought he was a decent guy."

Such exquisite hesitation. Ariana is certain now that Ellie knows more than she's telling. "Decent guy, my ass! You had an affair, didn't you?" At the blush that rushes into Ellie's cheeks Ariana becomes more persistent. "What was he like? Come on, I want details."

Ellie shrugs, ashamed at having spilled the beans. She wanted to say something that would catch the other girl's attention. Well, she's certainly succeeded in that.

"Did you suspect anything funny about him, Eleanor? Anything at all?"

Ellie nibbles on a fingernail. She painted some acrid substance on her nails again this morning in an effort to break herself of the dreadful habit, but despite the foul taste, she can't resist worrying away at an edge. She sees Ariana's frown of disapproval and returns her own inadequate fingers to the keyboard. "I've got a lot of work to do, Ariana. I'd rather not talk about it just now," she says. "If you don't mind?"

Ariana's own nails, resting neatly on the edge of the desk, are perfectly shaped and glazed with pale polish. They remind Ellie of pink-costumed chorus girls, lined up and waiting to burst into song. One, two, kick, razzle-dazzle.

"Actually, Elle, I do mind." Ariana adopts the half-teasing, half-petulant tone of someone who's used to getting her own way. "Whetting my curiosity like this and then clamming up. It just isn't fair."

Why can't Ariana understand? Ellie could damage her position at the *Chronicle* by being indiscreet. But besides that, Oliver doesn't deserve to have their brief affair ground into gossip. Just because he's in a tight spot at the moment doesn't mean that Ellie should kiss and tell. The refusal comes out more primly than Ellie meant it to. "I can't go into detail, Ariana. The guy's in trouble. It wouldn't be right."

Ariana's generous mouth collects itself into a slash of irritation. Her sigh as she swings upright is almost a harrumph. She saunters across a corridor of carpet to the financial news desk, where a tall man wearing suspenders is writing furiously on a legal pad. When he hears her coming, he sets his pad down and leans toward her, balancing on the rear legs of his chair. Ariana, with a backward glance at Ellie, bends and whispers in his ear.

The journalist responds with a low chuckle. In the quiet of the night shift, it can be heard halfway across the room. Ellie hears it and her face flames.

CHAPTER 25

Ellie can't help fretting about Oliver Nesbit. She gave her advice on the article about him without letting the editor know that he'd once been a boyfriend of hers. And then to compound her mistake, she chatted about him to Ariana when she should have kept her mouth shut. There's nothing between them now, of course; but nevertheless, it could look like conflict of interest.

She tells Odysseus all about the problem as she prepares a stir-fry for her supper. They make a right pair: Odysseus in a basket on the worktop, gnawing on a stalk of broccoli; Ellie in her bathrobe, fresh from the shower, with her hair wrapped in a towel, tossing bean sprouts and crushed peanuts into the wok.

"You see, Odysseus, I got it all wrong. I tried to make a bond with Ariana, you know, a good old girlie gossip, but then I realized that this wasn't fair to Oliver. And I ended up by saying more than I should and offending Ariana at the same time. What a chump!"

She sets the spatula down and tickles the hamster under his chin. He sneezes and settles back to his broccoli.

Her supper ready, Ellie piles it into a large bowl and carries it out into the garden. A midnight snack. The grass feels luxuriously cool on her toes. Only April, and already it's beginning to grow. She'll have to break out the lawn mower in the next few days.

Her garden isn't large, but it's lushly planted and very private, and there's a stillness that Ellie craves. The garden can echo to the sounds of children in the playground of the nearby primary school during the day, but at night, it's as quiet as the Cumbrian countryside, sheltered by high brick walls and protective shrubbery from the world outside.

Ellie is halfway through her noodles when the silence is broken by a clatter of footsteps along Hesperus Street. There's the jingle of coins in a pocket as the person dashes nearer.

Someone else farther away, chasing. A shout, rough and angry, the kind of meaningless outburst that you hear from Manchester Road at closing time. The kind of outburst that Ellie hates.

The footsteps slow and then a door closes with a formidable slam in the house next to hers. Someone stomps up the stairs. The balcony doors above the garden are thrown open. From inside the house, there's a growl.

"Jess!" The echo can be heard up and down Hesperus Street. "Fuck sake, Jess, answer me." Ellie shrinks back against her patio doors.

Another voice—tired, tearful, pleading. They're both on the balcony now, only a few feet away from Ellie, and she can hear every single word. "Tull, it's like I told you. It's peaceful down by the river. Sometimes I just need to get away, you know?"

"Whaddya mean, 'get away'? You were meeting someone? Is that it?"

"No, you idiot; you bloody well know I was looking for you. I'm worried about you." The words come out in bitter chunks. "That's the second time this week you've disappeared down by the river. What are you up to? I'm beginning to wonder if maybe you're dealing? Or thieving, perhaps?"

"Don't you say that, Jess. I don't never nick things, you know that—"

With a great choking sound, the girl begins to sob. Suddenly, Ellie thinks, she sounds much younger. She sounds as if she might have had far too much to drink.

"Yes, you are," she wails. "You are, you're stealing stuff, you and those crazy boys, and they're gonna lock you up."

Tull's boots thunder on the metal frame of the balcony. "Jess," he shouts, "fuck sake, don't. I got business, that's all, big-time business. Nothing to do with you . . ."

"You promised me you'd stay out of trouble." She's shrieking now, whether from rage or fear, it's impossible to tell. "You and your boys. You're nothing but a cheap bunch of thieves."

There's the sound of a scuffle. Then a slap, hard and resonant, wings into the night and a scream careers round the garden.

Ellie is glued to the spot with horror. She's trembling now, afraid to move, afraid to be heard. The blood throbs in her eardrums and she can't think what to do.

A minute passes before her courage rises. She slides open the patio doors and slips inside. She rings 999. "Yes," she says. "A fight. He hit her."

Ellie's not good at anger. Not other people's, not her own.

She lies down in the dark now with her fingers in her ears and waits for the police.

CHAPTER 26

He's sitting in the doorway, his coat slung over a pot of withered geraniums, when Jessica comes back out onto the balcony with two plates. Spaghetti rings on toast, her speciality. It's not up to much, her cooking, but Tull doesn't seem to mind.

He takes the plate. "Ketchup?" he says.

Jess fetches the sauce bottle and squeezes in next to him. They tuck into their meal in silence. It's cooler out here. The breeze ruffles their hair.

Tull tries for what could be the tenth time to make Jess understand. "I explained all that already, Jess. After my mum started using again, and I had to go to that foster home—the one in Beckton with the rottweiler, remember?—I had to take everything I owned in one black bin bag. My life in a bag! I won't live like that anymore. I'm not having you bringing up kids in some dung heap of a flat, either. We're going to have a decent home. We're going to have a house."

"Come on, Tull. Where're we ever gonna get the money for a house?"

"I got plans, Jess. I'm going to be somebody."

"Tull, what you said about kids. I don't know—"

A car rolls slowly along Hesperus Street. It stops. One door clunks shut and then another.

They fall silent as the sound of the brass knocker echoes through the house. Jess struggles to her feet and pushes past Tull. She comes back upstairs a minute later with two constables, a man and a woman. Tull gets to his feet and leans his back against the railing.

The police officers take their time, checking out the view from the balcony, looking around Jess's room, and making notes.

"Evening," the policewoman says. Strictly speaking, it is early morning, but the blackness outside makes it feel like evening.

Tull stares blankly at the officer. Jess stares at her feet. Neither says a word.

"What are you two doing out here, then, this time of night?" the woman constable asks. Her voice is casual.

Tull shrugs. "Just gettin' some fresh air."

"Lovely night," she agrees. She glances at her partner and back again. "You two live here?"

"Yeah," he says. He doesn't, but he has no intention of giving out his address. Even Jess doesn't know.

"Name?"

"Sanders," he says. "Freddy. And this is—"

"Jessica Barnes." She half admires his smooth ability to lie. (Not really lie, he says; I just don't like nobody poking about in my business.) "What's this about?"

"A neighbor reported some screams. A fight. The caller thought a woman might have been hurt."

"Screams? I didn't hear no screams, Jess, did you?"

A solemn shake of the head. Tull's fingers are digging into Jessica's shoulder, and she's annoyed. Does he really think she'd land him in the shit?

The policewoman turns her attention to Jessica. She passes a torch beam over her face. "You all right, miss? Looks as if you might have been crying."

Jessica does her best to firm up the edges of her smile. "I'm fine," she says, with as impish a grin as she can muster. "It's just the kind of face I have."

They both watch in uncomfortable silence as the constables radio in to headquarters, and then slowly, as if they have all the time in the world, leave the house. The minute they drive away, tears start streaming down Jessica's face.

"Fuck sake, Jess, what now?"

"I'm sorry, Tull, I'm sorry I accused you of thieving. I didn't mean it, really . . ."

Tull's smile is rarely seen, but when it appears it lightens his entire face. "Don't think about it now, babes, just hand me your plate." He reaches over and sets it on the floor inside the flat, on top of his own. "Now come here, you."

He wraps his arm around her shoulders. She leans her head against him and weeps.

CHAPTER 27

Ellie tiptoes out onto the lawn again as soon as she hears the police car pull up. She hears the whole exchange. Hears Jessica's sobs, too, after the police have gone away. Hears the man's shushing noises, apprehensive and tender. Hears the flick of a lighter and his deeply indrawn breath and catches the smell of cigarette smoke.

"Give us one," Jess says. There's a rustle as the packet passes between them, and the sound of the lighter again. Jess's sobs subside. Tull continues his gentle shushing sound.

Ellie gave up cigarettes when she started karate training. At the time, she didn't miss it. But now she lies awake fretting over Oliver Nesbit; should she, shouldn't she, let Clive know that he was a boyfriend of hers? About Ariana; why, oh why, did Ellie rebuff her attempts at conversation? Will Ariana hold it against her? Above all, for some strange reason, Ellie frets over tobacco. Alone in her bed, she is unable to banish the memory of the rich smell of the smoke that Tull and Jess shared, and she can hardly get to sleep for yearning for a cigarette.

CHAPTER 28

Karate runs, like the army or the navy, on discipline and hierarchy. Obedience to superiors smoothes the path to promotion. Punctuality is part of the deal.

This morning, for the first time since she took up karate, Ellie oversleeps. By the time she arrives for training, there's a hushed expectancy in the dojo and the karate-ka are standing in two immaculate lines. She hurries with eyes cast down to the section of the line where the purple belts stand. Vik makes room for her to squeeze in between himself and Tony, and the entire line shuffles to the right.

After the warm-up exercises, the novices are herded to the other end of the dojo. The littlest ones are working on *oi zuki,* a stepping punch, and having difficulty. Even the eight- and nine-year-olds struggle to make sense of the technique. Sensei calls Ellie over.

"Miss Porter."

"*Uss.*" Warily, she steps forward. She's about to be made to pay for her late arrival.

"This lot punch like amateurs," Sensei says, and it's true. Their shoulders follow the punch instead of keeping straight. Their instinct is to punch as they've seen it done in films—bouncing on the balls of their feet, fists raised in front of their faces, like boxers. Or sometimes like a street gang, with heads down and shoulders hunched. "Teach them what oi zuki is about."

"*Uss,* Sensei." Stalling for time, Ellie gathers the novices around her, youngest nearest the front, and searches for a simple way to tell a far from simple story.

Between China and Japan are a group of islands, Ellie begins. The largest is Okinawa. She speaks the word slowly, syllable by syllable. O-kin-a-wa. The little ones mouth it after her. O-kin-a-wa.

"In the fifteenth century the kings of Okinawa were rich, but their position was threatened by powerful feudal rulers who controlled much of the land. Each warlord had his own castle and his own army, and each could pose a challenge to the king. Then there came a new king called Sho Shin. Sho Shin issued a decree banning people from swearing loyalty to the lords, and then he sent his men out to confiscate every single weapon in the land. Sho Shin promised to execute anyone other than his own men who was found with a bladed weapon."

The youngsters, even the older lads, look rapt. None of them know where Okinawa is, and only one of them—a boy who reads widely and hides this from the others—understands the meaning of the word *feudal.* But they know the term *warlord* from computer games, and they know that an army without weapons is a very peculiar thing.

"But," Ellie assures them, "the warlords outsmarted the king. They developed a form of deadly combat that required no weapons other than hands and feet. That's where the name karate comes from: *kara* meaning 'empty' and *te* meaning 'hand.' As the old masters say, when we practice the art of karate—the way of the empty hand—our fingers must be knives. Our fingertips become arrowheads. The edges of our hands are swords and spears."

The children peep at their fingers, trying to envisage these homely appendages as deadly weapons.

"The fist on its own is weak," Ellie warns. "To give it power, you must drive it with the shoulder, with the hip, with the opposite arm. Like this." Her arm pumps forward like a piston, the sleeve of her jacket grazing the fabric of the torso so that it makes a whistling noise. As she finishes, she hears a soft chorus of *aahs*. Ellie can feel the admiration and it feels good.

She stops in the bar after the session and treats herself to a vodka and tonic, even though it's off the training schedule, and a little lad with slicked back hair calls to her through the open door. "That was wicked, Miss Porter." Ellie smiles. In the brief silence that follows, Sensei strides toward her. He is dressed in his street clothes, his hair still wet from the shower.

"Not changed yet?" he asks. "I'll wait a few minutes if you want a lift home."

"That's a pretty openhanded offer. I mean, you might end up driving down to Blackheath."

"You live just off Westferry Road, right? Not so far out of my way. Don't look so surprised, Eleanor. I make a point of knowing something about all my students."

If the truth be told, Ellie would rather make the short trip by DLR on her own. A conversation with Striker is bound to be a hard slog, and she's too tired to face that cheerfully. But she doesn't want to hurt his feelings. He is only trying to be kind.

As it turns out, she doesn't have to make an effort at conversation after all, because Striker—"Call me Lawrence," he says; "we're not in the dojo now."—begins talking about his job. He works for the Chartered Institute of Marketing, has a senior position, it seems, and there's a reorganization currently under way that is giving him trouble. Something about cutting out a level of management, and having financial control pass up the departments. Something like that. Striker's account is so convoluted that Ellie isn't certain what's going on, and she finds herself counting down the streets to home.

Ellie tries to persuade him to drop her off on Westferry Road, so as to save him the trouble of turning around, but Striker insists on seeing her all the way home. She points to number 8, and he edges up alongside a Mini that is parked by her door, and turns the motor off. Ellie has no intention of asking him in. "Thank you," she stammers. "You've been very kind and, I must say, it is good to be delivered right to my door." She swings herself out of the car and turns to pick up her gym bag. Striker has leapt out of the driver's seat. He reaches past her and extricates the bag. He hands it to her and gestures over his shoulder. "What's that?" he asks in a low voice.

"That?"

He jerks his thumb toward four youths who are occupying their habitual haunt on Hesperus Street, a couple of doors down from Ellie's. "That load of rubbish. Just look at them!" he says in disgust.

Ellie does. The melancholy group of lads are doing just what they do most evenings. Shuffling their feet. Cluttering up the pavement. Scraping slivers of paint off her neighbor's window frame. Irritating her neighbor's cat. Privately, Ellie thinks of them as the Hesperus Street Hellraisers, not for what they do—they do bugger all, as far as she can see—but for their piercings and tattoos, the chains, the air of studied disenchantment.

Striker positions himself between Ellie and the boys. "Not very nice for you," he says. "Quite threatening. I'll see them off." He takes a step toward them and they freeze.

"No! No," Ellie says, more quietly now. She laughs. "Honestly, Stri—Lawrence, they're just kids. They don't do any harm. Leave them alone."

And with a baleful glance in their direction, and a polite good night to Ellie, that's exactly what he does.

CHAPTER 29

Ellie's had to make a special trip in to the tower for a 10:30 AM meeting. There's been a high court ruling in the case of the model who sued a newspaper for revealing that she'd had an abortion, and Clive wants to make sure that all the legal staff are aware of the implications.

While Clive talks them through the case, Ellie's eyes keep straying to the compelling view through the window of the meeting room. When the meeting comes to a close—signaled by Clive tapping out a quick rhythm on the table with his fingers—Ellie takes a closer look. Away in the distance, she can see the silver pods of the flood barrier, like stepping-stones across the Thames. Nearer to, on the Greenwich Peninsula, is the startling white curve of the Millennium Dome. Clive joins her at the window.

"What's that new building going up opposite?" Ellie asks.

"Rumor is it's a new Waitrose. Every time I turn around, there's another set of cranes. They'll build so high and thick one day, they'll cut off our view of the river." He turns Eleanor away from the room, so that the two other lawyers who haven't yet left the room won't overhear. "Tell me, my dear, how are you settling in?"

"Fine, fine." Ellie realizes she's nodding repeatedly, like one of those toy dogs in the back window of a car. She tries for a more dignified response. "Put it this way, Clive. Haven't come across anything yet that I can't handle." She crosses her fingers and touches them to the wooden table just to be sure.

They are following the others out of the meeting room. It occurs to Ellie to mention the fact that she knows Oliver Nesbit, but Clive steps aside to let her pass in front of him. "Oh, by the way," he says, "apparently, someone was asking after you this morning. Did Marie tell you?"

Ellie stops in her tracks. "Someone? Who? Was he—Did he leave his name?" Will. William DeQuoyne. It must be Will.

"Sorry, no idea. I didn't speak to him. Listen," he says, lightly, "I was thinking of splashing out. To mark your arrival. Four Seasons, perhaps?"

"Oh, Clive, I'm sorry—" Will may be back. He may want to take her to lunch.

Clive's deft fingers make a dismissive motion in the air. "Of course," he says. "You've got other plans. See you for the handover this evening." He is jangling some change in his trousers' pocket, and the clink of coins follows Ellie all the way to the lift.

CHAPTER 30

Carl has not had a lot of luck in his life. There've been no lottery wins, not even modest ones. But just occasionally, Carl has been in the right place at the right time. Today, he sees the girl again, by chance, in the flesh.

Late this afternoon, Carl had been called to an emergency job in One Canada Square. He gave up his job as a locksmith when the tiny shop where he'd worked in Poplar had to close, but that doesn't stop him taking on the occasional freelance job. He likes to see the smile on Denise's face when he walks in with a fresh fifty quid in his pocket.

Carl tests the new system—works like a charm; he knew it would—at nine forty-five and locks up the broker's office a few minutes after. He steps into the lift with his aluminum tool case, and when he gets out again on the ground floor, the only person in the vast lobby, not counting himself and the security officers, is a trim young woman with copper-colored hair pulled back in a thick plait. Carl can hardly believe his luck.

She leaves the tower and heads toward the DLR, walking with quick little steps. Slowly now, don't rush it. Carl has a longer stride than his height might suggest, and he has to saunter to keep a decent distance between them.

Carl pauses to pick up a *Metro* so she can get ahead. She moves up the escalator to the platform; he tracks her bright head of hair out of the corner of his eye. He waits until he hears the train approaching and then takes the escalator stairs two at a time. He squeezes through the doors of the carriage just as they begin to shut.

For a second, Carl can't locate her and the anger rises up inside. What's the matter with him, anyway? Can't he even keep track of a girl?

But suddenly there she is, seated at the very front of the train, like she is pretending to be the driver or something.

Carl positions himself off to one side and two rows behind her, where he's rewarded with an unobstructed view. The narrow-boned face with the high forehead and up-tilted nose. The complexion, porcelain pale and shiny and dusted with freckles. The ceiling lights reflecting off her cheeks. She has a tiny gold earring shaped like a—whaddyacallit?—an ampersand dangling loosely from an earlobe, and that catches the light too. Everything about her seems to shine.

Carl is even more interested in her state of mind. Ill at ease, she is, if he's any judge. She sits as straight as a board with her document case square on her lap. She clutches the dashboard as if for protection. Carl cranes forward in his seat. Her fingernails are bitten to the quick and on one finger he can see where the skin has been ripped away.

As the train weaves through South Quay, she strains forward and follows the scene with her eyes. Then she settles back as if she's ceased to be aware of her surroundings. She lifts her hand and fiddles with her earring, twisting it to and fro. Her lips move fretfully. He strains forward, but he can't catch any of the words. She stops and starts her muted speech—maybe she's going over a conversation?—and an anxious smile plays around her lips. The earring falls onto the back of the seat, and she doesn't even notice.

As the train slows for Mudchute Station, Ellie leaps to her feet and moves to the door. Carl barely has time to avert his face before she glides past. As the train draws alongside the platform, Carl steps to the front and quickly passes his hand over the seat where she'd been. Then he dashes for a different exit, intending to catch a glimpse of her as she alights.

But when the doors slide back, a group of young men in hoodies are clustered on the platform. They press forward toward the door, blocking Ellie's exit. Ellie hesitates only for a second; then, clutching her document case in front of her chest like a shield, she steps firmly onto the platform. "Excuse me," she says in the kind of voice that's seldom challenged, and the men step aside and let her through.

She's alone now at the opposite end of the platform, standing still. She glances down and brushes at something on her skirt. Then she straightens up once again and trots down the slope toward Spindrift Avenue.

Carl doesn't follow—not this time—but his ears pick up every snick of her heels on the pavement. He imagines the slow progress of a bead of sweat trickling down her inner arm. He stands under the streetlamp and opens the fingers of his right hand. There, on his palm, showcased in the circle of light, is a small gold object shaped like an ampersand.

CHAPTER 31

The signs are there as soon as the train pulls into the Mudchute Station: Ellie Porter's evening is going from bad to worse. She'd been so jumpy at work—fretting over Will, over the fact that he'd come to see her and she'd missed him. What did he want? Would he return? She could scarcely concentrate on the day's stories she was so rattled. She wanted to rush to the lavatory, brush her hair until it gleamed, apply fresh makeup; but she daren't leave her desk for fear she might miss him again. Marie, the receptionist, had gone home with a dodgy tummy, so Ellie was unable to quiz her. Unable to confirm it was Will. But it couldn't have been anyone else, could it?

Ellie looks up as the train approaches Mudchute. Reflected in the broad surface of the window, a man seated somewhere behind her is staring. She walks by him as she makes her way to the door. His head is swiveled away, his collar turned up, but there's no mistaking him. The man from Island Gardens seems to be everywhere these days.

The doors open and Ellie is confronted by a group of young men who are wrapped up in their own matey world. She might as well be invisible for all the notice they take. They shoulder their way into the carriage. One of them brushes against her, leaving a trail of ashes on her skirt.

To hell with them. Home, that's all she can think of. She'll make a cup of hot chocolate and she'll drink it in the garden and everything will be fine.

But when Ellie turns onto Hesperus Street, she is met not by evening peace, but by an assault of harsh start-stop rhythms, like the revving up of a motorbike engine, and clashing guitars. And as she approaches her end of the terrace, she confirms with a sinking heart that this so-called music comes from Jessica's house. The upstairs window is open and noise thunders out into the street. Ellie surveys the street, astonished that the neighbors aren't assembled in protest. But apart from a cat whose neck bell tinkles into the distance, the street is still. No resident leans out of a window, aghast. No homeowner stands, hands on hips, in a doorway. Ellie is alone in the dark with her indignation.

She lingers a moment beneath the window, hoping that Jessica will notice her there and they can head off a row. Ellie could mention how warm it is for April, and point out the open windows on the street. She could suggest that Jessica might wish to turn the volume down. There's every chance that Jessica would smile her uneasy smile and then comply.

But Jessica doesn't appear. The old-fashioned net curtains at the window waver slightly and a voice wails above the bass and that is all.

Ellie raises the knocker on Jessica's front door and prepares to bring it down with a crash, but at the last minute, she chickens out. After all, it's not even midnight yet. In all probability, Jessica will have switched the CD player off before Ellie is even ready for bed.

Ellie unlocks her own door and slips quickly inside. Ignoring the gritty sound of Odysseus's wheel, she tosses her bag onto a chair and slides back the patio door. Widget, Jessica's cat, is there, twined around the base of the stone birdbath. Ellie crouches down and holds out her arms. The Persian cat rushes in and wraps himself around her neck and nudges her cheek with his nose. With one hand buried in his fur to steady him, Ellie stands and steps out of her shoes and plunges her feet into the springy grass.

She remains for a moment with her head tilted to one side as Widget kneads her shoulders with his paws. Thank heavens, that dreadful racket from Jessica's has stopped and, apart from the distant thrumming of a motor launch on the river, the garden is blissfully quiet. The cushion of grass beneath Ellie's feet feels exquisitely soft and cool. Her edginess begins to slough away like an outgrown skin.

And then, the drone of guitars from the next-door balcony windows crashes down into the garden, more earsplittingly than before. In one unconsidered motion, Ellie sets Widget on the paving stones and steps back inside, slamming the patio door so that it thunks resoundingly into the metal frame. Ellie hopes that the sound carries to Jessica. All the better to warn you with, my dear.

Ellie collects food from the fridge for Odysseus. There's a decent bottle of sauvignon blanc, cool and green, in the door of the fridge. She lays her hand on the glass and welcomes the chill that creeps up her arm. But, reminding herself of her target for the grading, Ellie doesn't lift the bottle off the shelf. She pours a glass of water instead, drinks it down, and sets to work.

Ellie's evening routine is as smooth and invariable as a prairie highway. She runs a finger along the stubby tips of her nails to check there are no snags, and then rolls down her stockings. She peels off her panties. She fills the basin with water and throws in a handful of soap crystals. She kneads the lingerie under the water and then leaves it to soak.

Ellie removes her jacket and puts it on a padded hanger, buttoning it all the way up. She winds a piece of Sellotape around her knuckles and lifts off some cat hairs. She clips her skirt onto a hanger and hooks the skirt and jacket up next to the shower so the creases will fall out as she washes. She removes her blouse and her bra and drops them into the drum of the washing machine.

Naked now, Ellie slips on a pale blue linen robe sprigged with delicate-looking flowers. She unclips her chain and her watch. She removes her earrings—correction, earring. Bloody hell! A diversion from routine as she searches the floor without success. Her earring is missing, and that's not the first thing she's lost recently, by a long chalk. Ellie wonders if she's losing her grip.

Forget it, she tells herself—Concentrate!—but the erratic rhythm from next door seems even louder now. It sets her teeth on edge.

Ellie removes her makeup and begins to brush her hair. She recalls, as a child, often watching her mother as she sat at her dressing table, brushing her hair. Annabel's hair was a more chestnut shade than Ellie's and smooth as honey. Annabel used to stare into the mirror as if the brushstrokes were the swings of a hypnotist's pendulum. Watching her gave Ellie the creeps. And yet, here she is, twenty years later, doing more or less the same thing.

Ellie submits to the shower with her head bowed and sighs with contentment as the warm pulse of water sucks the tension from her shoulders. The sound of the water drumming in her ears is like a tropical rainstorm. But the instant that Ellie steps out of the shower, the racket from next door is more intrusive than before.

Ellie picks up the directory and punches in the Barneses' number. The line is engaged. The unfairness of it! Jessica must be having a conversation while Ellie can hardly hear herself think. She slams down the phone.

Ellie dresses carelessly in jeans and T-shirt. She snatches the sauvignon blanc from the fridge and takes a long swig from the bottle. Then she bounds out the door and over to Jessica's.

Halfway there, Ellie has second thoughts. What if Jessica is not alone? What if she's surrounded by friends and allies? That girl with the terrible eczema? Those boys who stare at her on the street with speculative lust? What about her boyfriend, Tull? The others are little more than kids, but Tull is different; he looks as if he knows how to hate.

She leans against the rough brickwork, one eye on the street, and rehearses what she'll say. *Sorry to disturb you, Jessica.* (She's not sorry, not at all, but it seems the best way to head off a confrontation.) *Perhaps you hadn't realized that it's almost midnight, and I'm sorry but . . .*

No, no. Too many apologies. Try again. *Jessica, I'm tired, and I'm trying to wind down after work, and this music means that I can hardly hear myself think and—Goddamn you, you little bitch, who do you think you are?*

So much for contrition. The force of Ellie's anger seems a palpable thing, as if she had actually shouted *bitch* into the night. She looks guiltily around. She takes a long, slow breath and tries again.

Now, Jessica, perhaps you aren't aware of how late it is, but I'm sure you'll agree that it's not fair to your neighbors—me included—to play your music at this volume. If you can't be more considerate, I'll have no choice but to contact your parents . . .

Jessica's parents. Jessica's father is a weary-looking man who always gives the impression of being in a frightful hurry. When the Barnes family first moved in, a couple of years ago, he was polite but clipped, and the girl herself was all butter-wouldn't-melt. There was the emerald nose-stud, of course, buried in the fleshy part of her right nostril, that shot bright arrows into any shaft of sunlight, so that Ellie had to make an effort not to stare. But with her hair pulled neatly back off her face and dressed in a denim jacket and jeans, Jessica looked almost demure, like the kind of teenager who might babysit your little brother.

Then Jessica's father accepted a posting in Hong Kong and her mother went, too, and it was only a matter of weeks before everything had changed. (She's like me, Ellie thinks, a chameleon, but then suppresses the fugitive thought.) First, it was that rough-looking boyfriend, who wears an overcoat even on the warmest days. The hours became more nocturnal; the volume of the music went up a notch. Then the friends: The boys were leather-jacketed and spike-haired. The girls had blocky black hair and looked as if they'd just got out of bed.

Jessica's wardrobe became increasingly bizarre. She took to wearing peculiarly unflattering dresses, tubes of black lace through which could be glimpsed shreds of shabby underwear.

But all of those changes were nothing compared to what happened to Jessica's face. Its youthfulness was hidden beneath a veneer of white chalk. Jessica took to wearing lipstick in purple or brown—since the girl rarely leaves her house in daylight, Ellie can't be sure of the shade—but lipstick so dark that it made her mouth look bloated and predatory. Staring, fascinated, at that mouth, it once crossed Ellie's mind that if Jessica were to grin, she might reveal teeth that had been filed to a series of points.

The Barneses' doorstep is worn stone. Ellie raps sharply on the door. She forces herself to peer through the frosted glass panel and thinks she sees a strange flicker of orange light. She knocks again, more loudly, determined to make herself heard. But music drills into the mild night air, and nothing moves in the darkness behind the door.

There is a scraping on the street behind. Driven by a sudden breeze, a cardboard fast-food carton bumps along the tarmac. Ellie shivers.

Feeling like a Peeping Tom, she puts her eye to the keyhole. The inside of the house comes rushing out to meet her. A male vocalist shouting words that sound like *Fire*—or is it *Liar*? Erratic drumbeats. Furious guitars.

Ellie summons up her courage for a final time and struggles to bring the inside of the house into focus. A blast of heat pricks the surface of her eye. The light from a cluster of candles creates shifting shadows in the darkened room, but the corners are great black voids and Ellie can make out very little. But the music shrieks on and the smell—the cloying smell—convinces her that the house is thick with blood.

Ellie turns and runs. Her bare feet fly along the pavement. She bursts into her own home. She rushes to the shelves next to the fireplace, snatches up a wooden box, and takes out the long-barreled key that the Barneses left with her in case of emergency.

She rushes back, unlocks the door, and steps over the sill into the darkness.

CHAPTER 32

It's Carl's break. He's leafing through an old copy of the *Wharf* when Richard sidles up to him, pretending to be friendly.

"I saw you limping down the corridor on your way in," says Richard. "What's the matter with that foot of yours?"

"You trying to tell me you really care?" Carl mutters.

"Beg your pardon?"

Carl relents and shows Richard the blister on his heel. What with all the walking he's had to do lately, it's the size of an old penny now, and infected.

"You better get some antiseptic cream for that," Richard says. "There's a new chemist opened in Cabot Place West."

A new chemist. A new fitness center. A new restaurant. That's Canary Wharf, for you. Every bloody day, something new.

Carl isn't a man to stand in the way of progress. He accepts that by the late 1970s, even before the developers took over, the docks were gone and the swinging cranes were still. Island people were leaving, always leaving, in search of better jobs—any jobs at all—and better homes.

Carl left, too, for a time. He was a very young man when his father's sister, who ran a café in north London, offered him a job as a short-order cook and a room in her house. Carl wanted to be where the action was, away from the island, and so he jumped at the chance to move. He wandered the streets of the West End and wondered at the crowds. He stood alone in strange pubs with a lager and lime in his hand and marveled at the girls with their leg warmers and their rough-cut hair. He bought a pair of stonewashed denims and a skinny tie.

Carl began to imagine a different kind of life. He worked hard, and saved his money. He began working out with weights. He took the big step of applying to join the Metropolitan Police. He was young, and full of possibility, and life was exhilarating.

Until, that is, he met Eleanor Porter and his life fell apart.

Carl retreated to the Isle of Dogs. He told his aunt he missed the island, and it was partly true. He missed the tiny pubs along the riverside, and the boats' sirens, and the breezes that skipped across the Thames. The bombing had left an open landscape and in those days you could see a quarter of a mile to the river; in north London, amid the tight lines of terraced houses and the press of people, he felt confined.

But the truth is that Eleanor Porter had a lot to do with his leaving. If it hadn't been for her, he wouldn't be what he is today. Nothing.

CHAPTER 33

Ellie takes only two steps into the house and stops dead.

It's the smell. Air that's stale, and hot and heavy, in spite of the open windows. A gamy taint like that of an animal in pain. And, above all, the smell of blood. Not everyone would recognize it, but to Ellie the metallic tang of blood is as familiar as burnt toast.

Ellie masks her nostrils with one hand and fumbles along the wall with the other. She flicks a switch. There is a blue flash as a fuse blows and then flickering blackness again.

Ellie shuffles her way toward the stairs. "Jessica?" Music blasts from the upstairs rooms, but there's no reply.

At the top of the stairs is a short corridor with three doors opening off it. Ellie enters the first room. Her eyes are adjusting to the dark. The surface of a table, humped with bottles and books, begins to distinguish itself from the blackness. A bright blue line seeps out from under the lid of a laptop. Ellie is leaning toward the laptop, one finger poised to lift the cover, when she notices a sofa piled high with cushions and blankets. Something is bunched up underneath. Poking out beneath the blanket is an ankle boot. Ellie moves to the end of the sofa and leans forward, searching for the sound of breathing. Across the grain of the music, she can't hear a thing. She touches a waxy surface and recoils. Touches a finger to the surface again. It's a leather jacket being used as a coverlet.

"Jessica," Ellie whispers. "Hello, wake up." She somehow knows that it is useless.

Crack! Ellie jerks upright. Idiot! The door she'd left ajar has slammed in the breeze.

Ellie bends again and slides her finger gingerly along the slick surface of the jacket, tracing a body's outline. She finds the collar of the jacket, grits her teeth and peels it back in one fierce movement.

Seconds pass before Ellie can take in what she sees: a laundry bag. She strips the jacket back further. A rucksack and a heap of cushions and jumpers and a pair of boots—carelessly, not even artfully, scattered. At that moment, just as she begins to relax, above the crashing of the music there's a splintering of glass and a faint and menacing hiss.

The room at the back of the house is completely dark. The hot odor of newly extinguished candle wax greets Ellie in the doorway. She steps to the balcony, carefully—the carpet is greasy underfoot—and pulls back the heavy curtains. Through the open balcony doors comes the smell of the river.

Ellie can see her own garden. It's deserted. For a brief flash, she sees herself there as she was a short while ago, burying her toes in the grass, with the cat coiled around her neck. Sees herself glancing in annoyance at the source of the dreadful music. If only, Ellie thinks. If only I could still be out there. If only I had never undressed, never had a shower, never entered the Barneses' house, never climbed the stairs.

Come to that, Ellie needn't have returned home at all. What was to stop her from spending the entire night at the office, perhaps curled up in the managing editor's big comfy chair, watching the sun come up over the river? By the time she came home to Hesperus Street, all of this trouble might have been sorted.

But it's too late. Ellie's here now. She can't run and she can't hide.

She turns slowly and faces into the room. The first thing she sees is the glitter; a slice of light from the moon picks out bright fragments of glass on the carpet.

Then the winking green lights of the CD player making a silent counterpoint to the music.

Finally, reluctantly, the bed.

Jessica is sprawled there. At first Ellie supposes she is naked, but in fact, she is dressed in the briefest of briefs. In the moonlight, her skin is pearly pale. One gleaming arm is flung over the side of the bed, palm up. The hand is smeared with something dark, and from the fingers, poised as if pointing to the floor, blood drip drip drips onto the rug.

And now it is unmistakable: blood everywhere. Blood streaks across the carpet as if Jessica had dragged her wounded body to reach the bed. Blood lies in a shallow pool between her thighs. It stains the sheets. It soaks the towel that trails from her breast to her knee.

Ellie kneels among the fragments of glass and lays her ear alongside Jessica's lips. Is that a ragged intake of breath? Ellie puts two fingers across Jessica's windpipe, but the beat of the music makes it impossible to pick up a pulse. Ellie fumbles for the CD player. She jiggles the buttons until the dreadful noise is gone. In the sudden silence, she imagines she hears the gushing of Jessica's blood.

Ellie breathes from her diaphragm and presses her panic down to where it can hardly be felt. Not now, she thinks, not now. She slides the towel aside and examines the ugly wound on Jessica's thigh where a flap of skin has been peeled back to form a window into her flesh. Jessica's thighs are slick with blood. The wrinkled sheets are pooled with it. Blood is matted in the hairs that curl around the crotch of her panties. How much blood has she lost? A cupful? A pint? Could it be more?

Ellie struggles to pull a sheet loose where it is screwed up at the foot of the bed. Try as she might, she can't tear it into strips. She folds it instead, as a washerwoman might, in half and then into three, and presses the thick pad of cotton against Jessica's thigh. She lifts Jess's foot and wads a blanket underneath. Even with the leg raised, blood keeps pumping out. Ellie finds a dressing gown on a hook and jerks the belt free. She knots the belt around Jessica's thigh. She counts to ten. When she lifts the cotton pad and peers underneath, thank God! the fountain of blood has slowed to a trickle.

Ellie feels her way back into the other room. The telephone receiver lies on the floor away from its cradle. Ellie places the receiver back in place and jiggles it up and down until she gets a line. Dials 999.

By the time the police give permission for the paramedics to load Jessica into the ambulance, a small crowd has gathered on the street outside her house. The Hellraisers are there, though not, Ellie is relieved to see, the boyfriend. A couple who seem by their unsteady gaits to be making their way home from the pub lean against the brickwork and watch as if it were an episode of a soap. Two or three neighbors huddle in dressing gowns and slippers. "Not another burglary?" one of them asks Ellie. "No," Ellie says. "No, not as far as I know."

Ellie walks alongside the stretcher, and holds Jessica's hand. Jessica is conscious now, but she isn't saying a word. She isn't even crying. She is as limp and unresisting as a rag doll. Once she is secured inside the ambulance, Ellie says her farewells.

"Well, I'd better go now, Jess. They'll take care of you at the hospital. You'll be all right now." Ellie hates herself for speaking such drivel, but her brain can't come up with anything that is more honest and still reassuring. "I'll take care of your cat." She moves carefully to try to free her hand from Jessica's grip, but as she bends forward over the bed, there's a sudden stirring. Ellie's hand is gripped with astonishing force, and Jessica's eyes flash open.

"Uhhh," she says. It's a grunt, more than anything.

Ellie leans closer. "What is it? Can I help?" And then Jess's voice, husky with disuse, rings out, but the words are clear.

"Ellie, help me. Please help me. Promise?"

"Help you, Jess? With what? What is it you want?" Ellie's mind races to find a way out of this. Responsibility is the last thing Ellie wants. A crazy girl with self-destructive urges is the last thing that she needs.

And it is at precisely that moment, as she scans the crowd, trying to think of a way out, that she sees, at the edge of the crowd, the strange man who's been following her. He is staring, not at the vehicle into which Jessica is disappearing, but at her.

"Promise!" Jessica's voice is raised. The paramedic steps up to the back of the ambulance and begins to close the doors.

"I promise," Ellie says.

CHAPTER 34

Ellie sees Jessica off in the ambulance, but the horror of the evening follows her home. She fills a glass with ice cubes, pours vodka over the top, adds a swirl of Tia Maria, and sits down at the kitchen table. Odysseus keeps her company, hunching in the center of the table with whiskers twitching. Then he decides to play his favorite game: kamikaze hamster. He races forward like a lemming to a cliff and hurls himself over the edge of the table. Ellie reaches out and scoops him to safety.

She finds the number for Jessica's parents in Hong Kong and begins to dial. Odysseus leaps into the air, all four legs flying off the table, and makes another dash for freedom.

With the receiver still to her ear, Ellie leans to the side, stretches out her arm, and catches Odysseus in her palm. "Odysseus," she whispers to his face, as someone picks up at the other end. "You adventurer."

It's a man's voice, dry and businesslike. An answering machine. Ellie leaves her name and number. "It's about Jessica. She's going to be all right, don't worry." How glib is that? Ellie doesn't say that it's urgent. She doesn't have to. It's the middle of the night.

Jessica Barnes is a lucky girl. That's what the hospital says when Ellie rings two hours later. A lucky girl. She'd not had to compete with multiple victims of stabbings or fires or automobile crashes, and she is lying right now between crisp white sheets in the dusky nighttime of a hospital ward. Listening, perhaps, to the soft swish of the nurses' uniforms and the squeak of their rubber-soled shoes.

Ice cubes tinkle as Ellie swirls the Black Russian around in the glass. She bends her head back and lets the liquid, all the liquid, slide into her mouth. The ice burns against her lips. She mixes another Black Russian and returns to the table just in time to save Odysseus from a collision with the floor. She places him gently into his cage. The ice cubes rattle for a final time as she drains her glass, sets it in the sink, and heads off to bed.

Ellie is almost asleep when the willow tree in her garden shivers in a gust of wind and she has a sudden image, sharp as a Stanley knife, of the dark open maw of Jessica's balcony doors. Reluctantly, she jumps up, pulls on some clothes, and makes her way next door.

Inside the front door, she flicks the switch. "Bugger it!" The sound of the curse hangs in the empty house.

There's still a strong taint of blood in the air. Ellie puts her hand over her mouth and feels her way to the kitchen. The plastic cover of the fuse box is gritty with grease and dust; it sticks at first and then swings open. One click of a switch, and the room is lit by the harsh glow from a central bulb in a wicker shade.

Ellie tiptoes up the stairs, turning lights on as she goes. She marches past the sofa; the hump doesn't look much like a body now. Past the desk where the thin blue light from the laptop beckons. Ellie puts out her hand and then snatches it back. There is something disconcerting, something stealthy, about a computer humming away on its own. The hospital had confirmed what Ellie had suspected: that

Jessica's wounds were self-inflicted. What had the girl been doing on this very computer just before she stuck a knife into her flesh?

Gingerly, Ellie picks up a sheet of paper that's propped alongside the laptop. University headed notepaper. Missed assignments. Unauthorized absences. One last chance.

Shame on you, Eleanor Porter. A personal computer is just what its name says, personal. And correspondence is, or should be, private. Ellie puts the paper back where she found it and moves swiftly toward the door. As her fingers touch the brass handle, she halts. She ought at least to turn the laptop off.

She returns to the table and slowly, using only her forefinger, raises the laptop lid. The screen blazes in the dimly lit room. When Ellie can finally open her eyes, she sees on the screen a blue sea against a sun-hazed horizon, and one line of text:

"death is like surfing in wonderful waves in a place where the sun always shines"

Ellie's hand flies out and closes the computer down.

A cool gust of wind hits her as she enters the back room. She shivers and looks around, feeling suddenly exposed. She sees now, for the first time, that the ceiling is draped with swathes of fabric that billow like the folds of a tent. A bolt of Indian cotton sweeps across the sofa, and on the bookshelves, facing Ellie, there is a trio of dummies, each topped with a wild and wonderful hat.

For a moment, Ellie stands on the tiny balcony and stares down into her own garden. Soon the borders will be as thick and dark as a jungle; at the moment, they are just beginning to fill out. She steps back inside and closes the doors and drives the bolt home.

Ellie returns from Jessica's house and is asleep within minutes. It doesn't last. The phone rings. She snatches it up, but the line goes dead. The caller's number has been withheld.

Ellie rings Jessica's parents and gets the answering machine again. She mixes another Black Russian. She drapes a rug around her shoulders and sits in the rocking chair, with her bare feet pulled up under her, waiting for their call. It is five AM before she finally returns to bed. She crashes into a restless sleep and her dreams are full of blood.

CHAPTER 35

Eleanor Porter, you're a lucky little girl. That's what her parents said to her, singly and together, on her eighth birthday, in 1981, and only a fortnight later, she killed her father.

The shock of it left her with only disconnected images. The patent leather shoes that her father bought her for her birthday; she believed that the rhinestones on the front were diamonds, and she loved the way they glittered when she walked. Her mother in nursing uniform, about to leave for evening shift, crisp and cool and angry as she slammed a casserole into the oven. A neighboring garden, and a terrier with an inquisitive snout chasing autumn leaves.

Her mother and father quarreled a lot, and Ellie remembers that well. She used to hide under the kitchen table and shut her ears against their rows, convinced that she was in some way to blame. They were short of money; she realizes that now. Her father's overseas contract had lapsed; her mother resented having to go back to nursing to pay the bills. Her mother was cold, and her father was sulky. Ellie tiptoed around them, braced for the inevitable explosion.

The day her father died began with a visitor. The doorbell clanging. Someone standing on the doorstep, speaking to her, urging her. The details of who or what have been wiped away, and all she remembers is a terrible sense of dread. "Get your coat," her mother snapped. "It's time for school." She slid away, and hid behind the curtains in the sitting room window, from where she could see what happened and could hear the low rumble of the visitor's voice and the icy tones of her mother's replies. And then it began. The shouting. The mother of all rows. Just recalling it now, Ellie's hands begin to tremble. *Stop it! Stop it!* Ellie hides under the kitchen table while the accusations echoed back and forth through the sitting room. The stairs. The bedroom. The voices, sometimes high and anguished, sometimes low and furious, and sometimes—the most horrible—no voices at all, just the sound of pushing and shoving and some kind of scuffle and her mother's muffled screams.

And then nothing until the bang. The terrible, thunderous noise. She was almost in a dream, trancelike, when it happened. But there was a part of her that saw it coming.

The explosive sound, and then she was stalking toward him, her ears ringing. Her mother, distraught, rushing past her, frantically waving her away. Stay there. Don't come any closer. Don't come any closer—to where Ellie's father lies, his body contorted, his head and his chest bathed in blood. Ellie follows slowly behind, her little legs reluctant to carry her further. She reaches the place where her father lay still and smashed. Mother shoots her a look that is filled with accusation and despair, and then buries her face in his bloodied shirt. "Oh, God," Mother sobs. "What have you done?"

CHAPTER 36

Ellie throws herself into her work. She wants a hard copy of the latest Tory Filbert story. The printer runs out of paper and the job stops halfway. Ellie leans over, lifts a clutch of paper from a drawer, tries to slide it into the printer tray, and drops it. Sheets of paper tumble everywhere. As she pushes back her chair and stands, Jonathan appears at her shoulder. He bends over and scoops up the paper in two long sweeps. He squares it up and places it in her printer. Then he leans against the edge of the desk.

"Is something wrong?" he asks. He is particularly smartly dressed, Ellie notices. His trousers even have a crease. Ellie, by way of contrast, has removed her shoes while she's been working and is in stocking feet. Standing alongside Jonathan without her heels on, she feels exposed. Not to mention short.

"Wrong? With me, you mean?"

"You seem a little—well, rattled." The printer shoots out the final page of the story, and Jonathan catches it. He skims the first paragraph before passing it over. "That poor kid," he says. "This story isn't giving you trouble, is it, Ellie? No, I didn't think so." As he watches, puzzled, Ellie slides back into her chair. His mobile makes a sound like someone grating nutmeg. Jonathan whips the phone from his belt and snaps it open, but his eyes never leave Ellie's face.

"Eleanor?"

Ellie doesn't know what to say. "My next-door neighbor was injured last night. I found her, covered in blood and—"

His mobile rings again. He ignores it. "How did it happen?"

"I don't know for sure, but it looked as if she's been self-harming and she overdid it. Either that or she tried to kill herself." A third ring. Jonathan is looking at her with such a kindly, concerned expression on his face that she can't help but tell him the rest. "There was— all around her room, all over her bed—an amazing amount of blood. I—I know this sounds foolish, but it's left me feeling rather queasy."

Jonathan turns the phone off and snaps the case shut. His eyebrows level out into a frown. "I'm not surprised. Anything else?"

Ellie shakes her head. An image of the man who'd been watching the ambulance pops into her head, but she pushes it away, and concentrates instead on squeezing her feet back into her court shoes. An ache settles in just behind her left temple.

"Come." Jonathan beckons with both hands for her to stand up again. "Come with me. Time for a cup of tea." He takes her arm and steers her toward the corridor. He signals to one of his juniors to ring him if anything comes up.

"Tea!" Ellie laughs. "The British solution to the world's problems." But she suddenly feels ravenous. She hasn't eaten all day.

They head toward the door. Ellie is just noticing how quiet the newsroom is this evening, even more than usual, when the sound of laughter reaches her. In the corridor a group of people are knotted together, three men clustered round a woman. The woman has her back turned, but Ellie recognizes Ariana's silky voice.

Apart from the voice, everything else about Ariana is different. Instead of her loose and graceful way of standing, she is ramrod straight. Her chin is tilted up, which gives her face a haughty expression. In a tone that manages to be both anxious and prim, Ariana says, "Oh, no, I cannot possibly say. It just wouldn't be right. Oh, no."

There's a gust of appreciative laughter at Ariana's mimicry, and almost at the same moment, the group becomes aware of Ellie and Jonathan moving toward them. The men look furtive. Their eyes dart from side to side, searching for a means of escape. The truth lands on Ellie like an avalanche. That was supposed to be her. It was her whom Ariana was impersonating. Making her into a figure of fun. The effect is like a punch to the belly. With an effort Ellie prevents herself from doubling over. She wrenches her arm away from Jonathan's and pushes her way past the group in the corridor, staggering blindly on.

A heavy silence falls around her, and then, at her back, she hears Jonathan's voice, low and angry, remonstrating.

Ellie stumbles against the door to the lavatory. She enters a cubicle. She sits on the lavatory with her head in her hands and—for the first time since she left hospital—her tears flow like rain.

CHAPTER 37

A week has lapsed since that awful incident in the corridor, and Jonathan still feels sorry for her, Ellie can tell. Ever since that appalling moment when they were confronted with Ariana and her gaggle of admirers, he's been particularly gentle and attentive. Bringing her hot chocolate. An orchid for her desk. Making sure she's included in plans for the office summer party.

Jonathan is a dear man, but Ellie doesn't want his sympathy, or, for that matter, anyone else's. She doesn't want to be a victim. There's enough of that with reality TV. *Wife Swap, Big Brother, Pop Idol, The Weakest Link*. Ritual humiliation posing as unscripted truth. Ellie has to admit that once she starts watching, she can't turn it off; but she doesn't like it. The sob stories she finds most unsettling. *I was a hopeless drunk. My lover killed my mother. I lost my family in a fire*. Tragic as these stories are, and however sincere their tellers, Ellie squirms at this baring of souls. It's one thing to unburden yourself to a friend, but another to share your misfortune with the world. To let everyone see how damaged you are. To wash your soiled linen in public. Uh-uh. Not Ellie's thing at all.

"I'm fine, Jonathan. Really, I am. Up to my ears in work"—she gestures at the list of entries on the screen—"but fine. How about you? How did your committee meeting go?" Jonathan is on the board of trustees for a local church that is something of a heritage site. There's been a storm of controversy over how best to protect the pedigree. Over coffee the other day, Jonathan had given such a vivid description of the various factions involved that Ellie had giggled in spite of herself.

Jonathan wheels a chair over to her side of the desk and makes himself comfortable. "Frankly, Ellie, the meeting was a nightmare. Discussion totally derailed. Halfway through the agenda, someone mentioned the tourist—you know, the one whose body was found near Saunders Ness—and before you could say 'Hang on, we've got business to get through,' the entire committee was off and running. Murder? On the Isle of Dogs? Terrible, tut-tut. Tarnishes the image of the place."

"Tarnishes the poor tourist a whole lot worse, I would have thought."

"Absolutely. I blame Van Druten."

"Pardon?"

"Horace Van Druten. Chair of the committee. Should have stopped the discussion before it began. I didn't get home until half-past ten." He pauses, and his sandy eyebrows knit into a frown. "Joking aside, Ellie, until this killer is caught, I hope you're careful. I don't particularly like the idea of your traveling home on your own late at night. Especially since you've had someone following you. Why don't you order a taxi? I'm sure the paper will pay."

"Not necessary, Jonathan. It's only twenty minutes, door-to-door. And actually, I enjoy the journey home."

Sitting on the train, playing the conversation through again, Ellie reflects that it would have been more truthful, perhaps, if she'd used the past tense. *Enjoyed.* Until last week, I enjoyed the journey home. But not now. Things seem to have changed. It's not the man with the weird voice. Not exactly. After all, as she tells herself, he's only a man, not a monster. He hasn't actually threatened her. Not in any concrete way.

It's the combination of things. It's the murder. The police think the tourist's body was dumped in the river where it washed ashore again with the incoming tide. They believe he was killed on the island. Killed within a mile of her home.

And it's finding Jessica, like that, awash with blood. It makes Ellie wonder—she can't help it—what will be waiting for her this evening when she gets home?

Ellie stops in at the shop to pick up some tins of cat food and a copy of the *Wharf*. On the front of the paper, there's a black-and-white photo of the spot where the body was found.

Al drags his eyes away from the telly. "American," he says. "On vacation. Touring old industrial sites, can you believe? His wife was on the news tonight, appealing for help in finding his killer."

"Terrible," Ellie agrees. "Al, may I ask you something?"

Al stiffens, but his silence is a kind of acquiescence.

"You're open late. Every night, you're here alone. Do you ever get nervous? You know, worried about robbery. Or something like that?"

Al flexes his massive forearm. "I been robbed twice since I been here. First time, they used a knife and emptied the till. Second time, I beat the shit out of them." He reaches under the counter and pulls out a compact club. Ellie recognizes it. Her father used to take such a club with him when he went out fishing. "Today, I'm not so much worried about armed robbery as I am about those kids emptying my shelves when my back is turned."

Ellie knows what he means. At lunchtime children swarm over the shop like ants, feeling, touching, calling, darting from one display to another. And, in some cases, undoubtedly, pocketing whatever comes to hand.

And sure enough, when she leaves the shop, late as it is, a group of children are cycling aimlessly up and down on the pavement in front. Skinny little things. They can't be more than ten or eleven years old, and one of them lights a fag. She looks away, not wanting her dismay to show. He flicks the match in her direction, and she hurries on.

Ellie doesn't pause this evening to take in the scent of the river. She doesn't check out the details of new buildings as she passes. She moves quickly, one carrier bag loaded with cat food in each hand. She flicks her eyes into every nook and cranny. She listens for footsteps.

She's approaching the public lavatories. The doors are locked this time of night, but alongside the antiquated building there's a dark passage that runs from the pavement to somewhere behind. Ellie keeps her distance. She senses a shuffling movement from deep inside the passage as she passes by, but no one emerges. Probably someone shooting up, she thinks. Or a homeless person bedding down for the night. Ellie thinks how fortunate she is to have her own little house, but somehow the thought doesn't make her feel safe.

She's almost reached Harbinger Primary School when someone steps out from the shadows on the other side of the road. It's a man and he's moving straight toward her. Ellie tenses as he breaks into a run. Her legs continue to move, but she stops breathing. He's almost on her. Ellie's legs are pumping, her arms are swinging, and suddenly she knows what to do. Deliberately now, she angles her body toward him and lengthens her swing. She propels her right arm forward with as much force as she can. In that split second the man leaps up over the curb and onto the pavement and with one smooth sideways movement, steps around her, as her cargo of tins crashes through the point where his balls would have been had he continued in a straight line. He doesn't break stride. He carries on down the street, his trainers *thump thump thump*ing on the pavement.

A jogger. A jogger! Christ, Ellie, get a grip. She almost felled him. She has to set the carrier bags down on the ground and take a series of deep breaths before she is steady enough to make the hundred meters home.

Ellie's heart is still racing when she locks her front door behind her. She stands still just inside the door and listens. It's not Odysseus she's listening for this time; it's for anything untoward. Any sound that doesn't belong.

Ellie forces herself to do what's required. She feeds the hamster. She feeds Widget, the Barneses' cat. She looks out of her patio doors for a moment, vodka and tonic in hand, and stares blankly at the darkened garden. Then with two decisive tugs, she pulls the curtains closed and shuts herself inside.

CHAPTER 38

Don't let it get to you. That's what Ellie tells herself as she runs through her kata. *Don't sweat the small stuff. Don't let the buggers grind you down. Don't let it get to you.* "It" being that man who is following her. Jessica. The tourist who's been murdered. Everything.

But though she tries—though she jogs for four and a half miles before lunch, and throws herself into training—it gets to her still. Her kata isn't sharp enough. Sensei isn't satisfied. *And again, Miss Porter. And again.*

All the way home she is on edge. She runs her eye over the occupants of the carriage before she gets in. She walks along Westferry Road, rather than the shorter Spindrift Avenue route, and keeps well away from shop doorways. Routine precautions, she tells herself. Simple common sense.

But it's not routine to study the face of every man she sees, watching out for one. Her image of him is indistinct. Could she pick him out in a lineup if she had to? Would she recognize him if he came to her door claiming he was from the Water Board? Why does she feel that she's seen him before?

It's not common sense that makes her spin round at the sound of a footstep. Her sudden movement frightens a woman who is backing out of a telephone kiosk and who flinches in alarm.

"Sorry. I'm really sorry." Ellie hefts her gym bag higher and rushes on.

The phone is jangling away as she unlocks her front door. She doesn't race for it. She waits for the answering machine to click in.

"Ellie? Ellie. Come on, pick up the phone; I know you're there."

Ellie drops her gym bag with relief and answers straightaway. "Harriet! Sorry to keep you waiting. I've just this second come in from karate . . ."

"Really? Every time I ring these days, you don't answer and then you interrupt me halfway through a message. I'm beginning to think you're reluctant to take my calls."

"Don't be silly. I've just crossed the threshold, honest. Had to dash for the phone. Listen, Harry, I'm so glad to hear your voice . . . How are you? How are the babies?"

"Later. First, tell me. I got your message. What's this about a neighbor?"

"Jessica her name is. I went over the other night to check on something and I found her covered in blood. She'd been cutting—you know, self-harming—and she really injured herself."

"Self-mutilation? Terribly common, I'm afraid. She's how old, did you say?"

"I didn't. She's nineteen."

"That's the age group that's most at risk. I read about it just the other day. It's a compulsion. They can't stop themselves."

Ellie—who has always hated injections, who has to steel herself before every visit to the dentist—is appalled. To choose to cut yourself? "They must be mad," she says. "Temporarily, I mean."

"Not at all. It's a coping strategy. A way of expressing pain. A way of managing distress."

"With all due respect, Harry," Eleanor shoots back, "surely slicing yourself with a knife would cause distress rather than dispel it?" She hates it when Harriet gets bogged down in psychological claptrap.

"Oh, no, Ellie, not at all. What you've got to understand," she says with emphasis, "is that the person who cuts is already suffering. Cutting soothes, like a tranquilizer, I suppose. While the blood flows, she feels calm. She feels relief. And," Harriet continues, warming to her topic now, "it gets to be addictive, you see. It's soothing, and the relief draws people back to it time and again. A lot of the time it has to do with childhood trauma."

Ellie fidgets during this lecture. The glib claim of therapists that they understand what other people mean, better perhaps than the people themselves, makes her prickly with rage. She had her fill of this kind of thing in the hospital. "For Christ's sake, Harry, give it a rest. It's enough that the poor girl feels so miserable without you trying to reduce her to a type. A victim. Yet another case of childhood abuse."

"Hang on." Harriet uses her most imperious voice, the one that makes even taxi drivers shut up and listen. "What's the matter with you, Eleanor? You hardly know this girl. Is it something else—work, maybe?"

"No, no. Sorry I snapped, Harry. The whole thing, finding her like that, just seems to have set me off. I've had awful nightmares, and—"

"You poor pet. It's the shock. You're overwrought. I know—what you need, precisely what you need, is a holiday."

"Out of the question, Harry, I've only just started this job. I can't disappear just like that now."

"A long weekend. My cottage in Dorset in May, while we're away in Majorca—that's the ticket. It will do you a world of good. I'll even lend you the car. And stop worrying about that little Goth next door. Concentrate on the job. You don't want to let Clive down, now, do you?"

Ellie heads off another lecture by quizzing Harriet about the baby's feeding habits and Alexis's ballet. But before she finally rings off, she brings the subject back to Jessica.

"One last question, Harry. Do they ever actually kill themselves?"

"From time to time," Harriet says, her voice as bubbly now as if she were drinking champagne.

CHAPTER 39

A gangly young man and a girl with hair the color of chocolate are playing double bass and violin as Ellie sweeps down on the escalator into Cabot Place East. They're playing something somber. Shostakovich, maybe. Ellie likes the melancholy music, but she is surprised that the Canary Wharf management allow it. Too downbeat, too reflective, she would have thought. Too at odds with the upmarket shops that line the circular hall.

Ellie is fascinated by the way the violinist sways and rests her cheek against the wooden instrument. Can she possibly be as unselfconscious as she seems, standing there among a crowd of strangers with her eyes closed?

Ellie hears a male voice call out. Has he called her name? She turns with surprise to the bassist, thinking it was he who spoke, but he appears to be thoroughly absorbed in the music.

The escalator is approaching the ground floor. Ellie shifts her shopping to her right hand, and twists full circle. That's when she sees William DeQuoyne. He is on the escalator that moves upward from the subterranean mall. He sails past her, oblivious, and glides on toward the upper levels.

"Will!" The exclamation escapes her lips before she has time to bite it back. She waves her free hand.

He turns casually, in his languid way. His gaze sweeps over the men's outfitters and the handmade toiletries shop and the chocolate-haired violinist. Finally, it touches on Ellie.

Even at this distance, she reads the astonishment in his eyes. "Wait there," he mouths, as she is bounced off the escalator, and she does. He leaps off at the top and makes his way round and down again toward her. Ellie barely has time to compose herself before he is bending over and pressing his cheek to hers. Minutes later they're settled in armchairs with iced lattes in their hands and the hiss of the espresso machine in their ears.

"Lucky you spotted me," Will says, explaining that his work on the supplement hasn't finished. "Some disagreement about which development to feature. Behind-the-scenes politicking and all that. Nothing to worry about."

"But didn't you see me first, Will? I heard you call."

"Imagining things again, Eleanor?"

She doesn't press. Clearly, whatever he says, Will is worried about the problems with the supplement, because he goes on about it for some time, but he is careful to make it sound as if he himself has no emotional investment in the outcome. It's a long-standing trait. Will's way of pulling back from strong feeling. When they'd been together, Ellie had found it both endearingly transparent and infuriating.

There is a pause in the conversation. Ellie can't stop herself from asking. "How are you, Will?" with an emphasis on the pronoun. It's not the job she wants to know about, it's him. His personal life.

Whether he is contented. Whether things are going well for him. How his marriage is working out.

Will picks up his cup and swizzles the ice. He drains the last cool drops of liquid. "Kim has left me," he announces. "Just last week. She loaded Molly's things into the back of the Cherokee and drove off into the country. I came home to find the nursery empty."

"Oh, Will. I am so sorry." And in spite of herself, she is. "But why? I mean—" She pulls back. *Will was your lover,* she reminds herself. *You're the last person he'll confide in. You have no right to ask.* And yet the story—the way he'd told it, cutting straight to the chase—calls out for questions. "What I mean is, did you have no idea this was coming? Had Kim never hinted? Never threatened?"

Ellie realizes as she speaks that the same inquiries were directed at her when Will ended their relationship. Did you not see this coming? Weren't there unanswered questions, canceled meetings, averted eyes? And, the unspoken question: Did you really believe that a love affair with a married man could last? Ellie blushes. The color washes over her chest and neck and climbs to her forehead.

Will stares. His gaze follows the course of the color from her throat to her scalp. He watches as Ellie fiddles with her jacket. As she decides against removing it and, instead, holds the iced latte glass to her cheek. Then he leans forward. "D'you know," he says, "the color of your skin against your hair is glorious when you blush. I always remember that. It makes your eyes even brighter."

Will pushes himself into a standing position and approaches the bar with two long strides. He tweaks a package of cookies from the display case. Catches the eye of the girl behind the till, who is serving someone else, holds up a two-pound coin, places it on the counter, and sits back down.

"After the baby was born," he says, "Kim just seemed to change. She became so—" He searches for the word. "So narrow in her interests. So tired and distracted. As if I hardly mattered to her anymore."

Will peels the cellophane off the biscuits and offers one to Ellie, who declines. He shrugs and eats it himself. "Now," he says, inspecting his watch, "I've got five minutes left. Tell me about you. What's it like, being a night lawyer?"

Ellie struggles to turn her attention to the question. She does her best to make her job sound intriguing. She aims for a lightness of tone but doesn't quite achieve it.

The cashier sidles up to their table and hands Will his change. She has a small-toothed smile like that of an eight-year-old. "Charming," Will says, after her retreating back, and his accent is more pronounced than usual.

People sometimes guess that William DeQuoyne comes from New Zealand; they are searching for an accent that is English in origin, and less familiar than Australian. But they're wrong. He grew up in Zimbabwe and has traces of southern African planters' twang. This was one of the things Ellie had in common with him. Underneath his cultivated air, Will had about him, like her father, a whiff of the forest.

Will breaks into the flow of Ellie's conversation. She stops speaking at once, flustered to think she's been wittering.

"No friends there, yet?" he asks. "At work. No lovers? Old Clive hasn't made a move?"

"Clive? No, not at all." And for some strange reason, Ellie finds herself confiding to him how Ariana and the others had humiliated her. She would have held back from revealing the punch line—Ariana, posing as Ellie, declaiming "Oh, no, I cannot possibly say"—but Will looks at her with such sympathy in his eyes that she finds herself rushing on to the end.

He leans forward and reaches for her hand. He looks at her fingers as if inspecting her nails, as Ariana had done, but with a tenderness that Ellie had almost forgotten. He meets her eyes. "I think you'll make a great success of this job, Ellie. And believe me, anything said by an airhead like that is best forgotten." He kisses her cheek, and the pressure of his lips lasts longer than kindness requires. He lets go of her hand, picks up his change off the table, stands, and is gone.

CHAPTER 40

Will had never made a secret of his wife. Ellie knew right from day one that he was married. He used the term *we* in conversation to describe things that he and Kim did together. The scraps of information were never enough to enable Ellie to build a coherent picture of their marriage. In her mind's eye Mr. and Mrs. DeQuoyne were frozen in little vignettes. Will and Kim attended salsa classes. Will and Kim visited friends in Newbury. Kim shopped for groceries; Will did the cooking. That was all.

Ellie always believed that, given time, Will would leave Kim DeQuoyne and come to her. He never said so, never even hinted. He was scrupulous; he gave her no words of false hope. But how could he love her as he did, with such yearning, such desire, and not want to have her to himself?

And then came the day she'd waited for. Will's company was bidding on a commission in Vienna and he was taking Ellie with him. It wasn't only the weekend away or the elegant hotel, far beyond what his expense account would bear, that convinced her of his intentions. It was something in his manner. An intensity; she caught him staring at her when he thought she wasn't looking, as if he were searching for something. So she was prepared, in a sense, for a radical change.

Ellie didn't go into it all starry-eyed. She didn't assume it would be easy. She could see that he was charged with strain. She was tempted to lift the burden from him, to say: It's all right, Will, I know, you are going to break all your own rules now. I know that leaving Kim will cause pain to her and therefore to you. But yes, yes, we must be together.

They were to meet at the airport. The day before, throwing caution to the winds, Ellie had whirled into Covent Garden and there, in a shop that displayed only a narrow range of styles in an even narrower range of sizes, she was thrilled to find not one but two perfect outfits that fit her and flattered her and made her look closer to slender than she'd ever looked before. She teamed them with outrageous strappy shoes in lavender-colored suede that made her think of Ginger Rogers. She charged the entire purchase to her credit card; she had never before spent so much money on clothes in a single shot. She was prepared, in short, never to come back. Or only to come back as a new woman in a new world.

The details of the weekend ahead didn't concern Ellie at all. She made no demands. She didn't require flowers or diamonds. She didn't require Will on one knee to convince her she was loved. Nor did she care how the break with his wife would actually be accomplished; she was quite prepared to take things as they came. But nevertheless, as she danced back to her house layered with shopping, she found herself picking through the possibilities.

Maybe Will would telephone Kim from the hotel, and while he stuttered out the truth, Ellie would comfort his palm with kisses. No, she decided, that would be too cruel, and it was unfitting that their happiness should be built on a brutal moment. Better that he should write—with a fountain pen on pale gray paper, a long letter, a gentle and regretful letter—and then they would remain where they were until Kim was over the worst. Or maybe—Ellie liked this one best— maybe there'd be no communication at all. Maybe she and William DeQuoyne would simply take a high-windowed flat above the boulevard and remain in Vienna forever.

But it didn't happen in any of the ways that Ellie imagined. Instead, after they had climbed the magnificent staircase at the Schönbrunn Palace, after they'd visited the Secession and found themselves alone in a room with a shining frieze of golden images where they kissed as tenderly as children, after they'd had a delicious meal on the balcony of their hotel, Will broke the news. Kim was pregnant. "With my child, Ellie," he said solemnly. Kim had issued an ultimatum, and Will's affair with Ellie was to end.

"Why have you brought me to Vienna?" Ellie had shouted, unable to make sense of the words that fell from his mouth. "What are we doing here?"

Will laid constraining hands on her upper arms, and she hit out blindly, burned by his touch. "Sssh, shh," he said, trying to usher her inside, off the balcony, so that passersby wouldn't witness her despair.

He wanted to escort her back to London the following morning.

He wanted to see her safely home. *Safely?* Ellie thought. How shall I ever be safe when he has abandoned me?

Ellie refused his offers of help. She made her way back to London alone, and by the time she got there, the tears that stained her face had left a coarse patch on the beautiful lavender shoes.

CHAPTER 41

Nick Ross holds a clipboard to give the impression of late-breaking news as he reads his lines from the Autocue.

"The kettle's boiled," Denise Hewitt says, uncoiling herself from the sofa. Carl strains to see around her. He doesn't want to miss a single moment.

It's the part of *Crimewatch UK* where Nick Ross sums up the questions to which the police need answers. Carl likes this even better than the earlier part of the show, in which the crime itself is dissected, reconstructed, and deplored.

"Have you any knowledge"—the presenter's voice is appropriately solemn—"of the rape that took place in the car park of the Royal County Hotel in Durham last February thirteenth? Were you perhaps drinking in the Castle or one of the other pubs nearby?"

Carl watches every broadcast of *Crimewatch,* and Ross's manner never fails to impress. The presenter knows that violence matters and he makes you know it, too.

If there's one issue—besides his loyalty to the Isle of Dogs—that gets Carl going, it is law and order. When people get away with robbery or rape or murder, he says, it's a nail in the coffin of the civilized world. Carl isn't confident with words, but on law and order he can be positively eloquent.

Ever since he was a little lad, he's had one secret desire. One *aspiration,* Denise would say. Carl yearns with all his sober, middle-aged soul to catch—well, a thief would do, at a pinch, but better still would be a killer or a rapist—and bring him, or her, to justice. That, of course, is why Carl maintains his secret notebook. Because, whatever Denise says, you really never know.

Carl's eyes dart this way and that, but he settles down again to the telly once he's located his notebook. It's on the sideboard, a Biro attached to the front by a rubber band.

"Did you see a young man in jeans and matching jacket making his way through the nearby streets shortly after midnight?"

Carl knows that in homes all over Britain, people are wondering if the man in denim could be someone they know. But he can't shake off the feeling—the same feeling he had last week and the week before—that Nick Ross is inviting Carl, in particular, to sit up and take notice.

"Look at this face."

Carl strains forward, elbows resting on his knees. The Photofit shows a youngish man with a pointed chin and a prominent brow.

Nick Ross speaks over the image. "Perhaps you know a man who looks like this. He may be someone you work with, maybe even someone in your own household. If so, the Durham police would be very happy to hear from you."

Well, now. Carl does know a man who looks like this. In point of fact, he knows two. Neither a perfect likeness, but then Photofits are only as good as the witness's information and frightened victims often get it wrong.

Denise, returning with two mugs of tea and a bowl of toffee popcorn, detours past the telly to take a closer look. "That's the rapist?" she asks. She has removed her house socks and slipped into a pair of flip-flops instead. There is bronze-colored polish on her toenails. She hands him a well-brewed mug of tea. "Ugly-looking bugger, isn't he?"

Denise was twenty-five years old, assistant manager of a ladies' clothing shop in Greenwich, when two youths with stocking masks had threatened her with a hunting knife. Carl, who'd been fitting a mortice at the back of the shop, heard shouts and foul language and without even thinking had come out to tell the lads not to use words like c—— in front of a lady. The knife brought him up short. He was as surprised as Denise when the youths shouted a few final obscenities and then dashed away.

Denise and Carl began to date. She was a vivacious girl, with lovely brown hair, and her admiration of him—her insistence on his heroism—was so intoxicating that within weeks, Carl proposed, and she accepted. But over the years, Denise's admiration has trickled away. All that Carl can see in her manner now is a weary disappointment.

"That rapist," Carl says, "I know two men right here on the island who are a lot like him. One's a courier; he works in the mail room of the tower, you know, down in the basement. He's got the eyebrows."

"And the other one?"

"A bartender at the Fine Line."

Denise makes a snort of derision. "The rape took place in Durham," she says.

Carl picks up his notebook and jots down a reminder. He has no reason to believe that either the courier or the bartender was in Durham in February, but . . . "It can't hurt, can it, to ask a question or two?"

Carl and Denise's lounge—their sitting room, she calls it—is fresh and new, transformed by Carl's do-it-yourself skills and Denise's imagination and drive. The frieze two-thirds of the way up the wall was her idea. So were the patterned curtains and the matching tiebacks. She knows what's she's doing, all right, Carl thinks; she's got a sense of style. It's not Denise's fault that he feels more comfortable in his own little cubbyhole upstairs.

The program ends and Denise flicks through the channels. "What d'you want to watch, Carlie?"

"Whatever," Carl mumbles. He is going over in his mind what happened this afternoon.

He'd been surprised at first to see Eleanor Porter in Cabot Hall. She works nights, and she isn't the sort to hang around the Wharf outside working hours. She doesn't sit in bars, like some of them, her skirt sliding higher with every drink.

So Carl was taken aback when, in a routine afternoon scan of Cabot Place East, he caught a glimpse of her making a dash into Boots, her bag heavy with purchases from Waitrose. She hadn't been stocking up on pastries, that's for sure. She must stick to salads and fruit. How else would she stay so slim? Or maybe she's one of those sushi types. He tried it once, sitting alone at the curving counter in a

Japanese restaurant, confused about how you're supposed to order from a menu that isn't like any menu Carl'd ever seen before, and eventually choosing a dish almost at random. Carl reckoned he'd never before paid so much for so little. No wonder the Japanese were small, he mused. Probably never got a decent meal, poor buggers.

Eleanor Porter is small, too. One line for the body and four for the limbs, like a matchstick girl. Add a mane of scorching red hair and a shake of freckles and you'd have her. Only her breasts—they are the only part of her that has the kind of generosity that Carl prefers in a woman. She never wears a top that gives too much away, but there is cleavage under those silk sweaters, he can tell. The place where the breasts come together will be warm and smooth and . . .

Oh, shit.

Carl slams his right fist against the side of his skull. The pain bursts across his head.

Shit, shit, shit.

"Carl? Carl!"

Carl slams the fist once more into his skull, just above his ear. He starts thinking sensibly again.

Thinking about the narrow skirts. The close-fitting jackets. The blacks and grays and navy, Wharfwoman's camouflage colors, but always, in the case of the Dancing Queen, with a thin scarf in some girly kind of color or a silky top in pink. Even when she dresses in baggy pants and a cropped T-shirt, she looks ladylike. Not to mention gorgeous.

Concentrate, Carl tells himself. No imaginings now. Just concentrate on what you saw.

Carl's powers of observation really pay off at a time like this. He watched the monitors, and then—when Richard wasn't around—he replayed the tape once more, for himself, until it was all fixed in his memory. It starts with the moment when Eleanor Porter rushed out of Boots. She's always in a hurry. She's not what his grandfather used to call one of life's meanderers.

Except at night, when she thinks no one is watching her. Then she slows down. Carl smiles, thinking of the first time he saw her, dancing in the foyer of the tower. Then he goes over their last encounter again.

Eleanor Porter rushed out of Boots with her document case in one hand and a bulging carrier bag in the other. She stepped onto the down escalator. She was distracted for a moment by some musicians, but she soon lost interest.

Halfway down the escalator, quite suddenly, something cut through her poise. She swiveled to left and right. She craned her neck. She switched the carrier bag to the other hand and peered over the side of the escalator. Her expression lit up and then she waved her hand excitedly, like someone trying to flag down a passing motorcar.

A lanky man came bounding toward her. Carl leaned in closer to catch every detail. Arrogant-looking, Carl recalls. Poncy, too. What could she possibly want with a man like that? A lover? No, Carl decides, they were too awkward with each other, too restrained, to be lovers. The giveaway on that score was that moment's hesitation when neither of them was certain whether kisses were in order. But—and the memory of this makes Carl wince—Mr. Oh-So-Sure soon took charge. He bent over and pressed his cheek to Eleanor's. Then he swept her toward Starbucks, where the two of them remained, absorbed in conversation, for the best part of half an hour. Not lovers, Carl decided, as he studied their to-and-fro. The way the man focused on her lips as she spoke. How she gazed after him when he reached over to retrieve something from the counter. How, at one point, her face softened and she moved as if to touch his fingers, but then stiffened and pulled back.

Not lovers. But perhaps lovers-to-be. The thought gives Carl a sudden burst of shivers.

"Cold, Carlie?" Denise asks. "Perhaps you'd better put your fleece on."

Carl doesn't hear her. He's thinking of Eleanor Porter in a clinch with that man, and he feels like being sick.

CHAPTER 42

In the waiting room of the doctor's surgery, Ellie finds herself sitting opposite a blank-faced couple who are arranged side by side on plastic chairs. They hold hands and stare ahead bleakly.

Ellie leafs through the pages of a battered copy of *Hello!*, but she thinks about Will. About how he looked: his grace, his demeanor, his tenderness when he touched her. About his openness—how quickly he revealed to her what was going on in his life. About the simple and overwhelming fact that he is free. "Kim has left me." That clear announcement plays like music in her head. Aware of the couple sitting opposite, Ellie makes an effort to ensure that her expression doesn't betray the elation that she feels. "Kim has left me." Just like that.

At the umpteenth rehearsal, something in Will's remembered tones registers for the first time. It jerks her upright. He doesn't sound angry. How strange that is. He doesn't sound wounded. He doesn't even sound hugely concerned. Has he finally come to realize how little he cares for Kim? How ill-matched they are? Is her departure not a blow but a liberation?

Ellie lets the magazine fall to the floor as a more sinister possibility strikes her. Will didn't actually say—not in so many words—that the marriage is over. Could it be only a spat? Is he aiming to win his wife back?

To hide her shaking hands, Ellie picks *Hello!* up off the floor and pretends to skim a story. Her mind is working overtime. When Kim left, Will said, she took the baby. She took the baby's furniture. She wouldn't do that, surely, if she were intending to return. And even if she were, the whole sordid episode—flouncing off like that without even a decent warning—is bound to take the scales off Will's eyes. To make him see that this marriage hasn't got a future. Surely he recognizes that already. Why else would he have told Ellie that Kim had bunked off? He's such a private person, but he was keen as mustard. He clearly wanted her to know. Surely he wouldn't want to open up old wounds? Why would he want her to know unless he had plans, had hopes, and they included her?

"Miss Porter?" The doctor is holding open the door for her. Ellie leaps up and gathers her things. "And how are you today?" the doctor inquires as she slips under his arm and into his office.

Ellie turns to him with a dazzling smile. "Just fine," she says. "Quite wonderful."

CHAPTER 43

Ellie is checking her kumite against a demonstration video when a minicab pulls up on the street outside. Peeping through her shutters, she sees Jess tumble out of the back. Ellie deliberates until lunchtime. Should she, shouldn't she, do the neighborly thing? Should she knock on Jess's door? Should she offer sandwiches, advice, a shoulder to cry on? Or should she leave well enough alone?

Although she is touched by Jess's neediness, if Ellie's brutally honest with herself, she'll admit she doesn't much like the girl. Doesn't like her clothes. Her boyfriend. Her sullen ways. What's more, Ellie has enough on her plate right now. The grading is looming over her, it's still early days at the new job, and that man with the weird voice rang twice last night and hung up each time she answered. Enough already.

But then, Ellie reflects, Jess is so alone. She looked terribly frail in the ambulance, shrinking away under the hospital blanket. *Promise me. I promise.* Ellie has broken a promise before, one she'd made to her father, and she's vowed never to do so again.

Ellie pounds on Jessica's front door, her anxiety notching up with each unanswered knock. Finally, the door opens. Jessica nods at Ellie, then leaves the door ajar in silent invitation and slumps her way upstairs. Her feet are bare. She moves as if her own weight is an almost intolerable burden.

Jessica reaches the room with the balcony without uttering a word. She is wearing a silky nightdress with long sleeves that trumpet out at the wrist. Without her usual layers, with kohl-rimmed eyes and no other makeup, she looks thinner and more fragile. She curls herself up in a fetal position on a rickety sofa, and puts her thumb in her mouth. Her eyes are open, but she is as still as a block of ice.

Ellie had worked herself up to walk smiling into Jessica's presence. She meant to offer practical help: to do the shopping; to clear out the fridge; to arrange to have the carpet cleaned. She meant to stay no more than an hour, and to leave without having touched on any topic more challenging than the latest bust-up on *EastEnders*. But when she sees how forlorn Jessica is, she can't bite back the question.

"You didn't intend to kill yourself, Jess. Did you?" Ellie has always been of the view that you shouldn't mess around with suicide. If you're going to do it, then make a damn good job of it. A final job. Otherwise, lay off.

Jessica's head snaps up. The whites of her eyes are enormous. "No. It was just a cut. I screwed up, okay?" Then her head flicks toward the staircase.

Ellie smells him before she sees him. The top step gives a groan, and as she whirls she is assaulted by the odor of something like diesel fuel. It's clinging to Tull's overcoat.

His face hardens at the sight of her. The accusation comes shooting out. "What are you doing here?" He doesn't wait for Ellie to answer. "Jess? Where've you been? I wanna take some pictures of you," he says, waving a video camera at the girl on the sofa. "What the fuck's she doing here?"

Ellie is impressed by the energy Jess musters. "Leave her alone, Tull," she says, in a voice unexpectedly strong. "Don't you dare touch her. I've been in hospital, that's where I've been. I cut too deep. If Ellie, here, hadn't found me, I might have died or something. She saved me. And," she says, "where were you, you bastard? Gone again, off on one of your shady deals."

"Jess, oh, Jess—" He tries to wrap his arms around her, but she swats him away. "I'd no idea. When did this happen? Was it Wednesday? I was on my way to meet you, I was, but then Kristoff—"

"Fuck Kristoff, Tull. Do you hear me? And fuck you!" Once again, she pushes him away. "I don't want you here. I don't want you in my life. Get out!"

Tull makes a noise like a sob in the back of his throat, and then he turns and clatters down the stairs. The front door slams. Jess stands by the balcony window, hugging herself. Ellie doesn't know what to say.

After a couple of minutes of silence, long enough that they both watch Widget leap up onto the garden wall and disappear into the shrubbery, Jessica breaks the silence. "I met him, you know, at a pub on Westferry Road," she says. "He bought me a drink. And another." Her laugh is sardonic. "And another. We talked, a lot. He told me I was cool. I was flattered; I figured that for Tull, a compliment like 'cool' was the equivalent of a dozen long-stemmed roses."

"Are you saying it was love at first sight?"

Jessica leans her forehead against the window and ponders the question. "We had a lot in common," she says, after a moment. "That's what I thought at the time. He understands what it's like to feel trapped. I told him about my parents pushing me to go to university. 'Fuck it,' he said. 'What good does university do? Students spend three years in the bar, learning to talk pretentious crap. Then they end up working as a clerk in the local benefits office and owing thousands to the bank.' That made me laugh," Jessica says. "Thanks to Tull, I felt less frightened. Or maybe it was the drink that gave me that wonderful sensation that it bloody well didn't matter anymore."

Jessica's breath condenses on the glass and blurs the scene outside. She raises her arm and rubs the window with her sleeve. Half a minute passes with no sound except the whining of a bus on Westferry Road. Finally, Ellie breaks the silence. "Will you show me your arms?" she says.

There's another long pause. Then Jessica whirls around on the balls of her feet, and Ellie shrinks under her furious gaze. She sees Jessica as a fiery blur silhouetted against the light slanting in from the balcony, her hair, her nightdress, her fingernails, blazing black to match her blazing eyes. Then a cloud brushes across the sun, the intensity fades, and Ellie gets a grip. A child, Ellie reminds herself. She's only a child. A quick rush of sympathy is followed straightaway by the prick of tears.

Jessica stares. Her breathing quickens. She wanted to tough it out, but she hadn't bargained on this. She turns toward Ellie, and slowly, like a sleepwalker, she raises her arms straight out in front of her. There's only a hairsbreadth between her fingertips and Ellie's face. She could reach out and touch those tears, but she doesn't.

Instead, Jessica grasps the left sleeve of her nightgown, and with a single jerk, yanks it up all the way to the shoulder.

Ellie knows what she will see, but knowing doesn't save her from the shock. A mass of wounds, laid out parallel to one another like headstones in a graveyard, each cut short and sharp. The oldest incisions straddle the biceps, and the scar tissue there, pale and shiny, hardly shows. Farther down, the gashes are more visible. Near the wrist, they're so angry-looking that they put Ellie in mind, absurdly, of a baboon's bottom.

"So, it's true," Ellie whispers. "You do this to yourself."

Jessica's face flares as red as her infant scars. She begins to tug the sleeve down again, but Ellie puts out a hand. "Wait." Ellie places her forefinger tentatively on Jessica's upper arm. She slides it down, slowly, softly, fingering each hump and depression, registering the gristliness and the tenderness of the scars themselves.

"This one?" she says, touching a scar that is particularly lurid. "How did you come to do this one?"

Jessica's eyes follow the course of the scar, as if she can read its history in the flesh. She is silent for a moment and then she speaks.

"I was home alone one afternoon. Everything was quiet and still, like maybe there'd been a cloud of toxic dust and the entire population of London was dead. It felt as if my heart might explode from fear. You ever felt like that?"

"Yes." Ellie nods. "What did you do?"

"What did I do? I went looking, all through the house. In the shed, where my father keeps his tools, I found a little saw with jagged teeth." Her hand sketches a shape like a hatchet in the air.

"A hacksaw," Ellie says. Her father had had one, too.

"It looked like a little animal. I laid it across my forearm and I dug it in, slowly, and I pulled it toward me."

"It must have hurt like hell."

A small smile is playing around the corner of Jessica's mouth. She looks up at Ellie. "Pardon?"

"The pain. It must have been dreadful."

Jessica runs her finger over the scar again. "No. Not really. It only lasted a second or two."

"For Christ's sake, Jess, you might have cut an artery. You might have died."

"But I didn't, did I?" The tone is clipped. More like her old self.

Ellie is fascinated, in spite of herself. "But why, Jess? Why take such a risk?"

A pause. "I don't know, Ellie; it's just that everybody else seems so together. Like they know who they are, who they belong to. Like I'm the only one out there all on my own." A shrug. "I don't know why I'm telling you this. You couldn't possibly understand."

"What makes you say that?" Ellie is genuinely taken aback.

"It's obvious. You're a lawyer, aren't you? You've got your own home, your own life. You're somebody." Jessica leans her back against the glass and goes on without waiting for the objections that spring to Ellie's lips. "And you even look good. Your hair is quality."

The blush fans out from the V of Ellie's shirt all the way up to her hairline. "Oh, sure," she says, in an attempt to play down the compliment, "gorgeous and successful, that's me. Small and struggling, more like."

Jessica contradicts. "Small and perfectly formed. That's how my friend describes you."

Ellie doesn't know whether to be uneasy at the thought that she's been a topic of conversation for those creatures of the night or to be flattered.

"Let's face it, Ellie, you've got it made."

"You wouldn't say that if you knew."

"Knew what?"

No answer. Ellie is straining toward the balcony window now. She loosens the scarf at her neck with one hand, absentmindedly, and her eyes are narrowed. Jessica twists around and follows the direction of Ellie's gaze. There is a movement in the bushes where the wall between the houses has crumbled away, but nothing else.

"Ellie?" Jessica repeats her question. "I wouldn't say you had it made if I knew—what?"

"What?" Ellie tears her eyes away from the window. "Oh," she says. "If you knew what I did to my father."

CHAPTER 44

Odysseus is waiting for Ellie when she gets in from the *Chronicle* that night, emerging from a pile of bedding like a mouse shaking off a mound of snow. Ellie lowers herself until they're nose to nose. She reaches a hand into the cage. "Come on, Odysseus. Come on, baby. Come to me." She slides her hand around his delicate body. With one smooth movement, she lifts him free of the cage and rests his soft flank against her cheek.

When she returns the little creature to his cage, the house feels empty. Ellie switches the video on. She sets out to prepare her supper, washing the vegetables while a recording of *Who Wants to Be a Millionaire?* plays in the background. You should be ashamed, Ellie tells herself, using the telly for company. Like Muzak, that's what these quiz shows are. Filling in the silence. But then a question intrigues her, and the next thing Ellie knows she is craning to see the screen as she slices a red pepper into strips.

"Is the answer (A) William Blake, (B) James Watt, (C) Alexander Graham Bell, or (D) Isambard Kingdom Brunel?"

Ellie's father was an engineer, so she plumps for *D*.

"You happy with that answer?"

"Completely," Ellie says. She is facing the telly now, with a finger of ginger in one hand and a knife in the other. Seconds tick by. The presenter draws out the suspense. Ellie steps closer. In the instant of waiting, she all but convinces herself that there's some trick to the question. She should have selected James Watt, after all.

"Isambard Kingdom Brunel is—the right answer!" The presenter's smile is smug. The contestant's face glistens under the lights. And Ellie herself is unaccountably delighted.

"We got it right, Odysseus."

From the floor of his cage, where he is gnawing on a strip of red pepper, Odysseus yawns.

The doorbell rings as Ellie is tucking into her final forkful of stir fry. "A minute," she calls. She flicks off the television and shoves the trolley back against the wall. She snatches up her dishes and deposits them in the sink. And, at last, she approaches the door, and peers through the spyhole.

There on the pavement in front of her house, standing on one long leg like a stork, is Ariana. Ellie's first impulse is to hide, but Ariana will have heard Ellie call and will know she's there. A refusal to answer the door would just provide another thing for colleagues at the *Chronicle* to laugh about.

Ellie edges open the door and waits for Ariana to make the first move.

Ariana is bursting with apology. The words come out in a rush. "So sorry . . . calling like this, no warning . . . You're probably entertaining . . ." Ariana cranes her neck and peers into the cottage. She can see all the way to the back wall of the large room, which is conspicuously empty. Through the door, Ariana had heard a man's voice, so she's puzzled to discover that Ellie is alone.

Ellie, for her part, doesn't know how to respond to this unexpectedly friendly approach. Her cheeks flame at the memory of her humiliation. "No, no, not at all," she murmurs, but she remains in a position that bars the entrance to the house.

"May I come in?"

"Come in?" Ellie has few visitors and even fewer casual callers. Casual hostile callers. She feels dangerously unprepared. It occurs to her to tell Ariana that she's busy. But Ariana flashes her a radiant smile, and Eleanor relents.

And once Ellie steps aside and lets Ariana bounce past her into the sitting room, she begins to feel a certain pleasure in the fact that Ariana has come calling. That she's dropped in without warning, as if Ellie were a close friend. Ellie has to rein herself back. She's almost dizzy with the sense of possibility.

It turns out to be easier, far easier, than she might ever have imagined. Ariana flings her mohair jacket down on the bentwood rocker and makes herself at home. She steps ahead of Ellie and begins to explore.

"Oh, look at that!" she squeals. "A rolltop desk." She curls the top up and down, admires the smooth workings of the mechanism, bumps her finger over the slats. She examines Ellie's notebook, touching a tentative finger to the letters that spell out Ellie's name. She keeps up a running commentary on the house and its contents. She might have been an estate agent, Ellie thinks. Or perhaps a prospective buyer, sizing up the goods.

"Lovely place you have here, Ellie," she says, peering at a group of photographs. "How ever did you manage to find a house on the island? A proper house, a solid brick terrace, built to last. What is it, anyway, Victorian?"

Ellie slips into a space in the flow of words to explain that these three terraces were built for dockers and their families.

"Old, and pretty, too. How clever of you," Ariana says, as if Ellie had designed the house herself. She wheels around and looks directly into Ellie's eyes. Ellie tries to ignore the fact that the heels of Ariana's red mules have made an indentation on the planks of the wooden floor. "But then you are clever, aren't you?" Ariana continues. Her voice is speculative, her gaze intent. "You're a thinker. Not like me."

Ellie doesn't feel clever. Clever people are the ones who are quick, who bounce back with the swingeing comment or the brilliant remark, but Ellie has always been too shy to make that kind of an impact. When she got a First in her Part Is, her undergraduate tutor was astounded. "A dark horse," he said, jocularly, but she also detected an undertone of deprecation, as if she didn't quite deserve it. "There she was, sitting quietly, absorbing everything," he remarked to the rest of the tutorial group. As if Ellie were not really clever at all, but merely an intellectual sponge.

Before Ellie can think of anything at all to say in response, Ariana slides past her and takes up position near the patio doors. She peers out into the darkness. "And a garden! I expect in the summer you're out here on a hammock, naked as the day you were born? Lucky you. Me, I've only got a balcony the size of a bath mat, and you wouldn't see me for pigeon shit if I tried to catch the sun. You decided to leave the garden wild?" she asks, dragging the doors open and stepping out onto the grass. She walks on the balls of her feet, so that her heels won't sink into the turf. She heads to the corner of the garden where Ellie has a small shed.

"I love it like this," Ellie protests, and it is true. She'd like to explain that the garden is no trouble at all to care for, and secluded, and lush, and that is how she prefers it, but she stops. She is not at all certain that her visitor is listening.

Ariana has placed her face close to the grimy window of the shed. "My God, Ellie, whatever have you got in there?"

"A loom," Ellie replies quickly. The thought of the loom always brings a sudden pang of guilt. Ellie's mother accuses her of picking interests up and putting them down again like teacups. *You never stick to anything, Eleanor,* she says. "I used to weave wall hangings, once upon a time." Once upon a time was when Will was the center of her world, and weaving was a way of coping with his absences. She was waiting for him to call—always waiting, that's how it seemed—but when she sat at her loom, she felt purposeful and in charge. Will, on the other hand, didn't like "her little hobby." He thought it took up too much room. He was offended by the tufts of wool that floated through her flat. Finally, she put the loom away. "I'm too busy now," she says.

Back in the sitting room, Ellie suddenly wakens to her responsibilities as a hostess. "May I make you a cup of tea?"

Ariana's lazy eyes widen, and Ellie realizes her mistake. Tea? At this time of night? How old-maidish it sounds.

Ariana has other ideas. From her shoulder bag, she produces a bottle of wine. "Why not?" she says. "If you've nothing better to do?"

Ellie's hand creeps upward and she begins to twine a strand of hair around her finger. She had promised herself a week without booze. She's been drinking a lot lately, and it's not doing her training any good. But seeing Ariana's disappointment, Ellie locates a corkscrew and opens the bottle. She pours two glasses. "Why not?" she echoes.

Ariana leads them both back into the sitting area and takes a seat in the armchair. Ellie positions herself on the small sofa with the coffee table between them. Ariana then unwinds herself from the arm-chair and snuggles down on the other end of the sofa, with her body angled toward Ellie. They begin to talk. Ariana leaps from topic to topic like a jackrabbit, picking up an idea and chasing it until another catches her attention. It's a way of speaking that is alien to Ellie. "Pardon?" she says at one point, having utterly lost the thread.

The laughter that Ariana comes out with then is a cross between a chortle and a snatch of song. "You're right, I'm all over the place, aren't I?" she says. "I'm afraid you'll have to get used to that. When I talk it's always unfocused. Like a scattergun, or so Rick—he's my boyfriend; well, really, my ex—used to say."

Ellie remembers the man who stepped out of the shadows at Island Gardens.

Ariana gives her companion a shrewd glance. "It's not you, though, Eleanor. Not your style at all. You use words differently."

Ellie is stunned. It's so rare for someone to show an interest in what she's really like. "Differently?" she stammers.

"Mmmn. I just toss words around and hope that some will land in the right place. You're different. You deploy words, that's what you do, like a general on a battlefield. You use them as a kind of defensive shield."

Ellie is trying to decide whether or not this is an insult when Ariana continues. "That's one of the reasons," she says, "why the law suits you so well."

She's right, Ellie thinks. I never knew it before, but she's right. A shield. And then she feels a burst of shame. With all the force of a fall downstairs, she is flung back to that dreadful moment in the corridor at work. *I cannot possibly say!* But Ariana gets there first.

"Eleanor, listen. I actually had a reason for coming here tonight. I came to apologize. For what I did—you know, that day at work." Her speech increases pace as she explains. "I'd had a bad day—a really blond day, full of mistakes. First, a contact had clammed up on me—I'd spent ages, grooming him; it was such a waste—and then I'd been told off by my editor. And after that . . . Well, I'd thought about that conversation with you, Ellie—the one about Oliver Nesbit—and how you'd rebuffed me and something just snapped. It just came over me on the spur of the moment. It was absolutely the nastiest, meanest, most horrible thing I've ever done, and I'm really ashamed. It was just spite on my part, believe me. You're not like that at all—You're really cool." She reaches across and clasps Ellie's fingers in her own. "I'm so totally, totally sorry. Please say you forgive me."

A great wave of relief washes over Ellie. She no longer has an enemy at work. She might even—who knows?—have found a friend. "Of course I forgive you." She squeezes Ariana's hand and smiles.

And from then on, Ellie is quite able to manage the flow of conversation. Under Ariana's generous attention, she relaxes like a cat in the sun.

When they talk about holidays, Ellie confides. "Harriet, a friend of mine—my best friend, really—has a cottage in Dorset. I'm welcome to use it, she says, for the third weekend in May. It sounds nice, don't you think? You know, a bit of hiking along the cliff tops during the day, and curling up with a book and a glass of wine in the evening. The cottage has a view of the sea and an open fireplace."

"Lucky you," Ariana says, picking up the wine bottle. "I'd adore a few days in the country. Never been to Dorset, how sad is that?" She refills their glasses.

Ellie blinks. That's a hint if ever she's heard one. "I don't suppose, Ariana, you'd be interested in coming with me?"

Ariana doesn't hesitate. "Sounds marvelous," she says. "You're on. Round about mid-May? I'll get my diary out on Monday and we'll confirm." Ellie's almost dizzy with the ease of it. The whole thing is settled just like that.

After that, they turn to more intimate issues, and again, Ariana leads the conversation. She questions Ellie.

About her career. What jobs had she done before, and where?

About Will. How long had they been together? When had they split up and why? Ariana hazards a guess that Ellie wants to get together again, and Ellie stoutly denies it.

"I can tell you still like him."

"No, that's all in the past." There is a limit to openness, Ellie feels, even now.

And, especially, Ariana quizzes her, with a barely contained glee, about Oliver Nesbit. "Do you know," she says, wide-eyed with scandal, "it's turned out that the photographs of a naked child were of Nesbit's daughter. Janey Nesbit, her name is. Only three years old. What do you think of that?"

Ellie can scarcely contain herself. "It's absurd, Ariana; the whole thing's absurd. Since when is bathing your child a crime? And what of his family?" she says. "No one, not even a celebrity barrister, deserves to have every Tom, Dick, and Harry dishing the dirt."

Ariana is not deterred. She teases and prods and pokes at the subject like a matador with a bull, veering away and then swooping again for a fresh attack, until finally Ellie is forced to confront her memories of the man. Since Harriet introduced the name of Oliver Nesbit, the image of his face has sharpened and settled. His long jaw. His pale skin, white to the point of blue, and prone to unruly stubble. His dashing dark-fringed eyes.

Against her better judgment, Ellie finds herself searching for something to say. "Oliver Nesbit was given to bluster, but popular in spite of it, Ariana. Confident, cheerful, sociable," she says, "at least on the surface. The kind who sweeps people off to impromptu parties." She recalls a boisterous Oliver, brimming with bonhomie, leaning over a scarred table in the library. His voice is muted. *It's Dixon's birthday. We're off to the Cat for lunch.* He wins agreement from a boy who jerks awake from a nap, and a horse-faced girl with a very tight sweater. Oliver turns his head toward Ellie's end of the table just as she happens to look up. Their eyes lock. The pause that follows is uneasy. "Oh, ah—" Oliver says, struggling to remember her name, "I don't suppose you want to come?" "No, no," Ellie demurs. "Far too much to do." For the first time, Oliver Nesbit favors her with his wide buoyant smile. It was the following week that he sought Ellie out in the dining hall and invited her to a film.

Ariana gets up and pours herself another glass of wine. "Let's cut to the chase. Was he involved, even then, with underage girls?"

Ellie is still wearing the jumper she'd put on when she arrived home. She wishes she'd changed into something cooler. Widget has left a few hairs scattered along the sleeve of the sweater and Ellie plucks them off one by one. "I haven't the slightest idea."

"You can figure it out, can't you?" Ariana says. "A clever girl like you?" She tops up Ellie's glass. "What was he like as a lover? Could he get it up for you?"

Ellie takes a long sip of wine. "Let's put it like this, Ariana. We were both rather inexperienced. He was no better and no worse than me. We only saw each other for a few weeks, anyway, and not long after we split up, I heard he was engaged."

"Ah-hah! What was she like, the fiancée?"

There is a pause. Ariana kicks off her shoes and swings her legs up onto the sofa. She rubs her feet back and forth on the cushions as if trying to use friction to light a fire. All the while she looks impatiently at Ellie.

"Her name was Hester, as I recall," Ellie says at last, plucking a little harder at the cat hairs. She drains the last of her wine. "She had a very pretty complexion and a posh Scots accent."

"Whether she was Scots or not is ducking the issue. Did she look prepubescent?"

Ellie flushes. "Ariana, don't you think that's stretching things a bit? As it happens, Hester had rather a maternal air. You expected she would make a good cock-a-leekie soup."

"Which reminds me," Ariana says, setting her wineglass on the floorboards. "I'd better call a taxi."

The taxi arrives shortly before midnight. "Stay where you are," Ariana insists. She slides her feet into her shoes and dashes outside to speak to the driver. Like a whirlwind, she retrieves her jacket and bag, plonks her glass in Ellie's dishwasher, and is off.

But not before the oddest thing occurs. As she is making her exit, Ariana bends over with her back to Ellie and retrieves something from the floor.

"Late delivery, sweetie," she says, handing Ellie an envelope. "It was lying on the mat."

Then with a final hug for Ellie, she disappears into the night.

CHAPTER 45

Ellie remains in the doorway watching as the minicab pulls away. Ariana leans toward the driver, gesturing in the direction she wants to go. When the cab pauses at the junction, she turns back and gives Ellie a jaunty wave.

The thump of the engine fades away, but Ellie lingers, savoring the silence of the street. Except for a couple of bags of rubbish that lean against a house like drunks, the pavements are empty. The terrace is bathed in darkness. Ellie cranes her neck forward as far as she can, looking first in one direction and then the other. Nothing. No one. Nada.

Nothing equals peaceful, she tells herself. Not cottage-in-the-country peaceful, of course. Not as serene as Harriet's cottage. And at the thought of the cottage, of her and Ariana tucked up in front of the fire there, Ellie hugs herself with secret delight. It's almost too good to be true. And then somehow, when she looks around again, surveying the street by moonlight, with the traffic reduced to a trickle and wisps of illegal smoke curling up from a few chimneys in the row, even Hesperus Street has a touch of the idyllic. All the islanders safely tucked in their beds, while visions of—

Ellie stops and looks again at the school whose rear elevation backs onto the street that runs beside her house. Harbinger Primary, a grim Victorian structure, tall and forbidding, encased by strong iron railings. All the lights are out. The small windows that look out onto the paved play areas are dark. The gates are locked. But she's certain that in the darkness she saw a shifting of a shape, which was all the more conspicuous because the street outside is so very, very still.

Deliberately, Ellie turns her head away. On the count of ten, she flicks her gaze back to the school. Sure enough, there is a figure standing inside the iron railings. A face pressed to the bars. She doesn't register any more than that before the shape moves off around the side of the school and out of sight.

It's probably nothing, she tells herself. Nothing. No one. Nada.

The school has a caretaker. Does he live inside the gate? Surely not. He's in his early thirties, a nerdy-looking man who wears black T-shirts with slogans on them that she doesn't understand. When she heads for the office in the evening, she often sees him clearing the last of the stragglers out of the play area, returning the basketball to the games shed, locking the gates. They were introduced once by a neighbor. He seemed reluctant. Ellie had offered her hand, and the caretaker, his expression wary, had inspected his own hand as if he'd forgotten what it was for before matching Ellie's gesture. After shaking hands, he'd inspected his palm again, like someone checking for germs. Since then, there has been nothing more than fleeting smiles between them. So why is he watching her now, at half-past twelve at night? And why does he try to hide it?

Don't be ridiculous! Ellie tells herself. She's become fanciful in the past couple of weeks, and it has to stop. The caretaker—if indeed it was him—was simply drawn to the gates by the sound of the minicab, and Ellie happened to be standing in his line of vision. By now, he is probably tucked back up in bed, with splashes of turmeric from an Indian takeaway on the trademark T-shirt.

"You take everything so personally, Eleanor." That's what her mother says. "Just because someone's looking, doesn't mean he's looking at you."

Ellie glances up and down the empty street a final time and then slowly, almost reluctantly, steps back inside. She goes through her little ritual—close the door, check the lock, put the chain on.

The envelope that Ariana found is propped against the juice extractor. MISS ELEANOR PORTER, it says. Will sometimes, teasingly, called her that—when, that is, he didn't call her *little one*. But the handwriting isn't Will's.

Ellie doesn't rush to open the envelope. She rinses her supper dishes and stacks them in the dishwasher. She sluices out the wok. She pours a glass of cold water and forces herself to drink it down.

Finally, Ellie leans her back against the worktop, picks up the envelope, and examines it under the light. Cheap-looking paper underscored with gray, like dingy teeth. She uses the tip of the corkscrew to rip it open.

At first Ellie believes the envelope is empty. Then she crimps it and shakes. A morsel of paper, intricately folded, drifts out and settles on her palm. She tightens her fingers around it.

Her reluctance is a cramp in the pit of her stomach, like period pains. But they can't be period pains, because Ellie hasn't had a proper period, nothing more than haphazard spotting, for the past two years.

The cramp is a warning. Don't open it. Don't read it. Throw it away. Eleanor uses her toe to lift the flap of the kitchen bin. She could toss the note away, just as it is, unread. Life would then go on quite as if the envelope had never slithered through her letter box. As if Ariana had not spotted it on the mat, had not stooped over and picked it up. As if the note had never arrived. What would be the harm? Letters go missing all the time. If they're trivial, good riddance; if they're important, the writer tries again.

She opens her fingers and stares at the scrap of paper in the palm of her hand.

She crouches down next to the cage. "What do you think, Odysseus? One nod for *yes,* two nods for *no.*" She purses her lips and puffs a sharp stream of air into the mound of bedding. There is a sound like a miniature sneeze. Then the heap of white stuff shivers and shakes and is still again.

"I guess that's a yes, eh?"

Ellie slowly, deliberately, unpicks the folds. Opening each pleat reminds her of a schoolyard game, in which a sheet of paper was folded many times to form a pyramid with numbers or colors or predictions for the future embedded on each surface. One child put her fingers inside; each time she moved them, different facets were revealed. Another child made selections from the colors and numbers, until, at the lifting of the final fold, her fate would be revealed.

Smelly poo! might be written there. Or: *Kisses boys.*

Or: *Dance the night away.*

Or: *Soon to die.*

Ellie has come to the final fold. In front of her lies an A5 sheet of paper that is etched with a tracery of lines like a dried-out mudhole. With the side of her hand she presses the creases away, slowly ironing the surface until it is as smooth as that of a bowl of milk. Then she takes a breath and flips it open. Centered at the top is Ellie's address.

To: Eleanor Porter
8, Hesperus Street
Isle of Dogs
London E14

What is written below, in a firm but inelegant hand, is neither as brutal nor as ugly as her imagination had feared.

Mr. Tinkle calling Eleanor Porter.
Twenty years is long enough to wait. This time, you can be sure,
Justice will be done.

Reflecting afterward, Eleanor cannot remember actually reading the words on the page. Not if reading implies some deliberate concentration. Eleanor doesn't read—she *consumes* the words. Devours them. Sucks them up into her skull.

Justice will be done.

The handle of the cabinet scrapes along her spine as she slides to the floor. She sits with her arms around her knees, clutching the note. Consumes, devours, is penetrated by it, all over again.

And at last the questions follow. Twenty years, he's been waiting—for what? and what on earth does he mean by *Justice?*

Ellie staggers to her feet, grabbing at the edge of the glass tabletop to steady herself. She scrambles in the cupboard and digs out a fresh bottle of wine. Both of her wineglasses are in the dishwasher, so she reaches for a mug and pours the pinot grigio into that. Then she remembers the package of biscuits; they are squirreled away in the top cupboard, out of sight, as a test of willpower, much as an ex-lush might keep an unopened bottle of whiskey in the house. She pulls a chair over to the cupboard and extracts the chocolate digestives. They make the wine taste sour, but flavor is the last thing on her mind.

She crawls into bed with the mug in one hand and the bottle and the biscuits in the other.

Even after Ellie has gulped down the wine, and refilled her mug, and gulped again, the questions won't stop.

Who, for God's sake, is Mr. Tinkle?

CHAPTER 46

When Ellie wakes up, she is sharing her bed with an empty wine bottle and the cellophane wrapper from the biscuits she'd gnawed her way through the night before. Her head hurts. She drags herself to the mirror. Not a pretty sight.

She rings her mother, which makes the headache worse.

It takes a gentle run to Greenwich and a two-hour training session before she feels she's taken possession of her body again. As she works out, she runs through the imaginary conversation with her mother that she didn't manage to have over the phone.

"Nothing much to report, I suppose, Mummy. Things are quiet here. Well, of course there's the murder of the tourist that took place just around the corner. I don't know if you heard about that. And the man who's been following me. I should be brave; I shouldn't let him bother me. He looks like a pretty ordinary chap, not like a serial killer or anything." Ellie tries to laugh at her own joke but only manages to cough. "But he scares me, all the same. Not knowing what he wants. He looks at me with such intensity, as if I had something of his, something he needed. And the really frightening thing is, he looks familiar. Like someone I know from somewhere. He has these hands, big hands, too big for his height, and . . . Well, there's something horribly familiar about him. If only I knew. But I almost don't want to know. You understand?"

She passes through the foot tunnel, her T-shirt damp from sweat. *Come on, Ellie, get a grip.* The message means nothing. It's probably some kid, out for a laugh. Or an anonymous loony who pushes identical notes through every nineteenth door.

But the fear doesn't go.

She keeps picturing the bone white face in the schoolyard, and the way the darkness shifted as she turned her gaze toward it. She keeps picturing someone slinking through the night to her door—someone who's been waiting twenty years for Eleanor Porter.

CHAPTER 47

It is Annabel Porter's birthday and she has the entire day mapped out. She woke up at nine o'clock, after Andrew had already scooted off to work. Fond as she is of him, she prefers it like this. No slithering out of bed so he doesn't see her face without its war paint. No distracting comments while she sleepwalks through her morning routine.

Annabel sits at her bamboo dressing table and examines herself in the mirror. Her skin has been cleansed and sprayed with Evian water. Her hair is scraped back with a band that shows off her generous temples. She turns from side to side, inspecting her profile in the mirror. Not bad for fifty, she thinks. A crisp jawline; only the slightest droop in the region of the jowls. Skin that's smooth and tanned. The neckline sags a bit, but Annabel refuses to concern herself with that. Why else were scarves invented, for pity's sake? Some cavewoman with the Big 5-0 looming looked into a Jurassic pond, baulked at her reflection, and snatched up a saber-tooth pelt. Bob's your uncle— cavewoman in a fur collar, off for a night on the town. A night on the rock pile, Annabel amends, and cracks up with a case of the giggles.

Back to the mirror. What else does she see? Big eyes. Soulful eyes, that's what they always say. Her eyes make people (men, that is) believe that Annabel has hidden depths. Not that they particularly want to trawl those depths. In Annabel's experience, most men admire a woman's brains only insofar as they make her a more discerning audience for their own holdings-forth. Annabel has this down to an art form. She can appear engrossed in a man's description of his golf game, can nod and exclaim in all the right places, while she's settling which of her frocks she'll have altered for the coming season.

Annabel leans forward and gazes more intently at her image. There's something about those soulful eyes this morning. A new tinge of tiredness. Maybe they know she's fifty-one. Or maybe—Annabel sighs—maybe that strained look is what comes of having been widowed in your twenties. Having had to raise a child on your own. And what a child!

Annabel dabs on her favorite perfume. The advertisements for this scent feature gorgeous young men and women with expressions of sullen misery. Why these dreary images induced Annabel to buy the perfume, she'll never understand, but they did. Or rather, they induced Annabel to hint to Andrew that it would be marvelous to own a teeny-weeny bottle of said scent. Andrew demurred, of course. The people in the ads look as if they're dying, Andrew said; hardly a recommendation. And anyway, he'd read a report that showed that most of the price goes on the fancy bottle. The perfume inside is probably only worth tuppence ha'penny, he said.

Prosaic, that's the word for Andrew. A concrete, practical man. Annabel assumes that it comes of being a dentist. Probing about in people's mouths all day has taken the romance out of his soul. But with that tuppence ha'penny nonsense, he'd given her the opening she'd needed.

"It would be worth a great deal more than tuppence ha'penny to me, Andrew," she said.

Well, that got him thinking. Poor Andrew! He's so easily manipulated. But then most men are, aren't they?

Annabel Porter, née Kidd, had been the village beauty. Her parents owned a shop that sold trinkets and household linens, haberdashery and recordings—a sort of miniature Woolworth's without the chain. Annabel was always good with money. Customers remarked upon the pretty little girl who perched on a stool behind the counter, ringing up their purchases and taking in the cash. The pretty little girl coasted with scarcely a blemish into puberty. From the time she was thirteen, the local boys took to visiting the shop as often as they could, seeking out her sidelong smile and hoping that her fingertips would brush their skin as she counted coins into their outstretched palms.

Annabel was aware of their adoration, and she looked at them enticingly enough to bring them back, but she didn't become involved with any of the locals. Oh, no. She was saving herself for better things. Her parents' hard work and unceasing thrift taught her three crucial lessons that she intended never to forget.

Be prudent.

Don't take unnecessary risks.

Make full use of everything you've got.

What she'd got, in Annabel's case, was a heart-shaped face and violet eyes. And out of long hours of boredom and a taste for attention, Annabel had come up with a fourth rule that topped the other three: escape the village as soon as you are able.

She went up to London to train as a nurse. She liked the idea of a trim uniform, of her bare arms smoothing the sheets for a handsome young banker. She liked the idea of living in residence and sharing clothes and late-night gossip with other trainees—though when it came to it, the way she was treated by men outside the hall turned out to be more to her taste. She liked the idea of marrying a doctor.

Annabel learned many things during her training besides how to administer an enema. She learned tennis from a man with pendulous ears who ran a car franchise. He wanted to marry her. He wanted to show her off to the other members of the tennis club. But one of the other members was a civil engineer named Tom. Watching Annabel as she spun and teased and pouted, Tom fell head over heels in love. Annabel, who hadn't managed to land her doctor, took up with Tom, and within a month of her qualifying, the two of them were married.

And, Annabel adds to herself, less than a decade later, she was a widow with an eight-year-old daughter on her hands. A daughter who didn't seem to have her mother's common sense. A daughter who'd always made the business of growing up and getting on in the world much more complicated than it needed to be.

The telephone rings. Annabel plucks it from its stand on the bedside table. She uses her singsong voice. "Annabel here." It will be An-

drew, calling to wish her happy birthday. He'll have left his first patient sitting in the chair in order to get his greetings in bright and
early.

"Mummy?"

Oh, God, she's using that voice, the one that means she's upset
again. There's only one way to deal with Eleanor when she's like this.
Brisk and breezy does it.

"Eleanor, pet, is that you? So sweet of you to ring. I knew you'd be
the first."

"Happy Birthday, Mummy. I've bought something for you. I'll
bring it around later today. What have you got planned?"

"A lovely day, pet, of course. Andrew insists that I must have a little luxury just for myself, for a change. So I shall pop into the Sanctuary and lounge about by the pool, and then, when I've had a massage
and a facial and I'm really relaxed, then Andrew and I will do *The
Phantom of the Opera* and supper at Bertolucci's. What do you think?"

"Lovely."

"You don't sound convinced." Annabel holds the phone in her left
hand and begins applying a light layer of foundation with her right.
So what if she's having a facial later on? No need to show up at the
Sanctuary looking like a tramp.

"No, really, it sounds like a perfectly splendid birthday. Only, I
wondered . . ."

She sounds so hesitant that Annabel is almost moved to help her
out by asking whether there's something she needs. Almost. But then
Annabel puts too much makeup on her cheekbone and it spreads onto
the delicate skin beneath the eye. "Damn it." She snatches up a tissue,
dampens it with the tip of her tongue, and dabs the surplus off.

"Mum? Are you all right?"

Making a mountain out of a molehill, as usual. Why wouldn't
Annabel be all right? Annabel knows, of course, that Eleanor's
painfully apparent insecurity is not entirely Eleanor's fault. As a little
girl, she had been lively and charming and caring to please. But after
her father died, she changed. After the accident, she withdrew into
corners. She ate more and more, taking food from the fridge without
permission. She went from a well-shaped child to a pudgy one.

Annabel tried her best. She pleaded. She pointed out that charm and style could take a girl further than the books in which Eleanor liked to bury herself. Warned her time and again of the consequences of neglecting your looks in a world where appearances mattered. All to no avail. Eleanor stubbornly, sullenly, went her own way.

And even now, Eleanor—with a foot on the career ladder again, and with her figure as trim as it's ever been—is mooning around like chief mourner at a funeral. Tom has been dead now for what? My God, twenty-two years? It's time to shake all that off. Time for Ellie to get a grip.

"Mummy, answer me. Are you all right?"

"Of course I'm all right, Eleanor. Why on earth wouldn't I be? Greenwich is not exactly the African jungle, you know. Though come to think of it, sometimes when I see the foreign names on all those shops and restaurants in the high street, I think it might be."

"For heaven's sake, Mother!" Ellie deeply disapproves of Annabel's lazy, lighthearted racism. They have quarreled on this issue more than once.

"I made a mistake with my makeup, Eleanor, that's all." Armed now with a pair of tweezers, Annabel sets the telephone receiver gently on the dressing table, and bears down on a stray shaft of brow hair. Eleanor is leading up to a complaint of some kind, and Annabel resolves to head her off.

"And what are you up to this week, pet? Anything nice?" Chance would be a fine thing, given that fighting in some sort of pajamas seems to be Eleanor's idea of a good time. "Ouch!" Got it.

"Mother, I need your advice."

Aaah, now that's better. Annabel loves to give advice. If only Eleanor would take her mother's advice about jobs and love life and beauty routine, she would be a much happier girl. Annabel picks up the receiver again and places it to her ear. "All right Eleanor, I'm listening."

"It's just that . . . Last night, Mother, I received a letter. A threatening letter. And I don't know what to do."

"A threatening letter, last night? What are you talking about? There's no nighttime postal delivery in London."

"It was delivered by hand. A visitor found it on the mat. Mummy, I wouldn't have rung except that I'm really rather frightened."

"Was it Harriet? This visitor?" Annabel had met Harriet once, and it wasn't a happy encounter.

"Just someone from work. A girl I know." Eleanor doesn't want her mother to get the idea it was a man or she'd never hear the end of it. "Look, the crucial thing is the letter. What do you think I should do?"

Annabel wipes her tweezers with a tissue and puts them away. "Read it to me, Eleanor."

"I've got it here." Ellie could have recited the message from memory, but reading it aloud makes her feel more in control. She waits for a reaction. "Mother?"

"What do you want me to say, Eleanor? Mr. Tinkle, indeed!" In a way, though, Annabel is not surprised. Eleanor is that sort of girl; she attracts weirdos like a magnet, always has done; when she was a child, if there was a drunk on the corner, or a bully in the playground, they'd make a beeline for Eleanor. That's probably what's happening here.

"Eleanor, the whole thing sounds like a child's game. Like whispers down the phone: *I know who you are and I know what you did.* The only thing that's accomplished is to make someone with an overblown conscience feel very twitchy indeed."

Ellie bites back a caustic reply. No, she won't let her mother wind her up today. "So you don't think I should take it to the police?"

A deep sigh, the kind that Annabel has always felt makes her bosom heave enticingly. She parts the lapels of her dressing gown and sighs again, checking the mirror. Yes, still effective. A bit of boning is a wonderful thing.

"Honestly, Eleanor, the police wouldn't be the slightest bit interested. Give them some credit, won't you? And look at it sensibly. This message—where's the harm in it? I'd hardly call it threatening."

"Mother—"

"If you ask me, it doesn't really say anything at all."

"Mother, tell me: who is Mr. Tinkle?"

"Why don't you just ring off now, pet, and give me a chance to get dressed."

CHAPTER 48

There's a ritual to dressing for karate—how you fold the belt, how you knot it, and so forth—but that silly note about Mr. Tinkle has thrown Ellie off balance and she doesn't seem able to do anything right. She bows her way into the dojo, hoping that Sensei won't notice that her left trouser leg is longer than the right.

Tony Mannix stops his stretches and moves to her side. "What's the matter?" he whispers. "You look flushed. You all right?"

Tony sounds genuinely friendly; that's a first. Ellie takes stock. Sensei is working on his kicks in a bubble of isolation at the far end of the dojo. They've got a minute or two.

"Tony, someone has been following me." She throws an involuntary glance toward the door. "Every time I turn around, on the train or by the river, this man is just behind me. Most nights—round about one or half-past one—I hear him stop outside my door and just stand there."

"How long has this been going on?"

"I'm not sure. Two, three weeks, maybe? I laughed it off at first. But now I've had an anonymous note and it's really spooked me." She recites the contents of the note, but she doesn't mention Mr. Tinkle.

Mannix's rippled forehead creases further with concern. It seems that Ellie has misjudged him. "A stalker, then. Any idea who he is?"

Does she know who he is? Ellie spent half the night scouring her memories for a possible connection. "No," she says, and that's the truth. She has intuitions, but that's all. Nothing solid.

But if she doesn't know him, why does the mere thought of him make her insides clench with panic?

Mannix pats her shoulder. "You need to protect yourself. You live alone, is that right? How good are your locks?"

"I've got a chain on the front door," Ellie says, hopefully. He doesn't look impressed.

"You know that I work for Lock and Key, the security company?

We mainly do new builds, but I'd be happy to look over your house and give you some advice."

"Oh, would you? That would be such a help. But listen, I don't want to put you to any trouble. I'm sure you've got enough to do."

"Don't be silly. Let me help you, as a friend."

Ellie puts her finger to her lips as Sensei gives the signal for the warm-up to begin. She and Tony join Vikesh. Minutes later, when their hearts are pumping like pistons, Sensei steps to the front. The longer he remains silent, the more discomfort there is in the room. "I'm disappointed in you," he says.

He speaks softly, but still the hairs on Ellie's arm stand on end.

"As a class," Sensei continues, "you're not pulling your weight. There's too much—" Sensei has a commanding manner, but words are not his forte. He searches for the right phrase. "Too much—"

What Ellie does next is as instinctive—the urge to help—as it is foolish. "Too much slack, Sensei?" The dojo falls deathly silent.

Sensei pounces. "Did I ask you to speak, Porter? Did I? What makes you think you can put words into my mouth?" Sensei's hands are clenched. Several karate-ka in the front line take an involuntary step back.

Ellie doesn't retreat. "*Uss*," she says. "I apologize, Sensei, for speaking out of turn. I shouldn't have done that." Her voice is as dignified as she can make it.

Sensei glares around the group as if seeking out troublemakers. Then he resumes his position at the front of the class. "As I said, this class is out of order. There's too much slack." He narrows his eyes at Ellie. "Too much—"

This time no one tries to help.

"Too much—" They're all willing him to get it. "Too much easy-come-easy-go," he says, with triumph in his voice. Around the room, faces crack into expressions of relief. Sensei goes on about how the class needs bucking up. They need to be hungrier, he says. To focus on their training even when they're not in the mood. "You're tired," he says. "You're stressed. You push yourself; that's the time you'll have a workout that will bring you further on."

Ellie realizes with a sinking heart that he's speaking to her. The grading is stealing toward them, and he's picked up on the way she's let her training schedule slip. He's worried that she'll show him up in front of the other regional instructors. And who can blame him? He's done her the honor of selecting her for grading, and she is letting him down.

"Some of you may move on to a higher level soon—if, that is, you reach the standard. But there's no cause to be complacent. No cause to adopt an attitude of—"

Tension hangs like morning mist in the air. No one breathes a word.

"Been there, done that. Isn't that what they say? *Been there, done that, tick it off.*" A dark smile of victory bursts over Sensei's face. He hasn't been beaten by those frigging words. "No room for slacking." He stares at the seniors with hot blue eyes as if trying to burn the thought into their memories. His gaze comes to rest on Ellie. "What are you going to do, Miss Porter?"

Ellie draws herself up to full height. "Demand more of myself, Sensei."

"Say it again!"

"*Uss.* I must demand more of myself."

"And again. As if you really mean it."

Ellie squares her shoulders and bites back her tears. "Sensei. I must do more. Must work harder. Must demand more of myself."

"Well, Miss Porter, I'll be watching for results."

CHAPTER 49

It's Jonathan's day off. Ellie doesn't fancy a visit to the Tate Modern, but she can't resist his invitation to join him for a bite to eat before her shift. They take a table in the Café Rouge in Canary Wharf. Even at this early hour, there are a scattering of couples and one small friendly group of workmates chatting and smoking and munching on breadsticks.

"Come on," Jonathan urges. "On Tuesday evening you seemed set to go through a whole shift with nothing more than a cup of coffee. You're not dieting, are you?" He looks frankly appalled at the idea. "You certainly don't need to."

Ellie can see that dieting wouldn't be Jonathan's sort of thing. Sitting across from her, he looks big and solid, a man who likes his food and has the physique to carry it. Ellie suddenly realizes that she does feel hungry. She orders french onion soup, and a generous-sounding salad. It's good to be out and about and to be surrounded by people. The café is busy and brightly lit, and Jonathan is watching her back. No need to look over her shoulder here.

"Not dieting, Jonathan. I've just had rather a lot on my mind."

"Such as?"

"No, no, I'd rather forget it for the moment. You talk to me, won't you? I'd like that. How long have you worked here?"

"Here? You mean for the *Chronicle*? Or in Canary Wharf?"

"Either. Both." She laughs. "Give me the full story, no holds barred."

"The full story is rather more colorful than you may have bargained for. I came to work for the *Chronicle* on February tenth, 1996. Don't look so surprised, I have a good reason to remember the date. I was just settling in when out of the blue there was an almighty boom—as if Concorde had broken the sound barrier right inside the newsroom."

"Oh, February 1996? Was that was the day—"

"Exactly. We all rushed to the window, and there was this huge pall of smoke, everything was black, you could hardly see. And hundreds of alarms began to go off, and sirens everywhere. All these piercing noises cutting through the haze. I took the lift—there was no other way out of the tower—and ran toward the explosion. People were swarming out, blood running down their faces from shattered glass. A woman was screaming somewhere. I couldn't find her."

"What a start to a new job," Ellie says. "As far as I can recall, the IRA had abandoned a lorry loaded with explosives near South Quay Station. It's astounding that only two people died." She thinks for a moment about what it must have been like. "It may sound callous," she says at last, "but there's an upside."

"To the bombing? You're kidding."

"Security in the Wharf has been designed to match the threat, you know? No one drives into this area except on legitimate business. No one moves through the mall without CCTV surveillance. No one gets beyond the foyer of the tower without a pass." And, though she doesn't say it, there are no empty side streets where intruders can lurk. No letter boxes through which lethal messages might be slipped. No overlooking windows bathed in shadows. "I've heard it said that passes into the tower are like gold dust in value, and I, for one, fervently hope that it's true."

Their drinks arrive. "Cheers," Jonathan says. "Leaving bombs aside, how's work been? How do you rate Clive as a boss?"

"Oh, he seems like a sweetie pie. The practice where I worked before had the most dour senior partners. It's lovely to work with a man who has a sense of fun. Although, I must say, I can't always read him."

"Clive? He seems pretty straightforward to me."

"Well, maybe I'm being silly, but you see, I did a really bad interview. I was sure I wouldn't get the job. Clive seemed less than impressed, and I've never really understood why he appointed me."

"Why wouldn't he appoint you?"

"Because I was hopeless," Ellie says. She tries to think how to explain without exposing the full extent of her idiocy. It started about ten minutes into the interview. Clive had been smiling, dimples on full display, and out of the blue he pounced. "What did you think of last week's march against the war on Iraq?" he asked.

"A million marchers is no joke," she said. "How can the government fail to take it seriously?"

"Indeed. However, for us the issue is how seriously should the paper take it? The *Sun*, for example, chose to relegate it to a back page which, presumably, will suit government interests very well. Tell me, my dear, how exactly would you advise our journalists to handle the story?"

Ellie doesn't remember in detail what she said, but she knows that her response was clumsy and overemphasized the need for caution. When she'd finished stammering out her hastily gathered views, Clive remained silent, simply staring at her in a thoughtful way, until she felt she might scream. Then, he reached out, gave her arm an avuncular pat, and smiled.

"Well, you know, my dear," he said, "it's not quite as simple as that. On a newspaper like ours, it is the journalists who write and the editors who edit. We—the legal department—are the security men. The shotgun on the stagecoach. The muscle, if you like." He chuckled at his own joke. "Our role is defensive. That's what you were getting at, I suppose?"

Ellie's skin must have been as pink as a lobster. There was a pause that lasted for several seconds, and again it felt like hours. Then he nodded briskly, as if he'd just completed a sum in his head, and steered her toward the lift. "Well, Miss Porter," he said, "assuming you're free to start, we'll see you on Tuesday." Just like that.

Ellie gives an abbreviated version of the interview, and Jon listens in a way that makes it easy. "So," he says, when she's finished, "Clive seemed skeptical of the views you gave in the interview, but he hired you nonetheless. Is that it?"

Ellie nods.

"Look, Ellie, Clive has been around for a long time. He could see through the nerves of the interview, I bet, to what a first-rate night lawyer you'd make."

"And what if he changes his mind?"

Jonathan laughs. "You haven't had any complaints, have you? Well, then. Everyone knows you're doing a great job. All you need now is to relax. Cheers!" he says, nudging her vodka and tonic with his bottle of beer.

Ellie clinks drinks happily. She takes a deep, contented breath as relaxation begins to unpick the knots in her chest.

CHAPTER 50

When Ellie reaches the familiar bustle of the newsroom, the blinds are closed against the lowering sun. Clive is bouncy and warm, and Ellie is ashamed of herself for having questioned his sincerity in her conversation with Jonathan. But at the end of the handover, she thinks she detects a change.

"Oh," Clive says, and there's a shrill note in his voice like the scrape of a bow on a violin string. Ellie has noticed it before when something excites him. "Oh," he says, as if a thought has just occurred to him. "Remember the story about that telly barrister, Ellie? The one who was reported to the police by a Boots technician? It's hotting up."

"The last I heard, the story had turned out to be hogwash. A father bathing his child. No offense involved. Do you mean to say the police have found something substantial?"

"Well," says Clive, with a grin that colonizes the lower third of his face, "read for yourself." Clive fidgets as Ellie takes her seat. He watches impatiently, running his tongue back and forth along the inside of his upper teeth, as she raises her chair and slides the footrest into place.

Ellie refuses to be hurried. Only when the angle of the monitor is precisely right does she finally click on to the day's stories. NESBIT INVESTIGATION is first on the list.

Clive rereads the piece over Ellie's shoulder, mumbling the words aloud like a child.

The headline itself pulls no punches. BARRISTER IN CHILD ABUSE CASE. Ellie winces. She steels herself to read with due care and attention, fighting against the pull of Clive's voice.

Sources close to the Metropolitan Police say that a warrant has been drawn up and a search made of the home of the barrister accused of taking indecent photographs of a child. Police officers were seen this morning going into Oliver Nesbit's luxury home

near Wimbledon Common. Two hours later, they removed a computer and a dozen or more cardboard boxes and loaded them into
a police van.

Attached to the article is a pair of photographs: Oliver entering the
police station looking confident, his shoulders squared and head held
high. Oliver leaving hours later, a sinister streak of black shadowing
his lower jaw, his eyes averted from the cameras; he looked smaller,
somehow, and furtive.

"This Nesbit must be a real pillock, wouldn't you say, Eleanor?"

"Clive, I haven't finished reading."

Police are refusing to comment, beyond saying that no charges
have yet been laid. But it is understood that they are currently
interviewing Nesbit's friends and colleagues.

"You all right, Elle?"

"Perfectly, Clive." Ellie drags herself on through the article, line
after line. The words are blurred and indistinct and the newsroom is
bursting with distractions. Ariana purring to another journalist near
the watercooler. The chatter of a printer. The minutiae of Clive's appearance: his well-cut navy trousers, his mismatched socks, the dark
hairs on the back of his knuckles.

She has to read the concluding paragraphs a second time before
she finally takes them in.

Meanwhile, our reporter has attempted to speak to friends of
Oliver Nesbit to find out more about the celebrity barrister. So far,
colleagues are maintaining a tight silence. One who refused to give
his name said, "I never would have thought it." Jim Matthews,
whose son Zane was murdered two years ago after members of a
pedophile ring took pictures of him being abused, was more forthright in making a statement to our reporter. "Perverts like him deserve a bullet in the back of the head."

The article ends on a pious note.

The *Chronicle* has always deplored vigilante action. But we support the police in their attempts to bring this shocking case to court. The sooner men like Nesbit come to understand that children are off limits for their sexual games, the better.

With an enormous effort, Eleanor finishes reading and clicks the file closed.

"Finished, finally? What do you think?" Clive flashes the familiar smile, but when Ellie glances over, she thinks she detects for the first time a deeper touch of malice.

"A moment, Clive, please." Why is he so eager for her reaction? Why so keen on her opinion? To cover her confusion, she opens the piece again, and pretends to skim it. Ellie is upset by the piece on principle and on personal grounds. And from a legal point of view, that final paragraph simply won't do. But what call has Clive got to be so worked up?

He is still leaning over her, one forearm now propped on the back of her chair. She glances up at him.

"Clive?"

"Umm?" He drags his gaze away from the screen and looks at her. She notices for the first time how his eyeteeth gleam.

"Do you know this fellow? Nesbit?"

"Wouldn't know him from Adam, my dear Miss Porter." Clive had called her Miss Porter throughout her interview for the job, and then, as now, it sounded less than cordial. "However—" He smiles at her, and again she thinks she sees that hint of spite. "I understand that you and he are old pals."

The heat bursts out on Ellie's chest and skims its way up her neck. Her cheeks are flaming. It's a test. He knows she knows Oliver Nesbit. He thinks she's compromised—that she can't be impartial. That she can't do her job. She turns her head away, wanting to escape from Clive's interrogative stare, and looks across the wide desk and straight into Jonathan's eyes. Jonathan doesn't smile. He doesn't speak. Slowly and deliberately, he winks. Ellie wills the blushes to retreat. She turns back to Clive and looks him full in the eye.

"Clive? Who told you that I'm acquainted with Oliver Nesbit?"

Clive grins and taps the fleshy part of his nose with his finger. "Let's just say I have my sources. More than friends, that's what I heard."

Ellie is very careful in her reply. "I knew him at university. We dated for a few weeks. That was all."

"And you haven't seen him since?"

"No. No, I haven't. Clive, can we talk about this later?" Ellie pushes her chair back.

Clive steps aside with elaborate politeness as Eleanor swoops up her handbag and heads for the lavatory. She needs time to think. She takes off her jacket and hangs it on a hook. She fills the basin with cold water and splashes it on her face, her eyes, her neck. She freshens her makeup and powders her face.

This isn't bad, she tells herself. Not half as bad as, say, a karate grading. On the day of her first grading, she was sick with apprehension. She couldn't eat breakfast, couldn't sit still, couldn't think. She felt physically undisciplined and mentally chaotic. There were one hundred and fifty candidates crowded into the dojo, and she felt intimidated by the men who towered over her; by the boys, even, who were taller and stronger than she. And yet, and yet—*remember this, Ellie Porter,* she whispers to herself, *remember that you passed.* She went from white belt to blue belt and later all the way up to purple with white stripes. She knew her katas and her kumites. She did everything that was asked of her and she did it well. Just because she's scared, it doesn't mean she's going to screw up.

She puts on her jacket and smooths it down. One coppery strand of hair won't be patted into place. She plucks it out and heads back to the newsroom.

Clive is chatting to Jonathan when she returns to her desk. Ellie notes the fact that he maintains a respectful distance. He doesn't lean his weight on the editor's chair, and he keeps two decent paces between them.

"Better?" Clive asks her as she circles the end of the desk toward them. He tries to include Jonathan in a small amused glance, but Jonathan keeps his eyes on Ellie.

"Oh, much better," Ellie replies. "Shall we finish with the Nesbit piece?" This time when Clive positions himself, he doesn't crowd her, and it seems to Ellie that his eyeteeth have lost their gleam.

CHAPTER 51

Ellie wakes up with the taste of blood in her mouth. She opens one eye and lifts her gaze to the window, where there's a border of light around the edges of the blind. She's overslept. It must be ten AM.

She tries to burrow down again under the duvet, but images from a dream skitter through her mind. She drapes her dressing gown over her shoulders and shuffles downstairs to the refrigerator. Looks at the carton of milk, the yogurt, the bacon, and decides that she can't face breakfast. Puts the coffeemaker on instead.

Maybe there's still a chance to get the day back on track. She rummages in a basket that sits above the desk, looking for music to wash away the aftertaste of the dream. She puts the soundtrack from *O Brother, Where Art Thou?* on the CD player and dances to the strains of bluegrass banjo while she makes a piece of toast. The sound of the banjo fades away, and the dream comes flooding back.

It was the girl in black again. Ellie thought for a moment she was Jessica, though the face has a more androgynous cast. The girl is dressed as always in a black leather coat with a chain that dangles from the pocket. There is a slice of black leather cinched around her throat. Her eyes are rimmed with kohl, her cheeks as chalky as milk of magnesia.

The most noticeable thing about the girl this time around is not the black, but the red. One pitch-colored tight has been sliced off at the ankle and rolled back, to reveal a porcelain calf, shapely and strong. As Ellie watches, helpless, a knife plunges into it again and again, with a terrible slicing of flesh and ripping of tendons. Blood gushes from an artery and fills Ellie's vision. Blood pools in a scarlet mass on the carpet. Blood oozes in runnels down the walls. There is a watercolor print of an English landscape hanging at the head of the bed; splashes of blood transform the gray-blue sky above the English downs to purple. Ellie can't get close enough to save the girl. There is a wall of glass between them. Soon, through the blood that sheets the pane, Ellie can see only the stare of kohl-rimmed eyes. Then the blood clears away like the lifting of a fog, and the eyes are the eyes of her father. Their gaze is dark with accusation.

Ellie leaps up and silences the Soggy Bottom Boys. With a fierce shove, she shifts the rocking chair out of the way, and then, wearing only the T-shirt and briefs that she slept in, she begins swinging her arms and lifting her knees toward her chest. Left, then right; left, then right. When her hair flops onto her face, she snatches up a scrunchie from the desk and ties it at the back of her neck. She races through a sequence of jumping jacks. Her bare feet, conditioned by training, make a hollow thump each time she lands. She pumps her legs and arms like a cross-country skier until the warmth rises to her shoulders and up into her face.

Her hips and her spine and her hamstrings stretched, Ellie swings into the kata. She extends her left leg forward and rests most of her weight on her right, working to get her center of gravity as low as she can. She blocks an attacker who is going for her head. Moves into horse riding stance. Strikes hard to the side with her elbow, followed by a close punch, full force, upward into the solar plexus. Her movement is not tight enough, so she does it again. *Breathe out, tense the body, rotate the fist—so.*

Ellie works with her eyes partially closed, the better to focus on the sequence of movements. Occasionally, she pauses to peer at the list that's tacked to the bookshelf: Hidari Nami Ashi. Kiba Dachi, Sokumen Hidari Uke. Migi Nami Ashi. Kiba Dachi, Hidari Sokumen Uke. Kiba Dachi, Koshi Gamae. Kiba Dachi, Morote Zuki, KIAI. She says the names aloud as she performs each move, spitting out the syllables in a vehement style reminiscent of Striker's.

Ellie completes the kata for the fourth time, panting hard, and suddenly aware of the perspiration that soaks her face and chest. She strips off her T-shirt, wipes her brow with it, and tosses it on the floor. Her brain is blissfully empty of dream fragments now. She begins again.

CHAPTER 52

Annabel Porter is convinced that Eleanor is harboring a secret. Her daughter seems to be ringing every second day—that's not like her at all—and she keeps going on about this man who she says is following her. But really, Annabel tells her, what do you expect if you will take a job that brings you home in the wee small hours of the morning? *After ten, Mother,* Eleanor shoots back. The girl is such a stickler for detail; no wonder she went into law. But let's face it, after ten is getting on for pub closing time, and Annabel knows only too well what men are like when they've had a few drinks. That's why she allows Andrew only one whiskey before dinner and a glass of wine with. Tom had learned to drink far too much during his years in the bush, and look what came of that.

Annabel snaps on a pair of rubber gloves. Pink, with a lacy frill around the cuff. See? She does have a sense of humor, whatever Eleanor says. Annabel spreads a bath towel over a section of carpet at one end of the room. She places a wooden armchair alongside the bookcase, and climbing upon it, she removes books from the shelves, three at a time, and stacks them on the towel. Then she begins the job of wiping the bookcase down. Annabel has a cleaning lady, but she's convinced that if she wants anything done out of the ordinary, she's got to tackle it herself.

You'd think a girl like Eleanor, a clever girl—her father always said she had a mind like a trap, whatever that means—would be able to decide what has to be done and then to do it. Mind over matter; that's Annabel's way. Eleanor, on the other hand, has always been one to make a mountain out of molehill.

Look how she took her father's death. She could hardly speak for months. Of course, she was only a child, poor pet. But it wasn't Eleanor, it was Annabel, who had to face the dreadful aftermath of his death on her own. Eleanor was spared all that. She wasn't forced to spend hours with a dingy CID officer picking over the details of Tom's death. She didn't have to identify the body or organize the funeral or—in some ways, the worst of all—sort out the mess with the insurance and the will. And Eleanor didn't have to go back home to a newly empty bed and spend sleepless nights in a rage with Tom for going and spoiling everything and leaving her all alone.

The bookcase is clean now, not a trace of dirt, and dry. Annabel begins putting the books back on the shelves. Tiny puffs of dust rise up as they settle. She sneezes and opens a window and takes a duster to the nooks and crannies that the cleaning lady seems conveniently not to notice.

Annabel had learned to manage at an early age, and she cannot understand why Eleanor doesn't do the same. When the family didn't have enough money to keep the heaters going, she wore extra vests underneath her jumper to block out the cold. The humiliations—having to wear a secondhand school blazer with sleeves that were too short, having to skip the school trip because there wasn't money for the coach, being discovered in the school lavatory trying out makeup that someone else had thrown away—Annabel managed. She held her head high and cultivated an air of not caring, and if it didn't win her friends, at least it protected her from pity.

She managed even when her mother left. Annabel's mother had been a stout good-looking woman who felt keenly the deprivations of her life as a shopkeeper's wife. She didn't ask much; she wanted to enjoy life, to go out from time to time and have a few drinks. For a number of years, she had her few drinks with a man named Mr. Copley. He would swing around to pick her up in his sleek blue motorcar and off they'd go. After Mr. Copley ceased to call, Annabel's mother deflated like a punctured balloon.

Annabel came home from school as usual. Her father had gone to Tunbridge Wells to see a supplier. Her mother should have been there, greeting customers, shifting stock, keeping the lid on the freezer closed. But instead, the shop was locked. Annabel, perspiring in the blazer with the too-short sleeves, raced up the back stairs and found the flat empty. She never read the sheet of Basildon Bond that was propped up against the sugar bowl. She didn't need to. She could tell by the silence in the flat, by the way that the shadows lay across the windows, that her mother would never return.

One of the things that drew Annabel to Tom Porter was that Tom had laughed, the way her mother used to laugh. He had a sense of fun that could fill up the room. While washing up, he'd advance on her, hands dripping with suds, and she'd squeal and run, but she didn't really mind when he caught her and left wet paw prints on her dress, because however badly he behaved, she'd loved him so.

Annabel and Eleanor are surprisingly alike. Physically, that is. Now that Eleanor has finally succeeded in shedding that weight, the resemblance has come to the fore. The same milky skin. A red tinge to the hair, though Ellie's is burnished to a brighter copper, and falls into intense little curls, while Annabel's is as smooth as a sheet of toffee. The same delicacy of features: small, bright eyes, neat little nose, and pointed chin. But the resemblance is only skin-deep. Apart from a mutual liking for Ginger Rogers and Fred Astaire, Annabel and her daughter have little more in common than a history. And it's a strange thing to say about your own flesh and blood, but Annabel's own daughter is a mystery to her, and that makes Annabel uncomfortable.

She has tried different theories—pinning them on Ellie like a home-made dress to see if they would fit—to explain why a girl who has looks and education seems merely to drift through life. The break-down was bad enough. But now that she's well again, what does she do? She does evening work for a tabloid newspaper, hardly a proper job. What's the good of being clever if you never go anywhere or do anything? If you live on your own? If you haven't got a boyfriend, let alone a husband, no one to look after you? No one except your mother, that is.

Annabel flicks viciously at the back of the television with a duster. Annabel's number one theory is that Eleanor lacks ambition. The girl's been too amply cushioned from the hard facts of life. She has no sense of the rat race—how if you don't scrabble to get somewhere, you'll end up at the bottom of the heap. She doesn't know what it's like to lose everything. She has never come home from school to find her room and the rest of the flat stripped bare: to find her radio gone, and the little dressing table with the flower-sprigged skirt, and even the box in which she kept her costume jewelry—all taken by the bailiffs. Eleanor, by contrast, has always had everything a girl could want. But she takes it all for granted. Is prepared to drift through life, rather than make the effort to find security. Rather than marry.

It seems that Eleanor hasn't realized that if a girl doesn't improve her standing, she will surely go down. Annabel lifts a drawer off its runners and heaves it over so that its contents clatter onto the towel, and then begins to wipe out the inner surfaces. "Surely go down," she mutters to herself darkly, as she plies the J-cloth with hard, sharp strokes. Bottom, side, side, side, and the drawer is done.

"Surely go down," she mutters again.

CHAPTER 53

Clive isn't in the office when Ellie arrives. "Picking up the girls from a birthday party," Marie explains. "He said he'll stop in and see you before he takes them home."

"Thanks, Marie."

And sure enough, when Clive appears, Lily is leaning against his leg, keeping a tight grip on the loot from the party, while the younger child, Rose, has her sleepy face buried in his shoulder.

"About Oliver Nesbit," he says. Rose whimpers a little.

"Yes," says Ellie, "I've seen the story. Anonymous comments from ITV officials—very dicey."

Clive is in constant motion, one hand patting Rose's back, rocking her gently by flexing his knees. "You'll have a hard time convincing the editor to cut. It's a juicy story."

"Don't worry, Clive. I've already got him to agree on an angle." Ellie is determined not to be spooked, as she was the other evening, by Clive's concern. When she consulted the editor, she managed to reel off her views like a high court judge accustomed to sweeping opinion before her. *Seventy-five percent of winning your point is looking the part;* that's one of Will's proverbs that was spot-on.

Ellie crouches down beside Lily. "What a lovely, floppy flower," she says, pointing to a swirl of bright fabric attached to the shoulder of Lily's dress.

"My mummy made it for me," the girl replies with bashful pride.

Ellie carefully takes the ribbon that is offered her and tugs to make the helium balloon bounce. Lily laughs and Clive beams.

For the rest of the shift Ellie is buoyed by newfound confidence. Jonathan has already left, which is a pity. Other than that, everything is shipshape and Bristol fashion. As her final official duty of the night, Ellie signals her approval of the front page by putting her initials on a yellow Post-it—*Legal O.K.*, she writes—and then deposits a copy in the legal office. But she does one more thing before she leaves; she has a quick check in the library for other recent cases involving allegations of child pornography, and gathers the photocopies in a file, ready for the next day. When she returns to her desk, the newsroom is empty. She shrugs into her jacket and heads for the exit, but at the door to reception, she finds herself face-to-face with Ariana.

"Ellie!" A squeal of surprise, followed closely by laughter. "Oh, my God, I should have realized you'd be here."

"And what about you? It's half-past ten. A little late for the sports desk, isn't it?"

"Oh, no, I'm not working." Ariana launches into a breathless account of how she'd just finished dinner—"you know, with some friends." She discovered that her phone wasn't in her coat pocket, so she's just popped up to the newsroom to see if she left it there, again. "Blimey," she exclaims, scanning the vast empty room, "it's sort of creepy, isn't it? I've never been in here when everybody else is gone. Do you mind hanging on for a second while I check my desk?"

It has never occurred before to Ellie that the newsroom might be in any way sinister, but now that Ariana raises it . . . Well, she's right. It is rather eerie. In this soft gray light, one beige piece of equipment runs into another. The edges disappear. If you narrow your eyes, the room looks abandoned, as if the furniture has been draped with dust sheets. And if you looked for long enough, you might begin to wonder what those indistinct objects really are. That hump that sticks up above the surface of the desk—what is it, really? You might even begin to sense that some of the so-called furniture is moving.

A hand on her shoulder makes Ellie start. Ariana's fingernails, pink and white and perfect.

"A quick drink?" Ariana asks.

"Definitely. Maybe two."

As they swing down in the lift, they are absolutely alone. No one else gets on or off. The lift slides to a halt at the seventh floor, and they step back expectantly to make room, but the carpeted corridor is empty, and after a few seconds' delay, they plunge on alone.

Ellie feels justified in drinking; she handled things in the newsroom so well tonight, and it's been a tough week. With the very first sip of wine, the ache in her temples begins to ease. She has a second in quick succession, while her friend fills her in on office gossip, much of it about names to which Ellie can't assign a face. Ellie doesn't mind at all. The lighthearted chatter is a relief. When she returns from the bar with their third round of drinks, Ariana suddenly asks, "Who's the secret admirer, then?"

"What do you mean?"

Ariana wags a playful finger. "You know perfectly well, Eleanor Porter. The letter on your doormat. Hand delivery at midnight—ye gods, sounds like a service in a bordello, doesn't it?" Ariana laughs at her own joke, and Ellie joins in, less merrily now. "Don't tell me it wasn't a love letter or I shall be terribly disappointed."

"Brace yourself for disappointment, then. Not a love letter, Ariana. An anonymous letter. From someone who says he has waited twenty years. It didn't sound loving at all."

"No name? No initials, even?"

"The only name mentioned was Mr. Tinkle. '*Mr. Tinkle calling Eleanor Porter.*' How's that for creepy?" Ellie finishes off her sauvignon blanc. "I haven't got the faintest idea who sent it."

Ariana blows gently on the flame of the candle that sits between them. "Waiting twenty years," she repeats. "It's almost romantic!"

"Be serious, Ariana. It's spooky. Someone I don't even know . . ."

"You must know him. Come on now. Think. An old flame?"

"How could it be an old flame? Twenty years ago? I'm only thirty now."

"Started young, then, didn't you?" Ariana chortles.

A shiver passes through Ellie. Is she being silly? Overreacting? Her mother certainly seemed to think so. And now Ariana does, too. "So you don't think I should report it to the police?"

Ariana raises her hands in front of her. "Whoa, Ellie, hang on. I didn't say that. If you feel so strongly about this Mr. Tinkle—You sure that name means nothing to you?"

As Ellie shakes her head—no—the first droplet of uncertainty forms in her mind.

"Well, if you feel so strongly, maybe you should go to the police. What can be the harm? Just don't expect a big manhunt. Without a name and address, without anything—you know—concrete, what can they do? They've got their hands full anyway, what with all these robberies and that body in the Thames—"

"You mean the tourist?"

"Mugged for his camera, that's what they think. Apparently he'd been flashing it around in one of those horrid little pubs off Westferry Road, and next thing you know, he was dead. Isn't it dreadful?"

"Hardly bears thinking about. Which pub, do you know?"

"I'm not sure. The Ship, maybe? Blimey, Ellie, that's just around the corner from you."

"I wish I hadn't asked." Ellie shudders. "You want another drink? Oh, come on, one for the road. And when I come back with the drinks, you can tell me what you think of Clive."

Ellie bought a bottle this time—so much cheaper in the long run. "There's something I wanted to ask you. Now, what was it?"

"Clive," Ariana reminds her. "Oh, he's all right," she says. "A little touchy, maybe. Mention anything that sounds even vaguely like a criticism of the babies, Jocinda or—What's the other brat's name?—"

"Rose. It's Lily and Rose."

"Lily. How virtuous. One skeptical word about the children and he's down on you like a tiger. But I suppose he can be good fun." She smiles to herself and twirls her wine in her glass, and Ellie wonders for a fleeting moment whether Ariana and Clive might ever have dated. It doesn't seem likely. But then, particular pairings never do seem likely, do they? Maybe she'll find a tactful way of probing the subject when they're in Dorset. Thinking of which . . .

"Ariana, we've got to decide about Dorset. How are you fixed for the third weekend in May?"

"Sounds good, Ellie, but I've got a little something brewing, though, and I'll just have to check it out first. I'll let you know by Monday."

"Sure. That's great. No hurry." And at the thought of a weekend in the country—with a friend—Ellie is encased once again in a warm glow.

CHAPTER 54

The warm weather that graced the early part of April looks set to stay. Ellie comes in from a run and has to throw the patio doors open to let in some air before she can answer the phone.

It's Harriet. She's concerned about Dorset. "I wouldn't pester you about it, Eleanor, except that the car really needs servicing, and I thought I could arrange for you to drop it into the garage before you go. Unless you've changed your mind? Decided that our cottage isn't good enough for you?"

"Don't be silly, Harriet. I'm just waiting to settle dates with Ariana."

"That's the glamorous one you mentioned before? I wouldn't have thought she was quite your cup of tea."

"She's loads of fun. She's never been to Dorset, and she loves the idea."

"If she's so keen, why hasn't she confirmed yet?" Harriet sounds tetchy. "You can always go on your own, you know. It's perfectly safe."

"I don't know, Harry. I'd enjoy it so much more with someone else." Ellie spent two illicit weekends at the cottage with Will, and being there alone would conjure up the ghosts of the past. "I'll let you know by Friday. Promise."

Harriet's voice is clipped. "Friday it is, Eleanor. I'll hold the brother-in-law off until then. Don't let me down."

Don't let me down. On her way in to work, Ellie ponders what it is about that phrase that reminds her, unhappily, of home. When she says *home*, she doesn't mean Annabel and Andrew's house on the

edge of Greenwich. No, home can be traced to the urban valley below
Alexandra Palace where Ellie grew up. There a row of terraced
houses curved up a steep hill like plates on the spine of a stegosaurus,
and Ellie's home was perched near the peak. It had four bedrooms
arranged off a central landing, a tiny cellar, and an ancient wisteria
that made a magical perfume in spring.

Ellie's window faced away from the palace. She looked out on a
scrabble of railway lines and a group of council flats.

Ellie's happiest memories of home are of playing with her father.
He used to spend hours stretched out on a worn carpet helping Ellie
to arrange her men and women and animals into a facsimile of a
working farm. Farmer Phil, her favorite, was stout and green-wellied
and buttoned his yellow mac tightly against the cold. On fine days,
when her father flung open the curtains and the sun broke through,
Farmer Phil would strip down to his overalls, and would sing at the
top of his lungs as he tossed buckets of slops to the pigs.

Annabel Porter never joined them in these games. She'd never been
the playing sort. Ellie's mother had two modes of engagement: flirta-
tious (with either men or women, for Annabel needed to be admired)
or embattled. The battles began with domestic work. Annabel treated
their home as if it were a wayward child: never clean enough, never
neat enough, never fresh enough in its trim. Always needing to be
licked into shape.

After domestic work, there were the battles with neighbors. They
let their garden go to rack and ruin; they played their music intolera-
bly loud; they boasted too much about a son's success. "Who do they
think they are?" Annabel would fume. It was a rhetorical question
and the unspoken answer was perfectly clear. They were nobody. Nobody at all.

On one occasion an intrepid neighbor, a young man who lived in
the house uphill from theirs, dared to argue with Annabel on her own
doorstep. Ellie doesn't remember what the row was about, but she remembers perfectly well what it looked like. The young man laid out
the problem, hesitatingly, doggedly, his face stiff with concentration.
Annabel grew increasingly pale until Ellie feared she might faint, and
then, suddenly, she rallied. She pushed her face as close to his as the
difference in their heights would allow, and spoke to him slowly and

emphatically, as if he were simpleminded. Before she'd finished lecturing him, the man had slunk away.

Ellie herself isn't the fighting sort. Her mother's ferociousness killed her appetite for conflict. But she was central to her mother's battles. When Annabel spoke to outsiders, Ellie was always the accomplished and compliant daughter, but in private, she always fell short. She didn't look right; her grooming was sloppy, her clothing ill-chosen, her hair too tarty (when she used straighteners) and too frumpy (when she didn't). Ellie was careless when she did the washing up; she left egg on the spoons and stored the saucepans in the wrong place. Ellie was bright, but she didn't work hard enough, and—the worst sin of all—Ellie thought she was clever. Being clever was a good thing in Annabel's world, oh, yes. Being clever earned awards and admiration. But thinking you were clever? That was very, very bad.

In spite of all her mental meanderings, Ellie arrives at Canary Wharf early and turns in at the newsagent to buy a packet of Smints. She is deep in thought; she doesn't notice Will until she steps up to the counter. There he is, just ahead of her, slipping a packet of cigarettes into his pocket.

"Ellie," he says, spreading his arms in a welcoming gesture. He glances at his watch. "So keen to work? You're early."

"Just came from my mother's."

"Aaah," he says, as if that explains everything. He takes a step backward and examines her in a forthright way. "Are you all right?" he asks. In his pocket, his hand is jiggling the newly purchased packet up and down.

So, Ellie thinks, not quite as relaxed, as sure of himself, as he seemed at first glance.

"Why wouldn't I be?" Ellie hopes that her question sounds confident and perhaps just a little playful. She is thinking of the time now. Half an hour to go before her shift begins. Does she dare to suggest a coffee or a walk? Or should she leave it up to him?

Will realizes as he stands near to Eleanor, with her bright expectant face shining up at him, how much he misses their conversations. Misses, even after all this time, her understanding. She knew how to focus on him, on the real him, not just the person he presented to the outside world. She knew how to listen. Not many women do. In Will's experience, they are mostly waiting for compliments, waiting to be wooed. They want a man to comfort and reassure them. They want a man to be a *man,* a strong confident partner, with no fears or anxieties of his own. Ellie wasn't like that.

"I've been—" He can't seem to find the right words. She looks at him, beaming now, no longer trying to make him feel bad just because he felt a sense of obligation to his wife. He reaches out and flicks the copper curls on her forehead. "I never wanted to hurt you," he says.

She shakes her head. "Please, Will. You don't need to say it." Ellie is surprised at her own generosity of feeling, but she means it. The last thing she wants is to contaminate their future with hurts from the past.

"Oh, but I do. I need to explain everything. I need to come clean with you. But"—he looks at the clock on the wall—"I can't do it right now. I have a meeting in the City."

Ellie resists the urge to insist on an appointment here and now. She doesn't want to pressure him. William DeQuoyne is not generally an apologizing sort of man.

"There's no need for you to rush, Will." All the care and the love she has been saving up since Vienna is in her smile. "You and I— we've got all the time in the world."

Then, in a moment that Ellie knows she will never ever forget, no matter how many other wonderful moments there are in her life, William DeQuoyne leans toward her and kisses her forehead. Gently, reverently, lovingly.

"I'll call," he says. And then he's gone.

CHAPTER 55

Colleagues at the *Chronicle* have never before seen Eleanor Porter in such a buoyant mood. She swings through the glass doors and flashes a smile at Marie on the reception desk. She sings softly to herself and giggles at a George Dubya joke that is doing the rounds by e-mail.

Ellie has no illusions about her job. "Night lawyer" may sound interesting—enigmatic, even—but in the legal profession it's near the bottom of the heap. It requires a lawyer who is prepared to work on a part-time basis and during hours that are anything but social. But it does for her. She loves Canary Wharf, she loves the Isle of Dogs, she loves the sense of being part of a team. It all works for her, makes her feel for the first time since she was eight years old that she belongs.

Clive greets her with his overcoat already buttoned. "Good shape tonight, Eleanor?" He is whistling "Light My Fire" as he passes her the documents. "Your Oliver Nesbit story's been quiet," he says.

"My story?" She glances sharply up at him, but sees no indication in his face that he is getting at her. Perhaps those gleaming eyeteeth were merely a product of her paranoia. She awards Clive a silent apology.

"The police are still trawling through his paperwork, so there's nothing much of interest there. Most of the other pieces are pretty routine. School truancy, local government scandal, another celebrity divorce. They're more or less finalized. You'll have a quiet evening." And with a wave Clive is off. Lily is playing recorder in a school concert and he is anxious not to be late.

Ellie floats from task to task. The humidity has been building up all day. When the thunderstorm breaks, she and Jonathan dash to the big window off the cafeteria to catch the play of lightning across the dusky sky.

Even her anxiety about arrangements for the cottage seems to have faded. Ariana has already left the office when Ellie arrives, so she resolves to pop into Ariana's favorite bar on the way home and see if she can find her. The Henry Addington: fantastic views of the water and a huge screen above the bar that's permanently tuned to Sky Sport 2. Ariana isn't there, but Ellie recognizes two other journalists from the *Chronicle*. They beckon her to join them. Surprising even herself, Ellie buys a round and joins in as best she can with a conversation that seems to circulate around rugby and films and the price of flats. She dares to hint at a mysterious lover to her colleagues. She is elated. It is all so unexpectedly easy.

Shortly after eleven, Ellie leaves the bar and walks up toward the square. The night air is soft and warm and getting warmer. In the square, Ellie savors the solitude. The warning light on the top of the tower winks at her. The waterfalls are summer winds sighing in leafy woods; their droplets of water shimmer on the pebbled walkway. Ellie plonks herself down on a marble bench and raises her gaze up above the light-sprinkled trees, above the buildings that crowd the corners of the square, until she can see a pristine chunk of night sky.

She hasn't been alone, outside, at night and felt so good—so wrapped in safety—for a long time. It's Will. She knows it is. Seeing him like that—the look in his eyes, his kiss, his promise to call her—has put everything, but everything—Oliver Nesbit, Clive, Mr. Bloody Tinkle, whoever he may be—into perspective. She and Will are going to make it work this time. Not just good, but better than before. What are all her silly worries compared to this one truth: Will is coming back, and this time, it will last. Her eyes adjust to the darkness, and she is granted a vision of a sparkling trail of stars.

The air is becoming more humid by the minute as Ellie heads toward home. She opens her shirtdress at the throat and rolls the sleeves up to her elbows. There's going to be another thunderstorm. From the train, she sees flashes of lightning far off to the west. She pictures great flat drops of rain splashing on Bermondsey, and people stepping to their doorways for the sudden sense of cool.

But the rain hasn't yet reached the Isle of Dogs by the time Ellie arrives home. With one quick glance over her shoulder to make certain there's no one behind her, she turns the key in the lock, opens the door, and steps into the stuffy house. Trickles of moisture pool in her armpits. She removes her tights and tosses them on the floor. She opens the door to the garden and inhales the heady perfume of the lilacs and the smell of the grass after rain. She follows her nose out onto the lawn.

It is completely, eerily quiet outside. No distant shouts from the doorways of nearby pubs. No rumble of conversation from the street. Perhaps the thunder has chased everyone else indoors.

It's the lull before the storm. A gust of wind shakes the bushes, and moisture from their leaves peppers the ground. Then it is so still once again that Ellie hears the echo of her own breathing.

She lifts her arms. Much cooler this way. She stands on her toes like a ballerina and stretches. She begins to sway. She moves slowly and precisely, imitating the motions of a tai chi exercise she'd seen at the gym. Soon she shifts instead into an impromptu dance, something sinuous and flowing, something suited to her mood. It feels like an opening up, an invitation. Perhaps it's a moon dance, she thinks, except that the moon has hidden behind a layer of cloud. After a minute or two, Ellie raises her arms above her head once again and then winds herself down like a corkscrew, tumbling into a delicate heap on the grass.

The grass is wonderfully cool and damp, but the heat of the evening is still trapped under Ellie's skin. Slowly, she undoes her buttons, beginning at the throat and letting her hands glide down. Slowly, she rolls out of the dress. It lies on the grass in soft drifts, as if her body had simply melted away.

Then slowly, infinitely slowly, Ellie begins to roll over on the grass, over and over, picking up pace as she goes. She longs for a hill where she could go faster, as she loved to do when she was a child, her hands clutched to her chest, her sundress flying around her little legs, and her father standing at the bottom to swoop her up and swing her through the air. Then it was hot and dry and summer. Now it is warm and humid and spring, and it's a relief to feel the damp of the grass licking at her calves and the cool earth sending shivers up her spine.

She can see the dark gray folds of her dress in the light that shines from inside the house. Tenderly, she draws it toward her. She arranges it so that it trails along the length of her body like a dancing partner. She can feel its soft stroke along her thighs. She pulls it closer to her heart, and is strangely disappointed to find it empty and inert.

She sighs deeply and shakes off the garment and begins to stand. That's when she hears the scratching noise. A scrape of weft on warp. Two fabrics brushing together.

Ellie's eyes fly open. Her glance stabs into the corners of the garden. She can make something out now, a dark mass, crouching by the willow. Oh, my God, why didn't she see it before? See him before? He turns his head slightly and his eyes glitter in the light from the patio doors.

Ellie drops her dress and leaps to her feet. Spins on the ball of one foot and dashes for the house. She slips, struggling to keep her balance. The bushes crash behind her. There's a snapping of twigs and a shout. She throws herself through the open door, whirls around, and pulls the door to. She puts the stopper in place just as the man hauls himself up the wall. He wedges his knee on the top line of bricks, and scrapes himself over. He falls with a crash and a cry into the bushes below.

That cry stays with her. It had fear and pain. It had the tone of desperate measures. Ellie, too, might have uttered just such a wail when she threw herself through the door.

But this intruder who lurked beneath the willow tree. Who saw Ellie fumble out onto the lawn. Who watched as she slipped out of her dress, as she lay down, as she touched herself. What did he want with her?

That's what the police wonder, too. It's just short of three AM when they finally arrive, two constables. The man is in his thirties, bulky and jocular. The woman is younger than Ellie, and looks at the world through narrowed eyes.

By the time they arrive, Ellie has lost her fear. The man in the garden has gone and not come back. A nutcase, she insists; a Peeping Tom, an aberration. Whatever he might have been up to, he certainly isn't here now.

While Ellie waited for the police, while her heart rate returned to normal, she'd checked that the blinds on the upstairs windows reached all the way to the bottom of the sills. She'd stuck a piece of masking tape over the spyhole in the door. She'd made a promise to herself. She'd see to security. Tomorrow.

While Ellie waited, she went to the loo. She felt soiled, and shivery in spite of the heat, and would have dearly loved to take a shower. But she didn't dare in case the police were to show up while she was in the bathroom. For the same reason, she didn't ready herself for bed. She wiggled into a clean jersey dress, and belted a kimono over the top to keep herself warm. She turned on the heating. The night seemed chillier now.

She ate some leftover pasta salad while she waited, and drained one glass of red wine and poured herself another. She turned on the telly and sat in front of it, waiting for the police.

When the fear had subsided, she turned off the lights, and stood for three or four minutes just inside the patio doors, watching for movement in the garden. When she'd convinced herself that no one was out there, she managed to open the door and dash onto the lawn and retrieve her clothing. She put it in a bag for the dry cleaner.

She felt a little better. She hadn't abandoned her favorite dress to a Peeping Tom.

So the fear has faded. Not the anger, though. That still flares inside her, bright as an Olympic torch. The bastard, she thinks. The pervert. Sneaking up on her like that.

At last, a knock on the door. Ellie peels the masking tape aside and looks through the spyhole.

She shrugs off the dressing gown and hangs it on a hook before opening the door.

"Miss Porter?"

"That's right. Eleanor Porter," she says, and steps aside to let the police officers enter.

CHAPTER 56

The visit from the police somehow makes things worse. Before they came, Ellie had been frightened, and then angry. But they bring their bright, patronizing questions and undermine her confidence.

"Do you live here alone?"

"Yes." Trying hard not to sound apologetic. Somehow, for the first time, living here alone seems like a risky thing to do.

"What were you doing in the garden, Miss Porter?"

"Doing? I have to account for being in my own garden?"

"It was just a question, miss. It was midnight, after all."

All right, Ellie, calm down. They've got to ask. It's their job. For God's sake, you know that, you're a lawyer.

"Look, I work for the *Chronicle* in Canary Wharf. The evening shift. I finished round about nine thirty and had a drink afterward with some colleagues."

"Some women colleagues?"

"No, as it happens, two men. Journalists. Mike Turner and Aidan Neil. We talked until—oh, it must have been eleven. Then I came home." She hasn't brushed her teeth. A drink, she said, but actually it was two. And since then . . . Can they smell the alcohol on her breath?

"You travelled by DLR? To Island Gardens Station?" This from the man. His biceps strain at the short sleeves of his shirt, but his forearms are undeveloped. Popeye arms, she thinks.

"To Mudchute. And on foot from there."

"Did anyone follow you?"

It is an obvious inquiry, but the question startles her, nonetheless. Did anyone follow her? She'd taken a quick look around from the station mound before descending into Spindrift Avenue. Two passengers had alighted separately from other carriages, but she'd lingered under the lights until they'd tramped off in another direction.

"Miss Porter?"

"No—no, at least I don't think so."

The man with the Popeye arms is sweating as he sits at her table with a mug of tea between his palms. Ellie is shivering again. Surely the house is cool?

"Perhaps something made you uneasy?" He speaks more gently, as if trying to coax words from a frightened child.

Ellie has been spoken to like that before. She remembers another police officer, a woman, who hunkered down next to her as she crouched on the pavement. All around them lights were flashing, and cars parked at every which angle, and people shouting questions and commands. She can hear the sound of engines idling and smell the heavy fumes in the air. There are car horns hooting and cumbersome footsteps all around her, and she is covered with blood. Her shorts are streaked with blood. Her tie-dyed T-shirt is wet with it. There is blood in her Barbie's ponytail, and Ellie dabs at it hopelessly with a tissue.

The long-ago policewoman watched her in silence for several moments, and then asked her, in a tone of infinite concern—like the tone
this man is using now—if she was all right.

Ellie begins to weep. She knows she ought to do her best to convince the police officers that she is in control, to replace her anguished
demeanor with a bright and purposeful one. But before she can get a
grip, the tears take hold and the words come out in a rush.

She tells them about the letter. About everything he said, or rather,
everything he wrote. She tells them how it was hand-delivered, and
how her friend found it on the mat, and she explains what a shock it
gave her to think that someone has her in their sights.

"Any idea who it might be?" This is the policeman again. The
woman officer, the one with the jaundiced expression, has taken out a
notebook and is jotting something down.

Who it might be?

The shadow in the garden. Was it him? Is he aware of Ellie's late-
night visits to the garden, or is he merely an opportunistic voyeur?
Is he watching her, studying her, simply out of interest? Or more
purposefully—as an entomologist might study an insect before impal-
ing it on a pin?

"Miss Porter?"

"No. No, I don't know."

"May we see the letter?"

"No. No. I'm afraid—I was upset, you see. It gave me the creeps.
So I ripped it into shreds. I threw it away."

There's a pause in the questioning. The two officers exchange a
glance. Then the policewoman puts her notebook away and stands
and takes a few steps into the sitting room.

"You've just moved in?" she says. Her air is weary.

Ellie looks around, trying to see her flat through a stranger's eyes.
The painted floorboards. The simple blinds. The minimal furniture.
Even the kitchen consists of little more than a freestanding cooker
and a worktop and a table. "No, no, I like it like this. Traveling light
through the world," she says, airily.

The police officer shrugs. "So could you go over it once again?"

It? Ellie looks at the officer blankly.

"The garden. The man in the garden."

Ellie goes through it again. How she'd come in from work, and taken off her shoes and tights, and fed the hamster. She touches the cage, and the two police officers look at it curiously, as if they hadn't noticed it before. Ellie explains how she'd gone out in the garden to cool down. How she'd been doing some exercises—

"In that dress?"

Ellie sees immediately what's meant by the question. The dress she'd put on after she'd rung the police is Lycra-rich with a skirt so tight that her knees are practically glued together. Hardly the thing for exercise.

"No, no, not this dress, another one. A shirtdress, much looser." She is babbling now. "It's over there, in that bag, ready for the dry cleaners."

The woman is pacing around the room with a slow deliberate step. She interrupts Ellie's flow. "You were expecting visitors? This evening, I mean? After you got home?"

"No. Of course not."

"Then why change? Midnight is bedtime in most people's books. Why put a fresh dress on?" She steps across to the door where the laundry bag is suspended from a hook.

"I know that must seem silly of me," Ellie says, "but you were coming, so I couldn't get ready for bed and the dress I was wearing was soiled and so I— What are you doing?"

The policewoman lifts the canvas bag from the hook. She opens the drawstring. She looks inside. She reaches in and takes out Ellie's gray dress and gives it a shake. She holds it up in front of her for her colleague to see. Her hips protrude around the edges and the legs of her trousers stick out below. "Just having a look. You don't mind, do you?" she says to Ellie.

What can Ellie say?

The dress is a linen in a pale pearly gray, and beautifully cut, with a skirt that flares slightly from the hips. Ellie wore it with a rose-colored scarf. But now it's lost its charm. The front is streaked with grass stains and the dress is as damp as a dishrag.

"How did this happen?" the woman asks. "How did the dress become soiled?"

Ellie realizes with a rush of surprise that they think she was assaulted in the garden; they suppose she needs help to face the fact of an attack. She tries to set the record straight. Explains about how hot she was and about taking off her dress, and lying down. How it was only then that she heard him. And saw him. The intruder.

When she finishes her breathlessly told tale, there is a few seconds' silence.

"You were naked?" Popeye asks.

"What? Of course not! I had my—I was wearing underclothes."

"Otherwise naked?"

She nods and looks away.

"In the garden? At midnight? Wouldn't you say that was a little—unusual?"

Ellie cannot wait for them to go.

They make a cursory tour of the house before they leave. Shine their torches around the garden. Point out the place where the wall has partially collapsed, as if Ellie didn't know.

"I'd arrange to have a better lock fitted on that shower room window," Popeye says. And then, they are gone. She can hear them in the street, talking on their shoulder radios, telling their story—her story—to someone at headquarters, long after she's closed the door.

CHAPTER 57

"Jess!" Ellie knocks for the second time, much louder than before. "Jess, are you awake? I need a word." Ellie feels exposed standing out on the street like this. She wishes the girl would hurry up and answer.

Suddenly, the door flies open and Jess is there with her black night-dress and her hair all spiked up from sleep. "Yeah?" She yawns. "Sorry to take so long, Ellie, I was—"

"I can see you were asleep. Sorry to wake you. I just wanted to see how you're getting on. And also, to warn you about something."

"It's all right, Ellie. Come on inside." Jess turns and pads toward the kitchen. "You want a cup of coffee?"

"Sure. I was up too late last night. I could do with a shot of caffeine." Ellie follows her into the kitchen. It is decorated in a 1970s style—cork floors, mosaic worktops—that hasn't worn well. Ellie washes two mugs from a stack of dirty dishes while Jess gets the percolator going.

"Did you have fun?" Jess asks. She's rummaging in the fridge for a safe pint of milk.

"Pardon?"

"Last night. Up late, you said. A night on the town? Fun?"

"No, Jess, not fun at all. And that's what I wanted to warn you about. Last night, I had the police around." She is interrupted by the sound of footsteps, as someone clatters down the stairs, taking them two at a time. Ellie hadn't expected Tull; she thought Jess had sent him packing. But here he is, his bulk making the cottage seem smaller than it is.

"You called the police?" he asks. He places an arm around Jess's shoulders, but his wary eyes are fixed on the visitor. "What you want to do that for?"

"You haven't even said hello," Jess flings at him. She wriggles free from the proprietorial arm. Tull buries his hands in his pockets. He avoids Jess's gaze and turns to Ellie instead.

"What're you doing here?"

Ellie can see that this conversation is going nowhere. She directs an I-give-up gesture at Jess and turns and heads for the door. Suddenly, a thought leaps into her head about the intruder in the garden. She might have made a big mistake in thinking that her Peeping Tom was Mr. Tinkle's friend. The answer to the mystery might just lie a whole lot closer to home. She turns back, taking her courage in her hands. "Oh, one thing, Tull? That is your name, isn't it?"

"Whaddya want now?"

Clearly a bully, Ellie thinks. Well, he may have a hold over Jess, but she's older than Jess and more experienced, and he's not going to terrorize her. "Tull." Her voice is almost commanding. His belligerent expression fades to one of astonishment. He's not accustomed to being spoken to like that. "Tull, one other thing. Those boys you hang out with. Your little gang. You tell them to keep away from my garden, do you hear?"

And she swings smartly on her heel and leaves the house, slamming the door satisfyingly behind.

CHAPTER 58

"Hey, there. You're Eleanor, aren't you? Eleanor Porter?" The new pair who are assigned to the diary column corner Ellie the minute she walks into the office. At the *Chronicle,* as at many other newspapers, the task of finding tidbits for the diary is given to the most inexperienced members of the staff. They're expected to nose out juicy stories, establish contacts, and provide a whiff of scandal. It's good training for them, and popular with the readers; but their gung-ho approach can generate headaches for the legal department. So when Ellie finds Nikki and Guy at her desk, fretting over a paragraph of text, she braces herself for trouble.

"How's it going?"

Nikki looks up through chic black spectacles. "Thank heavens it's you. We've written a terrific piece on Ken Livingstone's second-in-command, but him in there"—she gestures crossly in the direction of Clive's office—"insists we do it all over again."

"He's gutted it," complains Guy. "And now he says he's off to do something with 'lilyrose,' whatever that means."

"Lily and Rose," Ellie explains. "His daughters. Look, just hang in there. I'll check in with Clive and then I'll be right with you."

Clive tells her, as Ellie knew he would, to keep the youngsters under her thumb. "You'll see what I mean. They're in a rebellious mood. Good luck," he says, and dashes.

Ellie does see what he means. The diarists have penned a piece which, in its final paragraph, alleges that the deputy mayor of London has business dealings with a man recently convicted of embezzlement. "It's like this," Ellie says, drawing on her most authoritative voice. "You can set the information about the embezzler within the paragraph, if you like, and leave readers to draw their own conclusions; but unless your evidence that the politician has deliberately swung a decision the way of the embezzler is foolproof, you had better abandon the claims of mayoral links."

At the notion of rewording their precious entry, Guy and Nikki are appalled. They are outraged, alarmed, dismayed. Ellie, they suggest, is out to quash their quest for Truth.

Ellie is amused at first; but she has a trayful of work to be getting on with and their charm soon wears thin. She tries twice without success to disentangle herself from their clutches; they seem determined to wear her down by sheer persistence. Just as Ellie is despairing of an end to the discussion, her printer leaps into life and Ellie seizes her chance. She dashes over and snatches the sheet of paper from the printer. The message therein reads: "You've been called away. It's terribly urgent. Put the toddlers in their playpen and meet me in the coffee room in five."

On the far side of the table, Jonathan stands and stretches and makes his way toward the stairs. He doesn't look at her, and she doesn't look at him. It's all Ellie can do to keep from smiling.

"Nikki, Guy, sorry. Got to run."

"But, Eleanor—"

"No buts. If you've fixed the piece by the time I get back, I'll sign it off. Otherwise . . ." Ellie raises her palms in the air and shrugs. Comply or take the consequences. Goodness, she thinks, as she makes her way out of the newsroom past the crestfallen diarists, if only everything in life were that simple!

Jonathan is perched on a stool in the caf next to the huge windows that look out over Canada Square. He has prepared a hot chocolate for Ellie. She smiles her thanks.

"You're a hero, Jonathan. For the chocolate, and even more, for rescuing me from Nikki and Guy."

"Eager bunnies, aren't they? The diarists are always like that at first. They imagine they'll make their names by turning up a tidbit that goes straight to the front page. Hardly ever happens. And in a year's time, they'll be calm and rational—"

"Cynical, you mean? Worn down?"

"Let's just say their enthusiasm will have been blunted by contact with reality. Then they'll be moved on to a real journalistic post."

Ellie considers as she blows on her cocoa. Under the creamy topping, it's still scalding. "I rather like the fact that they're so keen, Jon. That they're still after the Holy Grail."

"That they're after Truth, you mean? With a capital *T*?"

"It's a hell of a lot better than Lies with capital *L*, wouldn't you agree?"

Jonathan's chuckle echoes around the room, and Ellie warms to the sound. He's so—easy, she thinks. So at ease with himself. She'd love to have even a tenth of his talent for taking things as they come.

"Jonathan, you know, you amaze me. Stressful as things get at work, you always seem to enjoy yourself. How do you do it—stay so relaxed, I mean?"

Jonathan breaks a gooey cookie in half and offers her a piece. Ellie expects a flippant reply to her question: "Drugs are my friends" maybe, or "Excuse me. It's time for my injection."

But instead, to her dismay, Jonathan clears his throat and looks pensive. "You know, Ellie, it's funny you should ask me that, because just last evening I was thinking how much I'd calmed down in the past year or so. Before that—before my divorce," he adds, "you wouldn't have described me as relaxed at all. I fretted over everything: deadlines, money, car breakdown. Whether or not to have kids." Jonathan chuckles again when he sees the expression on Ellie's face. "Don't look so surprised. Blokes hem and haw over the issue, too."

Ellie doesn't know whether surprise is her dominant feeling, or dread. She meant to thank Jonathan for rescuing her from the diarists, to exchange a bit of banter, and then get back to work. She didn't want confessions. Didn't—doesn't—want things to get heavy between them. Jonathan Roberts is a helluva guy, but it is William DeQuoyne who's the love of her life, and she's not the kind of girl who plays around. She looks at her watch. "Jon, I've got to get back soon. I haven't even started on my in-box yet."

"Of course, Ellie. But just let me finish, please. What I wanted to say was that when I bounced back, after my divorce, I found that day-to-day anxieties didn't bother me much anymore. The experience of something much more shattering had brought me to my senses. And I swore then that if I ever had the opportunity to make another, better, relationship, I'd seize it with both hands."

Ellie slides down off the stool. She fixes the lid on her chocolate. "Good for you, Jon. I'm sure that's exactly the right attitude, but look, I've got to get back to work; I really do. Will you walk me back to the newsroom?"

His hand is gentle on her arm. "Ellie, please. Will you have dinner with me? Saturday?" He must have seen the hesitation in her eyes. "Any day, then—Friday? Sunday? Christmas Eve?"

He looks so hopeful, and so vulnerable, that Ellie has to resist a sudden urge to throw her arms around him. She sets her cup down on the table and says what has to be said. "Jon, listen, I like you a lot. You've been a real friend at the *Chronicle*. I don't know how I would have managed without you." His hand is lying limp on his thigh now. She picks it up and holds it between her palms for a second. God, this is difficult.

"Oh, look up there," he says, withdrawing his hand and pointing to the ceiling.

Ellie can't see anything.

"Come on, Ellie, I see a great big *but* hanging in the air. Spare me the trimmings. Out with it now."

Ellie's laugh is touched with pain. "It's the timing, Jonathan. Since I came to work at the *Chronicle,* my old boyfriend has come back on the scene. He's someone I've been—committed to—for a long time. So you see, I'm not really single anymore. I hope we—you and I—can still be friends."

The color of Jonathan's eyes darkens to indigo, and a sadness creeps into his expression. But he smiles gamely as he accompanies Ellie out of the room. "Of course we will," he says. "But Ellie?"

She turns and looks at him.

"Next time, you pay for your own hot chocolate," he says, with a grin.

CHAPTER 59

It is because of Denise—Denise and dinner—that Carl is almost forced to abandon his plan. Denise wolfs down her dinner like someone afraid that the plate might be whipped from under her nose. She is serving up the salad before Carl is halfway through his chicken nuggets. Carl takes heart from this, assuming that soon she'll trot off to her meeting. But Denise insists on hanging around. She spoons salad onto Carl's plate and helps herself to seconds. She makes two mugs of instant decaf. She lights a cigarette, puts her feet up on a chair, and gives him a long, inquiring look.

Denise wants to talk, but not the uninhibited chatter that he misses so much. She wants a solemn discussion. A heart-to-heart. "You've got to open up, Carl," she says. "Something's wrong, I can tell."

Carl has been such a good boy where smoking is concerned. He has stuck to his doctor's orders for months now. But sitting near Denise, with her wanting to know and him unable to say, he gets the urge. He reaches across without asking, and shakes a cigarette out of the pack and lights up. He sucks in a great lungful of smoke and closes his eyes.

"Carlie?"

"No, Denise," he says, suppressing a cough. "Nothing wrong."

"It doesn't look that way from where I'm sitting. You've hardly spoken two words to me for the past week or more. If you're not shut away in that room upstairs, you're out all hours of the night. And look at your plate; you don't eat enough to keep a flea alive." Denise picks up the ashtray and shakes it gently so that the ashes drift from side to side. Over the edge of the ashtray, she is watching Carl.

Carl avoids her eyes. It's a betrayal; he knows that. Taking time off from work without telling her. Lying about where he goes. Deceiving her again. Carl has never been able to bring himself to tell her the truth about Eleanor Porter, not even on his fortieth birthday, when the whole thing started to come back to him again.

A chilly December day his birthday was, with a low gray ceiling of cloud, and Carl was in the back garden setting up a laundry line. Through the kitchen window he could see Denise preparing lunch. Carl raised an arm to steady the line with his gloved hand, and as he did so, the washing line disappeared and instead, in front of him was a young girl who was reaching out toward him, her bony wrists protruding from the sleeves of her duffel coat. The image of the girl, as clear as crystal—the coppery frizz, the frightened eyes, the droplet of liquid at the end of her red nose—superimposed itself on the outline of Carl's house. Standing in the winter-dead garden, Carl began to sob. The next thing he knew, Denise was beside him, unhooking his hand from the laundry line. She reached under his fleece, feeling the racing of his heart, and she held him until the image of the little girl had fallen away. After that, Denise had kept Carl close beside her while she finished the supper preparations. She'd fed him sliced apples intended for the crumble, and tiny lumps of sugar and butter, and she'd regaled him with stories about the shop, until Carl could scarcely remember why he'd cried.

Then and now, he'd never explained. Never said a word. The story might have less of a hold on him if he shared it, he knows that, but he couldn't risk losing what was left of Denise's good opinion. Not for Eleanor Porter; not for something that, as he thought, could never be put right.

"Carlie?" Denise stubs out her cigarette. Carl follows suit. Now is not the time to confess, he's sure of that, no matter how many questions Denise throws at him. It's not words that are needed now; it's action.

Denise finally gives up on Carl, heaving herself out of the chair with a reproachful sigh. Carl waits just long enough to be sure she's left for her meeting, and then he bolts upstairs, grabs his things, and sets off again for Canary Wharf.

CHAPTER 60

The headache starts as Ellie comes to the end of her shift. Not a headache, really; not yet. But an arc of lights flashing at the edge of her vision. Enough to make it difficult to see. Enough to warn her of a migraine on the way.

She must have overdone it this morning. Two hours work on her kata, followed by an hour running around the island perimeter in the sun, must have been too much for her. Especially after that bottle of wine the night before.

She enters the house, drops her things on the floor, and dashes straight up to the bedroom. The bed looks all soft and silky. There is a gentle indentation in the quilt, almost the shape of a body, that seems to invite her to lie down. Ellie scrabbles through the basket on her bedside cabinet, looking for her migraine medication, but the strip is empty. She remembers now; she took the last two tablets on the morning after the police had visited. She hasn't yet ordered a new prescription. Ellie searches the cabinet thoroughly, just in case she'd salted away another strip of tablets, but no luck. She'll have to do without them.

She lies down on the bed, fully clothed, in the dark. When she closes her eyes, the white lights seem to burn into her brain. Minutes later, they are still dancing on her eyeballs.

Ellie switches on a lamp, easing the shade so that the bulb faces away. She won't sleep with this pain, so there's no point in torturing herself. She reaches out and turns on the radio. A news bulletin is just coming to an end. It's four minutes past midnight, the announcer says.

Four minutes past midnight. That means it's Friday already. She's due to pick up her navy suit from the dry cleaner's. And she absolutely must get hold of Ariana; she promised Harry that they'd settle things by Friday.

Perhaps she should ring Ariana now. What, after midnight? Well, why not? Ariana describes herself as a night owl. Five hours sleep, she says, like Margaret Thatcher; lucky girl. Ariana, that is, not Mrs. T.

Ellie adjusts the pillow behind her head and lifts the phone onto her tummy. She presses *Redial*. Before she left the house for work this afternoon, the very last thing she did was to leave a voice mail message on Ariana's mobile. Ellie hears the deep-deep-dip-dop-deep of the mechanical dialer and then the sound of Ariana's phone ringing. Ellie is used by now to failure. The phone will ring and ring and ring until, finally, the voice mail cuts in, and Ellie will leave yet another message and then close her eyes once more.

So she's taken aback when someone answers. A real person not the voice mail. "Yes? Who is it?" a voice says.

"Ariana?" She knows it's not. Not with that strong east London accent.

"What?" the voice says.

Ellie hesitates. "I want to speak to Ariana, please. Is Ariana there?"

"Ariana? No. You've got the wrong number. And it's after midnight. You should be more careful with your dialing."

"I'm sorry, I really am. I hope I haven't woken you." Ellie replaces the handset and looks at it in astonishment. It's impossible. Did she just dream that conversation?

Her hand is shaking slightly as she lifts the handset and once again presses *Redial*. It's picked up immediately at the other end. "If you're playing silly buggers—" Ellie slams the receiver down, but not before she reads the phone number on her LCD screen.

The number hits her like a ton of bricks. It pushes even the arc of white lights out of the forefront of her mind. It's a London number, but it's not Ariana's. Not the last one Ellie called before she left the house today. Another number, one Ellie doesn't know. One Ellie's never called.

She searches desperately for other explanations, but there's only one that fits. Someone made a call from Ellie's phone, from Ellie's house, during the day while she was out. And that means—there's no getting around it—that someone was here, oh, God! Here, in her bedroom. Using her phone. Looking at her private things. Perhaps even—

oh, God!—Ellie leaps to her feet and backs away in horror—perhaps even sleeping in her bed.

CHAPTER 61

Carl has often complained about the way that One Canada Square dominates the skyline, but what he does not like to admit is that the building gives him the shivers. All that bloody marble. On the floor of the foyer, pale and glittering like ice. On the gigantic rose-colored pillars. Marble from Italy. Marble from Guatemala. Ninety thousand square bloody feet of it. Enough to make headstones, Carl calculates, for an entire city of the dead.

As Carl walks across the foyer to one of the waiting areas, he feels the nasty slipperiness of the marble under his feet. The chilliness of it, like the skin of a dead baby. The dull way it reflects, like the unfeeling eye of a great white shark.

Everything about the Spike—that's what Carl calls the tower—reminds him of death. The vases of pallid lilies give off a sickly perfume. They are stiff with rigor mortis. They're foreign corpses, harvested in South Africa, flown to the Netherlands, trucked to London, transported across half the world in refrigerated planes and lorries, so that even in death they don't decay. The foyer of the Spike is cool enough that putrefaction will be kept at bay for a week or even two, but Carl isn't fooled.

Carl perches awkwardly on one of the leather benches near the barriers through which Eleanor usually exits. It's 9:15 PM. He hopes he hasn't missed her. He looks at the screen set into the pillar and pretends to study the stock market news.

Share prices plummet in New York and Tokyo. Well, at least that's one thing that Carl doesn't have to worry about. The value of shares might sweep downhill faster than an avalanche, but Carl doesn't stand to lose a penny. Maybe there'll be a few more falls off apartment balconies in the next few months. Carl, for one, won't be flattened by grief.

Carl smiles in grim amusement at the accidental appropriateness of the word *flattened*. They think they're so smart, with their flash cars and their expensive clothes and their waterfront apartments. So high and mighty. Well, more fool them.

Suddenly, he spots Richard, his supervisor, still in uniform, coming up from the mall. A muscle in Carl's jawline jumps. Carl has taken two shifts off in the past three days, claiming his throat is playing him up again, so he shouldn't really be seen out and about. But Richard walks right on by, and his eyes pass over Carl as if he were a stranger.

Saved by the suit, Carl decides. He looks down at the unfamiliar expanse of black wool with its faint gray stripe: his funeral suit. Far too heavy for a warm May evening like this, but the only suit he has. It has hung in his closet since his grandfather's funeral service. The rain was so fierce that day that mud splattered up his trouser leg as he trudged to the crematorium. Funny in times like that, you are overwhelmed by intense feeling—*bowled over by grief,* he remembers somebody saying, and that's just how it felt—but at the same time you're taking in lots of mundane details. Like the birds that hopped excitedly around the edges of the puddles. Carl couldn't give them a name, and that made him feel bad, because his grandfather had tried to teach him to recognize different species of bird and he'd never really listened. Carl recalls the small number of mourners who'd attended. He doesn't even have to count to come up with a number, there were so few. Mrs. Yelland and her husband, she struggling with her knees when the time came to stand. Tiny Ken Timlin, in his brown suit, his back skewed so sharply that he had to twist his head sideways if he wanted to look Carl in the eye. An attendant from the nursing home where his grandfather had lived for his final eighteen months. Mrs. Stimpson, who managed the newsagent's before Al took over. Only five people, apart from Carl and Denise. Not a lot to show for a life. And Mrs. Stimpson didn't really count, because she went to every funeral on the island in the hopes of catching a glimpse of her son, Teddy, who had disappeared decades before.

When he arrived home after the funeral, Carl had wiped the mud off his trousers with a damp cloth and covered the suit with a bin bag and put it away at the back of the wardrobe. He got it out today for camouflage. He wants to fit in with the office workers in the tower, so that colleagues like Richard, who have never seen him looking smart, won't recognize him. And it works.

Carl has chosen a good spot. He has a perfect view of the trickle of people who are passing through the barriers at this time of the evening. A businessman hauls his tie off in one smooth movement as he exits. Another cradles an extension cord under his arm. A young woman trips through in sequined top and killer heels. The sensible shoes that she wore in the office are in her tote; that's Carl's guess. And then, just as the fascinating question pops into Carl's head of whether the girl has changed her underwear, too, Eleanor Porter glides through the barrier, pushing her ID back into her document case in one smooth motion.

Carl follows her toward the DLR. From here on in, it's all down to timing, and Carl has it planned like a military campaign. When he gets near the station, he loses sight of her for a moment. But he leaps up the escalator, shouldering other people aside, and arrives at the platform just in time to see Eleanor step swiftly into a waiting carriage.

Carl enters and takes a seat without so much as a glance in her direction. But as soon as the train leaves the brightly lit station, Eleanor Porter's face, her fascinating face, appears in the front window. Her slender features are framed by a mandarin collar, with her hair tied in a sort of love knot on her neck. Her shoulders are squared and her back is as erect as that of a soldier on parade.

Carl takes a breath and swings his head casually to the left. His gaze sweeps slowly over a group of boys in skater shorts, and a drunk, and a woman with a drooling toddler, before brushing across Eleanor's lower half, across her lap and her legs and her feet, and coming to rest on the window again.

A sigh of satisfaction. Yes, it's as he thought. Knees pressed together. Legs parallel, slanted to the right. She sits like a woman posing for a photograph, with her face composed, cool, giving nothing away.

He longs to disrupt that composure. To stand in front of her and take her by the shoulders and grip her so tightly that she can't get away. He wants to say to her: *You can stop pretending. I know the truth.*

But first, he has to be sure.

There's a kind of responsibility that goes with knowing. All these years, he has kept it to himself. Hasn't told a soul. His guilt has held him back. But now that he has found her again, the questions have welled up. Every single day, he's had to walk from one end of the island and back again, hoping to exhaust himself out of this obsession. He's rejoined the gym. He has gone back to his old pastime of composing doggerel in an effort to empty his mind.

> Eleanor Porter, Eleanor Porter,
> Living in the southern quarter.
> Hoping she's safe with bricks and mortar
> I'm the man who's gonna sort'er.

None of this helps. His need to know is stronger than his shyness and more powerful than his fear. He needs to know everything about her. Where she goes. How she feels. What sort of person she is. She looks so fresh, almost innocent. How can that possibly be?

> Eleanor Porter, Eleanor Porter,
> On the edge of the river water,
> Tom and Annabel's only daughter,
> Frail and small. A lamb to the slaughter.

In the reflection in the window, he sees her eyelids flicker and close, but only for a moment, as if she's trying to remember something. Or trying to forget. There's a slight trembling of the features as if she might be going to cry. And then the eyelids fly open again, and her eyes dart from side to side, startled. No, more than startled: terrified.

Carl pops a stick of Juicy Fruit chewing gum into his mouth and keeps his eyes trained on her wavering image in the window. She shifts her weight. Straightens her legs. Plucks at something on her skirt. As the train rocks past Millwall Outer Dock and into the darker area around Mudchute Park, Eleanor Porter stands. She pulls down her skirt and adjusts her case and positions herself near the door. She steps off and heads along the platform and up toward the mound. He crouches down on the platform and pretends to retie his shoelace. Eleanor disappears from view. Carl reaches the top in three great strides and looks wildly around.

Normally, when Carl passes through Mudchute, he is thinking of its layered history: of the lake formed by silt that was pumped out of Millwall Dock, of allotments bursting with vegetables and flowers, of the guns blasting during German bombing raids. Now what is there? Only the darkling green lawns of an urban park. From the station mound, Carl can see the lights along Globe Rope Walk, and for a moment he thinks he has spotted Eleanor, but the figure he is following turns out to be a man.

She is rounding the corner onto Spindrift Avenue by the time Carl locates her again. He runs pell-mell down the stairs and takes up the pursuit. Once he has her retreating figure in his sights, he slows and retrieves his copy of the *London A–Z* from his carrier bag. If she should turn around, he hopes she'll see nothing more than yet another tourist who has lost his way.

Carl doesn't think of himself as a stalker. It's not ghoulishness or malice that makes him follow Eleanor to work and back again. It's a desperate need to fill in the blanks. Like when the telephone rings and you don't answer it in time and it nags away at you—who was that ringing? What did they want? You need—what does Denise call it ?—*closure*. It's the not knowing that is most difficult to take.

He needs to know the details, however unpalatable. Was her childhood stunted and her adolescence overshadowed by what she did? Or did she just brush it out of mind? And which, he wonders, would be more terrifying? If she was deeply, darkly, irremediably affected? Or if what she did didn't trouble her at all?

Carl examines her again over the top of his *A–Z*. Eleanor Porter is a good-looking girl, but she doesn't have her mother's sexual confidence. Eleanor's back is a little too straight. Her walk is a little too clipped. Her features are strained. She looks, Carl concludes, like she's clinging to a secret.

And if Carl exposes that secret, what will happen? She'll deny it, of course. Why after all these years of silence would she confess? The worst scenario, from Carl's point of view, is that someone will tell the tabloids—twenty-year-old crime exposed—and then it will be his word against hers. She's a lawyer—people will believe a lawyer; courts will, anyway—and Denise will say he's gone and made a fool of himself again. Carl clamps down on his bottom lip and carries on.

They follow Spindrift Avenue for most of its length. Past the former site of the Millwall Graving Dock. Past streets in the new development with names—Whiteadder Way, Taeping Street—that speak of tall ships and faraway ports. Carl is trying his damnedest to stay in the present. When Eleanor dips in toward the Docklands Medical Center, he hangs well back. She slips something in through the letter box, and carries on down the main road.

But not before she turns, with an awkward, apologetic movement, and looks directly at Carl, who has come to a halt under the streetlamp. He is holding his *A–Z* toward the light, running his finger down the page. She stares for a moment and then hurries off, but not before he glances up and catches the desolation in her eyes.

Carl is furious with himself. He's blown it now. She's had a good look at him. It will be harder to follow her in the future, and she hasn't yet taken him where he wants to go. He remains under the streetlamp, trying to control his fury with himself, until Eleanor disappears onto Westferry Road. Then suddenly he knows what to do next. He moves out of the glow of the streetlamp and into a duskier patch. He crouches down and reaches into the bushes. He snaps off a twig, and then another, until he comes up with a branch that is long enough and strong enough. He spits out his gum, presses it onto the end of the stick, and makes his way back toward the darkness of the medical center, chanting under his breath.

> Eleanor Porter, Eleanor Porter,
> What shall it be?
> Shall we lock up the villain, or hang, draw, and quarter?
> Someone's gotta sort her.
> And it's gonna be me.

CHAPTER 62

Ellie was eight going on nine when her father was killed. She has a newspaper cutting—she carries it in her handbag, always, folded up into a tiny talisman—that reveals in stark and inaccurate prose the "facts" of her father's death. She has a handful of blazing images—visual memories—but these fragments are disconnected and incomplete. What she recalls most coherently is what it felt like.

It was November. The sixth of November. Bleak, wintry weather. Ellie was wearing her woolen tights for the first time that winter, and she couldn't stop scratching her legs, in spite of her mother's warning about scars. *Get your things together,* her mother instructed, *while I just pop upstairs and finish putting my war paint on.* That's what her mother always called her makeup; she called it war paint; Ellie thought it was funny. Then came the knock at the door. Tentative at first and then more insistent. Her parents were busy upstairs. Ellie pushed her schoolbags to one side and reached up and opened the latch.

At the sight of the man's face, icicles formed inside her. She could feel a stalactite melting, ever so slightly, and glacial drops sliding down her spine. She tried to shut the door, but he blocked her. He spoke to her in an urgent whisper, telling her things, making her promises, the substance of which she can't remember now. What she can remember is the terror. The terror of him. The terror if her parents should find out.

She struggled to make him understand. She begged him to go. He crouched down and held her by the arms and said: *You know I can't leave you. Don't worry, it will be all right.* But it wouldn't be all right and Ellie knew it.

Suddenly her mother appeared, her face twisted with anxiety. The man talked to her. He tried to explain himself. He was determined, and he was dogged, but he was no match for Annabel. Ellie's mother overwhelmed him, her face white with fury, her advance so implacable that he stumbled more than once in his retreat down the steps and along the path.

From behind the sitting room curtains, Ellie saw him go. She raced out into the corridor and clutched at her mother's hand. *Mother! Mother! I'm frightened. Stay with me! Please don't go.*

But her mother went. Ellie heard Annabel's footsteps snap up the stairs and along the landing, and then the rows began.

After her father's death, Ellie enjoyed an uncomfortable celebrity at her primary school. Other children were part of single-parent families, but she was the only child whose father had died on active service, so to speak. Her classmates buzzed about her nervously for a few days, and then lunch menus and games became the priority again, and everything went back to normal. For the rest of the children, anyway.

Annabel said as little as possible about her husband's death. *A road accident* was her standard response to the rare explicit question; *too painful to speak about.* The details of Tom's death became a family secret, one of many, hidden in the end even from Ellie herself. Now when Ellie conjures up the image of Tom Porter's crumpled, bleeding body, she can't even be certain that the memory is real. What is real is the horror she saw in her mother's eyes. The accusation her mother flung at her: "Oh God, what have you done?" And the fact—hideously, undeniably, real—that her father is dead and that there is no one but Ellie to blame.

CHAPTER 63

"Something's happened, hasn't it?" Tony Mannix says. "I could tell by the sound of your voice when you rang. What is it? What's happened?"

"Nothing. Nothing, I'm fine." They are sitting at the kitchen table having a cup of tea. Her karate colleague is concerned, she can see that, and it's generous of him to give up his time to advise her on security. But Ellie doesn't want to talk about the man who's been following her. Or the Peeping Tom in the shrubbery. Even less does she want to talk about the person who broke into her house. Who's been sleeping in my bed? She doesn't want to know. She just wants him to go away.

They start upstairs. Tony doesn't say much; he looks closely at the frames of the sash windows in Ellie's bedroom and makes a few notes on a clipboard as he goes. At one point, he sends Ellie off for a stepladder. He climbs on the top platform and pulls himself up into the loft access with his arms. "What's it like up there?" Ellie asks when he's back on terra firma.

"Open," he says, brushing dust off his hands. "There's no proper partition wall between this house and the others in the terrace. I'm surprised the fire inspector hasn't been down on you. A fire in one house would just rage all the way down the street." It turns out that Mannix is full of cheering thoughts like that.

When he has completed his survey upstairs and down, he wheels around and fixes Ellie with a stern expression. "Like an invitation to burglars, this place, Elle. Did you know that?"

"That good?" Ellie asks. Mannix is doing her a favor, and she's grateful, but it would be nice if he would lighten up.

"An invitation," he repeats. "Open house for the criminal crackheads." Tony is particularly scathing about the ground floor. He relates the weaknesses of her house with gusto. Her improvised locking system for the patio doors gets short shrift. He demonstrates how easy it is to dismantle the door and lift it entirely from its runners, leaving the back of the house exposed. "Out goes your stereo system, your jewelry and anything else worth having."

Anything else worth having? It's personal safety that concerns Ellie, not the prospect of supplying merchandise for someone's car boot sale.

"And it's not just the value of the goods that matters here," Tony says, as if picking up on her thoughts. "How d'you feel if you came home and your house was trashed? I've seen it, believe me." He makes a slow sweep of the scene with narrowed eyes. "This beautiful floor, covered with graffiti. A pile of cra—excuse me, Elle—human excrement, steaming on your sofa. Your cushions slashed and the spines of your books broken and a fire burning on your bedroom floor."

Eleanor has imagined plenty of dreadful things in the dark moments of the night, but her rational mind rejects the idea. "A burglar would have to hate me an awful lot to do such despicable things." As soon as the words are out of her mouth, she wishes she hadn't voiced them. What someone who hates her a lot might do is a thought she'd rather steer away from.

Tony Mannix marches solemnly to the door and throws it open. Hesperus Street is quiet and dark. He turns his head from side to side, sniffing the air, while the night tries to push past him and shoulder its way inside. He speaks in a soft and menacing tone. "You have no idea how much hate there is out there."

Ellie calls him, softly, to come back inside. She wants him to stop this kind of talk. He seems not to hear her. "Mannix!" He wakes from his trance and steps back inside the house, brisk and business-like again.

"I'll make a proper list, and send it to you, Elle. But for now let me talk you through it. Look, if you want effective security, the first thing you have to do is to see the world through the eyes of a perp. Come on, I'll show you." He puts his hand under her elbow, like a man guiding a woman onto the dance floor. Ellie holds the clipboard and takes notes on what's to be done while he leads her around the house. Fit new locks on the windows and repair a damaged frame. Mount an additional Chubb lock lower down on the door. Anchor the door chain more firmly by moving it to a better position. Install an alarm, and give it two separate panic buttons, one by the front door and one next to her bed.

"Don't want you having any nasty shocks in the middle of the night."

They go into the garden. Mannix propels her gently across the lawn to the willow tree. "There," he says, pointing back toward the house. "What do you see?"

Ellie has always loved the view of the house from the back of the garden. The steeply pitched roof under its armor of slates. The vine-covered walls, tall and commanding on one side, dipping picturesquely on the other. The homely image of light shining through the patio doors. But looking at it as Tony wants her to, with the eyes of an intruder? "Strong brick walls," she says. "The garden, I mean, and the house, too. Patio doors in need of attention. A sash window that could be opened by anyone with an arm."

"And a party wall that begs to be climbed."

"It already has been," she admits, and tells him for the first time about the intruder in the garden. She doesn't mention that she was in her underwear at the time, but even so, her blushes give it away.

"Job number one. Get a builder in to repair that wall. Add a barrier at the top. Angled spikes would be best; barbed wire or broken glass would be better than nothing."

"Sounds expensive."

"Look at this way. An opportunist burglar, a kid maybe, will smash through the front window of your house, snatch up your laptop, and be off. But an intruder with a more—shall we say, sinister—purpose won't draw attention to himself. He'll want a little privacy for his project. He'll come in through the back, and when he's in, these garden walls will work in his favor. They make you feel safe? They'll make him feel safe, as well."

Is that how the man felt as he stood pressed up tight against the tree in her garden? Safe? Ellie looks up at the sky. It's overcast and the clouds press down on the tops of the trees. She hears the wail of a siren somewhere on the island.

"No prying eyes," Tony continues. "He can settle down and do a proper job of whatever it is he's come for."

Whatever it is he's come for. Ellie crouches down and sniffs at a leaf. There is a tiny cache of water pooled on its surface. The little hairs on the underside are tender.

He comes and stands behind her. "A stalker, Elle. A man who wants you, not your possessions. A man like that will be coming in the back way." The squat outline of the shed catches his attention. "He'll want a ladder. Is there one in there?"

She nods.

"Get a padlock," he says. "A strong one. And use long screws to attach a board—two boards—across the window. I'll do it for you if you like."

Ellie runs the palm of her hand over the earth. She can hear the tiny, soft sucking sounds that come after the rain. Things moving in the soil, coming to the surface, insects and earthworms and other crawling creatures, easing up out of their flooded burrows to feed in the moist night air.

"Are you listening?"

She's offended him now. It's clear from his tone. He gave up his free time to help her, and here she is, ungrateful cow, recoiling from his comments.

Ellie tilts her head back, so she can glimpse his face. Even in the dark, she can make out the frown that knots his brows.

"Am I listening? Every word, Mr. Mannix." She smiles up at him. "The wall must be armored and the garden shed fortified. Right?" She smiles again, hoping to lighten the atmosphere, but she only succeeds in upsetting him further.

"It's not funny. A woman who lives alone is at risk." He punctuates his words by stabbing the clipboard with the pen. "Isn't that why you asked me to help? Because you felt at risk?"

A woman living alone? Well, yes. But what about all the others? Ellie wants to say. What about the two little girls who were murdered in Soham? Or Millie Dowler? Heather West? None of them lived alone. And living with their families certainly didn't save them. And as for the risk to women . . . "Tony, what about the poor chap they pulled out of the Thames the other week? He was certainly at risk."

"What are you talking about?" Mannix hunkers down next to her. "Look, Elle, you're not taking this half seriously enough. You've got to get a few things straight."

Ellie hasn't got the energy to argue. She nods and carries on attending with half an ear. But she's really listening to the moisture that drips from the surface of the leaves onto the soil beneath.

"Think about it. What is a garden shed from the point of view of an intruder? It's a ladder; it's easy access to your house, as I said. But worse than that—are you listening?—worse than that, it's an arsenal. There's twine to tie someone up. Sacking to place over her head. Chemicals to disable her. Glue."

"Glue?" Ellie echoes. She thinks of nursery school. She thinks of clouds of cotton wool glued to a sheet of sky-blue paper.

"Oh, come on. Don't tell me you haven't heard of the rapist who made sure he wasn't recognized? Who took his victims' eyelids and superglued them shut?"

"I didn't need to know that," Ellie says.

Tony grabs her wrist. She twists in an effort to pull away. He grips her so tightly that it hurts.

"Tools," he says. "Screwdrivers, pliers, bolt cutters. Intruders can use 'em to break into houses. Can use them just as easily against someone they hate. Do I need to go on?"

"I'll fit a padlock," Ellie says. "A strong one."

He releases her wrist. She rubs it where it hurts. "And one more thing, Elle. This business of stepping out into the garden after dark. I've got something to show you." He helps her to her feet. "Just go inside. Turn your back, count to five, and then come out again."

Ellie stands in the kitchen with her back turned and her head bowed and longs for the whole ordeal to be over. When he calls, she turns reluctantly toward the door, steps over the sill, and takes two paces into the garden. Then she stops dead. Where is he?

There's a flash of movement and suddenly—"What the—?"—she's grabbed from behind. Her arms are pinioned to her sides. The grip is just above the elbows, hard to break. Ellie twists and turns and tries to put a few inches between them so that she can deliver a kick, but his hold is too firm.

Tony whispers in her ear. "I was there, Elle, just next to the door. Flattened against the wall in the shadows." He nods. "You wouldn't see an intruder until you'd already left the safety of your house. And then," he adds, "it's too late."

He is still hanging on to Ellie's arms as if waiting for her to do something that will win her release. Ellie has no strategy, no plan, only a desperate cry that wells up and bursts out and fills the garden.

"Let go of me," she wails.

Later, tucked up in bed with the hot water bottle clutched to her chest, Ellie is overcome with shame. Mannix's behavior in the garden was insensitive, but her own reaction was worse. Her cry exposed the humiliation and the helplessness she'd felt. She'd felt like a baby, and it had showed.

Tony had been aghast. She'd seen it in his face. He made extravagant apologies. He fussed over Ellie, preparing a hot water bottle and making her promise to ring him at any time if he could be of help.

"I didn't realize," he said, shaking his head. "I didn't know how frightened you were."

Well, now he does know. And what is much, much worse, Ellie herself knows, too.

CHAPTER 64

Ellie wakes out of a restless sleep and struggles on to her side, and there normality ends. Her throat is locked. Something is blocking it.

Disbelieving, she tries to draw a breath. No movement in her windpipe. Her chest expands, but her lungs are empty.

She scrabbles out of bed, throwing back the covers. Catches her foot in the sheet and tumbles to the floor.

On hands and knees, she wrenches out a violent cough. She thrusts her desperate fingers into her open mouth and claws at her throat. She gags. Bile shoots up and her stomach heaves. She still can't catch a breath.

Ellie crawls to the phone. There are pins and needles in her hands and feet. She fumbles and drops the handset. She sweeps the floor with her palm until she finds it again and dials 999.

Her words to the operator—little slaps of consonants—have no proper sound behind them. *Hesperus Street* comes out as a series of whistles.

"Crosspress Street?" the operator asks. "Cypress? I'm sorry, I can't hear you. Please say it again."

Ellie begins to shake violently.

She tries one more thing. She searches her memory. Yes, she still knows it. She picks up the receiver and punches in Will's home telephone number.

It is three o'clock in the morning. The phone rings and rings and rings.

Finally, a voice answers. "Hello?" A familiar male voice, warmer-toned than in the day and muzzy with sleep. "Hello, who the hell is this?"

An explosive cough. Ellie's throat clears.

She breathes.

And breathes.

And breathes.

CHAPTER 65

The knock is so loud that the echo can be heard up and down the street. It's so hard that the side of Tull's hand is sore. "Jess!" He pounds again. "Jess, for fuck's sake, I've got to see you."

Tull doesn't usually get tanked up in the middle of the day, doesn't usually pick a fight with a stranger. But then it's been a fucking awful week, what with Jess dumping him like that, and then disappearing. He knows she doesn't mean it. She's just playing hard to get. Trying to get him to come around to her way of thinking on Kristoff and all.

He laughs as he walks along, recalling the bouncers who had been dispatched to see him out of the pub; at the sound of his laugh, which is more like a snarl, two young women steer their pushchairs to the other side of the street. Security, my ass. Tull could recognize their kind a mile off. He ought to, enough of his pals from the care home ended up just like that. Ex-army lads, couldn't take army discipline, but didn't have what it takes to make it in any other field. You scrub 'em up, put a uniform on them, but they're still the same tossers as before.

He knew the bouncers wouldn't call the police. Couldn't be bothered, most like. Anyway, as it turned out, one of them remembered Tull from a snooker game in Lewisham, and came over all matey. "Nice-looking piece," he said, gesturing with his shaved head toward the door where Jessica had exited after he'd tracked her down and she'd refused to speak to him. Tull pretended to trip then, and slammed into the ex-squaddie so hard that the man's shoulder crashed against the wall.

"Sorry, mate." After the other man had stopped rubbing the injured shoulder, Tull added: "That *piece* you were talking about . . . she's my girl."

"Not from what I heard," the bouncer mouthed to his partner as Tull walked away.

The bus comes and Tull jumps aboard, shouldering aside two kids whose rucksacks are blocking the gangway. He takes the first empty seat, rests his elbows on his knees, and puts his head in his hands. His thinking position, Jess calls it.

Tull would never admit it to anybody—hasn't admitted fear since a beating by his father at the age of six—but Jess saying she wants to split has scared the shit out of him. At first he thought she must be ill or something, maybe cancer, like his mother had. Couldn't believe she just plain wanted out. "But, Jess, we're so good together," he protested. He hated it when she walked away.

He looks up and sees that the bus is passing Asda. Three more stops to go.

There's a lesson in what happened today. You're bound to screw up when you're angry. Wait until the anger passes. Uncle Vince used to say that, and he was right. Tull always makes his worst mistakes when he's scared or upset. The past few weeks prove that.

Uncle Vince wasn't Tull's real uncle; he was his foster dad. After Tull's mum became too ill to look after him and his baby sister, Tull had three foster families. One was a mechanic and his wife and children. Kind, they were, and the wife always cooked up a storm, but their son became ill, really ill, and they couldn't manage the extra child anymore. Then there were the Whitstones. They were an older couple, gentle-seeming, but only with outsiders. To Tull, they were cold, and experts at the kind of small cruelties that you never forget. And then finally there was Uncle Vince.

Uncle Vince ran a contract cleaning company. He and his Mrs. Vince had three children—"the lasses," he called them—and they applied to social services for a foster son when the girls were in their early teens. Want another man around the house, that's what Vince said. From the beginning, he and Tull got along like a house on fire.

They played cricket together in summer and kicked a ball around in winter. Sometimes the youngest daughter, Tessa—a tomboy if ever there was one—would join in, but usually it was the men on their own. They played darts on a dartboard set up on the back fence, and on cold days the air outside would be misty with their laughter. They made tall ships from balsa wood and floated them in the dock. Uncle Vince had dozens of them. The shed where he kept them was done up like a showcase; he was that proud of his ships.

The trouble came when things began to go missing. "You're sure you haven't seen my new porcelain figure?" Mrs. Vince asked one day. A week later, it was a pendant belonging to the eldest lass. But the final straw came when Uncle Vince left the shed door unlocked; the next morning, his favorite ship, a model of the *Cutty Sark* that he'd built with his own father—perfect down to the slightest detail, it was—had disappeared.

"I can't see who could have done it, if it wasn't you, lad. I'm disappointed. I never took you for a thief."

Tull pleaded, but it didn't do a bit of good. They put him in the car. Uncle Vince looked very sad, and hugged him, but couldn't look him in the eye. Mrs. Vince cried and cried. But they had to draw a line, that's what they said. And it was only after Tull had gone away, back to a shared home that wasn't a home at all, back to a feeling of emptiness that was ten times worse than hunger, that he remembered how Tessa, the tomboy daughter, with her ginger hair, had watched out of the window as he was driven away, and how there was a hint of a smile playing around her mouth.

What upsets Tull now almost as much as Jess having dumped him is not knowing what's going on with her next-door neighbor. "Ellie," Jessica calls her. How come she's so tight with Jessica, then? A few days ago, one of Tull's young mates saw a woman—a real looker, he said—coming out of Ellie's house sometime after midnight. There was lots of hugging and stuff on the doorstep. Course with women you never know. They're touchy-feely by nature, Tull reckons. But Nick, the kid, had another idea.

"Lezzies," he sneered. "Why do you let your Jessica hang out with a lezzie? Maybe that red-haired slag has her eye on Jess."

Tull exploded at that. "Don't be such a fucking idiot. Jess isn't like that. And if that bitch so much as looks at her . . ." He outlined in graphic terms what he would do to Ellie, outrage lending him inspiration. The others listened, impressed, maybe a touch appalled, and he was soothed.

He can feel it still now. That explosion of rage isn't gone; it's just submerged. But it's chilly around the edges now, as if dread is creeping in where the anger was before. And now that Jess has dumped him . . . She's only trying to get a rise out of him, he knows that, but he doesn't like this playing hard to get.

Tull stands, shakily. He takes out his Zippo and lights a cigarette to steady himself. Other passengers give him disapproving stares. He waits until the bus slows down, and then leaps off and heads for a pub in Lewisham where a man is waiting to do business.

CHAPTER 66

Carl is finding Eleanor Porter harder and harder to predict. The minute he saw her with that poncy bloke in Cabot Place East he figured they were lovers. It was just something about them, something unmistakable. But as far as Carl can tell, she's seen the geezer only once since, and that was fleetingly in the newsagent. What's going on there?

And then last night, there was this thin, nervy bloke. Knocked on the door smartly, like a salesman, and Eleanor welcomed him in. He stayed a long while, almost an hour and a half, but by the look on his face when he left Hesperus Street, Carl had the distinct impression that it didn't go well. At one point, they went out into the garden and Carl is pretty sure that Eleanor ordered him to let her go; whatever games the Thin Man had in mind, Miss Porter wasn't playing. Carl followed him to Poplar, to a small shabby flat with a yellow door, before he made his own way home.

Is Eleanor Porter having a scene with one, maybe both, of these men? Denise would know. She understands relationships; she always has. But he can't ask Denise, because Denise isn't speaking to him, ever since they had a row about his late nights.

"You're never home," she'd screamed at him. "Out all hours. Early morning, late at night." She was wearing her lilac top, the one he liked, and she would've looked really lovely if she hadn't been so angry. "What the friggin' hell are you doing, Carl Thomas?" When Denise uses phrases like "friggin' hell," it means that she's really lost her rag.

"Denise, like I told you, I can't sleep. What else is there to do in the early hours? Walking makes me feel better. Anyway, you're so busy with your book club and all, I'm surprised you even noticed."

As soon as the sarcy comment was out of his mouth, Carl regretted it. Making up was out of the question after that.

So here is Carl once again on Hesperus Street in disguise. An anorak and a baseball cap, this time. He trudges along past Eleanor's house, and catches a glimpse of her out of the corner of his eye. She is standing in the middle of the sitting room making strange jerky movements. Reminds Carl of karate, but he doesn't dare pause for a longer look. By the time he returns, minus the baseball cap, her shutters have been closed, so that he can't see inside at all.

Carl rings in to work. His voice is always rough and scratchy and he strives to make it more so. "Richard? Throat's still playing me up. I'll be off for a day or two." Richard mumbles his displeasure; Carl takes no notice. A man like that, a man with no natural authority, has no right to be running a surveillance room.

Carl can't linger in the area without calling attention to himself. He keeps on the move, following a circular route that takes him past Mudchute and Island Gardens stations, down toward the river, and back again. Sticking to this course, Carl reckons, gives him a seventy-to-thirty chance of coming across her wherever she goes. They're not perfect odds, but they're good enough to keep him at it.

The third time he approaches her house, he's in luck. He's just rounding the corner when the light in the sitting room flicks off, and seconds later, Eleanor Porter steps out onto the street. Carl manages to back out of sight while she locks up. She has a good look up and down the street, and then sets off in the direction of the station.

Carl takes the roundabout route, jogging in spite of the still-tender spot on his heel. He arrives in time to jostle himself into position in the carriage next to hers. Their journey takes them north. They change trains. Through the glass panel in the door at the end of the carriage, he catches occasional glimpses of his quarry. She stands in the central aisle, dressed in a corduroy jacket and suede trainers, looking blankly at the tube map on the wall.

The train is unusually full. At every station, there is pushing and jostling as people get on and off. Carl is forced farther back into the carriage. A man with dark hair gelled straight back from a high fore-head, the skin on his cheeks etched with acne scars, pushes into posi-tion by the door, blocking Carl's view. Carl cranes his neck until he spots Eleanor's cloud of red hair. The man with gelled hair bends to peer out the window; that's when Carl sees the overcoat and recog-nizes Billy the Kid.

At the next stop, Eleanor Porter gets off the train and hesitates, looking up and down the platform, before setting off with quick little steps.

Carl leaps out of the carriage just as the doors begin to close. Someone pushes past him. Lo and behold, it's Billy. The Kid strides confidently up the platform. His boots make a scraping noise as he walks, and people edge away, so that he's surrounded by a bubble of space. For several seconds, to Carl's annoyance, he blocks Carl's view of his quarry. They turn into the central tunnel, and Carl loses Eleanor in the crowd. He spots her again just as the escalator spills her out at the top and she disappears off to the left. The Kid is only five or six steps farther down.

Carl squeezes past suitcases and bounds up the escalator, half pulling himself by the handrail. He locates Eleanor standing by one of the station kiosks, scanning the front page of the *Evening Standard*. The story—Carl's already read it—is about that tourist who got himself murdered a while back. Tourist's family, poor buggers, are ap-pealing for anyone who saw him after he left the Ship to come for-ward. Carl has worked out that he himself was in the Ship that night, but as he told the PC who came to interview him, he can't remember seeing the tourist. He must have had a mini-seizure, because for the life of him he can't remember anything at all.

Carl pauses in the newsagent's and makes a pretense of scanning the sweets. Billy the Kid is there ahead of him. He drops a packet of cigarettes and scoops them up again from the floor of the concourse with one clean movement.

Carl blinks. He hardly knows the Kid, but he's seen him make that gesture—seen him pick something up with one long sweep of his arm—before. His memory leaps to a moment by the river and in his confusion, Carl almost misses Eleanor as she sets off for the high street. Carl whirls around to follow her and narrowly avoids crashing into the man in the long overcoat. The Kid is oblivious to the near collision because—finally, Carl gets it—his gaze is fixed unswervingly on Eleanor Porter.

CHAPTER 67

"You've got to hype yourself up, girl." In the corridor outside the changing rooms, Vikesh Patel, one of the other purple belts, is giving Ellie a pep talk. She has forced herself to come to today's training session, but she couldn't feel less like fighting. "Focus on your opponent, girl. Find his Achilles' heel, that's the thing."

"What if he hasn't got one?"

"Everyone's got a weakness, girl. Go for his eyes, his solar plexus. Go for his goolies, pardon my French." Vik speaks quickly, reeling off these suggestions in a voice that's a perfect imitation of Eddie Murphy.

"I've been working at it, honest, Vik. But I've got this feeling . . ." She sees Tony Mannix coming down the corridor toward them. She tries to catch his eye, but he pushes straight past them without saying a word. All she can think about is her embarrassment over her babyish behavior in the garden. No wonder he's not speaking to her now. "There's Sensei," she says. "We'd better go in."

Vikesh steps in front of her. "You've got a feeling?" he says. "What's that supposed to mean?"

"It's simple." Ellie shrugs. "Some people can fight and some people can't."

Striker is in a ferocious mood. Two red belts fail to follow instructions during warm-up and he has them doing fifty press-ups.

If Ellie was nervous before, now she's like a mouse cornered by a cat. She throws herself into a kata, giving it everything she has, making her turns swifter and her blocks harder than before. She takes comfort in her own sharp punches, but it's a cold comfort. Some of the men—though not in front of Sensei—refer to katas as "line dancing." They're a doddle, they say, compared to sparring.

Sensei signals them to clear the floor. They're assigned their sparring partners. For Tony Mannix, a burly Asian brown belt. Vikesh squares off against a fresh-cheeked public schoolboy, inexperienced but aggressive. Ellie holds her breath while Sensei surveys the remaining brown belts. Finally, he pairs her with a stocky man, taller than her by only a few inches, but as wide as a barrel, with a face that is deeply lined and utterly composed.

Elie searches out her opponent's weakness. He is powerfully built, but he might be slow, she decides. She'll concentrate on speed.

He attacks first, but she counters effectively and swings onto the offensive. Her stance is too flat. Before she has time to correct it, he has swept his leg around and thrown her to the ground.

When she jumps up, Sensei is looming over her. "Again," he orders.

Ellie faces the brown belt again. He can be defeated. She says it to herself, over and over, but her opponent looks faster to her than he did before, and taller, too. And her mind is only half on him. The other half registers the muscle that's dancing in Sensei's jaw.

She makes only two moves before her opponent brings her to the ground again.

The telling off is worse than she feared. "Disgrace . . . I'd expect better from a sixth kyu . . . I wouldn't have put you in for the grading if I'd thought . . ."

Ellie is sick with a sense of failure. She'd like to run away and hide but manages to take her punishment like a woman.

"Deplorable technique," Striker barks. "Why did you hesitate in your defense? What's the matter with you?"

It's all Ellie can do not to burst into tears. She hides out in the changing room after class, waiting for the others to disperse, hoping to escape unseen. After fifteen minutes, she emerges into the reception area and, desperate for a drink, feeds a pound coin into the drinks machine. There's a series of clunks and whirrs, but no bottle is released.

"Not working, is it, love?" says a woman who has formed a queue behind her.

It's the final straw. Ellie pounds the machine with her fist. More clunks, more whirrs; no water. She squeezes her eyes shut to force back the tears and marches toward the reception desk, with her sports bag in hand. Halfway there, she sees him. She sees the ponytail first, streaked with gray. That man, her stalker, is standing at reception, writing out a check. His awkward fingers struggle to grip the pen. He uses his other hand to adjust the angle of the Biro. He hasn't yet caught sight of Ellie.

She spins on her heel and races for the exit.

The woman who'd been behind Ellie at the vending machine calls after her. "Hey! Here's your coin!" Ellie keeps going.

Halfway down the stairs, on the landing, Sensei is leaning against the wall alongside a scraggly potted palm. She nods at him, struggling to keep her expression neutral, and continues her flight.

"Wait, please," he says.

She glances back toward reception. No one is following. Reluctantly, she comes to a halt in front of the instructor, with her eyes cast down.

"Miss Porter?" He's trying to be lighthearted, but he doesn't wear it well. "Bet you're glad that's over with, aren't you?" The word *that's* comes out oddly because of his lisp.

She nods but refuses to look up. "I'm sorry, Sensei. I'm hopeless." Might as well say it, before he does. "I won't be ready for the grading."

Striker is dressed in a navy blue tracksuit with the club's official logo on the front. He sets his Puma bag on the landing and takes her by the shoulders. They have never touched before except as part of a karate move. She recoils from the intimacy, and he quickly drops his hands again.

"I was too hard on you. You were moving too quickly, not following through firmly enough, but you weren't hopeless. No," he says, shaking his head, "far from hopeless."

Ellie steps aside as two girls career down the stairs, badminton rackets poking out of their rucksacks. She waits until they're out of earshot.

"I can't fight. I just can't do it."

"Let's talk about it," he says. "A drink? The bar on the corner should be quiet now."

A drink? God, she hopes he isn't coming on to her. Striker has always fascinated her, it's true, but in the weird way that a shark might fascinate or a member of the Mafia. She's impressed by his strength and his single-mindedness. She's never thought of him as human.

"Thank you very much, Sensei—"

"Lawrence."

A pause. "Lawrence. Thank you, but no, I can't, I have to . . ."

The door at the top of the stairs flies open as if someone struck it with a fist. Ellie and Striker look up. The man is standing there.

She puts out a hand and grabs the cuff of Striker's tracksuit as he prepares to leave.

"Yes, yes, thank you. A drink, that would be nice. Let's have a drink."

There is puzzlement in the twist of his chiseled face. He frowns as he glances at the fingers entwined in his cuff. "Sure," he says. "If you like. All right. A drink."

CHAPTER 68

Carl is blending in with a queue of people at a bus stop when his luck turns sour. Along comes Pat Mahoney. "How's it hanging?" Pat asks, his hands buried in his pockets as always. "What's Denise up to these days?"

"Hello, mate. Good to see you." Carl can't slough him off. He's known Mahoney since school days, and the poor bloke's been through some hard times. So they chat on like a couple of washerwomen, about Denise, and Pat's wife, Teresa, who died of breast cancer last year, and

Millwall's chances this season, and out of the corner of his eye Carl watches the Queen stride off out of sight, with Billy close behind.

Seeing her disappear into the distance puts Carl distinctly out of sorts, but he can't be cross with Mahoney—he's a good guy, and it can't be nice to lose your wife to cancer. No kids either. He must be lonely. They say good-bye with promises to have a drink together sometime, and Carl sets out along the high street at a run. Just when he thinks it's hopeless, he should give up and go home, he catches a glimpse of her. There she is, with her gym bag slamming awkwardly against her leg, ducking into the big leisure complex on the corner, the one where he comes sometimes on the weekends. Yes! Carl punches the air with his fist and follows.

What an evening! First, Billy the Kid. Where did that guy come from? And what's his interest in the Queen? She might have been a winning lottery ticket the way his eyes locked on her as she walked along the high street. No sign of the Kid now, though. He's probably taken off, and good thing, too. A man like him would stand out in a leisure center like a birthmark on a baby's cheek.

And speaking of standing out, what was that memory he had back there in the tube station? What Denise would call déjà vu—thinking he'd seen the Kid pick something up off the floor before. Carl scrolls in memory through the occasions when he's seen Billy on the monitors in the surveillance room, but nothing fits. It'll come, he tells himself. It'll come.

"You're the weights room, aren't you?" The young thing at the reception desk has hay-colored hair and would be pretty except for the exhaustion in her face. She has a baby, Carl knows. *Two under the age of three, poor thing,* he's heard the other ladies say. Carl feels an urge to sympathize, but he has no idea what to say. So instead, he picks up his pass and pops the question. "Listen—" There is a name tag on the right-hand side of her blouse. On her breast. He stammers as he reads the name. "Lo—Lorraine, I'd like to know—That is—"

"Ye-e-es," she says. The word comes across as a great big question mark.

"What classes are there today?"

"What sort of thing are you interested in?"

"I—I don't know really. Depends on the schedule, I guess. How it fits in with my job. What have you got at this time of day?" He glances nervously around. How long do ladies like Eleanor take to change? Denise is very quick, at least in the mornings. She lays out her work clothes the night before, and she's usually up and ready for breakfast before he's boiled the eggs. On the rare occasions that they go out in the evenings, she takes a lot longer. "Starting in the next ten minutes, say?"

It's the kind of challenge that makes Lorraine's tired eyes spark into life. "Most of the classes run on the half hour." She consults the screen. "Oh, here we are. How 'bout men's volleyball?"

"No, no. Not my thing."

"There's karate. You interested in martial arts?"

Carl feels the excitement mounting in his chest. "Is it a mixed class?"

"Uh-huh." She looks across and gives him a friendly wink. "Here," she says, tipping her chair backward and reaching to a shelf on the wall behind, "I'll get you a brochure." She hands him a sheet of paper folded lengthways, with a picture of a man in a gi on the front. SHOTOKAN KARATE, it says. LEARN THE ANCIENT ART OF SELF-DEFENSE.

Carl can hardly believe his good fortune. "Tell me," he says, "I think I've got a friend who might be in that class. Do you keep a copy of the register?"

"All on here now." Lorraine taps the screen. "Makes things a lot easier, except of course when it breaks down. Computers!" she says. "Your friend's name?"

"Have you got a Porter on your list?"

"Now, let's see. Mannix. Nichols. Patel. Yes, Porter, here it is." A customer arrives and raps impatiently on the desk with the edge of a pound coin. Lorraine ignores him. "Eleanor Porter? Would that be her?"

"Definitely not. Not unless Eleanor Porter is six-two with a shaved head. Graham Porter, that's who. Maybe he's over at Holmes Place. Listen, Lorraine, if I wanted to sign up for karate, would I do that with you?"

"Oh, no." The exhaustion drops back into her features again. "No, registration is up to Lawrence Striker. He's the instructor. See, his phone number's on the brochure there. Why don't you give him a ring? Or," she says, brightening again, "just pop in and sit through a class, see if it suits. It's just over there."

Carl smiles back. He hasn't been doing a great deal of smiling for the past year or two, and the movement of his facial muscles feels awkward and unaccustomed.

When he turns away from reception, Eleanor Porter is there on the other side of the room, with a long purple belt knotted at the front of her gi. The first impression of crispness is sullied by the fact that one of her sleeves is shorter than the other.

She is huddled in conversation with a young Paki. Too pretty a face, in Carl's humble opinion. Probably a pouf. Pretty Boy points off down the corridor, and the two of them lope along into the hall.

"I won't go in," Carl tells Lorraine. "I'll just watch." He takes up position beside the porthole in the door to the gym just as the training session gets under way. The purple belts are positioned right in his line of vision, so he sees it all. Every movement she makes. The way her skin colors as she warms up. The awkward way she approaches semi-free sparring.

Carl learns all he needs to know. He learns that Eleanor Porter has strength and skill and speed, and that knowledge sends a shiver of pleasure through his belly. It's always thrilling when a woman can defend herself. Exciting, somehow. He also discovers that she doesn't have an appetite for fighting.

When Carl was growing up in Millwall, there was a lad who was something of a local legend. Can't forget a name like that: Jonny Pitcher. Can't forget the face, either. Jonny Pitcher was small and wiry, with silky hair and a sunny smile. In spite of his innocent looks, he had a streak of naked aggression. He was the unchallenged star of their tumble-about football matches. No opponent could stand against Jonny's tackles. Then one day, a group of lads from Lewisham tried to take the ball. When Carl and his mates resisted, they started in on Jonny. Started taunting him, calling him a pouf and a wuss and a pretty boy. Jonny ignored them for a couple of minutes as the tension ratcheted up. He ignored them some more. Then two of the boys lunged, and before you could say Jack Robinson, these Lewisham lads were running for dear life and one was up and over the embankment, squelching through the mud. Jonny had been smaller and younger, but he was a weapon of mass destruction all on his own.

Jonny had real aggression. Eleanor Porter hasn't got it, Carl can tell. Which is it, he wonders? Either the aggression has been knocked out of her, or there was never any there in the first place.

So intrigued is Carl by his discoveries that he doesn't keep track of the time. He's still in the reception area, renewing his gym membership, when Eleanor Porter comes shooting out of the hall. He keeps his back to her and hopes he won't be noticed. He dives into the weights room, to give her time to change and get off home.

But when he swings out through the double doors, lo and behold, there she is on the landing with the instructor. Carl goes to duck back out of sight, but before he makes a move, she looks over her shoulder. For an awful instant, her eyes seem to look right through him and the blankness there takes him back to what she did when she was a child. Carl has lain awake at night often enough, chilled to the bone by the memory. Does she, too, sit in the dark, shivering from the horror of it? Or has the fact that she was so very young saved her? Was it water off a duck's back? Does she regard it as something from the past, nothing to do with who she is now? Is she so . . . bloodless? These are things that Carl has wondered, obsessively, over the past twenty-odd years, but now he sees the emptiness in her eyes, and suddenly he knows the answer to all of his questions.

CHAPTER 69

By the time Carl emerges from the leisure center, he is a changed man. No, that's not quite right. It's not him that has changed; it's the world. The pavements are clean and just a little shiny. The air is sweet-smelling. The pedestrians move with a fluid grace. And Carl himself? Carl has, for the first time, a searing sense of certainty. If he were a writing man, setting out to describe himself in a phrase, he would say that now, for the first time in his life, he is a man of purpose.

The sheer unbelievable coincidence is what turned him. All right, so she's gone to the leisure center, his leisure center; big deal. She might be taking a spinning class or Pilates or kickboxing. They're the trendy things, now, aren't they?

But instead of that, Eleanor Porter is training in the only sport that Carl has ever excelled at. He was a karate senior brown belt. Still is, though he's not in training now. When it comes to the Dancing Queen, this is the omen he's been waiting for. A first-class, number one, undismissable, fucking A omen. And it can mean only one thing.

Carl should take action. And he should do it soon.

CHAPTER 70

They've reached the island now—Striker insisted on driving her home—and Ellie is casting around for a suitable pub. She can't, she won't, take him home. To ask him in for a drink might suggest a level of intimacy that she's keen to avoid.

With its fresh coat of blue paint, the Lord Nelson stands out like an oasis in the desert. Ellie signals for Striker to pull over. Inside, the Lord Nelson is humming with business. The balls on the snooker table click and snap. Roberta Flack croons "Killing Me Softly" over a scratchy sound system.

Ellie slides into a banquette while Striker gets the drinks. Men in denim jackets with marked east London accents trade sporting anecdotes at the bar. "Romany Rites rides out at Doncaster," someone says. "Three to one," a man on the other side of the bar chimes in. She tunes in to a conversation between two off-duty firemen who are swapping stories about extreme weather. One of them catches her eye and raises his glass to her, and she can't resist a smile.

When Striker gets back with the drinks, Ellie struggles to find something to say. "I'm sorry, Sensei, but I've forgotten what it is you do—outside karate, I mean."

"Lawrence," he corrects her. His coat is hanging over the back of the banquette. He pats the pocket and extracts a case containing thin cigars. He takes one out and taps it on the table.

"Sorry?"

"Lawrence. My name. We're not in the dojo now." He fiddles with a match and the cigar flames into light. Striker heaves a great sigh as the smoke hits his lungs, and then he puts his elbows on the table and bends his head toward her. He pitches his voice just above a whisper, so Ellie is forced to lean forward in order to hear. "I work for the Chartered Institute of Marketing. Have done for seven years now. Surely you remember?" He launches himself into his Guinness. His Adam's apple pumps up and down as he swallows.

"Oh, yes, of course . . ."

"The CIM is a big deal, you know. We set the global standard when it comes to marketing excellence. Fifty thousand members in over one hundred countries, can you believe? We provide training and issue qualifications around the world."

"Well," says Ellie, taking a long swig of vodka and tonic, "quite a mission." The smoke from the cigar drifts toward her the way a pussycat goes for the person who hates felines. She dodges the smoke, and the firemen come back into view.

"Certainly is. You should take a look at our conference center in Berkshire. You'd be amazed at the training programs we run there: everything from Advanced Copywriting for Marketers to courses in sponsorship metrics."

"We get more rain on the island now," one of the firemen says. "And it's going to get worse. It's not global warming that's responsible; it's the skyscrapers."

"I heard that, too," the other one says, nodding somber agreement. "Did you know that the annual rainfall increases by fifty millimeters when you're downwind from a tower block?"

Ellie drags her attention back to her companion. "Sponsorship metrics?" she asks.

"Ahh," says Striker, "you've hit the nail on the head. You see, in the U.K., sponsors invest around one billion pounds a year in sporting events alone. Like the Stella Artois Tennis Championships. You've heard of them?"

She nods.

"Good girl. But what you probably haven't considered is that much of that billion pounds may be wasted, because many sponsorships are poorly planned and characterized by weak targeting. Sponsorship metrics helps companies think about the most effective way to deploy sponsorship as part of a marketing mix." Now that he has her to himself, Striker is looking more confident. This is a situation—she is a situation—that he knows how to handle.

Ellie shivers and finishes her drink.

"You're cold. Come on, let me get you another drink." He's on his feet already. He reaches out.

She places her hand over the top of the glass. "No, sit down again, Sen—Lawrence. I'm fine, I don't need another drink." What she needs is a clear head.

"Oh, come on," he says. "End of the day and all that."

Ellie watches him at the bar and wonders how she can get away without causing offense. She doesn't want to hurt his feelings. And she doesn't want any complications before the grading, that's for sure. When Striker comes back, he slides around the plush bench and edges closer to Ellie.

Behind his back, one of the firemen is gesticulating in the direction of the river. "This whole island will be submerged," he says. "There'll be nothing but that bloody tower sticking up. Can't you just see it? The light still winking away on the top?"

The other laughs. He has a good laugh. His smile is even better.

"Listen," Striker says. "About training tonight. Like I said, Ellie, I kind of lost it in there. It's been a rough week. I guess I took it out on you." He doesn't say what made it a rough week, and Ellie has an uncomfortable feeling that it might be to do with his love life. Ellie hopes he won't start on about it. Striker talks away, explaining something, barely noticing that she's not. Noticing, that is.

Ellie is still listening to the fit fireman—"Progress? You call that progress?"—and wishing she were cuddled up with Odysseus in front of reruns of *Sex and the City*. What a bad drinking companion she is!

She volunteers to replenish Striker's glass and, on impulse, orders a whiskey for herself. She sips at it while the barman is pulling a pint, and the warm glow it provides is welcome.

Striker watches her as she circles around other customers on her way back to the banquette. She sits down, takes two more gulps of whiskey, and smiles. The butterflies in her stomach fold their wings.

"You know, you should do that more often," Striker says.

"What? Go to the bar? Pay for a round? Hey, are you calling me cheap?" she asks, with a smile.

"Let your hair down, loosen up a bit. You're a real babe when you smile, you know that?"

Ellie drains the last drop of her whiskey, and gathers up her things. "I really should be going."

"Hang on a minute." His tone is peremptory. Then it softens. "I'm not having you walk out into the night on your own. Not after getting you safely all this way! Listen, can you wait a minute. Just one minute? I have to go to the men's room. I'll be right back and then I'll drive you home." He sees that she is wavering. "Please," he says, and manages a look of humility.

He returns in three minutes, with a pint of bitter in his left hand and a large tumbler of whiskey in his right. He is chuckling to himself. "You're a popular girl!" he says.

"Pardon?" She waves the whiskey away. Is he referring to the firemen?

"That bloke," he says, "at the bar." He looks around and seems startled when there's no one standing near. "I could have sworn he was right behind me. Anyway, he's an old friend of yours, hadn't seen you in ages. Wanted to know all about you—took a kind of proprietorial interest, I guess. How long had I known you? Are you happy? Were we *close*? Cheeky bugger." He pushes the whiskey back toward Ellie. "Go on, one more won't hurt."

"What did he look like?"

Striker carries on talking as if he didn't hear the question. "At first I didn't think anything of it. After all, friends do turn up out of the blue. But after three or four questions, I thought, whoa, what's going on here? Who the hell is he, anyway?"

Ellie starts gathering up her things. "I've got to get home, Lawrence," she says. "It's late. Sorry, but I've got to go."

"Ellie? Is anything wrong?" Striker takes his cigar out of the ashtray, where it has almost gone out and draws three quick puffs in succession, his mouth working to hold it in place. A fog of smoke hangs around their table. The end of the cigar flares, winking like the warning light on the top of the tower. "Hang on a minute." Striker reaches over and puts an arm around her. "You're shivering again. What's the matter?"

Ellie reaches across the table for the double whiskey and drains it at a single go.

"One more thing," Striker says. "This man by the bar. He said he had a message for you. He said to tell you that he's almost ready. He said he won't be long. Do you know what he means?"

"Excuse me," Ellie whispers. She stumbles toward the loo. As she enters the empty room, the door of a cubicle swings lazily inward. A tap gushes tepid water into a basin. A hand dryer blasts hot air out into the empty room. Ellie pushes one cubicle door open, and then the other, checking to make sure they're empty. She pushes the bin so that it blocks the main door. She runs cold water and splashes it onto her face, not even caring that her mascara streaks. The lights above the mirrors create a perpetual evening. It's a nowhere land, and she, Ellie, is a nowhere person, with nowhere safe to go and no one safe to be. Ellie stands face-to-face with her reflection. She leans closer to the mirror and touches her face with a tentative hand. She places her hands on her belly and is flooded with relief. It's still her, Ellie. The last sound of a flush dies away. The tap stops running. The hand dryer falls silent. She moves the bin that is blocking the door and pushes her way back into the busy pub and to Sensei, who is waiting to see her home.

CHAPTER 71

Carl reaches her house in record time, half jogging, half walking. Not a minute to waste. She looks as if she won't be making her way home from the pub anytime soon, but even so. Better safe than sorry. He checks that the side street is empty in both directions, and then pulls out his tackle and secures it to the top of the wall. He makes it into her garden without anyone noticing. There's a light on in the kitchen. Lately, she's taken to doing that when she goes out, but the rest of the house is dark. So is the house next door.

It's a much easier job to scale the broken wall on the party side and enter the garden of that Goth girl. (Actually, he saw her this morning, and she wasn't Goth at all. She was wearing a cute little outfit with color in it. Hardly recognized her without the makeup.) Carl tucks himself alongside the gnarled base of an old buddleia, and waits for two minutes just to make sure there's no movement inside the house. Then he swings himself up and onto the balcony. The small bolt on the doors has been pushed to for once, but it takes only one wrench to open them, and he's inside. He moves purposefully through the upstairs of Jessica's house, avoiding the clutter on the floor. He picks up a wooden chair and positions it directly beneath the roof access. It's only a matter of seconds before he's up and speeding along among the roof joists until he's directly over the Queen's bedroom.

The last time he was here, he made a huge mistake. He'd misjudged the time and suddenly Dancing Queen was home. He expected her to mess around with the hamster, as she usually does, and potter around for a while, but no, she completely broke her pattern. She threw her things on the floor and rushed straight for the stairs. He barely had time to squeeze himself into the loft and pull the ladder up behind him before she turned onto the top landing. Carl dared not move. He lay with his ear to the floor of the loft and listened. He heard her plonk herself down on the bed. He heard her moan. He heard—and this is where his heart stopped—he heard her press a button on her landline.

Carl could have kicked himself. *What a prime idiot!* He and Denise had had another of their quarrels that evening, and it was preying on his mind, so he'd used the Queen's phone and dialed home. He knew as he did it that it was stupid, that he should have used his mobile instead. But it was the fact that it was her phone that made it so attractive; the idea of using the very handset that she used was just too appealing to resist. He'd only just dialed when Eleanor Porter came in and he'd had to leg it. And it was as he was replacing the door to the loft that he realized his fatal mistake. She might press *Redial.* She did press *Redial.* Oh, my God, he heard her speaking to Denise! Denise complained to him the next day about being woken twice, first by him and then by a wrong number. Jesus! Obviously the Queen hadn't figured out what was going on, but she might have. And certainly, now, she knows that he's been coming in and out of her house like it was a candy shop.

Eleanor Porter's house. He didn't get beyond her bedroom last time. He got distracted; too many interesting things to see. This time he starts downstairs. He daren't turn on the lights, and he can't see much with the torch, but what he does see intrigues him. The house is practically empty; no carpets on the floor; hardly any furniture; a kitchen the size of a cupboard. Maybe she's moving out? Or maybe, Carl decides, she is poorer than he thought. Carl had imagined that all lawyers made a packet, but the bareness of this house suggests that maybe he was wrong.

Or perhaps she cares for herself so little that she doesn't think she's worth fixing up a house for. Maybe it would be different if she had a husband, or even a boyfriend; maybe then she'd care enough to lay down carpets and to buy some decent furniture; maybe then she'd care enough to make this house a home.

Still, Carl can't complain. One good thing about a house without much furniture, he reflects; searching it is easy-peasy. He slides the torch beam over the shelves in the alcove, and checks out the wooden box he finds there—keys; they look like house keys—and then heads straight for the rolltop desk. With a sudden give, the lid flies open and he finds what he wants. A suede-covered notebook; the one she dropped in the foot tunnel. He props his torch in one of the pigeonholes and settles down to try to solve the mystery of Eleanor Porter's life.

CHAPTER 72

The sex wasn't bad, exactly. Striker was gentler than she expected. More concerned for her pleasure. But for all the effort he put in, it was as if he had memorized a list of tweak-heres and caress-theres. None of it seemed spontaneous. It didn't leave her with that feeling of well-being that comes when the sex is truthful. Still, whatever gets you through the night, Ellie babe.

She's fine until she thinks of Will. What would he say if he found out? Will loves Ellie's reticence, her discretion. *What makes you irresistible,* he once told her, *is knowing that you're wild only for me.* If he learns that she slept with Striker just like that—not even because she fancied him, but because she was scared, because she needed someone to stay with her, to hold her, to blot out the darkness outside—Will won't want her anymore. She'll be just another of those slags to him, the ones he always despised.

Ellie turns the corner onto Hesperus Street and steels herself to walk at a measured pace. The Hellraisers are gathered again. She's not afraid, she tells herself; not at all. But if she could have reached home without encountering them, she would happily have done so.

Ellie sizes them up as she approaches. A well-built bloke with ripped jeans lounges against the front of Jessica's cottage. It's close to midnight, but as usual, he wears dark glasses. The others cluster around. They scarcely move. They must know she's approaching by the click of her heels, but they avoid looking in her direction. From time to time, they scan the skyline, as if there might be a sniper concealed on the rooftops.

Ellie has no choice but to pass by them to reach her front door. Steady now. They're only adolescents, after all. Well, all except Tull, who isn't with them this evening. He's older than the rest, in his mid-twenties, and he's the one she really wants to avoid. The way he looks at her sometimes . . .

Ellie makes herself as tall as she can. She focuses on a point in the distance and sets her mind to running through an attacking movement. She has no intention of taking them on, but it can't hurt to look as if she could.

The members of the gang shift warily, like a herd of cattle, at her approach. They change the way they stand, the side to which they lean, the angle of their hips. They straighten and take their hands out of their pockets. They have one last drag on their cigarettes and pluck them from their mouths and grind them underfoot. And while they do these things, they watch Ellie out of the corners of their eyes.

Ellie steps off the curb into the street. Bracing herself, she passes within inches of the group; she won't give them the satisfaction of seeing her move farther out of her way. A sly voice mutters something like "Hey, baby," but she reaches her front door safely. She fumbles with her key. There's a grating noise and she spins around. The insolent-looking lad with the tear in his jeans is holding a flaming lighter and laughing as Ellie spins away again and plunges into the house. Like a diver who has shot to the surface after seeing a shark, Ellie leans her back against the door and gulps in lungfuls of air.

She can still hear them, outside, their voices, harsh and low, seeping into her house. And then she sees it. A cheap envelope, thin white paper, lying on the mat. Her hands are shaking. She picks it up and props it against Odysseus's cage, and stares and stares until she steadies. Then she takes a sharp knife from the kitchen drawer and slices the envelope open.

I know what Mr. Tinkle would have thought if he'd seen you playing the slut tonight:

> *Eleanor Porter, Eleanor Porter*
> *Someone's gotta sort her*
> *And it's gonna be me.*

CHAPTER 73

Ellie is proud of herself. Sure, she was shaken last night by that nasty little note, and found it hard to sleep, but she hasn't let her lousy night defeat her. Hasn't let it carry over into her day. Instead, Ellie has managed the morning as if nothing had happened. She's seen a representative from the Lock and Key security company and arranged for the installation of an alarm. She's popped in and seen Jessica, who has pieces of fabric strewn all around the sitting room and is busy running up some new outfits. Ellie has spoken to Harriet—put her off again about the weekend—and mowed the lawn, and gone for a run.

"Achoo!" Ellie breaks into a sneeze. Loose powder kills the shine on her forehead and tickles her nose. She takes the hand mirror to the window to check the effect in the afternoon sun.

She's prepared herself for the office with painstaking care. Putting on her war paint, as her mother would say. Putting on her mask, more like. She's followed the routine religiously. Every bit of her body scrubbed and filed and moisturized. Clean underwear, of course, and a fresh suit. It's no more foolish than footballers, is it? Didn't Ariana mention to her that that gorgeous Chelsea striker wears the same boxers all the time for luck?

Ellie stands at an angle so that her features in the mirror are washed with light. The face that stares back at her has bruises under the eyes. The makeup is askew, the foundation line obvious, the powder too dense. She has hectic circles of pink on her cheeks.

With furious strokes, Ellie removes her makeup and begins all over again.

CHAPTER 74

"I left it here on Tuesday," Ellie says. "It should be ready now."

The receptionist in the medical center has watery eyes with pink rims like those of a rabbit. The line of a contact lens shows on the surface of her eye. She makes a show of fingering through the scrum of prescriptions. She sniffs. "Porter, you say?"

"Yes." Ellie stifles her irritation. "Porter, that's right."

One of the doctors wanders into reception through an inner door. The receptionist turns to greet him. They have a conversation about a file for a patient named Pataki, while Ellie restrains the urge to shout at them to hurry up. The receptionist turns back to Ellie, the smile falling away. "I'm sorry, no prescription for you."

"But you were only halfway through the pile when the doctor came in. Could you have another look?" Ellie says. "I put it in on Tuesday. Your notice says prescriptions will be ready in forty-eight hours."

"I don't suppose you sent it by post?"

"No, I didn't."

"Because the post has been quite slow lately." The receptionist rolls her eyes to one side and then the other as if trying to clear an obstacle.

"I put it through the letter box myself on my way home from work."

"I'm sorry," the woman says, shrugging her sloping shoulders. She doesn't look the least bit sorry. "Perhaps it's with one of the doctors right now. Why don't you just pop back tomorrow?" She shrugs and looks over Ellie's shoulder toward a man in a boilersuit who is standing behind her. "Next?"

At that very moment, Ellie gets the first indications of a migraine. The dull sensation in her skull. The beginning of the aura. She has to take her medication. She needs it now. She takes a step sideways that blocks the receptionist's view of the man behind. She lowers her voice and speaks slowly. "Your policy," she says, pointing with one finger toward the notice board, "promises a two-day turnaround in prescriptions. It is two and a half working days since I submitted mine. I have a migraine coming on right this very minute. I need that medication. Now, either you find that prescription for me or you locate the original request and get it filled right now." Ellie nods toward the door through which the doctor has just departed. The receptionist understands what she means, and she understands that she means it.

"One moment," she says, tight-lipped. She disappears across the office and out the other door.

The man standing behind Ellie coughs and looks away. He takes a copy of the *Sun* from under his arm, opens it with a snap, and begins to read a story about Michael Barrymore's swimming pool.

The receptionist returns, smiling; on seeing Ellie, once again, her smiles fades. "What's the prescription for?"

The receptionist scribbles down the name of Ellie's migraine medication and wanders off again. Ellie, brimming with irritation, skims the other notices posted on the board. Support groups for sufferers of cystitis, head injury, alcoholism, incontinence. For mothers of toddlers and carers for the disabled, and for the recently bereaved. Ellie tries to imagine what some of these groups must be like. A room full of people with their heads shaved and bandaged, having difficulty speaking? Or a group of alcoholics, meeting in a church hall, each one holding a glass of orange juice and dreaming about a pint? Support groups sound like a good idea in principle, but Ellie isn't sure about the practice. Is a problem shared really a problem halved? Or does putting people together multiply the problem? Does it label them: I'm not a man with a computer business and an interest in motocross; I'm an incontinent. Ellie wonders whether there is a group for her. She did have cystitis when she was in college. Perhaps they'd welcome her into that group? Or would they only admit her if she were a current sufferer, doubled over in pain?

"It doesn't make sense to me," the man in the boilersuit says. He catches Ellie's eye and looks down at the newspaper again, pointing with his forefinger to an aerial photo of a large detached house with a substantial outdoor pool. "Why would he have a pool?"

"I beg your pardon?" Ellie hasn't the faintest idea what he's talking about. "Who?"

"Barrymore, of course. Michael Barrymore, you know."

She supposes she does know. An entertainer. A television personality. She's seen him on some quiz show or other. Quite a personable chap. But now there's been some horrid scandal and someone has drowned in his pool. The *Chronicle* ran a small story on it, but the *Sun* has better access, so the *Chronicle* is playing it down.

"He doesn't swim," the man continues. "Can't even float, that's what he says."

"Perhaps his wife uses the pool. Perhaps that's why they had it installed." Ellie desperately wants to stop this conversation, but she doesn't know how.

"Miss Porter?"

She turns and the receptionist is standing there, dabbing a tissue to her left eye. She pushes a prescription across the counter toward Ellie.

Ellie mumbles her thanks and turns to go. Her head feels now as if someone has scooped half the brains out and replaced them with sand. A head injury support group, perhaps?

The man touches her arm. Ellie pulls away. "I've got to go," she murmurs.

"That's where you're wrong," the man in the boilersuit says. His tone is relaxed, conversational.

Whatever does he mean? She must go. She has to make her way home, through the cutting, through Ambassador Square and down Hesperus Street. She has to take her medication and lie down.

"They're not married anymore. Haven't been for quite some time. She doesn't live there anymore." He reaches toward her again, but Ellie backs away, mumbling apologies. She pushes the door with her shoulder and swings into the parking area, and she can still hear his voice. "So what's he doing with a pool? That's what I want to know."

Lying in the quiet of her bedroom with all the lights turned off, and Shostakovich thrumming softly through the room, a sense of isolation settles on Ellie like a shroud. Her father is long gone. Her mother loves her, in her own self-centered way, but might as well be a stranger for all she understands. Clive is a sweetie pie, and Jonathan more so, but they haven't known her for long; they're not what she'd call close friends. Nor is Ariana; Ellie feels again the disappointment of Ariana's refusal—it can't be anything else—to take her calls. Her only true friend is Harriet, but Harry is so busy these days that Ellie scarcely registers on her radar screen. They even lose her prescription at the medical center. For a moment, Ellie has a sense of herself as only thinly attached to the earth, like a spider's web that clings to a twig by its corners. The only person for whom she's really special, the person who knows her better than any other, is Will. And Will is taking his time about getting in touch.

She squeezes her eyes tightly as the lights play across her eyelids. The two tablets she's taken have distanced her from the migraine, but they haven't stopped it, and the visual disturbance, once started, will last for hours. She tries to focus on the tones of the concerto. On a humming descent, deep and mournful, like a swarm of bees who've been dulled by smoke. A series of sharp staccato strokes. A soaring passage, the music breaking free of its earlier constraints and then mellowing.

But just as the strains of the cello slide inside her head, pushing the aura farther away, the ceiling above her bed gives out a long low sigh.

Ellie peels back the covers and slides out of bed. The sound, she's sure of it, is the sound of movement in her empty loft. Not a skittery movement like a mouse; nothing so small. This was pressure, the shifting of something—or someone—heavy. Ellie reaches out and switches off her CD player. Her arms grow cold, as she stands in silence, holding her breath.

Two minutes of silence. It was nothing, she tells herself. Nothing but the house settling down for the night.

Ellie is about to roll back into bed when there's a different sort of sound. It's coming from the house next door. In Jess's house, which should be empty—there are sounds of stealthy movement. Jess distinctly said that she'd be visiting a friend—The floor, with the faintest of moans, is shifting beneath their weight.

The noise starts up again, and stops. Perhaps he's looking for something. Searching Jessica's meager belongings: the table, with its stacks of books and papers; the lumpy sofa. He's in the bedroom now, Jessica's bedroom. Silence.

Ellie holds her breath.

Her eyes flick toward the stairs. Her own front door. Locked, she's sure she locked it. Didn't she?

Still no noise.

Then it starts up again, and this time, there's a harsh scraping of wood. Opening drawers, that's what he's doing. On Jessica's black lace tops. The plums and maroons and blacks of her makeup. Her underwear.

Ellie finds herself shaking with outrage at this violation, but the soles of her feet are rooted to the rug. She is stuck here, trapped, not by any tangible threat but by her own fear and anger. She longs to rush across the room and snatch up the phone and summon the police. To dial 999 and summon an entire squad of police constables—not like those two pathetic creatures who visited her after the Peeping Tom, but real policemen with riot shields and gas masks and submachine guns—who will burst out of the police van and batter their way into the house and pin him to the floor.

The searching stops. There's a crash as something is swept off a surface and running footsteps. Ellie picks up a chair and wedges it under her doorknob. She crawls back into bed and pulls the duvet up around her ears.

CHAPTER 75

Clive is in his glass-fronted cubicle, leaning forward into the screen and typing furiously, when Ellie skitters into the *Chronicle* offices.

"Clive?"

He types a few more words, slams his hands onto his knees, and whirls to face her. "Yo, Eleanor." He leans back in his chair and studies her face. "My dear, you look—would rattled be the right word? Anything I should know?"

The case against speaking up tumbles through Ellie's mind. What if he thinks she's making it up? What if he dismisses her as self-dramatizing and therefore unreliable? But she can't go on pretending that everything's all right. And, oh, the desire to confide in someone. Someone without an ax to grind.

She manages to give a plain account of the stalking. No embellishments at all. She simply lists the incidents: the silent phone calls, the notes, the man in the garden, the horribly suggestive message delivered to Striker at the bar. "I've seen him following me at least a dozen times, and God knows, there must be other occasions when he manages to stay out of sight. And he's been in my house. Creeping around. Touching my things. Using my telephone."

"Using your telephone? How do you know?"

"I redialed. I was connected to an unknown number."

"Did you make a note of it?"

It's so blindingly obvious that Ellie can't speak, stunned by her own stupidity. All she can do is shake her head, no. She was too frightened to do anything as rational as noting down the number.

Clive begins pacing up and down, an almost impossible feat in the cramped office. "The police," he declares, stopping suddenly in his tracks. "They must be informed."

"I called when he broke into my garden. They were useless. Worse than useless. I need to find some way of dealing with this on my own."

"Has he threatened you?"

It's the wrong question. "He says he'll sort me out, Clive. He says it won't be long. What can that be but a threat? The worst of it is not knowing what he wants. And anyway, just being followed is horrible in itself. Not being able to use my garden anymore. Not having any privacy. Feeling self-conscious. Having to think every day, every moment: Is he behind me right now?" She clutches at his sleeve. "Why do I need any further threat? Look at me, Clive, I'm a wreck!"

"Hush. Hush." Clive seems almost as distressed as Ellie is as he envelops her in a hug. "What are you doing here at the *Chronicle* when you're feeling like this? You must take some time off, little Elle."

Ellie hugs him back. "Oh, Clive, that's so sweet, but I've only just started this job. I can't be taking time off already. People will think I can't handle it. And anyway, I don't want you to have to stay in my place. What about Lily and Rose?"

He is adamant. "Their mum's getting them a DVD this evening. They won't even notice I'm not there. Take a taxi," he says. "Put it on the office account. I've told you before, you shouldn't travel on your own so late in the evening."

"No need, Clive. I'll take the DLR."

"But surely—"

"I don't like taxis."

She can see by the way his twinkle retreats that Clive is taken aback. But what can she say? She daren't tell him that the last time she tried to get into a taxi, she was gripped by a fear that the driver might, just might, turn out to be her stalker. She couldn't risk it.

"I'm sorry, Clive."

"For what?" he asks. His kindly face is wrinkled with concern.

For landing you with extra trouble. For refusing your kind, kind offer of help. For being a nuisance, instead of the cool, calm, and competent person I'd love to be. She lands a kiss on his cheek. "Just sorry," she says.

Ellie does a quick tour of the newsroom, weaving between the half-empty desks, before she pushes off. She has seen Ariana twice in the past few days, but always in the distance and always surrounded by other people. They've never managed to speak.

Ariana's diary is sitting on her desk. Ellie plonks a Post-it on the cover and writes a quick message. *I need a decision about Dorset by tomorrow.* She hesitates. It's true—she does need a decision—but it sounds too assertive. *Please, Ariana?* she adds and heads for home.

CHAPTER 76

Ariana was an only child. Her father used to play at rugby with her when she was little, with wild tackles and equally wild laughter on the back lawn, and rugby is still her favorite game. But even Ariana has had enough. Not *another* piece on Jonny Wilkinson, she'd said to her editor. But yes, another piece; and that's why she has spent the past two hours in the library, trying to find a fresh angle on the twenty-four-year-old who is said to have the best chance of bringing England to glory in the 2003 Rugby World Cup.

She swings into her chair, and the first thing that strikes her is the note from Eleanor. *Hell and high water!* A weekend with Ellie had seemed a more attractive idea when it was somewhere in the future. Besides, things have changed since they made that tentative agreement. Life has become—Ariana can't suppress a grin—more complicated.

Better get it sorted.

Eleanor isn't on the foreign desk. She isn't in the ladies'. She isn't in the caf. Clive is in his office, but Ariana's question triggers a grim tale.

"A stalker?" A theatrical shiver. "Oooh, Clive, it's our very own *Scary Movie.*"

"Sit down here." Clive offers her his chair and perches himself on the corner of the desk. The room is little bigger than a cloakroom.

"What's she going to do?" Ariana asks.

"I don't know. I suggested she take taxis to and from work, but she refused. Says she doesn't like 'em." He picks up a fat, black Waterman pen, and twirls it around his knuckles. "How well do you know Eleanor?"

Ariana glances at the photo of two little curly-haired girls on the shelf above his desk. They're wearing pastel-colored fleeces and patterned wellies. She shrugs. "We've talked a few times."

"Did you know—?" Clive pauses and lowers his voice, pulling Ariana's attention back from the photo. "Did you know she had a breakdown?" Gratified by the girl's sudden interest, he fills in the details. He learned about it from a friend who worked in the same practice as Eleanor when she was taken ill. He doesn't know about William DeQuoyne, but he tells her the rest.

"And you think this might have some connection with her story about stalking?"

"Have you ever seen a man following her?"

Ariana shakes her head. Her ponytail swings back and forth.

"Neither have I."

Ariana returns to her desk to draft the piece on Jonny Wilkinson. *While the others are taking a day off, Wilkinson, England's white hope, returns to the discipline that makes him the tops. . . .*

Her phone rings. *Eleanor P,* it says on the screen.

Automatically, Ariana answers. She hears Ellie's voice, anxious and strained. "Hello? Hello? Ariana?" Ariana says nothing. After an instant's hesitation, she switches off the mobile and returns to her work.

CHAPTER 77

Nikki and Guy, the diarists—greener than Ellie herself and still bursting with bright ideas—are lounging against Ellie's desk that evening when she slides into the *Chronicle*. They jump to attention. "We've been told to talk to you about our plans for the column," Guy says.

"Talk away." Ellie relieves herself of her scarf and briefcase, and turns on her monitor as she listens.

"We're going to transform the diary," Guy declares.

Nikki interrupts. "We're going to build in long-running narratives."

"Overarching themes. That way, don't you see, we'll get different stories from week to week and continuity, too."

"You've got some examples of these themes?" Ellie asks. She wishes they would move away from her desk so she could take her seat.

"The central theme," Nikki says, moving closer to Ellie and peering at her through sharp black specs, "will be the changing landscape of London." She makes gestures toward the other side of the office where the windows reveal the distant twinklings of the river. "That's where we'll plant all the gossip about local movers and shakers. Right, Guy?"

"Absolutely," says Guy. "We'll take the behind-the-scenes people who are shaping London and shine a spotlight on them."

"Sounds intriguing," Ellie says. "But you know, it's not up to me." It's up to the editor, and Ellie would lay bets that said editor will take a we-shall-see approach. The diarists won't actually hear the phrase "too highbrow," but everyone who pitches new ideas has to be braced for the *Chronicle* chorus: *Our readers won't go for that.*

Having no wish to snuff out Nikki and Guy's enthusiasm, Ellie merely alerts them to the legal pitfalls and then, at last, gets down to work. The time she's spent with the diarists makes for a late start and a later finish. It is well past ten when she rolls up the front page and secures it with a rubber band. *Legal OK,* she scrawls on a Post-it, adding her initials and then, as an afterthought, a flourish. She is threading her way through the empty newsroom toward the legal office when the phone on her desk strikes an insistent note. She trots back to the desk and puts the receiver to her ear.

"*Chronicle.* Legal desk."

"Eleanor Porter?" The voice is soft and clearly male. "Eleanor Porter, it is you, isn't it?"

"Who—who is this?"

"It's Oliver. Oliver Nesbit. Don't you remember me?"

"Oliver! Yes. Yes, of course I do." Remembers him with startling clarity, in fact. The dark-fringed eyes. The nose that might have taken a blow in rugby. The face that exudes good humor when he smiles, and falls back into watchfulness when he doesn't.

"So, Eleanor, what have you been up to during the past few years?"

What has she been up to? "Oh, this and that. I've moved to the Isle of Dogs—you know, the Canary Wharf area. And I've switched to media law." She doesn't mention the months she spent in hospital. She doesn't mention William DeQuoyne. "And you?" She wishes she could bite the question back. For a second she'd forgotten about the police investigation.

But Oliver seems not at all nonplussed. "Listen," he says, "you'll have seen that story about me and some photographs, yes?"

A relief. Ellie doesn't have to pretend she doesn't know. "Yes," she says. "I've seen it."

"It's a complete fabrication. A fantasy."

He is so calm, so confident. Surely, Ellie thinks, if he were guilty of the things at which the paper hinted, he would sound ashamed.

"I can't tell you how awful it's been," Oliver says, lowering his voice. "The police asking questions—again and again. My wife,

Katrina—she's been interviewed three times. Can you imagine what it's like knowing that everyone around you, neighbors and so forth, they've all read the papers and are thinking: *Hmmn. No smoke without fire?* I wouldn't be surprised if our nanny gave in her notice. The whole thing is outrageous."

"Poor Oliver. It's all very well believing that justice will triumph in the end, but in the meanwhile—Look, do you mind? There are some things I still don't understand. Like, your daughter was having a bath, right? A perfectly normal family activity. I can't for the life of me see why—"

He interrupts. "It's the way things are going now, haven't you noticed? Soon there'll be no such thing as private life."

"So you're telling me there's nothing else to explain the attentions of the police? No other photos, no downloads, nothing?"

"One minute." There's a rustling noise. Then a tapping. Then the whoosh of a lighter. He has lit a cigar. "What you have to understand, Eleanor, is how easy it is for outsiders to misconstrue what goes on in a family. You see it all the time. A father smacks a hysterical toddler in Waitrose and next thing you know, he's a child beater. Things get blown up out of proportion. Taken out of context."

Taken out of context. "Do you mean to say that something did happen? An innocent incident that might look sinister from the outside?" For a long moment, all she hears is the wet smack of lips as Oliver puffs on his cigar. Then, suddenly, urgently, he begins to speak again.

"Look, Eleanor, it was years ago, for God's sake. I was young, just out of university. Those so-called adult sites were popping up everywhere. I'm no different from any other chap. I glanced at them from time to time. That's all."

Ellie is perplexed. She's sorry for Oliver, but something doesn't gel here. Looking at pornography isn't a sin. It's not even illegal. But still . . . "So what kind of sites are we talking about? Photographs of children?"

"Don't be ridiculous!"

Ellie doesn't want to be ridiculous; not at all. What she wants is to drop the whole sordid subject, to leave the *Chronicle* offices and go home. But something in the vehemence of Oliver's response makes her continue. "All the models were over the age of eighteen?"

"Oh, come on, grow up, Eleanor. Have you seen those sites? Those chicks don't post their ID, you know. Who knows what age they are? College girls, they're called; they could be any age up to seventy, for all I know."

"Or anywhere down to twelve?"

He snorts. "That's it. If you're determined to judge—"

"Hang on," Ellie says. "This isn't about judging you. I'm just trying to figure it out. The police wouldn't show this much interest unless there was some indication of a serious offense. Would they?" She hesitates before putting the question. "There's a rumor, Oliver, nothing more than that . . . Do you have any links at all to child pornographers?"

"Shit!" For a second, she thinks he is going to hang up. Then he pitches his voice just above a whisper, so Ellie has to strain in order to hear. His voice is silky. It's the tone he uses on his television broadcasts. "Let's be honest, here, Eleanor. Is there anyone who doesn't have a murky secret? Something from their past that they feel ashamed of, something that has nothing whatsoever to do with who they are now? Surely even you, Eleanor Porter, have some— indiscretion, shall we say?—that you'd rather not have aired in public?"

Eleanor's heart has begun to thud. He sounds suddenly so confident. So sly. Is he threatening her? Has he found out something? Does he know about her father? She's got to end this conversation. She's got to get away.

"What do you want, Oliver? Why have you rung me?"

"Why wouldn't I want to renew my acquaintance? You're a lovely lady, Eleanor, and it's been too long."

The crude flattery enrages Ellie. "Cut the crap," she says.

Something catches in Oliver Nesbit's throat. There's a rustling and then a cough. "Please, Eleanor," he says. "Please, just tell me what they've got on me. Your journalist is like a dog with a bone. I'm not asking you to use your influence with him or anything like that. Not asking you to suppress the story."

"As if I could!"

"Exactly. All I'm asking is for you to let me know what he turns up. So I can prepare myself. Emotionally, I mean. Against the shock."

"Why don't you simply tell the truth, Oliver? Then there would be no shock. Nothing to expose."

"But I explained already, Eleanor. I'm innocent. If I can just have some time to weigh up new accusations before they're published, I can prove it."

Now Ellie knows what he is up to. Just before they run the story— it always happens—the journalists will come to Oliver for an admission or a denial. He wants to be in a position to discredit enough of their material to swing things his way in the press conference that follows. He wants to wriggle out of the accusations, and he wants Ellie to help him. It's as much as her job is worth, and he knows it. She picks up her document case.

"Oliver, please don't ask this. I'm sorry, really I am, for the horrid situation you're in. If there's anything else I could do to help, I would. But I can't do this." She puts the phone down on his flurries of protest. Ellie feels every inch the night lawyer, and is not at all certain that she likes it.

CHAPTER 78

Ellie is just emerging from the legal office where she dropped the front page when her phone rings again. She hesitates. Is Oliver going to hound her? It's almost half-past ten. She doesn't have to answer. But what if—?

She dashes back, sweeps the receiver off its cradle, and puts it to her ear.

"*Chronicle.* Legal desk."

Nothing. Not Oliver, then. In the silence, her heart begins to stutter. "Will?" Who else would it be, this time of night? He knows where she works and he knows when her shift finishes. He'll be in a bar by Fisherman's Walk, looking out over the North Quay, with a gin sling in his hand. She'll join him there. She can see herself standing next to him, leaning over a railing, with her hair hanging loose and the breeze from the water lifting it around her face. Instinctively, Ellie reaches up and begins to disentangle the band that holds her hair back.

"Will, where are you?" No answer. The line is crackly. Long-distance calls used to sound like that when her father called home from Africa, as if the voice had to hack through jungle to get home. A few more muffled syllables. She can't distinguish the words but there's a playful lilt—perhaps, more precisely, a note of mischief. The excitement fades: not Will, then, after all. William DeQuoyne doesn't do silly.

She finally succeeds in working the hairband off and shakes her hair free. The voice is obscured by static still, the teasing tone the only detail she can be sure of. Aaah, funny voices: it must be Tony Mannix. He's always messing around.

"Tony? Bad line, I can hardly hear you. Why don't you call me back on my mobile?"

She's beginning to make out the odd word. And *odd* is right. This isn't amusing, not anymore. "Tony?" Muffled noises. "Come on, I know it's you."

Suddenly the line is clear as a bell. The crackling is gone. For an instant, all she hears is silence. Then: "Are you sitting down?" he asks.

"No." Ellie can't keep the uncertainty out of her voice. "I'm standing by my desk, getting ready to leave. And that's precisely what I'm going to do if you don't stop messing around. Come on, Mannix, what are you up to?"

There's a laugh and Ellie doesn't like it. It's a sly, insinuating laugh. She doesn't like it at all. She casts a swift glance around the newsroom at the empty desks and the computer screens poking up like tombstones.

The voice is slow and low and deeply accented. Rural, by the sound of it. Eleanor isn't very good on accents, but she knows now from the timbre of the voice that this isn't Tony. She would hang up, except that something compels her to hear him out.

"What am I up to, my lovely? Do you really want to know?"

For the first time, Ellie catches her breath. "Who is this?" she asks. She despises herself for the fear that rings through her words.

"This is Steve, and you sound very sexy."

Steve? Steve? Does she know any Steve? She can't think. Her brain won't work.

"Steve wants you, honey, so badly, and he—"

Ellie flings the phone down. It scoots sideways off the cradle. She snatches it up again and replaces it, then leans her weight on the receiver, pressing it down.

It rings again. Ellie snatches her hands off. She begins to back away. But the answering device clicks in and the sly voice fills the air. "Hello, honey, I know you're there; I know you're listening. Pick up, there's a good girl. I'm waiting for you, and I've got my friend in my hand. You sound so sexy. Horny, too. I bet you're horny, aren't you? Why don't you help me?"

A long pause. Idiotically, she holds her breath so that he can't hear her.

"I'm waiting, honey. Playing hard to get only gets me hotter."

Another pause.

"All right, then, if that's how you want it. I've got other things in mind for you, but they can surely wait."

Click.

Ellie stares at the phone for the best part of a minute before she can bring herself to move. For the first time, as she walks to the lift, she feels fear dragging at her footsteps. Until now, the quiet of the late-evening corridors has been a comfort to her. She's enjoyed the fantasy of queen of the castle. Now there's another side to solitude.

In spite of herself, as the lift bumps to a stop and the doors glide open, Ellie trembles. What if there's someone waiting for her, inside? Steve, maybe, with his friend in his hand? She peers into the corners of the lift before she can bring herself to enter. The lift begins its descent.

One elephant, two elephant . . . What? The lift comes to an unprecedented halt on the eleventh floor. Ellie pumps the button for the foyer, but the doors glide open. Pale orange walls are the first thing she sees before a blue carpet and a reproduction Gauguin slide into view. Ellie edges forward, stopping the door with one hand, and pokes her head out. At one end of the compact corridor is a radiation symbol. At the other, a heavy glass door is slowly swinging closed.

Ellie pulls herself back inside and stabs at the controls. The doors remain stubbornly agape. She huddles against the back wall. The warm light from the corridor floods in and she feels as if she's in a showcase. Like an entry in a freak show. Here she is, folks, the little lady in the lift. Step right up. Come and get her.

There's a shushing sound in the corridor, and Ellie is about to press the alarm button, when the doors close and the lift shudders and moves off. Ellie collapses against the wall, and tries to control her trembling. Three elephants, four elephants . . . The lift slides to a stop on the ground floor. The open foyer, the lights, the security guards. The relief!

She pauses next to one of the security desks. "Evening," she says.

"Evening, miss."

And what if something had happened, she thinks? What if there had been a—a—an incident—in the lift? There are security cameras hidden in the lifts, she knows. How long would it be before someone came to her aid? How long might she be trapped with a madman before a guard would notice, and make his way up to the eleventh level, and prize open those doors? Could be minutes. Could be hours. Could it?

"Do you mind if I ask you a question?"

The uniformed woman behind the high desk has neatly cropped black hair and a pale, pudding face. She nods a yes, but her eyes are guarded.

"If there is an emergency—in the lifts, I mean—would it be you who would respond? Or is there a team of guards—like a SWAT team or something—whose job that is?"

"What sort of emergency, miss?" She speaks like a pupil confronted with a trick question.

"Oh, just, anything. A mugging, say. An attack of some kind."

"Oh, that." The guard is relieved. She's been desperately trying to recall the terrorist incident routine. "Yes, miss, interpersonal violence? The first thing we'd do? We'd ring the police. And then we'd call the main security center and they'd send men over on the double."

"And the main security center is—how far away?"

"I'm sorry, miss, I'm not allowed to say."

As Ellie walks out of the building into the twinkly lights of the square, the tower trembles behind her. The vibrations can be felt in her spine. The bolts that hold the steel cladding on the outsides of the tower begin to pop. Slowly, one by one, gigantic sheets of steel peel away, and crash like thunder to the ground. The skeleton of the tower—from its mail rooms and maintenance bays to its penthouse reception rooms—is exposed.

Hunched at their desks doing overtime, office workers run their hands through their hair or snatch paper from the printer; they haven't yet noticed that they're laid open to the night. Unaware that the tower is crumbling, cleaners and caretakers, handymen and porters, couriers and packers, and yes, security guards, go about their duties. For the first time Ellie recognizes that the nighttime tower is crawling with people. Men and women, silent and purposeful, on every floor: in lifts, riding up while she goes down and down while she goes up; behind office doors; under her feet, above her head. They're hidden behind the tombstone computers, behind doors in corridors with Gauguin reproductions on the wall. They've just stepped into the lift, just slid out of sight behind a glass door, just exited the building. The scent of their aftershave, the squeak of their shoes, the trace of moisture from their breaths, lingers. The air is thick with their absence. So many people. So many places to hide.

Ellie is no longer alone in the nighttime tower, and it isn't a comforting thought.

CHAPTER 79

The cottage thing has been stressful. Ellie can't let Harriet down; she can't go there alone; and Ariana clearly—there's no escaping the truth any longer—isn't coming. Ellie must have been pondering this problem all night, because she woke up suddenly this morning with the perfect solution. Now it's evening. Ellie is meeting Harriet in an hour's time, and she can't wait to tell her what she's decided.

On the way out of the house, she bumps into Jessica, who is wearing a lime green skirt and hat and looks terrific. A complete change from the deadpan Goth. She's bursting with a secret; something she's arranged herself, is all she'll say.

You and me both, Ellie thinks. "I hope it's something marvelous. Call me if you need me, promise?"

Jess blows a kiss and dances off.

Ellie arrives at the Trafalgar Tavern half a minute after Harriet. The interior of the pub is striking, with dark wooden paneling and elaborately framed oil paintings on walls of pillar-box red. Watching as Harriet maneuvers across the room, Ellie observes that her friend is heavier, her face a little fuller, her hips more matronly. She seems tired. But tiredness doesn't stop her from beating a group of tourists to a table overlooking the river. Harriet arranges herself on a wooden chair with an air of satisfaction while Ellie goes to the bar. She fetches a large glass of Chablis and some cashews for Harriet, and on impulse orders a pint of Flowers for herself.

Fatigue hasn't dimmed Harriet's inquisitiveness, either. "What's this?" she demands as Ellie sets down the drinks.

"What's what?"

"I've never ever seen you with a beer before." The tone is almost accusing. "What's come over you?"

Ellie laughs. "I saw the pump and I've never tasted Flowers and, I thought, 'Well, why not?' Simple as that." She takes a sip. "It's good. You should try it." She lifts her glass. "Cheers, Harry." Ellie is buoyed by her decision. The terrors of the previous night—even Oliver Nesbit's menacing questions—have receded. She doesn't object when Harriet leans forward across the table and begins to quiz her.

"So? How's the job? Have you been taking good care of the *Chronicle* for me?"

"Do you know, Harry, I like it. I mean really like it. The first couple of shifts, I was anxious about being wrong-footed. You know how it is."

Harriet softens. "Anybody would be nervous. But I spoke to Clive just last week—"

"Checking up on me?"

"Don't be silly. I bumped into him and the girls at a children's birthday party. We only had a moment, what with apple juice spills and magicians pulling bunnies out of hats, but Clive said you seemed to be settling in. He mentioned there'd been some challenges, though. What exactly did he mean?"

"Not sure." Ellie shrugs. "This so-called pedophile scandal—you know, the barrister and the baby thing—has been a headache." She looks swiftly around to make certain no one's listening and then leans forward. "He rang me, can you believe it?"

"Who, Oliver Nesbit? At the paper?" Harriet looks scandalized.

"Late last night. He wanted to talk. It was hard to shake him off."

"So what did he want?"

"Advance warning of stories we'd be running. No, no, no; calm down." In her anxiety, Harriet has scooped up a whole handful of cashews and tossed them in her mouth. "Of course I won't do it. Though I must say, Harriet, I do feel sorry for the poor chap. One slip, and he stands to lose everything."

"It's a rather big slip. If you had children—"

"All right. Point taken." The set of Harriet's jawline tells Ellie to change the subject. "Look, Harry, the important thing is that the job is going fine. Just fine." She resists the sudden sensation of trembling in her spine. The sound of sheets of steel crashing onto the ground. "I've handled several big stories on my own now, without any major problems. As a night lawyer, if I do say so myself, I'm doing okay."

Harriet shakes another handful of cashews into her palm and considers. So what's wrong here, she wonders. Ellie talks the talk, but she looks as if she hasn't slept in days and there's a hysterical edge to her good humor. Still, no point in pushing. Softly, softly.

"I told you you'd be perfect, didn't I?" Harriet says. "How about your colleagues? Clive is a lamb, wouldn't you say?"

Ellie doesn't answer. She is staring intently at a group of workmen who have taken up position near the bar.

"Ellie?" Harriet tries a stage whisper. "Ellie! What's so interesting? Surely you've seen a group of warehousemen before?"

One of the men wears a fleece with a forest scene running across the front. Ellie can't tear herself away. "Sssh. Harry, please." But just then, the man glances toward the bar and she sees that his nose is long and narrow and his hair is receding at the temples. He's not her man at all.

Harriet taps the bottom of her glass on the table. "Ellie, I asked you a question!"

"I'm sorry, Harriet. I thought I recognized someone. What did you ask?"

"I asked about Clive, what a sweetheart he is. But what I really want to know is whether there are any interesting men in the office." The question is accompanied by a wink.

Ellie grins. "Well," she says, looking forward to drawing it out, "there may be one. And I've had a brilliant idea. I'm thinking of bringing him with me to Dorset for the weekend. Ariana, the girl I told you about, is kind of busy." What Ellie doesn't say about her brilliant idea is that ever since it bounced into her head this morning, she's felt safe again. Before, when she was with Will, his love always made her feel as if she'd been wrapped up in a fleecy blanket; made her feel secure. It will be like that again. No more reason to feel afraid. It is the perfect answer to everything—to Harry and the cottage, to Ariana's reluctance, and to that horrible, horrible stalker.

Harriet is bursting with curiosity. "Go on, then, who is he? What's he like? I suppose he's one of the legals?"

"No, not at all. He's an acting consultant for the magazine. But he's gorgeous. Just sitting opposite him in Starbucks made me feel weak at the knees."

"Ho, ho. Now, this sounds like a go-er. Has he asked you out yet?"

"No-o. That's my fault. I wasn't particularly warm to him at first, you see, and I expect he's afraid to make the first move. Do you think I ought to take the bull by the horns and ring him up?"

"Now, hang on a minute, Ellie. Let's just get one thing straight. This fellow you're talking about. He's a nice fellow, right? A decent sort of chap? And unattached? When it comes to picking men, you know, your track record is abysmal."

"Oh, he's unattached, all right. His wife left him a couple of weeks ago. Ran off with the baby and half the contents of the house." She can't hold back any longer. "Can't you guess who it is?" She sees Harriet's features flood with suspicion and laughs. "It's Will, that's who. He's single again and we'll have a romantic weekend at the cottage."

"With that creep William DeQuoyne? For Christ's sake, Ellie! How can you even consider it, after the way he treated you? He strung you along and then he left you high and dry. How can you ever trust him again?"

A lump of dread rises in Ellie's throat. Oh, God, what if Harry's right? It could happen. Will could take his wife back. Ellie might be his beloved, but he is married to Kim. And he was unable to break with her before. Ellie gulps a mouthful of Flowers. She won't, she won't, fall prey to this negative thinking. It's what stops her from going after the things she wants. And this—Will—is the thing she wants most.

"He's changed, Harry. Believe me, I can tell. Before, there was an issue of loyalty. Even you must see that there was some—some—integrity about his refusal to abandon his wife and child. But now it's different. Kim has dumped him. He's on his own. And where is he first thing? Hanging around my office, that's where."

"You said he was a consultant," Harriet protests. "He might have bumped into you by accident."

"There are no accidents," Ellie shoots back. "Not where Will and I are concerned."

Harriet heaves herself to her feet and pulls her bag onto her shoulder. "I've got to go. The nanny'll be waiting. But you just think about one thing, Ellie. William DeQuoyne is trouble. You don't need another breakdown. Just take my advice and forget it."

Ellie grabs Harriet's arm. "Harry, Harry, I promise you, it's all right. What you don't realize is that I've changed, too. I'm different. Stronger. Forget the cottage and the weekend in Dorset. I don't need it. This—William DeQuoyne—is what I need." She stands and gives a resisting Harriet a fervent hug. "Don't worry, Harry. I'll still look after your car."

"All right," Harriet says. A second hug, this one more heartfelt. "But just be careful, Ellie. You're very dear to me." A pause. "You said he hasn't rung. Are you planning to make the first move?"

"Oh," Ellie says, dropping a few coins onto the table, "I couldn't do that."

But even as she says it, she feels her heart soar.

CHAPTER 80

Ellie knows now what she must do. Her hand shakes from excitement, not from fear, as she fumbles with the key to her house. She steps over the sill and closes the door gently behind her. Inside, the house is pitch-black. The lamp she left on must have burned out.

Ellie reaches for the light switch and is stopped in her tracks by a thump. A hard thump, like a staff hitting a plank. It seemed to come from the direction of the desk, but she can't make out anything beyond the rocking chair and the desk itself.

Ellie waits for a full minute. There are no more troubling sounds. Impatiently, she flicks the light switch. "Odysseus?" she calls. There's no response.

She flicks the light switch, but the darkness remains. Bugger it. The soft sound of something brushing against fabric. Oh, God, she hasn't made a mistake and let Widget in, has she? She did that once before and he almost gave Odysseus a heart attack. "Widget?" she calls, quietly still. She whistles softly. "Puss, puss, puss?" No padding footsteps. No soft fur rubbing around her legs. Nothing.

Thump! She whirls and peers with dilated pupils into the dark cavern of the sitting room. Again, the pounding of wood on wood. And movement this time: the bentwood rocking chair tips forward, grinding on the floorboards.

"Who is it?" Ellie's voice is reedy. "Who's there?"

No answer. But the chair picks up speed, the rockers grinding away, and Ellie gets a grip on herself just as she begins to feel a cold trickle of terror. The rocker from hell? What bollocks! She gives her head a sharp shake and races blindly in the direction of the fuse box.

She bashes her leg against a corner of the kitchen cupboard. Hops the rest of the way on one foot, clutching the injured shin. The pounding of the rockers drives her on. She yanks the cover of the fuse box down and runs her thumb beneath the switches, snapping them up. The lights come on. There's instant recognition.

"Kim!" she exclaims.

Mrs. DeQuoyne tilts her face and looks at Ellie with cold black eyes as if she were a curiosity in an aquarium.

"So you do know me," she says. She doesn't sound surprised.

They've never met before, not face-to-face; though after Will left, Ellie was wildly curious about Kim. Ellie stood outside their house for an hour, watching as Kim flitted across her line of vision, as she drew the William Morris curtains, as she maneuvered the baby's cot out of the car. And once, in desperation, Ellie phoned the house. She listened to Kim's voice on the telephone (*Hello? Hello? Who's there?*) and remembers it as being husky with sleep. She imagined that in real life Kim would have a smoky, sexy way of speaking. Instead, without the telephone between them, Kim DeQuoyne merely sounds businesslike and bold.

Now, Kim's eyes are narrowed behind thick, stubby lashes. She looks Ellie up and down.

Ellie tries to get away from that appraising gaze. It's only then that she notices what should have been her first concern.

"How did you get in?"

Kim's strong-looking hands are gripping the curved arms of the rocking chair so tightly that her knuckles are bone white.

"Where is he?" she demands.

Ellie ignores her. She races through the house, switching on lights as she goes. She ignores the chaos—the contents of her desk strewn about, the drawers from her bedside table turned out on the bed—until she finds what she is looking for. In the lavatory, the sash window is pushed up as far as it will go, and there's a streak of dirt on the toilet lid.

Ellie snaps on more lights until the house is clinically bright. She is shaking as she confronts Kim.

"You've broken into my home. How dare you!" Ellie may have

stood outside the DeQuoyne residence on one occasion, but her intrusions never went this far.

Behind the rocking chair, the shelves have been swept clean. Ellie's books have been thrown to the ground, their spines cracked open, their pages splayed; the carved figures her father brought her back from Africa, the file that holds her bank statements, her wooden boxes, all are lying in a heap. But Ellie has eyes for only one item. Kim holds Ellie's notebook in her lap and she is leafing through it.

Kim shakes her head. "You're wrong about that," she says. "The door was unlocked. In fact, it was ajar. Very careless, I thought. I just walked in. Thought you might welcome me, since we have so much in common."

Kim's self-certainty is so brazen it's clichéd. She is cool as a cucumber. Bold as brass. "He's not here," Kim says. "So where is he?"

"Who?" Ellie reaches for the notebook. Kim snatches it away. They grapple and suddenly—not before time—the penny drops. "Do you mean—?"

"Of course," Kim says. "Who else? My husband, Will."

"But you left him! You took your daughter and left."

With Kim's sardonic laughter beating in her ears, Ellie crosses the room and turns on the spotlights. The light bounces off Kim, and for the first time Ellie sees that her face has been hollowed out.

"William said you were naïve." Kim is more bitter now than bold. "He told you that I left? No way. One minute we were planning a summer holiday and the next minute, he was gone. He's done it before, you know. Walked out on me." She smiles broadly, though Ellie senses it's an effort. "But make no mistake. He always comes back."

Ellie's heart is hammering in her chest. She needs to get away. . . . "Look," she says, "I'm sorry you're so unhappy. Really I am. And I know you have reason to be angry with me, but believe me, I never meant to hurt you. Whatever I've done to you in the past, you can't break in here like this, causing chaos, rifling through my things." Ellie's on the verge of tears now. "Please, I think you should go."

Kim blinks with surprise and looks around. "Breaking in. You mean this?" She gestures toward the mess on the floor. "But the place was a tip when I got here. And I didn't break in. The door was open;

I already told you." Kim heaves herself to her feet like a much older woman. "I'll leave with pleasure the minute you tell me where he is. And not before."

"Why should I know where Will has got to?"

It's a bluff. Suddenly, thrillingly, Ellie knows. He's only a mile or so away in West India Quay. Will's friend James, who is often away, has a flat there and Will keeps the spare key. Will said once that every married man needs a hidey-hole, by which she understood that the flat was a secret to which Kim was never privy. Ellie went there with him countless times.

Kim steps forward. Her face is contorted with righteous anger. "Because," she hisses, leaning into Ellie's face, "you've stolen him away from me, you scheming little bitch." And she pulls her arm back and delivers a slap so hard that Ellie's head snaps to the side.

CHAPTER 81

Ellie's attention was snagged on Kim's words. She wasn't prepared for the blow. Her head snapped to the right and pain like an electric shock lanced down her neck. But it is not the blow, nor the pain, to which she reacts; it is Kim's words . . . *You've stolen him away.*

Yes! Ellie thinks. Yes! She doesn't retreat. She smiles. She steps forward. She stretches her arms in front of her as if warding off attack. She speaks in a tone of sweet reason. "Listen," she says. Kim's mouth is twisted into a hard line and the planes of her face bulge with fury.

Ellie advances in two long strides. Her palms strike like a pile driver just below Kim's shoulders. Kim stumbles backward and thuds against the bookshelves.

Ellie offers a hand to help Kim up. She isn't angry anymore. She just wants this to be over so she can get away.

Kim swings again, but Ellie grabs her wrist and yanks her to her feet. "I'm sorry. But you've got to go."

The hard lines of Kim's face melt under the force of Ellie's conviction. She stares in disbelief. She staggers to the door. She fumbles with the doorknob. With a bitter glance at Ellie, she drags herself down the street like a wounded animal.

Ellie flings back the door. She means to shout, but when she sees Kim's defeated retreat, she calls softly instead. "I didn't steal him! He came to me freely. He loves me, do you hear?"

Back inside, Ellie is surfing on a wild and mighty surge of hope. She unwinds her plait, and brushes her hair with rapid strokes until it drapes around her shoulders in gleaming waves. She is only a flowing dress away from a Pre-Raphaelite maiden; that was what Will used to say.

She brushes her teeth, sprays herself with a cloud of Obsession, and is gone.

CHAPTER 82

James, William DeQuoyne's best and possibly only friend, is a designer, with miles of creative talent but little skill at making money. He owns a small and stylish flat overlooking South Quay. There are two rooms, painted orange and hot pink and studded with oddities: a statue of a bleeding Madonna, a ferociously large map of the London underground, and a trio of stuffed ferrets, which Ellie always found unnerving. The counterpoint to all this showy eccentricity is housekeeping in the bachelor style—cases of Grolsch next to the armchair, kitchen cabinets defiantly bare. The bedroom contains only a king-size mattress and a mirror, but Ellie cannot remember another room anywhere in the world in which she ever felt happier.

As she races toward the flat, Ellie rehearses the meeting to come. She wants it to be perfect. She'll press the buzzer and linger under the overhang while Will slouches to the videophone. When he realizes it's Ellie with a dusting of rain like diamonds in her hair, he'll be incapable of hiding his feelings.

That's the point at which her vision blurs. What will she say to him? What *can* she say? *Will, we need to talk?* No, too commonplace. Not a good start.

Perhaps an indirect approach. *So, Will, I guessed that you'd be hiding here.* Lightly, airily, unconcerned. *Let me in. I'd like to remind myself of the view.* It would show a certain confidence, wouldn't it? Show that she doesn't doubt her own pulling power.

But Ellie does doubt. What if he has been dreaming about her, but now, face-to-face, he finds her less enticing? What if he hasn't yet cut the emotional ties to Kim? Leaving one's wife for a few days or even for a few weeks is not the same thing as a permanent break. What if he . . .

Stop it, Eleanor! Get a grip.

She is pacing now on a walkway beside the dock. Mushroom lights squat on either side. The *Lord of the Glens* is running its engines; there's a not-unpleasant smell of diesel in the air. She glances across the quay to the cluster of skyscrapers that seem to grow out of the water. They're like ladies, lifting their skirts to tiptoe into a lake. Lights blaze gold and silver in every window, their shimmering reflections turning the surface of the water into an open treasure chest.

At the top of the tiled steps, by a wall painted an improbable azure—the color of paradise—Ellie lingers. She holds her finger over the buzzer. It's late, but William will still be awake. He'll be dressed in a casual shirt and a chunky pullover; a thin man, he's sensitive to the slightest draft. He'll be slumped across the leather sofa, one arm flung along the back, a glass of bourbon in his hand. He'll be listening to Schubert, possibly, through the huge speakers, or watching *The African Queen,* and beating Bogart to his lines. When he realizes that Ellie has come at last, the lethargy will drop away. He'll fling the door open and his embrace will make everything all right.

Ellie's ready for the future. She presses all the buttons and waits. The wind is ruffling the water in the dock behind her, and a small motor chugs in the distance. She hears a hoarse voice call out far away, but before she can trace the source of the sound, there is an ear-piercing buzz. The door glides open.

So easy, Ellie thinks. Like magic. She sails through the lobby and heads for the third floor. Her tread on the carpeted stairs is light, each step taking her closer to where she belongs. She doesn't need to rehearse the route. She doesn't need to check the numbers on the doors. Her feet lead her straight to the flat where William awaits.

She rings the bell, and the door is flung open. Will is there, slouching. (Doesn't he always? How intimately she knows him). His eyes widen. His hand reaches out in an involuntary gesture. "Eleanor!" he exclaims, and at the sound of his voice she feels an explosion of warmth, so that for half an instant she fears she might have wet herself. She steps across the threshold and coils her arms around his neck. She kisses him so he can know that he's forgiven. So he can know that this start will be a fresh one.

From the end of the hallway, there's a click of nails on floorboards. A low and vicious snarl. Will jerks away, glancing nervously over his shoulder, and she sees for the first time the animal that is grinding its way toward her.

"Silky!" Will barks out a command and places his hand in front of the animal's muzzle, and the hound, still snarling at Ellie, snaps. "Bugger!" Will shouts, and the animal lets go and blood drips from Will's hand and Ellie recognizes the elegant dog. And at precisely that moment, Ariana emerges from the bedroom, with an ice-blue sheet draped across her naked self and her mouth a moist pink O of surprise.

CHAPTER 83

Inside Ellie, there's a colossal emptiness. The day before yesterday, she was frightened—terrified, even—but she had hope. She knew, with that kind of knowing that isn't as much knowing as it is a desperate longing, that Will and she would be together. She knew that when she and Will were together, everything else—the man with the voice of straw, Steve with his friend in his hand, even the ending of her love affair with the tower—wouldn't matter at all.

And now that hope is gone? Ellie feels as if she's been hollowed out. She spent all yesterday, and most of today, under the bedclothes, trying to shut her mind against the onslaught of fears that are scurrying in to fill the hollow place. She could have stayed in bed forever. But she doesn't dare miss another day of work. Doesn't dare risk losing her job. Being the night lawyer is the only thing she's got left.

Ellie isn't hungry, but it's been a long time since she ate. Maybe she could manage some bread. She picks up a small olive-layered focaccia in Carluccio's on the way in to work, and heads back out of the restaurant with her prize in a paper bag.

She presses toward the tower, bucking the throng that is streaming out. Her umbrella—she's left it behind in the restaurant. She wheels around and that's when she spots him. The middle-aged man, the same cheap trousers, the same patterned fleece. He is bucking the crowd, too, heading toward the tower.

Hordes of office workers swarm down the wide steps from One Canada Square, rushing for the train, steering toward Smollensky's, heading for Heron Quays. Ellie abandons the umbrella and launches herself forward against the tide. She swerves among them, stepping swiftly around one and then another. Taking a blow from a briefcase that hits her on the hip. Apologizing, hurrying on.

When Ellie reaches the foyer, she backs against a wall and scans the area behind her. She can't see him. That doesn't mean he's not there. He might have dashed ahead. He might be making his way right now to the *Chronicle* offices.

In her haste, she fails to swipe her card correctly and bashes into the barrier. "Miss?" She stops and does it again.

She stands tightly as a group of bankers shoulder their way out of the lift, and then steps on alone. What will she do if he tries to get in with her? She hears footsteps approaching. The doors close. A man's voice rasps out a curse as the metal panels slide together. The lift begins to rise: one elephant, two elephants. Faster, faster!

The receptionist straightens and smooths the front of her jacket as Ellie enters the offices.

"Marie," Ellie says. She stops to get her breathing under control. "Marie, there's a man." Ellie describes the slouchy face, the strong physique, the unwholesome voice. "Whatever you do, don't tell him I'm here." Marie glances nervously toward the heavy glass door and nods.

Ellie has almost reached her desk when Clive catches up with her. "No time for me, today, Elle?" Pinned to his waistcoat is a homemade badge bordered with red glitter. He sniffs the air. "What's that wonderful smell?"

"Here," she says, handing him the paper bag. "From Carluccio's. For you." She isn't hungry anymore. "Clive," she says, as he opens the bag and inhales, "he's there again. He's here, I mean. In the tower. That man, he's following me."

The bag goes down, the head comes up. Clive is instantly alert. He turns and examines the newsroom. He peers down the corridor behind them. He looks back at Ellie, and she can see that he is struggling to believe. How to make him understand?

"I don't mean he's in the office, Clive. Not yet, anyway. He's in the building. He followed me. He's coming here; I'm certain of it." Ellie reaches out to set her case on the desk. She sees her own hand and she realizes with a shock that she is shaking.

Clive's face softens. He takes her case from her and eases her into the chair. He sits down opposite her and encloses her cold, thin hand in his warm, solid one. Their knees are almost touching. "Give me a full description," he says.

Ellie does her best to give words to the image that's burned in her mind: the cheap trousers, the fleece, the sagging face. Clive nods as if he's taking it all in. He makes a move.

"No, wait." Ellie clutches at his arm. "Don't leave me."

Clive pats her hand and then releases it. "I won't be long. You're safe here. You last saw him—where?"

"He was right behind me when I came up the steps into. . . . Actually, Clive, I believe he tried to get in the lift with me."

"You believe?"

"I didn't see him. Not actually see him. I—I heard his voice. The lift doors closed and I heard him swear." Ellie rubs her hands along the sleeves of her jacket. The air-conditioning is too high. She is freezing.

Clive shrugs himself into his jacket and heads for the reception desk. Uncertainly, at a distance, Ellie follows. Through the glass door, she sees him speaking to Marie. Their faces are grim.

Ellie returns to her desk and clicks open a file, but the words congeal on the screen. She can't make them out. Clive will be back soon. No point starting work until then.

She looks around for someone, anyone, to talk to. There's a subeditor on an adjacent desk, but he's an edgy man with the kind of cheap confidence that Ellie can't abide. He calls every man his *mate*. Women are *love* if they're over forty, and *gorgeous* if they're under. Ellie loathes being called gorgeous.

But she needs to be with someone, just until Clive gets back. Desperately, she scans the room. In the far, far corner, she spies a mop of blond hair that glows white under the lights. A chunky pair of shoulders. Tristan! Tristan Blocombe! The pleasure of that first, affirming, e-mail comes flooding back. *Spot-on, Miss Porter . . . and welcome to the club.* She should have printed it out and had it framed.

She weaves her way between the desks to the opposite corner. She feels sharply conspicuous, the only thing that moves in the nearly empty room. She hears a noise behind her and whirls around, but there's no one there. She rehearses what she'll say. *Hey, I'm Eleanor Porter. You know, the night lawyer. I really appreciated your welcome message on my first night in the job. I should've thanked you sooner.* He lifts his head at her approach. She reaches his workstation and he swings his chair toward her.

Tristan Blocombe is in his early thirties with eyebrows so fair that his face looks bald. His grin is distinctly uncool and his face is all the more appealing for it. "It's about time we met," he says. "You're the night lawyer, aren't you? I'm a financial journalist. One of those chaps who knows all about money but is permanently hard up." He holds out a hand with ink stains on the flank. "Ronald Foster Clarke, at your service."

"I really appreciated your welcome message—" Ellie stops halfway through her prepared speech. "Ronald Clarke?" she says, stunned. Her cheeks beginning to burn. "You're not Tristan Blocombe?"

He laughs, a little too heartily. "Not as far as I know. Here, grab a seat." He indicates a nearby chair. "Better still, shall we go for a drink? I could murder a pint."

Ellie scarcely hears. She's looking wildly around the newsroom. "Where is he, then?"

Clarke is puzzled. "Who are you talking about? This Tristan person? Who is he, anyway?"

"He's an editor. You must have met him, surely."

Clarke fumbles in the filing drawer that's wedged beneath his desk, and pulls out a binder. He flips through it. "The staff directory. Updated only last month. See for yourself."

Ellie takes the binder in hands that can hardly hold it for trembling and runs her finger down the *B*s. Ball, Bledsoe, Brown. No Tristan Blocombe. No Blocombe at all.

"But he must be here! He wrote to me! His message came though on the printer."

"If you say so." Clarke shrugs, looking at the ledger on his desk. At the monitor. Anywhere but at her.

"But surely it was you! You gave me a thumbs-up when I looked at you."

"Hey, there." He raises his hands in a keep-your-distance gesture. "If I'd known you're the type who would read so much into a friendly wave, I'd have kept my paws to myself."

Behind her, Ellie hears a step. She drops the binder and spins around. Thank God, it's Clive. "Clive," she says, pleading. "Clive, you know Tristan Blocombe, don't you?"

Clive doesn't answer. He glances at Ronald Clarke, and then slips an arm around her shoulders. Ellie tries to shake him off, tries to make him look her in the eye, but his grip is too firm.

And then she remembers. "Clive, what about that man? Did you find him?" She glances apprehensively in the direction of the door. "Was he in the lobby?"

She struggles to get away from Clive's insistent arm. The sharp edge of his badge is digging into her.

"No sign of the man you described," Clive says, and all the twinkle has disappeared from his face. He seems grave and strained. "That's what I want to talk to you about." He steers her across the newsroom and into his tiny office and moves the wastepaper bin so he can close the door behind them. He releases her arm. Both remain standing.

"Elle, this man," Clive says. "This man who's been stalking you. Are you positive you've told me everything?"

"Told you everything?" Oh, my God. She stalls for time. "What—what do you mean?"

"I mean just that—well, perhaps he's not a stranger. Perhaps he's someone you have a closer connection with? An ex-boyfriend maybe?"

"No, no! I told you! The first time I ever saw him he was sitting on a bench in Island Gardens. We didn't even speak. He's been following me ever since. I'd never seen him before."

Ellie can hear the shrill edge in her own voice. Clive reaches out a hand to restrain her, but she shakes him off. Her own words are ringing in her ears. Never seen him before. Ellie is washed with a new and startling kind of certainty. Startling but undeniable, like the world turned upside down. She has told a blatant lie.

Ellie can see the man's features—that melancholy mouth, those large hands—looming down at her. It is him. And yet it isn't. It is someone very like him; someone slighter; someone younger; someone far less assured. She is wrenched by a feeling of nausea.

"Elle! Elle!" Clive shouts after her as she stumbles out of his office and down the corridor and past an astonished Marie in the reception area and beyond the once-secure outer boundaries of the *Chronicle*.

CHAPTER 84

Carl has perfect concentration. Fourteen monitors are banked up in front of him. The angle on the screens changes every five seconds. *Flick flick flick.* Asked for an instant report, Carl could tell you what's happening on any of the monitors at any point in time.

It takes something extraordinary to break his concentration and something extraordinary has just occurred. It's the Dancing Queen. What the bloody hell is she doing in the mall? It's less than an hour since she got to work. She shouldn't be wandering around like that. He zooms in just as she passes into Waitrose. She seems nervous; she's looking over her shoulder, and she's trying to hurry, taking short steps because of the pencil skirt. She looks a mess. A section of hair has worked loose from her plait and her scarf is missing. It's time he did something. Time he brought this to a close.

With his eyes still on the screen, Carl reaches over and picks up the lid from his bottle of Dr Pepper. He balances it in his palm, and then flips it into the air and catches it again. Tails.

He pushes his chair back so abruptly that it tumbles over. He doesn't care.

"Hey, Carl," Richards calls in his irritable voice. "Whatcha think you're doing?"

Carl is already at the outer door of the unit.

"Hey!" Richard calls again.

Carl doesn't give Richard an answer. He's too busy working out the quickest route to Waitrose.

CHAPTER 85

The hands, that's what it is. Those big hands. Ellie is astonished that she didn't see the resemblance before. Long ago, when Ellie lived on the hill near Alexandra Palace, she knew this man. He was younger then, of course. He must have been—what? Late teens? Maybe twenty? For a few months, he lived next door, with the lady who ran a caf on the high street. He might have been her son, or maybe her nephew. Ellie can't remember. She's not sure she ever knew.

He was lonely; even as a child she could recognize that. He used to like to talk to her. And she liked to talk to him, liked his tentativeness, his uncertainty; he wasn't plump with self-assurance like so many grown-ups. He came into her garden and sat on her swing. He walked the swing back and forth with his feet, his hands resting on his knees. It always looked to the little girl as if he were holding his knees in place.

The face is older now, but even then he had a rumpled look. How could she have forgotten? He was there the day her daddy died. She'd watched with trepidation every single step he took as he approached the house. Please, please, go away! She'd pushed the thought toward him, but no: on and on he came, moving slowly and with exaggerated care, the way she and her friends did when they walked a line chalked on the pavement. Suddenly, he looked up and saw her watching. He pinned her with his gaze. She struggled but she couldn't escape. She opened the door and whispered, "Please, please go away!"

His voice didn't croak in those days, not nearly so much. "Eleanor, you know I can't leave you," he said.

With a sudden sweep, Ellie's mother was at her back. She wrenched the door wide open and pushed Ellie aside, exposing the man who stood on the porch with wisteria framing his head. Annabel turned and shooed Ellie away. "Finish getting ready for school. Go on now, off with you," she'd said.

Ellie didn't go away. She couldn't. She watched again from behind the curtains. Saw the young-old man, speaking urgently to Annabel, his face a fist of concentration. Saw Mother try to stop him once or twice, try to turn away. Watched as the color slowly drained out of Mother's face, knowing that when her mother went white it meant that she was furious.

When he'd finished what he had to say, when he cocked his head higher as if waiting for a response, Annabel drew herself up and began. She had a way of speaking, quiet but forceful, so that the words drummed into your head. As Annabel spoke, the man seemed to shrink. He looked around with an air of desperation. He spotted Ellie and for an instant tilted in her direction. She crouched down. When she peeped out again, he was stumbling his way back along the path. He cast a despairing glance over his shoulder and then he disappeared.

He had confronted her mother and then backed away. Ellie had to face the consequences alone. To throw herself on her mother's mercy. To tell her mother every last thing that had happened. Annabel, grim-faced, said she would take care of it. She warned Ellie to have no further dealings with that dreadful man. She buttoned Ellie's coat and sent her off to school. But Ellie didn't go. She hid under the table, sick with apprehension, terrified about what would happen next. In her worst imaginings, her mother and father would go away, would abandon her as a wicked child, and she would be left alone.

Ellie had forgotten all this until now. How strange, how positively weird, that the episode comes back to her in crystal clarity, undimmed by the years, every detail intact, right down to the humiliation on his face as he slunk away.

Ellie pauses for a moment outside Waitrose before plunging in. The wide-open entrance is bright with fresh flowers and the perfume of the lilies almost overwhelms her as she rushes by. Ellie thrusts a carton of milk into her basket. She snatches up a packet of sanitary towels. She senses danger all around. In the assistant manager with his clipboard who looks as if he might try to interrogate her. The shoppers whose trolleys block her path. The carton of olives that, dropped, splashes garlicky oil flecked with red chillies all over the aisle. She jumps aside from the mess, but she is unnerved by the slick of oil on the soles of her shoes. She glances over her shoulder, and sees her own sticky footprints stretching out behind her.

So her stalker knows who she is. Who she was. What she did? No wonder he wrote: *"Twenty years is long enough to wait."* He was there that morning, the morning that her father died.

Standing in the aisle of Waitrose now, looking helplessly around for pasta sauces, Ellie can feel the terror and guilt in her gut as sharp as it had been when she was eight years old. But what's strange is that the emotions are alive, but not the reasons; she can't recall what his confrontation with Annabel had been about. Her father hadn't died yet. That came the same day, but later. So what had he said to Annabel? What had Annabel replied? What had passed between them to generate Ellie's sense of imminent catastrophe? What did he want from her then, and what is he after now?

In the center of Waitrose, among the housewares, Ellie loses her bearings. She skirts around a display of baking tins, and comes face-to-face with a rack of knives suspended from chrome hooks. Their blades are bright and shiny. She steps aside to let a trolley pass and stares again. She sets her basket on the floor and reaches out and runs her fingers lightly across the top of the display. She draws a long, thin boning knife from its plastic sleeve. She touches the pad of her finger to the tip of the blade. It draws the tiniest, weeniest drop of blood. She lifts her basket again, drops the knife into it, and heads for the checkout, sucking her finger as she goes. She's got to get home, and quickly.

She's forgotten her pasta-for-one, she realizes, as the cashier scans her purchases. But she's no longer hungry, anyway.

The cashier has a crunchy Jamaican accent. "Goodness me, that's a wicked-looking blade," she says, picking up the knife and sliding it back into its sleeve. "Sharp, too. A chicken won't have a chance against that."

"I hope not," Ellie says.

CHAPTER 86

Ellie's home doesn't feel like a haven anymore. She slides inside the house and stiffens. It's so hot in here. Something's different. Something's wrong. A smell. Her own fault; she hasn't emptied the bin in days. She hasn't tidied up. Her breakfast dishes are still on the table. The books, the bank statements, the African carvings that had been swept off her shelves still litter the floor. She turns on the lights in the alcove, but they just make things worse. Her big room, her white-walled, clean-lined room, doesn't look serene now. It merely looks empty. The light falls on blank unpeopled spaces. Loveless spaces. This could be a clinic. Or a car wash. Or a laundromat.

Ellie takes her shoes off and peels off her tights. Why is it so hot in here? She crosses her arms across her belly. The ache is starting up again. Maybe it's appendicitis. Or gallstones. Maybe it's cancer. She never rang for the results of her last cervical smear. Maybe it's too late already. God, the pain is getting worse. Maybe the sickness has already spread like a giant fungus into her womb. She crouches down against the kitchen cabinet.

A noise—a thud, like something falling—from next door. It must have been a car door in the distance. No more thuds. Now that she strains to hear, there is no sound whatsoever. No traffic from Westferry Road. No muttering from the Hellraisers. Nothing. Perhaps she is alone in the world. She will squat here, forever, with whatever it is in her belly eating her up from inside, and no one will come to her aid.

She's burning with heat. Her breathing is coming now in short, rapid bursts. Her pulse is racing. She's heading for one of her attacks. Oh, Christ, she's got to do something, quickly, before she stops breathing altogether.

Ellie feels for the plastic carrier bag that she dropped inside the door. She slides her hand inside. She pushes the sanitary towels aside and wraps her fingers around the knife. She peels away the plastic sheath and sets the blade free.

Ellie hefts the weight of the knife in her hand. It feels solid. It feels real, somehow, and true. She pushes her sleeve up and is astonished to see a flake of dried blood on her wrist. She hasn't showered since she saw Will. This must be Will's blood. He must have reached for her after the dog had bitten him. Must have brushed her arm with his hand. It's a sign. Will has given some of himself to her, left on her skin the last of him she'll ever have.

Ellie exposes the inside of her arm. She slides the smooth edge of the knife down her skin from the elbow to the wrist. Gently, with a soft teasing motion, she tests the razor-sharp blade against her flesh.

Like a flash of electricity, that's what Jessica said. It only lasts a second or two, and then—peace. Then you're not frightened anymore.

Ellie looks at the blade almost lovingly. Not frightened anymore. She clutches the handle of the knife and angles the blade against her wrist. She makes her first lovely little slit. She cuts a tiny mouth, the lips parting to reveal one drop, and then another, of rich red blood. She steels herself to slice more deeply and stops. A noise. Jessica didn't warn her about this. A high-pitched beeping. It's not loud but it's insistent. Something's wrong.

Ellie can tell only one thing. The high-pitched noise isn't coming from the street. It's inside Ellie's house. She looks wildly around. What is it? Should she run? Would she be safer in the street? She opens the door an inch or two, ready for a quick escape. The pulsing noise continues, louder and more demanding.

It's the kitchen, surely. Coming from the kitchen. Ellie moves toward the worktop. A pinpoint red flash draws her eye to the cooker. That's it! The timer, that's what it is. Ellie has hardly ever used it; she can't remember how it works. She crouches down for a closer look. There's a digital screen and it registers zero. Ellie punches each of the buttons on the front panel in turn. Numbers flash up, arrows appear and disappear, and then silence falls. She stands for a moment and listens with relief to the hush.

The house is quiet again. Still no pub sounds, no sounds of traffic, no voices, from outside. And inside, the clock is ticking, but nothing else. Slowly, Ellie pushes herself to her feet. "Odysseus?" she whispers. She steps toward the hamster cage. "Odysseus?" Nothing. He is silent, too, traumatized perhaps by the sound of the timer.

So hot. Ellie is in the middle of sloughing off her jacket when she hears something else. She whirls, her arm caught in the sleeve of the jacket, and sees the front door easing open. A hand seizes the doorjamb. A square, tanned face with close-cropped hair pokes around the edge.

"Jonathan!"

He leaps into the room at the sound of her voice and then draws back against the door, shutting it behind him. "Sorry! I'm really sorry." He checks his watch. "It's a beastly time to come calling. I didn't mean to startle you—God knows, you get enough of that without me adding to it—but you were so frightened when you left work tonight. I heard all about it. And I left a message on your phone—"

"I haven't checked for messages yet—"

"—And when you didn't reply . . . Well, I began to worry that something was terribly wrong." He stops and stares at the jacket dangling from Ellie's right arm. "What's that you're wearing? Oh, I see." Gently, he pulls Ellie free of the jacket and tosses it onto the sofa. "And I was on my way home from a dinner in the East End, and so I thought I'd just stop by and make sure you're all right. And then I saw your door ajar, and I'm afraid I rather panicked."

Ellie's heart goes out to him. He's so embarrassed. "It's very kind of you, Jonathan."

"And I thought, well, what if she has gone to bed and left the door open? And so I—" He straightens. Sniffs. Checks his watch. It's after eleven. "What are you cooking?" he asks.

Cooking? All of a sudden it makes sense. The heat in the kitchen; it's as warm as a bakehouse. The timer. Timers don't go off by themselves, do they? Someone has to set them. And the smell. That awful, gamey, smell. Ellie's stomach clenches and waves of sick try to force their way up. She reaches for the oven, but her head begins to whirl. Jonathan dashes toward her. She feels herself falling. He eases her into a chair. She tries to fight him off, to push him away, she has to get to the oven, but she is too nauseous. All she can do is bend forward when he urges her to do so, and put her head between her knees. "Oh, God," she whispers. "Oh, God. The oven."

"Don't worry," Jonathan says. "I'll get it." He wraps a tea towel around his hand. He opens the oven door. He pulls out a baking tray and stares at it for a long moment. "It's—it's—it's a—"

Ellie knows what it is. Every fiber of her being tells her what it is. She manages to raise her head so she can bear witness to the tray where the little bundle of fur lies steaming, before Jonathan drops it. Ellie's head is blazingly bright, but it is Jonathan, not her, who is sick on the kitchen floor.

CHAPTER 87

Ellie had made a bandage for her wrist as neat and small as she could, but it's clearly not discreet enough. When she's practicing moves with Vik, his glance locks on to the injury. He cocks one eyebrow quizzically. "It's nothing," she mouths.

Nothing. And everything. Ellie isn't certain why she came today, except for the conviction that if she didn't drag herself out of bed

now, she might never get up again. Jonathan stayed over. He refused—
quite literally refused—to leave her on her own. He slept crammed up
on the sofa, his large body swathed in blankets. And though she'd resisted, once she was under her own duvet, she was glad of his presence downstairs. In the morning, dressed again in his suit, he woke
her with a too-strong cup of coffee. She drank it gratefully and showered and dressed. Together, they dug a grave under the willow tree
and put Odysseus, the adventurer, to rest.

Jonathan drove her to the leisure center—again, he insisted—and
didn't mind one bit that she wasn't up to talking. She feels bruised,
like a piece of steak that's been tenderized, but it is her soul not her
body that is aching. When, on arrival, she discovers she is late—the
members of the class already gathered in a ring in the center of the
dojo—her impulse is to turn and flee. But then Sensei sees her dithering in the doorway and bows her in; Tony and Vik move a few steps
apart to open a space for her; and now, here she is, standing among her
colleagues while Sensei instructs them in the practice of Tameshiwari.

"What is Tameshiwari, Miss Porter?" No sooner has she caught
her breath than Sensei puts her on the spot. Testing her, she supposes.
Rebuking her for late arrival. Or, Striker being Striker, he may be concerned to reassure himself that their night together hasn't led him to
show her any signs of softness. Whatever the reason, Ellie is glad he
asks. She knows all about Tameshiwari, and it stops her dwelling on
Odysseus.

"Tameshiwari is the practice of breaking, Sensei," she says, and
bows. "Destroying objects with a blow, using the side of the hand, or
the elbow, or the sole of a foot."

As long, Ellie thinks, as that's all that he asks of her. History is fine.
Theory's okay. But please, please, don't let him ask her to demonstrate. If he'd seen her last evening, trying to escape from her own
problems by putting a knife to her wrist, he'd know she isn't up to it.

Sensei smiles with something approaching pride and turns back to
the group. "Precisely," he says. "With the proper technique, the body
can shatter any rigid object: hardwood planks, baseball bats, bottles, bricks. You name it. In competition, we are forbidden to use full
force against our opponent's head—but Tameshirwara shows us what
might happen if we did."

Breaking has been played down in recent years. Some karate prac-
titioners are convinced that it gives the sport an outmoded, karate-
chop, image. But Ellie, in her first season of karate, traveled all the
way to Bradford to watch a demonstration. She remembers the excitement in the arena, the sharp scent of pine as six planks of hardwood
were stacked with bricks as risers. Kukuto Sensei stood in front of the
obstacle for minutes, utterly motionless, his eyes closed. Then he cast
one glance in the direction of the ceiling and raised his arm. His hand
smashed all the planks with a splintering crash, and halted mere
inches from the floor.

Striker sweeps his gaze over the group. "In Tameshiwara," he
lisps, "there are four essentials for success. One." Left arm with fist
clenched high in the air. "Skill. Perfect technique. Two." Right arm
raised in place of left. "Conditioning. Work with breaking pads over
months and years to strengthen your bones and muscles. Three."
Both arms in the air now. "Complete concentration. Become utterly
aware of your object."

Ellie recalls that, before closing his eyes, Kukuto Sensei stared at
the stack of planks like a starving man facing a meal. Suddenly, a
wave of anger rises at her head and sweeps through her body as the
thought of a meal brings back the sickening image of Odysseus. Why
kill him? Why? Was it to punish her, Ellie, for the past? Well, punish
her then. Come on, punish her. *Punish me,* she thinks. I deserve it.
Punish me, not a defenseless little animal.

"Now I come," Striker says, his voice ringing out in the dojo, "to
the most important quality of all. The secret: kime. Kime—or focus—
lets you concentrate your power into a small area. Even a black belt
with years of training isn't as strong as a plank of hardwood, and in
a straight fight, he'd be defeated every time." Hand slicing down in a
punch and snatched back, in a pantomime of pain.

"But if that man focuses all his power into a single spot smaller
than the side of his hand, then he can defeat the plank." Slowly,
slowly, uncurling the wounded hand. Opening it out in a gesture of
defiance. "The man has kime and the plank doesn't. Because of kime,
the man will win." Striker is coming to the crux of the matter. "And
how does a man condense his power in this way?"

Or a woman? Ellie thinks.

"By punching through the target. If he aims at the surface of the plank, the blow begins to slow down even before contact. Though he doesn't intend it, the man will pull his punches. With kime, he is aiming at a spot behind the point of impact. When his fist or his foot connects with the target, it will be traveling at maximum speed."

Striker has finished. He straightens and his gaze sweeps the room. It comes to rest on the purple belts. Ellie is quivering. She knows this because she's looking downward and she can see the ends of her belt moving. She knows without looking that Sensei is staring at her. *No. Please, I can't do this.* There is silence in the room. Everyone is waiting.

Focus, Ellie. You can't smash a piece of wood if you just lash out at the surface. You have to go beyond. To aim deep. To penetrate.

"Miss Porter?"

Yes, Ellie, yes. You can't win a fight if your attention is all over the place. You can't get rid of a stalker if you're worrying about Jess, and the boyz in the hood, and the ex-lover who has betrayed you yet again. To tackle a stalker you have to make him and only him the focus of your attention. Go deep, go beyond the surface, and don't pull back, don't slow down, don't recoil, until the blow hits home.

Slowly, Ellie raises her eyes until they meet Striker's. He points at the big blue breaking board. She picks it up and hands it to him. He holds it across the lower part of his face. They exchange bows.

Ellie breathes deeply and exhales and breaths again. She closes her eyes. She fills her chest with air. She fills her mind with the mote of dust just behind Sensei's ear. *I will do it this time,* she thinks. *For Odysseus, this time, I will succeed.*

And then, she steps up smartly, and sends her fist flying with such force that Striker's iron arm, holding the pad aloft, shudders from the blow.

CHAPTER 88

Ellie doesn't get anywhere by questioning her mother. "Next door?" Annabel says. "Big hands? Whatever are you on about, Eleanor?"

Half an hour later, Ellie is in the newsagent's, dithering over whether to buy a Galaxy bar or a Lion bar, when—speak of the devil—the man strolls into the shop, his hands in his pockets, casually, apparently unconcerned.

Ellie happens to glance at Al and catches his nod of recognition. She manages to conceal her excitement while the man browses the magazines and watches her from the corner of his eye. His confidence appalls her. Ellie waits until he is paying for his paper and then races out of the shop and down the road and into the public lavatories. She stays therefore a full twenty minutes. Then she doubles back to the shop. She grabs a bottle of Coke and heads for the counter.

"Al, you know I was in here a short while ago? Do you remember a man who followed me in? He was browsing through the magazines."

Al displays what is as close as he ever comes to interest. "The one with the dodgy voice? That one? Why d'you ask?"

For a fraction of a second, Ellie is tempted to take him into her confidence. Al is solid and unflappable, and always there. Why shouldn't she enlist his help? But the memory of the disdainful eyes of the police officers is enough to put her off. She doesn't want the whole island coming to the conclusion that she's losing it.

"You know his name, Al?" Her heart was drumming in her chest. "You know where he lives?"

Al is glued to the telly. Some reality show, in which two women—one in a shell suit, the other in a crisp white blouse—are shouting at each other across a class divide.

"Carl Hewitt. He's—" Al cracks the faintest hint of a smile as one of the women hurls a dishrag to the floor. He pauses to follow the action on the screen. Ellie doesn't dare to interrupt.

At the commercial break, Al changes channels with the remote, tuning in to Laurence Llewelyn-Bowen, who is extolling the virtues of a plywood cutout. Al studies the designer with an air of resignation and picks up the conversation where he left off.

"He's an islander, I know that much. Used to deliver his paper when I was a kid." He shakes his head at a mural that Llewelyn-Bowen has designed for a bedroom wall. "To think people pay for that," he grumbles. "Just the other side of Millwall Park it was, near the Seyssel Street estate. Kingfield Street, maybe?

"Hey!" he calls after Ellie, as she heads for the door, "you forgot your shopping."

When Ellie gets home, she takes out a striped deck chair from the shed, and sits in the garden making her plans. Widget comes and snuggles into her lap. Her mood is lifted by a glass of red wine—only one; she is in serious training now—and she is just draining the glass when she hears a group of men approaching on the other side of the wall.

They're coming closer. They scuff to a halt. There's the flare of a lighter, a tang of cigarette smoke, and an exchange of harsh comments. Heavy footsteps slam their way round the corner to the door of Jessica's house.

There's a rattle as someone tries the doorknob and a shake as the door thumps against the frame. A second shake, harder this time, as if in anger.

A squeaky voice calls: "She's not here." A pause. "Tull? Maybe she still doesn't want to see you?" Nervous laughter.

"Fuck her," comes the response. "Let's get a drink."

The heavy footsteps join up again with the rest of the group. They don't move off immediately. Everything goes quiet.

Ellie hugs her knees more tightly and sits perfectly still. The longer the silence goes on—one second, five seconds, fifteen—the more uneasy she becomes. What can they be doing? Do they intend to wait, right here, never leaving her any peace, until Jessica succumbs? Or could it be—God, what a thought!—that they know that Ellie's here? Are they listening out for her?

Ellie stands and takes a step toward the patio doors, setting her bare foot down with utmost care, moving as quietly as she can. But on the second step, a shard of rage pierces her self-control. It is her wall, for Christ's sake. This is her home. Why should she be made to feel like this in her very own garden?

At that moment, there's a chorus of grumbling and complaint, and the footsteps begin to move off down the street. Ellie despises the lazy, scuffing sound they make.

She can't resist it. She turns toward the retreating echoes and takes a deep breath. "Bugger off," she shouts at top volume. She steps inside, and shuts the patio door with a defiant thud. Suddenly, unexpectedly, she feels a whole lot better.

CHAPTER 89

Almost midnight. Ellie has draped a throw around her shoulders, and curled up as best she can in the rocking chair. Her fingers tap an edgy rhythm on the bottle of wine that sits on the floor beside her chair. Her glass is empty. Ellie won't allow herself a drink until she has fixed all the details in her mind.

Harriet rings the mobile. "Ellie? You still awake?"

"I'm surprised you are, given the hour that the baby gets you up. Are you at the villa?"

"We arrived in Majorca at half-past nine. It took ages to get the children to sleep, but now Greg and I are sitting on the balcony enjoying a drink. It's heavenly to be here. Just so I can relax completely, Ellie—you won't forget to take the car in tomorrow?"

"I picked it up this afternoon, Harry, just as you suggested."

"Remember, Ellie, to get them to sign the service manual. It's in the glove box. And whatever you do, don't forget to put the keys back through the letter box when you're finished."

"Stop worrying, Harry, everything will be fine." Ellie pours herself a glass of sauvignon blanc. A very small one. She'll be driving soon. . . .

"Thanks, Ellie. How are things with you? Have you managed to stop obsessing about Will?"

"Will's the last thing on my mind right now. Listen, Harry, I've got to go. This call will cost you a fortune. Anyway, I'm on my way out. There's something I've got to do."

"Are you serious? Like what? It must be after midnight."

"I'm deadly serious. I'll tell you all about it when you get back. Bye, Harry. Lots of love."

Ellie puts a Mag-lite torch and a thin pair of gloves into a rucksack, picks up the keys to Harriet's car, and sets off.

Ellie creeps slowly along the road, accustoming herself to driving again. Apart from a knot of people saying their good-byes outside the Gaylord Tandoori, the island seems deserted. Metal shutters are pulled down over the window of Al's shop.

Kingfield Street turns out to be a short tidy stretch of road wedged between Millwall Park and the Seyssel Street estate. It has grass verges planted with holly bushes and trees that tower over neat little houses. Hewitt's house—according to the London telephone directory, the home of the only C. Hewitt on the island—has ivy growing up the front wall. Apart from a light shining through a small mottled window at the side, the house is in darkness.

Ellie drives past, does a three-point turn, and squeezes the Golf into a parking space some distance away. She slouches down in the darkness and fixes her gaze on the house.

A rising breeze gusts along the length of the street. It swirls wet litter up from the curbside and plops it down onto small neat lawns. Ellie finds some Chopin on the car radio, sets the volume as low as it will go, and sinks back into the seat.

Fog builds up on the inside of the car windows. Ellie cracks them open and the fresh air jolts her awake. She sits for ten minutes, twenty minutes, longer. The fog fades. Rain begins to beat against her windscreen.

At ten minutes past one, a light snaps on inside Hewitt's house. Ellie switches the radio off. Hewitt's door inches open and for a moment, a figure is silhouetted against a lighted hallway. The figure turns on the porch light and extends a palm as if to test for rain. Before he pulls up the hood on his anorak, Ellie confirms that it's Hewitt. Or the Bastard, as she thinks of him; *stalker* is far too neutral a term.

Hewitt steps outside and closes the door behind him. He bends over and fumbles about at the side of the path. Finally, he buries his hands in his pockets and sets off toward Millwall Park.

Ellie slides down behind the steering wheel, steeling herself for discovery. There's a shadow as Hewitt passes by her car. His head is bent against the drizzle and he doesn't even glance in her direction.

When Ellie pokes her head up, Hewitt is heading steadily west, moving, maybe, toward Ellie's house. He rounds the corner and is out of sight.

Ellie swings out of the car, closing the door again as quietly as she can, and shrugs herself into the rucksack. She brushes off the raindrops that shower onto her shoulders as she passes under a tree, and moves quickly up the concrete path to Hewitt's house. She places her finger firmly on the bell and holds her breath as a thin chime echoes through the house. Nothing stirs inside. Ellie feels uncomfortable in the glow from the porch light. She's got to get in and out as quickly as possible.

Ellie feels around near the base of an acacia bush until her fingers brush a rock. She lifts it and snatches up a key.

Inside the carpeted hallway of Carl Hewitt's house, the air is warm and still. The sound of the wind is replaced by the slow ticking of a clock. Ellie pulls on a pair of gloves. She takes the Mag-lite from her rucksack, and in its narrow beam, makes out a low-ceilinged hallway with a staircase straight ahead. To her left, through a plastered archway, she can see the eerie red glow of the standby button on a telly. The sitting room is plunged in darkness. Ellie circles slowly, her torch beam picking out a pile of newspapers on the sofa. Everything else seems to have been tidied away. No dirty ashtrays, though there's a lingering odor of cigarette smoke; no empty glasses; no notebooks or computers or files. Nothing that might explain what the Bastard—the name comes easily now—is playing at. Ellie moves over to a sideboard topped with an arrangement of artificial flowers. She squats, exploring each drawer in turn. There's table linen. Silver cutlery in a satin-lined box. Videocassettes: *Titanic, Band of Brothers, The Grapes of Wrath*. A set of London directories and a current copy of the *TV Times*. Ellie decides to give the kitchen a miss. Time is ticking away.

She creeps up the stairs, keeping close to the wall, moving silently. At the top, four flush doors open off a narrow landing. Ellie selects the first door on her right. It's a bad choice. The floor shifts at her step and makes a creaking noise that seems shockingly loud.

Ellie freezes. Her knees begin to tremble. She grasps for the post at the head of the stairs and hangs on for dear life. She's sure she hears a sound then, from behind one of the doors. A soft sound, like the air pressing out of a feather pillow. Like a child's sigh. Ellie's exit is clear, down the stairs and out. The desire to be gone, to end this wild escapade, is powerful, but her legs won't carry her.

Seconds creep by. No more sighs. Ellie regains the use of her limbs and is off again, more swiftly this time. She pushes the door open an inch at a time with her fingertips. The torch beam reveals an office the size of a boxroom with most of the floor space taken up by a wooden table. Ellie makes a beeline for a squared-off stack of plastic folders on its surface.

She opens the top folder and flicks through the contents. Clippings, and all of them, apparently, related to the O. J. Simpson trial. There are photos of O. J. going into the courtroom; stories before, during, and after the trial. Ellie replaces the clippings and glances at the other folders. Stories from the U.S., from Italy, from the U.K. About David Butler, who died in Washington, D.C., in 2000 and whose killer has never been identified. About, bizarrely, Jack the Ripper.

In the middle of the table is a glue stick and a cuttings book. Attached to the front cover is an image of Justice with her eyes bandaged. Inside, only one clipping: about proposals to set up a new cold-crimes unit in Britain. Suddenly, Ellie gets it. What Carl Hewitt is on about. What these folders signify. They are all cold cases, in a sense—cases where no one has been charged or where the person who was charged, innocent or not, has been set free. They all have one thing in common: getting away with murder.

Ellie raises her head, and suddenly she sees the small notice board on the wall. There is only one item pinned to it—an A4 manila envelope. Scrawled on the front in felt-tip pen are the words: *Tom Porter 1981.*

Ellie stiffens, and sure enough, there's a sound from downstairs. The opening and closing of a door. Scraping of shoes on a mat. Ellie snatches the envelope off the notice board and switches off her torch.

The tack that had held the envelope plinks to the surface of the table. With ponderous steps, someone begins to mount the stairs. Ellie looks desperately around. It's hopeless. Even a hamster couldn't hide in here.

The footsteps come to a halt.

Ellie is clutching the envelope so tightly that the paper crumples. She's holding her breath.

The footsteps begin again, but now they're heading back downstairs.

Ellie cracks open the door just enough to catch a glimpse of the top of Carl Hewitt's head retreating down the corridor toward the kitchen. She stuffs the envelope inside her jacket and steps quickly out of the office. Her step over the creaky landing, onto the top stair, is a giant one, and she begins to descend.

A voice behind her—a woman's voice. Loud and piercing; frightened. "Carl?"

The woman has thick blond hair mussed by sleep. She has the build of an opera singer and a voice with the volume to match. Her screams, high-pitched and increasingly hysterical, follow Ellie down the stairs and along the path.

Ellie is fumbling in her pocket for the car key when the front door of the house slams open and Hewitt comes tearing out. He spots Ellie hunched over the ignition of the Golf and makes toward her.

Ellie inserts the key at the wrong angle and stabs at it again. He is almost upon her before the engine finally leaps into life.

She accelerates. She is halfway out of the parking space when her door is pulled open. Hewitt is on her like a flash. He grips her shoulder with his enormous hand, tearing her arm off the steering wheel. The sound of his panting fills the car.

Ellie jams her foot down hard on the accelerator, and the car jolts away from the curb. Hewitt loses his grip. "Eleanor!" he shouts.

She grabs for the door handle and swings her weight so that the car door closes and shuts him out. "Wait!" he rages, stepping out into the street. "You can't run away from the past. I know all about your father." He slams his fist against the window, as the Golf screeches off in the rain.

CHAPTER 90

Ellie's hands are trembling violently as she unzips her jacket and releases the envelope that she'd stuffed inside. She leans into the light of the lamp: *"Tom Porter,"* it says. And *"1981,"* the year of her father's death. As she stands, hesitant—knowing she has to open the envelope, afraid to take that fateful step—she hears a scuff on the pavement outside. Someone raps on the door panel, and she drops the envelope and reaches the door in three long paces and slides the chain into its runner.

"Who's there?"

"Ellie? It's me, Jonathan. Are you all right?"

Ellie opens the door as far as the chain will allow and peers out. "Jonathan!" She closes the door, releases the chain, and flings the door wide open.

Jonathan steps inside, and plants a friendly kiss on her cheek. "I was worried when you didn't show up for work. After the other night—"

Ellie takes his mac and lays it over the rocking chair. "I'm fine now, Jon. It was just the shock of finding him like that—" She still can't bring herself to say Odysseus's name. "But I'll be off work for a bit because—well, I've got something important to sort out. Something that can't wait." She sits down and takes a long, hard look at Jonathan. She expects to see the usual grin, but instead his expression is anxious. Hangdog. Kind of shadowed. "Wait a minute; something's wrong. What is it, Jon? What's happened?"

Jon buries his clenched hands in his pockets. "Promise, Ellie. Promise you won't hate me."

"Hate you? Why should I hate you?" Is this some kind of joke?

"I was talking to some of the people at work, you see. And—and, I have a confession to make."

"A confession? What are you talking about?" Ellie's the one with the guilty secret, not Jon. "Whatever do you mean?"

"When you came into the office, Ellie, I took to you immediately.

The way you looked, the way you spoke, everything about you was so—hopeful, somehow. All bright and shiny. But you were afraid of failing, and I so longed to do something to help." He swallows. "Honestly, Ellie, I only meant to be encouraging."

"Jon, I don't understand. What are you on about?"

"Tristan Blocombe," he says.

There are two or three seconds of stunned incomprehension, and then Ellie leaps to her feet. "Do you mean to tell me that you made him up! That there never was a Tristan Blocombe? It was you all along?" Jonathan nods, miserably, and it's all the confirmation Ellie needs. "How could you, Jon? How could you be so patronizing? You must have known I'd find out."

To Ellie's consternation, Jonathan kneels at her feet and clutches her hand. "Ellie, it was stupid; I can see that now. A senseless thing to do. I hoped that you'd just get on with the job and forget all about it. I'd do anything—anything to make it up to you. To show you I'm sorry. Please, won't you forgive me?"

The sight of the substantial foreign editor kneeling on her wooden floor, hands raised in supplication, is more than Ellie can resist. A smile plays around her lips. "All right, Jon," she says, tugging on his hand. "That's enough. Come on, get up."

Jon stands, cheered to be forgiven, but then he stops and raises her palm to his cheek. "You're cold. Freezing." He looks around. "Shall I put the heating on?"

"It's two AM."

"I'll make a fire." And so he does, twisting newspapers into lighters, making a framework of kindling, huffing and puffing at the sparks, coaxing a fire out of the cold hearth. Watching him—how competently, how conscientiously, he attends to the task—warms Ellie even before the flickers of fire burst into flame. She comes to a decision and opens her very finest bottle of red wine. She makes her way back into the living room just as the flickers of fire burst into flame. She and Jonathan drag the sofa closer to the fire and sit down side by side.

"A toast," says Jonathan, lifting his wine so that the flames sparkle ruby and raspberry inside the glass. "To fire."

"To fire!" Elle echoes. This world—her world—might be going to hell in a handbasket, but first she'll have this one small moment of pleasure.

"Not so cold now?" Jon says. Happily, protectively, lightly, he wraps his arm around her.

"I've stopped trembling." Ellie relaxes against him as a bubble of delight works its way up her body. Can it really be so easy to feel safe? she thinks. She turns toward him, snuggling into his chest, and as she does her eyes sweep across the envelope that has wedged halfway under the sofa.

"What's the matter?" Jon asks. He feels the rigidity come back into her body.

"Nothing." Ellie pulls away. She picks up the envelope, holding it against her so the penciled words don't show. "Nothing." The envelope burns her fingers—not cold now, but flaming.

It's a warning. A sign. She can't let Jonathan into her life. He deserves someone better than her. Someone honest, someone pure. Someone innocent.

"Ellie? What's going on? What's in that envelope? Is it something to do with—your fellow? That chap you told me about?"

He stands and takes a blanket from the back of the sofa and eases it around her shoulders.

Ellie shakes her head. "No. I haven't really had anything to do with him for quite a while. Three years, I guess. More than three years." Ellie pulls the blanket tighter. "And now—"

"And now?"

"I thought he was coming back to me, but he didn't. Now I'm alone and that's how I have to stay. No, *ssshh,* Jonathan, please. I'm trying to be straight with you. You don't want to be mixed up with someone like me."

"But, Ellie—"

"I'm serious, Jon. I'm in trouble. Big trouble. I did something— monstrous—a long, long time ago—and the shit's just about to hit the fan."

Jonathan doesn't ply her with questions. He reaches out and lifts an errant strand of hair off Ellie's face. The gentleness of his touch makes Ellie want to cry. She stands. "I think you'd better go now."

She pulls away as he tries to put his arms around her. "No! Please, Jon, just go."

When she hears the sound of his car pulling away, Ellie collapses onto the sofa. She falls asleep right there, with the blanket around her shoulders and tears on her cheeks, in front of the fire. When she wakes later in the night, there is nothing but cold ashes in the grate.

But staying up has saved her from having to open the envelope. Her last thoughts before she crashes back into sleep: *Carl knows. He knows about my father.*

CHAPTER 91

"Sweets?" Denise says. She is cruising through the channels while she waits for *EastEnders,* and her eyes remain glued to the telly as she speaks. Denise took to calling Carl *sweets* when they were dating. Carl was as good as aniseed balls, she said, and aniseed balls are still her all-time favorite.

She never says things like that anymore, but the endearment remains, like stale grains of sugar in the bottom of a bowl.

She's obviously leading up to a question. Carl heads for the kitchen, pretending he hasn't heard.

"Carl?" she calls after him. "Three of the girls—you know, from the book club—are coming over to help me plan the program. We'll need the sitting room. D'you mind popping out to the pub, just for an hour?"

Denise always wants him to leave when her friends come over. It pisses him off. Why can't he sit in the kitchen and listen to the radio? Or take a glass of beer up to his study? Or—he grins sourly, imagining Denise's face were he to suggest it—why can't he join Denise and *the girls* for a cup of tea? But in the end, it's never worth the row, so he puts on his anorak and out he goes.

Carl trudges along the road watching the rain slicking the pavement, and returns to the topic of guilt. His guilt. A fragile-looking eight-year-old girl's—is it possible that she was on her own in the whole nasty business? Isn't it more likely that there was someone else involved? That's the really big question, and it's a question to which he doesn't have an answer.

Hoity-toity Mrs. Annabel Porter, maybe? Was the mother covering up? Trying to shield the daughter from exposure? Maybe she was simply in denial, unable to look open-eyed at the awful truth. What will she say now, how will she react, when Carl forces it all out into the open?

At the thought of Mrs. Porter, Carl feels a lump forming in the back of his throat. She's a tough nut. She'll jump to her family's defense the way she did before, he knows that for absolutely bloody certain. She'll point her finger at him, and she'll threaten him, and . . .

Carl is starting to feel unwell. He pauses outside the pub to catch his breath. A car pulls up next to him. To his surprise, one of Denise's friends steps out and starts toward the saloon bar. Then she notices Carl hunched over near the door.

"It's Carl, isn't it? Well, talk about coincidence! I'm just on my way to your place for one of our mini-meets."

Her laugh is sort of twinkly. It must be fun to be part of a mini-meet.

"I've stopped to get cigarettes. You?"

Carl puts his hand in his anorak pocket and pulls out his mobile. "Just making a phone call," he says.

She nips inside.

Yes, what a coincidence, bumping into one of the girls here. What *serendipity*, Denise would say. But then it's been that kind of a year. Ever since he came back to the Isle of Dogs, Carl has been searching for Eleanor Porter; this year he finally finds her, right here on the island. One of those scientist chappies, a statistician or someone like that, would point out that since the Canary Wharf redevelopment began, people have been streaming onto the island; finding the occasional person from the past is only to be expected. But Carl sees it differently. Their meeting, he prefers to think, was fated. As if someone planned it that way. Predestined. Inevitable. Meant to be.

Carl finds himself humming again. He concocts a tune, a snatch of a Beatles song, a touch of the Kinks, to match his favorite words.

> Eleanor Porter, Eleanor Porter,
> On the edge of the river water,
> Tom and Annabel's only daughter,
> Frail and small, like a lamb to the slaughter. . . .

Carl isn't taking chances. He keeps the number for *Crimewatch UK* right there on his mobile phone. He initiates the call just as the heavy door of the pub opens to release the odor of smoke and stale beer, and Denise's friend steps gingerly onto the wet pavement.

"Night, Carl," she says.

"Night," he croaks back.

He redials. Someone answers almost immediately. A woman with a motherly tone. Carl clears his throat. *Here I go.* There's no stopping now.

"I have something to report. A crime, you know. Yes. Yes, I'm a witness. To a death. No, actually, to a murder."

CHAPTER 92

A grumbling crash jolts Ellie awake as a delivery van drops a load of bricks outside her door. A night on the sofa has left her stiff, but at least she can greet her visitors fully dressed.

First comes the builder, and Ellie is glad to see him. He is going to repair the garden wall and embed glass along the top. He has only been there for half an hour when two technicians from Lock and Key arrive and begin work inside the house, laying wires for a panoply of alarms and security lights that will sit on Ellie's credit card for months to come. Ellie's morning is eaten up with mundane tasks: moving shrubs away from the garden wall; delivering Harriet's car to the garage; providing cups of tea. She writes a careful letter to Clive at the *Chronicle* and takes it to the post. Finally, there's nothing left to do. She can't avoid the envelope any longer.

Ellie climbs onto her bed, squashes the pillows into a heap behind her back, and takes the envelope from a drawer. *Tom Porter 1981*. As she works the edge of her thumb under the flap, a staple tears at her skin. She holds the envelope upside down and gives a gentle shake, and two snapshots slide out onto her satin coverlet. From the first, her father stares out at her, younger than she remembers him. His pose is casual, almost insolent, one shoulder resting against the trunk of a massive tree. He wears chinos and a slim-fitting shirt with pockets and a watch with a thick leather strap. He smiles toward the camera. Ellie half recognizes that careless, confident look, the lip just beginning to curl in a mischievous grin. Her eyes prickle with tears. She shivers and tugs the quilt up over her legs.

Ellie props the photograph of her father on the bedside table and picks up the other snap. She sees herself: little Eleanor Porter in a blue duffle coat with wooden toggles. She's standing in their tiny garden in Crouch End, the back wall topped by a wooden trellis that only partly blocks the view of the council flats behind. Her own face and body are half-hidden behind something that she's holding out toward the camera. It's an oversized doll with a rag body. Ellie stares. A pulse begins to throb in her throat, and in a rush, she remembers: the clown mouth; the body that folded like an understuffed pillow when she tried to sit him up; the rubbery smell of his face. What it felt like to sing loudly to him so as to drown out the noise of her parents' quarrels. This doll was her rock, her protection. How could she have betrayed him? How could she ever, ever, have forgotten Mr. Tinkle?

As Ellie struggles to capture the details of the photo, it strikes her that something's not quite right. The wall in the background is familiar, and so is the trellis. But where is her swing? Her swing should be there in that corner; in its place stands a greenhouse with dusty plants crushed up against the glass. And there's no lawn, only paving stones pocked with leaves.

Heavy footsteps on the wooden floor downstairs and a shout. "Hello? Are you up there?"

Where were they—she and Mr. Tinkle—when this photograph was

taken? At someone else's house? In a neighboring garden, perhaps? How did the photo come to be tucked away in Carl Hewitt's study?

"I'm coming. Just a minute." Ellie is weak-kneed with uncertainty as she drags herself downstairs to receive a demonstration of the workings of her new alarm. Already, a plan is forming in her mind.

CHAPTER 93

Not much longer now.

Ellie climbs to the top of the mound at Mudchute Station. May blossoms gleam white in the dusk of the park, and in the distance, three young women stroll arm-in-arm along Spindrift Avenue. The streets are otherwise deserted, the inhabitants of the island mostly enjoying the soft summer evening at home.

Ellie has been to see her mother. To try, one last time, to winkle something out of her about the past. But when she cautiously introduced the topic of Mr. Tinkle, Annabel launched into a scattergun attack: How thoughtless Ellie is. How obsessive. How paranoid. How pale. All the speeches that Ellie had prepared—the strategies to break through Annabel's shell, the subtle ways to soothe her—were abandoned. The last half hour of the visit was civil, the conversation stuttering over topics about which neither of them cared, but in the end, nothing has been learned, and the distance that separates Ellie and her mother is even greater than before.

Light spills out of the flats on the northern side of the avenue as Ellie walks toward home. A figure in a matronly cardigan is silhouetted for a moment against a window, the image so immediate that Ellie stops and stares. What if she were to march up to that door? What if she were to open it, to take off her shoes and walk in to where they'd all be comfortably arranged in front of the telly? They'd shift on the sofa to make room for Ellie and she'd curl up and become part of the family, just like that.

So intent is Ellie on this fantasy that she doesn't notice the man emerging from a nearby close until he is halfway across the street. A loose stone rattles, and she whirls around. It's as if he's come out of nowhere.

Ellie tightens her grip on her handbag and begins to run. He swings into step behind her. A quick glance around shows him running, too, and effortlessly. She's ahead of him but not by much. Ellie puts on a spurt, pumping her legs as hard as she can until all she hears is her own breathing. She looks around, at the street, at the thin line of saplings that glimmer in the moonlight. He has vanished.

The snicket lies ahead. A dogleg footpath, hedged about by blackberry canes and abandoned condoms and fast-food debris, one end obscured from the other by a jutting fence. An urban jungle. A hidden place. She looks wistfully at the three young women as they disappear, laughing, around a distant curve of the avenue. Then she takes a deep breath, and enters the cutting. This is what she has been waiting for.

She's nearly through. One more turn and she'll be in spitting distance of Hesperus Street. She takes the corner, and there he is, planted dead in the middle of the path. Ellie'd known he wouldn't be able to resist. She takes it all in at once: anorak zipped to the chest; eyes shadowed under the baseball cap; right hand buried in his pocket.

She advances within a few feet of him before she comes to a halt. She's not running any longer, but then, neither is he. He is standing stone-still, and staring hungrily.

Ellie's mouth is dry. She manages a few words. "Me and Mr. Tinkle. Why did you have that photograph? Where was it taken?"

"I had a camera," he says, and in spite of its grating quality, his voice is strangely gentle. "Bought it with my earnings in the caf. I took that photo, don't you remember?"

Ellie shakes her head.

"I took it in the garden of the house next to yours, where I lived with my aunt. There'd been a frost, the first of the season."

Ellie can feel it even before the image begins to form in her mind. "My legs were itchy. My mother'd made me put on winter tights."

"You'd come into the garden, drawn by the dog . . ."

"A terrier!"

She remembers perfectly how it raced round and round, excited by the frost, stirring up the leaves.

"We were both too shy to speak at first. I'd been an only child; I wasn't used to little girls. And you'd probably been warned not to talk to strangers. You were hugging that foolish-looking doll, and that's how we finally managed to talk. I asked the doll a question and you gave the response. *What is your name?* 'Mr. Tinkle.' *Who do you belong to?*"

There is a reluctant smile on Ellie's face as she supplies the answer: "Eleanor Porter."

"*Were you a birthday gift?*"

With little-girl solemnity, Ellie shakes her head. "A gift from my father," she says. "For being a good girl."

There's dead silence now in the snicket. Neither of them speaks. Behind Hewitt's pouchy eyes and sagging jawline, Ellie can see the features of the young man. She remembers what he did and she's struck by a bolt of anger. "You asked to have a closer look at Mr. Tinkle, and, like a fool," she says, "I lifted him up so you could see his face."

"Yes," Carl says. "You did. Only an instant's hesitation, and then you smiled your gap-toothed smile and held the doll up for me to see. But it wasn't the doll that caught my attention. Your thin white wrists stuck out of the sleeves of your coat like the bones of a bird. The mucky marks—the kind of marks that would be left if parcel tape had been wrapped tightly around and then yanked off—were shockingly visible. Some childish game? I wondered. But when I tried to examine your wrists, your panic—your determination not to let me see— convinced me that this was no game."

"The tape," Ellie whispers. "He used the tape to tie my hands above my head. '*Don't be frightened,*' you said to me. You crouched down close. Your breath battered at my face. '*Tell me who did this,*' you said. '*Tell me who did this! Trust me, Eleanor. I'll take care of you.*'"

"You were such a determined little girl. You refused to speak for the longest time. '*No,*' you said. '*I promised I wouldn't tell.*' You seemed frightened."

"Frightened? I was terrified." So terrified that she wet herself and the hot trickle of wee had oozed down her thighs, adding shame to fear. Ellie's mouth twists in anguish. "But you didn't stop your questions, not even then. 'Who?' you kept saying. 'Who was the terrible person who did this to you?' And then—"

"Then I let you go."

"No. Then you did the cruelest thing of all. You smiled a smile that was kindly. Confident. A smile that gave me a little flare of hope. Ellie looks up and makes eye contact. Her gaze is fierce now. "I dared to believe that you would help me. That everything could be made all right, back how it was before. That's why I broke my promise. The answer to your question just floated out on that flare of hope, before I could call it back. 'Daddy,' I said."

For a moment, they stand there in the cutting, facing each other as adults, but neither seeing the adult other. Then, quietly, Ellie begins to sob. Hewitt takes a step toward her.

"Stop!" She wipes her face roughly on her sleeve. "You bastard, why did you make me do it? I'd promised never to tell. Daddy hurt me badly that time, but he didn't mean to, and afterward he was so sorry. So tender. He reached into an enormous Hamleys bag and brought out the doll. Mr. Tinkle loved me just the way Daddy did, that's what Daddy said. Mr. Tinkle would watch over me. And Mr. Tinkle would know if I ever, ever told anyone what Daddy and I did when Mummy was at work. If I broke my promise, he said—if I ever told anyone, anyone at all—Daddy would have to go away forever."

Ellie pauses and stares at Hewitt, searching his face for clues. "Why did you pressure me into breaking my promise? And why have you tracked me down now? I've got—I had—a life that worked. The past was past. Why have you stirred it all up again?"

"But, Eleanor—" He takes another step forward and stops at a warning gesture from Ellie. "I—I wanted so badly to help you, you see. To fix things; to protect you."

"But you didn't, did you? You only made things worse!"

"But I tried, Eleanor. God knows I tried! It took all the courage I had to walk the long path to your front door. You opened it yourself, do you remember? I tried to talk to you, but you just kept telling me to leave. Your mother must have heard the commotion, and suddenly there she was, marching down the hallway like an avenging angel."

Carl takes his cap off now and bows his head. Except for the rubbish round his feet, he might be a man in church. "I managed to get the first words out—'Mrs. Porter I have something terrible to tell you, in private'—before she pounced. 'In private?' she said. 'Come now, Carl, anything you want to say can be said here and now, in front of the entire neighborhood.' I plucked up my courage and tried again. 'Mrs. Porter, have you seen your daughter's wrists?' I reached past your mother and took hold of your hand and pushed back your cuff. You just stared at the floor, all helpless and unresisting and two fat tears trembled at the corners of your eyes. I almost lost my nerve when I saw those tears."

Ellie can remember all of it now. "My mother told me to go inside, but I watched from behind the curtain. I could see you talking."

"You saw that I was trembling?" Carl asks.

Ellie closes her eyes, and then nods.

"I was shaking with fright, Eleanor. Your mother's face was pale and still, and her eyes glittered. She reminded me of an ice sculpture. I wasn't even sure that she heard me. But I told her everything. I have that at least to feel proud of. And then—then there was a deathly silence."

Ellie nods. "I feared Mother might faint, she was so white. But instead, she drew herself up and began to speak in a slow and emphatic way."

"I was sure that she would be heard over the whole neighborhood." Carl pauses, shaking his head.

"What did my mother say that made you run away? That made you not care any longer what happened to me?"

Carl lifts his head. His eyes seem lifeless. "She denied it all. My accusations were monstrous, she said. You'd never been hurt by anyone in your family, ever. She was silent for a few seconds after that outburst, and in the pause, I could see something like cunning rallying in her eyes. 'And what's more, Mr. Hewitt,' she said, 'I've seen you looking at Eleanor. Grabbing her hands, touching her. I know what you're

after!' My throat went all stiff. 'P-P-Pardon?' I said. I felt as if a puff
of wind might blow me away. But she didn't stop. *'Yes, indeed, I've
seen the way you look at her. Those marks you showed me, Mr. Hewitt. On her wrists. Maybe you did this, Mr. Hewitt. Yes, maybe
you did.'* I denied it; I told her the charges were ridiculous, but her
eyes were blazing and she wouldn't stop. *'You're a filthy pervert,
that's what you are. A child molester. One more word and I'll have
the police down on you. No more talk of a career in the Met for you
then!'* "

" 'In the Met'? What did she mean by that?"

"I wanted to be a policeman. I would have made a good one. But
if she'd said these things—my second interview was coming up—if
she'd made these accusations—why then . . . I wanted to save you,
Eleanor, that's all. I wanted to do the right thing, to rescue you, to call
your father to account. Instead, I behaved like a coward."

Ellie laughs—a small, unhappy laugh—and turns away. Carl
lunges. His large hand tightens around her wrist. She puts the other
arm up to block him, but he takes hold of that wrist, too, and twists
until her handbag falls from her grasp. Ellie thrashes. Hewitt delivers one hard shake that makes her head snap back.

"Listen to me," he rasps. "Every single day for twenty-two years,
I've had to face my cowardice."

Footsteps from the far end of the path. A boy in baggy trousers
comes into view. Ellie glares at the youth, and he backs away. She is
beginning to understand. "Are you telling me that you feel guilty?
That I'm supposed to feel sorry for your suffering? Is that what this is
about? Don't you talk to me about guilt! Don't you dare." She struggles, but he is holding her so close to his chest that there's not room to
kick. The second she subsides into stillness, he starts in on her again.

"Eleanor, I must have your forgiveness. Let me make it up to
you. Your father, tell me where he is. I'll find your father and—"

"My father," Ellie shrieks. "How dare you mention my father.
Talk about guilt! I loved my father, and because of you, I killed him.
My father's dead!"

"Dead?" Carl whispers. "Tom Porter dead?" His jaw drops and
his mouth, with its crooked teeth, hangs open. "It can't be true. All
these years—"

"He's dead and it is my fault. You pressured me into telling, and because I told, my daddy died."

"No, Eleanor! You were right to tell. What your father did was wicked. You've no reason to blame yourself."

"Yes, I do. If I hadn't told, my father wouldn't have got in a fight with my mother, wouldn't have dashed away, wouldn't have crashed. I caused his death. Even my mother blamed me. She was there, at the scene of the crash, cradling his head in her lap. 'Oh, God, what have you done?' That's what she said. She looked up at me and she cried out, 'What have you done?' "

There's a horrible silence. Both of them are breathing hard, like runners, in the evening air. Finally, still clutching Ellie's wrists, Carl speaks.

"What is it with your mother? She worked nights, right? She might not have known what was happening. But why, once I told her, did she attack me? What kind of mother—what kind of monster?—cares more about the family's reputation than she does about her daughter?"

Suddenly, pushing against his hold on her wrists, Ellie grabs at his shoulders. She yanks him toward her. As he falls forward, she slams her knee upward into his balls. He yowls with pain and his hands fly to his groin. She lifts her leg again and smashes her heel down onto the arch of his foot. He doubles over and sinks to his knees.

Ellie fumbles in her handbag for the newspaper cutting and throws it onto the ground in front of him. Without even a backward glance, she sprints straight down the middle of Hesperus Street, making for home.

CHAPTER 94

"Don't be frightened. Eleanor! Wait!" The howl echoes along Hesperus Street. Carl is following her as fast as he can. It's automatic, like breathing, except that each and every movement sends shock waves through his groin.

He presses his hand to the front of his trousers. There's a shooting pain. He should probably see a doctor, but the Medical Center will be closed by now. Hospital? Should he call an ambulance? What if Eleanor Porter has done some real damage to his down-there?

He leans against a house and watches from a distance as Eleanor Porter pushes her door open and stumbles across the threshold. No longer any point in Carl running. He'll shuffle, one foot in front of the other, like so. No jarring movement.

He puts his ear to the wooden panels of her door. "Eleanor?" he whispers. There's no sound. Strange; she usually turns the telly on the minute she steps in. He tries the doorknob. It's locked, of course. "Eleanor?"

She's there; he knows she is, just inches away on the other side of the door. He runs his hand over the panels. They're warmer in the middle. Is she leaning just there? Is that her body heat seeping through the wood?

"Dead." He breathes the word against the door. "Dead?" Can it really be?

Slowly, he opens his palm with the cutting inside and smooths its aged folds. He fishes in his pocket for a torch and shines its narrow beam on to the faded print. "CROUCH END MAN KILLED," he reads, "WITHIN SIGHT OF HOME." Killed? A car crash. "Thomas Porter, 38, died of head and spinal injuries on Wednesday after the car he was driving collided with a dustcart at the top of Uplands Road. His wife, Annabel Porter, witnessed the crash from the front of their home, and was with her husband before the ambulance arrived. His daughter, age eight, was also nearby. Police said the extent of damage suggested that the car must have been going at top speed."

The local paper is dated November 6, 1981—the very day that Carl had confronted Mrs. Porter. The day he slunk back, defeated, to his home in the Isle of Dogs.

Carl is shocked to the core. He can scarcely believe it. He doesn't want it to be true. He's been waiting all these years to see Tom Porter punished. To bring the bastard to book. To prove to Eleanor Porter that there is justice in the world. His own betrayal of the child who needed his help—no, let's face it, his spinelessness—has eaten him up.

He has longed to make it up to her; to rescue her, at last. Twenty-two years of guilt, twenty-two years committed to seeing Tom Porter punished—and all that time the man was already dead.

Carl throws back his head and lets out a howl. "Dead!" The cry echoes all the way down to the river.

He leans back against Ellie's door once more. Once a failure, always a failure. He should have known better than to hope for redemption. With a sigh, Carl presses his hand to the front of his trousers in an unconscious gesture of protection, and heads off to shuffle around the island one more time.

CHAPTER 95

Once she's inside her home—once she has locked up and stifled the alarm and turned on the lights—Ellie collapses against the door and closes her eyes and drinks in the merciful silence.

Her mind is in turmoil. Hewitt: all these years she's been frightened of him, without even knowing him, without knowing his name. He's been her bogeyman. The one who betrayed her. At first, way back then, when he'd come walking up to her house, with his jaw set and his large hands clenching and unclenching, she hadn't realized how dangerous he was. She'd seen him and her heart had bloomed with hope. She'd imagined for one foolish, foolish moment that he'd tell her mummy and her mummy'd tell her daddy and her daddy would understand, at last, how Ellie felt. He'd stop their "special" times and they'd be a proper family again. But Ellie didn't get her happy ending. Instead, after Carl Hewitt stammered out his speech, he'd staggered backward down the path and out of Ellie's life.

Ellie's heartbeat has just begun to steady when there's a scraping sound at the door. A fingernail scratching at woodwork, uncertain at first but becoming gradually stronger and more assured. She backs away as if the panels of the door are packed with explosives. Then she hears that sandpaper voice. Softly at first. "Eleanor." The voice scrapes across her consciousness like an emery board. "Eleanor."

Hewitt has never gone out of Ellie's life, not really. When she was eight years old, he'd hounded her to break her promise. *Who was it? Who hurt you?* He's been hounding her all her life, trying to force her to go back to that time and that place from which she's tried so hard to escape. She smashes her fist against the door. For God's sake, why did he have to go and remind her! Stirring it all up again when she'd almost succeeded in forgetting. It wasn't, after all, that big a deal. Ellie was very close to her daddy. She loved him. And he loved her, too, and because of that, he needed sometimes to be close to her in a special way. To put things inside her so he could be a part of her.

There's silence. One minute, two minutes, three minutes. She's not heard a peep from him but he's still standing there, pressed against her door; she's sure of that. Or perhaps—she glances quickly around—perhaps he has crept round to the back of the house. Along the top of the garden wall the newly laid shards of glass are supposed to stop that sort of thing, but—Her eyes widen as a sunrise blazes out from the security light beyond the patio doors. He's in the garden now. In a moment, he'll start calling again. *Eleanor. Who did this to you?* Calling, calling, as he's been doing all her life.

Darkness slides in and covers up the pool of light beyond the patio doors. She is alone. Alone—and empty. Will has gone. She's thrown away her job; she's not the night lawyer anymore, not *toute seule* or in any other form. Her relationship with her mother is wretched, based on vanity and lies. And, above all, there used to be a good daddy inside who kept her safe—who laughed and taught her to ride a bike and played farmers with her on the floor. But now, thanks to Carl Hewitt's stubborn insistence on telling, there's nothing inside. Nothing but guilt. Is this what it means to be grown up? To be your own person, not a child, not a victim? Is this all there is?

All those years ago, when Hewitt recoiled from Annabel's words, when he ran away, Ellie wasn't sad. She just felt hopeless, that's all. A profound hopelessness that began in her heart and crept outward until it reached every finger, every toe, every hair on her head. *So*, she thought, with a horrible sense of finality. *So, then, this is what happens when you tell.*

Yes: Ellie stands in the darkened room, with her back pressed to the door, and experiences again that feeling of despair. This is what happens when you tell. Ellie broke her promise and told; her mother despised her and her father died. In her mind, these dreadful truths are close-coupled. They go together like *Jekyll* and *Hyde*. Like *Frankenstein* and *monster*. Like *fe-fi-fo-fum* and *the blood of an Englishman*.

Eleanor hears footsteps on Marsh Street. The security light blazes again. Still watching where the light pierces through, Ellie runs her hand over the plastic domes that once were Odysseus's home, now all washed and cleaned and empty. She's been meaning to take the cage to the charity shop, but she hasn't gotten around to it yet. Maybe tomorrow. It's time to tie up those loose ends. And the day after tomorrow—her grading. Another loose end. She should just give it a go.

Ellie fishes her running gear out of the dryer and changes her clothes. She laces up her trainers. A run. One last run. Before her grading.

CHAPTER 96

Jessica has had a fucking awful week. The interview, it pretty well gutted her. Just a chat, that's what they'd said. A chat! When she got to the College of Fashion, a crowd was gathered there—like, four interviewers, can you believe? Four!—and they began plying her with questions. The questions about her own stuff were okay; she didn't mind those. *Why did she choose felt for the skirt, and not a more fluid fabric? Would anyone really wear a hat like that?* ("I would," she answered. They smiled at that.) It was the general questions that had bothered her. *What is fashion for? Pardon?* What is a question like that supposed to mean?

Jessica could kick herself for applying. It's all very well for Ellie to encourage her to have a go, but Jess is the one who has to take the flak. Felt quite the business when she went in, wearing her new skirt and hat. But by the time she'd been, like, interrogated, she felt like shit. Now she's got nothing to look forward to but another year of debits and credits and set asides.

That was yesterday. Today, the dentist. She hates the dentist, all that poking around in her mouth. And as if that wasn't enough, when she got home the police were waiting. Jessica knows that within the next few hours, she'll bottom out; she'll come over all weedy and depressed. But at this very moment, she's stalking down the footpath near Cubitts Wharf, on the lookout for Tull, and she's fuming.

She emerges at the small spit of land on the end of the island that pushes the river southward. It's late and it's low tide. A stretch of black mud gleams below the shingle. Where the river laps the mud, a swarm of tiny birds are swimming and dipping in the water. Tull is standing there with his elbows resting on the iron railing. He's looking across at the flames that flare alarmingly out of a works chimney near the Dome.

He hears a footstep, but she's on him before he turns.

"You dickhead," she shouts, and slaps him full across the face. "And I trusted you. I convinced myself that deep down under that vicious exterior you were really just a lost little boy. How dumb is that?"

The hem of Tull's coat flaps forward and back in a gust of wind, but the man remains rooted to the spot, his back against the railing, a cigarette stuck to his bottom lip. The smoke curls upward into his eyes. It's as if the slap has turned him into stone.

Jess is ashamed now, even though he bloody well deserves the slap. "Tull?" There's a hoarse shout on the far side of the river and an answering cry. The green laser light from the Royal Observatory slices across the darkening sky. "Tull, are you listening? The police came to see me today about the murder of that tourist who was dumped in the river. They think it's down to you. Want to know where you were on the night he was killed. Whether you come down to the river. Whether I'd ever seen you with a camcorder."

He moves at last. He plucks the cigarette from his lips and pinches the end and tosses it over the railing. He watches as the breeze lifts it and then drops it at the edge of the river. "What'd you say?"

"What do you think I'd say? I told them the truth. They'll find out anyway. The night of the murder was the same night I went to casualty. Remember? You were supposed to meet me, but you didn't show." She shrugs. "About the other things, I lied. But they'll find out soon enough." She hugs her arms across her chest to steady herself. "Did you kill him, Tull? From America, they said he was. An industrial-heritage enthusiast with two little kiddies. Did you kill him? Was it you who dumped his body in the river?"

Tull takes a step toward her. He puts out his arms as if to encircle her, but she shrinks back against the chipped white railing. She's shaking now, with fear as much as anger. Her voice drops to a whisper. "I saw you with that camera." He turns and starts to walk away. Jess screams after him: "Tell me the truth, Tull. You murdered him, didn't you? For a stupid camera!"

He whirls and is on her so quickly that she doesn't have a chance to run. He smashes his hands, and the iron railing judders. "Don't you start that again," he shouts. "It wasn't like that. I was just standing there, farther along the shoreline; you know, where we got drunk that time? Just minding my own business. Talking to someone."

"To Kristoff?"

Tull glares at her. "I told you we had business. He was letting me in on something big. And then this bloody tourist comes tootling along the path—I couldn't believe it, it's nighttime, what's he doing there?—and he's got this bloody night-lens thing. He's filming the river, filming me and Kristoff, as if we were part of the fucking scenery or something."

"So you attacked him?"

"It wasn't my idea. You should have seen Kristoff's face. He's paranoid about having his picture taken. 'Get the film, Tull,' he said, and walked off, just like that. So I stops the tourist and demands the film, but this asshole decides I'm trying to steal his camera and he hangs on like a maniac. And he's shouting, and there's an ugly little dog in that gateway over there, starts yelping and yapping. And that geezer goes on and on, calls me a mugger, a dirty thief, robbing him, he says—and I just lost it."

"You did kill him! And you're trying to say it's not your fault?"

"I didn't plan it like that, Jess. He just got me all wound up. I hit him on the temple and he fell down, but he's still bloody well clutching that camera, so I start kicking him in the head. And then I hear someone coming toward me, and I shout at the geezer to get up, and he's not moving or anything. He's got blood coming out of his ear-hole. I don't know what to do. So I picks him up, heavy he is, too, and threw his top half over the railing, and then I lifted his feet and legs and all of him toppled over. He landed just at the base of the wall," he says, staring at the river. "Just at the edge of the water."

"What about the footsteps? You heard someone coming."

"And," Tull says, as if she hadn't spoken, "then this bloke comes around the corner. I've seen him around. He always wears this naff fleece with a picture on the front. And I just snatched up the camera—couldn't leave it there, could I? It would give the game away—and ran."

The wind is picking up now. Jessica unwinds a cardigan from around her waist and puts it on. There's one more thing she owes him, and then they're done. "Tull?" she says. He's gone all still again. "Tull? You've got no choice now. It looks like this guy, the one who saw you here that night? Looks like he's gone to the police. You've got to give yourself up. Explain how it happened. Tell them that you didn't mean to kill anybody."

Tull rummages in his pockets. He takes out another cigarette and holds it in one cupped hand, shielding it from the breeze. He lights it with a flick of his Zippo. With the other he reaches out and slides his arm around Jessica's waist. He seems suddenly full of fire. "No way, babes," he says. "No way. That's not the life I got planned. I'm getting out of here. Off the island where they can't find me. And you—You're coming with me."

His arm is tight around her, and when he starts off down the path, she is dragged, wriggling, along. She lets out a loud piercing scream that echoes back and forth across the water, and then he hits her, hard, across the side of her head. For a second she can smell something burning as Tull's cigarette melts a strand of her hair, and then she passes out.

CHAPTER 97

One thing about running. Some people say that when they run, they use the time to sort things out in their heads. Not Ellie. Uh-uh. What Ellie likes about running is that once she's in her stride, her mind empties. It goes blissfully blank. She sees what's going on around her. But there's no analyzing, no judging, no anxiety. Mind like water, that's what karate teaches you. Where the surface of a lake is smooth, they say, the water will give off a perfect reflection of the forest in front; so it is with karate, too. When you face an opponent, if your mind is serene—not preoccupied with strategy but simply alert to the signals that the opponent gives off—then your response will be swift and appropriate. When Ellie is sparring, she's usually too tense to adopt the right attitude. But when she's running, mind like water comes to her naturally.

She slides into her front door feeling close to human again. It's late, but she doesn't care. She is standing by the fridge, downing a tall glass of orange juice, when she hears a shriek. Probably kids—she shrugs—horsing around. She is about to layer some peanut butter on a fresh slice of bread, but she stops, knife in hand. Another shriek. Ellie puts the peanut butter away. She walks to the back of the house and unlocks the patio doors. It could be something serious—God knows, it doesn't sound like someone having fun—but she can't tell where it came from. She steps out onto the lawn, bread in hand. She hears a siren in the distance and an engine, maybe the night bus, chugging its way along Westferry Road. And then, not a shriek, but a grunt and a thud, from next door.

"Jessica!"

Ellie tosses her slice of bread into the bushes and, reaching inside the house, she grabs the mat off the floor near the door. She races to the wall and throws the mat on top. She scrambles up the wall, slides stomach-first across the mat, and lands in an untidy heap in the Barneses' garden. She raps her knuckles on the kitchen door. A fresh shriek slices to a finish as if a hand has been clapped over a mouth.

"Jessica!" Ellie puts her shoulder to the door, and shoves. It holds firm. She lifts her foot and sends it crashing down onto the panel. It shudders and holds. The next time, there's a splintering sound. A third time, and it splits.

Ellie tumbles into the house. No screams now. Only labored breathing from upstairs.

When Ellie reaches the bedroom, at first all she sees is the tall figure of Tull, standing at the foot of the bed. His back is to Ellie and his arm is raised. There's something, Jessica's lime green skirt, lying in a heap at his feet.

Then she hears Jessica's moans. The girl is nearly naked, her face buried in the bedclothes.

Tull hears Ellie behind him and swivels to face her. His flies are unzipped, his arm half raised, his neck bulging with rage.

Ellie ignores him and moves toward the bed. All she can think about is Jessica. Tull's fist shoots out and thumps down onto Ellie's breastbone. The punch lifts her clear off the floor. For half a second she is suspended in the air. Then she slams against the doorframe. The molding gouges into her scalp. She's lucky not to knock herself out on the metal doorstop.

Her lungs clamp shut. She has a spasm of choking. Then she takes in air in great gulps like a diver coming to the surface. The first breath sends bolts of agony coursing through her body.

She staggers to her feet.

Tull is stuffing his limp dick back inside his jeans, zipping with one hand, pulling at Jessica's arm with the other.

"Leave her alone!" Ellie's voice is shaky. She reaches him in two unsteady strides and aims a punch at the side of his head.

In a fury, he straightens and turns on her. He's so much taller that she misses, her hand whipping the air. He's moving toward her. He pulls his fist back like a street fighter and aims squarely at her face.

Ellie doesn't wait for the punch to connect. She spins around, and delivers a high kick that slams into his ear. His own movement doubles the force of the blow. He shakes his head slowly like a wounded animal, then straightens and lunges at her. Ellie doesn't flinch. She isn't thinking about Jessica now—she's not thinking about anything—she's watching him. Mind like water. She plants her leg firmly across his path. Tull crashes into it at full speed and flies up and lands face-first against the foot of the wardrobe. He curls up like a fetus, groaning with pain.

"Jessica!" Ellie croaks. She leans over. Jess's face is obscured by wet strands of black hair. "Jess!"

Tull attacks from behind. He grabs a handful of Ellie's hair and twists his fist and tugs her head backward. His other arm snakes around her throat. His forearm presses like a stone on her windpipe. Ellie is wedged against his body. She can feel his chest, his hip bones, the muscles in his thighs. He tightens his grip. She feels his erection returning to life.

Ellie closes her eyes, and what she sees is Sensei demonstrating Gankaku. Crane on a rock, she tells herself. Poised to strike. Ellie stops struggling. She lets herself go limp. She starts to sink to the floor taking all her weight on one leg. Tull loses his grip. He tightens his arm. The pain in her ribs is breathtaking.

Poised to attack.

Tull needs to adjust his position so he can hang on to her slumping form. He releases his grip on her hair and in a split second, Ellie drives her arm up and back. Her elbow smashes into his windpipe with a crunching noise. Tull gags. Slowly, almost delicately, he lets her go. Ellie whirls on her bent leg and cracks the other like a whip, from the hip, up and out, fracturing his nose with the sole of her shoe. She snaps her leg back out of his reach and takes a long step toward him. One arm pumps forward and the other back. The punch lands dead center on his face. Blood gushes over his jaw and flowers across the front of his T-shirt. He falls to his knees.

Ellie whirls around to the figure on the bed. "Jessica. Come with me. Come on!" She senses the ragged rise and fall of the girl's breathing. "We've got to get out of here." She picks Jessica's skirt up off the floor and begins to dress her.

Jessica turns like a woman drugged, and mutters something. As Ellie twists forward to listen, a hand closes round her ankle. She struggles to get her balance, but a sharp tug sends her crashing to the floor. Her head collides with the bedframe.

The room is whirling. She tries to lift herself off the floor, but everything spins faster. She hears a footfall and then—crunch!—a kick that flips her onto her side. She flops back to the ground. Her eyes close and she prays for unconsciousness, for an escape from the pain.

There's a scream. A scuffle. "No, Tull, leave her alone. Don't!"

The kick this time is so effective that the new pain merges in with all the rest. A rib, Ellie thinks. At the least, he's broken a rib. Maybe my spleen. She's surprisingly calm. Surges of color like an Arizona sunset blast through her brain.

The shrieking continues. "Tull, I'll come with you. For God's sake, leave her alone!"

Tull gives one last, halfhearted, kick. He turns away from the woman crumpled on the floor.

By the time he speaks to Jessica, he's a different man. "You all right?" he asks in a tone of bewilderment. Rage has been replaced by compassion and fear and need.

Jessica struggles to a sitting position. She wipes her nose with her sleeve.

Tull strokes Jessica's temple. He places under her chin a finger that is stained with his blood. He tilts the girl's face up and studies the flaring marks across her cheek. His eyes prickle. He hasn't felt like crying since the day Uncle Vince ordered him to leave.

"Baby, baby, that mark on your cheek. I didn't make it, did I?" He kneels down next to the bed and envelops her in a clumsy embrace. "You know I wouldn't never hurt a hair on your head. You know that, don't you, babes?" Tull buries his face in her lap. "Come on, Jess, come on. You gotta tell me that I didn't hurt you."

Jess sits limp and unresisting. "Ellie is my friend."

Tull looks up at her. He tightens his grip on her arm and doesn't even notice when she winces with pain. "She took you away, Jess. Right from the beginning, that's what she was up to. She tried to change you, make you into something you aren't."

On the floor, Ellie draws her legs up to her chest and moans.

Tull shakes Jess's arm and tries again. "Listen babes, what I'm trying to tell you, it's all her fault. If it wasn't for Ellie what's-her-name, we'd be back where we were before. Happy." He rises briskly to his feet. "We're going now." His confidence has returned. In spite of his bleeding nose, he takes a Gauloise from his pocket and flicks open his lighter. "It'll be great, Jess. Just like I said. Without fucking busy-bodies like her—"

The odor of cigarette smoke brings Ellie to her senses. For a few groggy seconds she is a little girl, sitting on her father's lap as he smokes a ciggie. Then Jessica's voice brings her back to the present and pain rushes in again.

"No, Tull, let me go."

Ellie manages to turn over, biting the inside of her mouth to prevent herself crying out.

"Never mind about . . . Jess, just put your coat on; you can change later." He sweeps a pair of jeans off a chair, and pulls a struggling Jessica toward the door. She is straining against him, her feet slipping on the carpet like a dog resisting the lead.

Ellie forces herself up onto her hands and knees. With a mighty effort, she stands. She sways. Mind like water. No longer serene. This time, a destructive force: a raging sea, a flood, a tsunami.

Tull's back is inches away. He is focussed on Jessica and his expression is darkening. He pulls Jess toward him and slaps her hard. Jess screams. Ellie picks up the metal doorstop and with a flick of her wrist brings it down fairly and squarely on the crown of his head.

CHAPTER 98

Ellie is starving. "One, two, three." She arranges the strips of bacon in the pan. There's room for another. "Four." Since she got home from Jess's, she has been so restless that sleep is out of the question. She hasn't even been able to sit still, though she did try, picking up a copy of *English Passengers*—she's always wanted to read it—and putting it down after five minutes to dash to the fridge.

She beats three eggs in a glass bowl and adds a dash of milk and a snipping of tarragon. The aroma of the bacon makes her ravenous. And no wonder. The confrontation with Hewitt; the run, pounding the pavements and pushing herself hard; then the fight with Tull. No wonder she's depleted. In fact, she thinks, as the bacon spits and the eggs firm up and the cherry tomatoes and button mushrooms braise in butter braced with garlic, she's surprised at her own resilience. There's an underlying exhaustion there, but on the surface, she's all go.

Ellie tucks into her impromptu supper with gusto. She corrects herself: impromptu full English breakfast, more like; it is, after all, four in the morning. She is aware that at some level, she is hurting. She hasn't dared to look in the mirror to see what state she's in. There's a dull ache in her back and at various points on her body, where the kicks collided, and not all of the splashes of blood on her T-shirt are Tull's. But she's mobile—no ribs broken after all—and her mind is bouncing about like a kid on a pogo stick. Like a kid on a pogo stick, she suspects, she'll crash at some point. For now, she's riding a wave of adrenaline.

The police took Tull away. To the hospital, first, for an X-ray; she'd hit him pretty hard. She would've hit him harder—would have killed him, most likely—if she'd known then what she found out later: it was Tull who had broken into her house and killed Odysseus, aiming to punish her.

There was little doubt that he'd face charges for the murder of the man from Des Moines, and if found guilty, he'd get a hefty prison sentence. How could he not be found guilty? The police told her that they have an eyewitness, a local man who saw Tull bundling something substantial over the railing. He hadn't come forward earlier because he'd suffered an epileptic attack round about the time of the murder, and it was only later that he put it all together. Then there is Jess's statement about the camera, and Tull's failure to meet her on the evening of the killing. Jess didn't want to press charges of her own. She refused utterly to give police details about the rape. "I'll only testify about the camera," she insisted, "if you agree never to raise the question of rape." Jess seemed to be unexpectedly in control. Ellie is guessing that the girl's relief at having Tull well and truly out of her life is greater than her horror at what he'd done.

Ellie polishes off the last of the bacon. She feels satisfied now, no longer hungry, but her brain is still buzzing. So she undresses and slowly plunges her aching body into a hot bath with half a jar of bath oil tossed in for good measure. She stretches out, chilled glass of vodka and cranberry juice to hand, closes her eyes, and breathes in the lovely, old-fashioned scent of tea roses. Her mind begins, at last, to calm.

The sound of her mobile shatters the moment. Who would ring at four-thirty in the morning? Ellie debates with herself whether to go to the trouble of reaching over and drying her arm on the towel so she can answer, but curiosity—and a vague, residual feeling that something might be wrong—calls the shots.

"You still awake, Ellie?" It's Jess.

"If I wasn't before, I would be now," Ellie says dryly. "What's up? Are you all right?"

"I couldn't sleep. So I did some sketches, and surfed the Web, and then I remembered that I hadn't checked the post. And there, in the middle of tons of junk mail, is a letter from the London College of Fashion. Ellie, you'll never guess what."

"You've got a place on a course?"

"You must be psychic. How in heaven's name did you know? Ellie, what's that noise? I hear water, and—Are you giggling?"

"You hear my bathwater, Jess. And as for psychic powers—with the way you sound on the phone, what could it be other than good news? Your voice is full of sunshine."

"Ellie! I'm so over the moon. I'm in! I'm going to be a designer!"

Ellie runs her hand around until she finds the plug and pulls it out. She raises her voice over the gurgle of the water. "What about your parents, Jess?" she says, reaching for the towel. "What about the accountancy course?"

"No worries. This time I'll make them understand how important it is to me. They'll come round. I know they will."

Jess burbles on for a few minutes, happily. When she finally rings off, Ellie trundles off to bed and falls straight into a deep sleep.

CHAPTER 99

A solid object—Ellie's mobile, as it happens—has become scrunched into a valley in her bedclothes. She rolls over, lands on top of it, and is jolted into a consciousness that seems to come from a million miles away. Heart thudding in her chest, she scans the clock. Eight AM. She's had—at most—four hours sleep. Ellie takes a sip of water, tosses the mobile onto the rug and snuggles into sleep again.

The landline this time, and it seems shockingly loud. Ellie gropes for the receiver. "Hello?"

"Ellie? Thank God, it's you. You've had me worried. I must have left a dozen messages on your mobile. I finally got Marie to give me this number."

"Jonathan? I've been asleep. My mobile's turned off. What time is it?" She sits up and winces at the stiffness in her muscles. She avoided checking her injuries last night, but the fight with Tull has left a legacy of aches.

"It's nine AM. Where on earth have you been? What've you been doing?"

"What do you think I've been doing? Honestly, Jonathan! I've been sleeping. It's what I do most nights." Her ribs hurts. The physical discomfort makes her more irritable than she meant to be.

"All right, sorry. I guess I shouldn't have bothered you. I only wanted to wish you the best of luck today. I hope it goes well."

"Best of luck?" Ellie's upright now, trying to ease her way into her dressing gown without knocking the phone off its perch. "Jonathan, what are you talking about?"

"I'm talking about karate. Your grading for brown belt. It is today, isn't it? Saturday, June the seventh, that's what you told me."

"The seventh of June. That's right, Jonathan. Tomorrow."

"Not tomorrow, Ellie. Today."

Ellie dives for the alarm clock. The dial lights up with a sickly green glow. "Oh, my God, it's Saturday. I must have slept for twenty-four hours!"

Suddenly, Ellie is wide awake. "Sorry, Jonathan. Got to go."

She's gathered up her soiled uniform and is scribbling a list of all the things that have to be done when there's a sharp *tip tap* on the front door.

"Ellie, darling, are you in there?"

It's her mother. Reluctantly, Ellie opens the door.

Annabel Porter stands on the pavement with her handbag held demurely in front of her, and smiles as if impromptu visits were routine. "Well? Aren't you going to ask me in? I'm up early," she continues, waving Ellie aside, "because I have to trek into the West End to have my hair colored. But I thought, as it's on my way, we could have a nice little chat." She glances at Ellie, who is stuffing her gi into the washing machine. "What's the matter with you, anyway?"

"Sorry, Mummy, but I've rather a lot to do this morning. It's my grading at one o'clock, you see, and I overslept. I have to practice my kata and I haven't even had breakfast yet."

"That's all right, dear. You go right ahead with your breakfast. I'll just have a cup of tea. But first, don't I even get a kiss?"

Ellie shuts the washing machine door, touches her lips to Annabel's cheek, and quickly turns away. She switches on the kettle.

"Ellie?" Annabel's voice is suddenly more tentative. "Ellie, what have you done to your head?"

In her exhaustion last evening—correction, the evening before—Ellie threw herself into the bath but couldn't be bothered to wash her hair. She avoided looking at herself in the mirror, avoided checking the damage. Now she wishes that she had.

Annabel's fingers tease their way through her daughter's hair. She finds a crust of blood on the scalp. "What's this?" She is gentle. Ellie is reminded that her mother was a nurse.

Desperately, Ellie sets to work chopping up an apple for her muesli. "It's nothing. A scratch, that's all."

"Nothing? That's a sizable wound for nothing." Annabel lifts Ellie's hair off her neck. "And you've got a huge bruise just here, behind your ear." She notices for the first time the lump on Ellie's temple, the abrasion on her leg. She reaches for the opening of Ellie's dressing gown, but Ellie moves quickly out of reach.

"No!"

Annabel's gaze sweeps Ellie's hair, her face, her features, as if she's seeing her daughter for the first time. "For the love of God, Ellie, what have you been doing?"

"I don't want to talk about it, Mummy. It's not karate, if that's what you think." She stands stiff and unyielding as Annabel tries to hug her. She knows her mother means well, but she can't help herself; her mother's embrace feels like a straitjacket. "There's nothing to worry about."

Annabel makes one final try. "Darling, why don't you just let me clean up your scalp and that wound on your leg? You can't go to your grading like that. It might start bleeding again. You might get an infection."

"No!" *No motherly gestures, thank you. It's a little late for that.* "I just need to get on, Mother. Time is ticking away."

"You're sure you're all right, then?"

"Perfectly," Ellie mumbles, setting a bottle of skimmed milk and two teaspoons on the table.

"Only I wanted to ask you for a bit of a favor, darling." Annabel takes off her jacket and folds it neatly over the back of a chair. She starts to sit but changes her mind. She takes a jug from one of the kitchen cabinets, transfers the milk into the jug, and finally sits down, talking all the while. "Lindsay—you know, Marcus's wife—says that Gavin, their son, you know, the one who's at Dulwich College, is interested in reading journalism at university." Daintily, she dusts a few crumbs off the table. "Anyway, she and Marcus think it would be a good idea if Gavin were to work at a newspaper for part of the summer. You know, for the experience. Would look good on his UCAS application, don't you think?"

Ellie's head is occupied. She should be thinking about the grading, but memories of the recent past keep getting in the way.

"Ellie? I'm asking you a question. For heaven's sake, say something. Gavin should get some newspaper experience, don't you agree?"

The kettle boils. Ellie adds tea bags and boiling water to two mugs and sets them on the table. Annabel looks suspiciously at the darkening fluid.

Ellie seats herself. "Mother?"

Annabel dangles a tea bag in front of her. "What am I supposed to do with this?"

"Mother, that man who was following me. That stalker. I knew him when I was a child. I knew him, Mother. And so did you."

"Stalker?" Annabel rises from the table and plops her tea bag in the sink.

"His name, Mother, is Carl Hewitt."

Annabel takes a noisy sip and sets her tea down again. "No, Ellie. Randall. Gavin Randall. Marcus and Lindsay's eldest boy." Annabel puts on a seductive smile. "What I thought was, if you would have a word with your boss—Clive, isn't it?—you could ask him to find a place for Gavin. Just for a fortnight. Just long enough so that Gavin can—"

"I can't speak for anyone. I haven't been in to work in days, Mother. I've sent Clive a letter of resignation. I'm not a night lawyer anymore."

"You what? But, Ellie, you're doing so well, you're a great success in this new job, you . . ." Ellie suddenly rises. Annabel stops speaking and stares.

"Carl Hewitt, Mother. He lived next door to us in Crouch End. You must remember."

Annabel stirs her tea noisily. The spoon clinks against the side of the mug.

"Oh, yes, you do, Mother. This Hewitt—he was a young man then, just a teenager, really—befriended me. He persuaded me to tell him a secret that I had never before told anyone else. Then he came to our house and told you the secret, too. He told you that Daddy—"

Annabel squeezes her eyes shut. Ellie notices, for the first time, the fans of fine lines that frame her eyes. "That's enough!" Annabel shouts, clamping her palms over her ears. "Stop this nonsense. You're being hysterical again, Ellie. You're making something out of nothing."

"Not nothing, Mother. It was only too real. Do you want me to tell you what he did? All the details?" A sharp pain skewers Ellie and she presses her hands to her belly. Oh, God; she'd forgotten how much it hurt. "For God's sake, Mother, I was only eight years old.

You should've protected me. But you—you—didn't want to know. You didn't care."

Annabel shoots to her feet. The kitchen chair teeters for a moment and then crashes to the floor. "Didn't care!" she cries. "I loved you more than anything else in the world. I would have done anything for you. Anything! But you didn't tell me. Why on earth did you tell that horrible boy and not me?"

Now Ellie's tears come, sheeting down her cheeks. She stumbles to the sink, groping for the tea towel. Annabel is there, placing the cloth in her hand, stroking her cheek, taking the tears onto her own fingers. Ellie shakes her mother off.

"Don't you understand, Mother? If you had cared, if you'd stood up for me, then maybe everything would have been all right. But you didn't, and so Daddy had to die, because of me."

Ellie stands rigid as her mother's arms encircle her. She hasn't been held like this since—well, she can't remember when. She is overwhelmed by a scent, light and citrusy and vaguely familiar, but try as she might, she can't place it. How strange, Ellie thinks. For the first time ever, I am talking to my mother about the most important event in my life, and all I can think about is her perfume.

Annabel gentles Ellie into a chair. She crouches beside her. "He didn't die because of you, darling. He died because he'd hurt you. And because he was planning to hurt you again."

"Mother, what are you talking about?"

"Carl Hewitt. Yes, I do remember Hewitt," Annabel says. She clears her throat and half a minute passes in silence before she continues. "Do you know, even before he spoke, I had a premonition of disaster. A trickle of ice down my spine. People who were in London during the war describe that horrible moment of silence before a doodlebug landed—you know?—and that's what it was like. And then he told me those terrible things." She rises from her crouching position, slowly, painfully, like an old woman. "He might as well have plunged a knife into me. The thought that Tom—my husband—might have harmed you in that way—"

"So you chose not to believe Hewitt. You assumed that I'd lied."

"Not to believe him?"

"You were furious with him for revealing the truth. You threatened to blame everything on him. That's why he gave up. That's why he slunk away."

"No, no, you don't understand, Eleanor. I had to shut him up. I had to have time to think. To decide what to do. So I got rid of him any way I could and then I rushed upstairs and—"

"And?"

"And there was your father. He walked out of the bedroom, demanding a clean shirt, just as if nothing had happened. I screamed at him: "How could you hurt Ellie? How could you do such a thing?" Didn't believe him? No, you're wrong there. The worst thing of all was that I knew it was true. As soon as that Hewitt boy said he had something to tell me, I knew it was true, even before he spoke."

"You mean that you'd known all along—?"

"No, not known. There'd been signs, intimations, that's all; I could have tried to make sense of them, but I'd swept them aside. So when Hewitt forced me to face up to the truth, I was ashamed of myself for having tried to wish it away."

"What did he say?"

"Your father? 'Crazy,' he said. The boy next door was crazy. I was crazy. He'd never hurt you, that's what he said. So I asked him why he'd given you Mr. Tinkle without even a mention of the gift to me, and do you know what he did then? There was a long, calculating pause and then he said, 'Pardon?' It was all there in that *Pardon?* I knew for certain then that he had lied."

Annabel lowers herself into a chair. She looks older, somehow, her shoulders more stooped and her face less crisp. "He may have gone a bit far with you, he said, but he hadn't really hurt you. It was a mistake. A once-only mistake. It would never happen again. He told me that he loved me, that I was his girl, that this would never have occurred if we hadn't been so distant and unhappy over the past year. He insisted that he and I could make a go of it. He swore up and down that he wouldn't touch you again."

"You believed him?"

"No. But I wanted to. And, you see, darling, I hated myself for that, too."

"*You* hated yourself, Mother? How do you think I felt? If I hadn't let the truth slip to Carl Hewitt, Daddy wouldn't have raced out of the house like that. He wouldn't have driven off at top speed. He wouldn't have died."

"Stop it, Ellie." Annabel picks up her mug and drinks down the tepid tea in one long draft, like a woman who is parched. She slams the mug back onto the table. "You're not responsible for your father's death. When he died—well, you must remember. He and I had been arguing for hours. It felt like forever. He made one last attempt to win me over and when I told him that I could never trust him, he became indignant. All right, he said, if that's how I felt, he'd be off. What I hadn't been expecting was that he went straight for you. You were hiding under the kitchen table, and he picked you up and carried you to the front of the house. But he stopped to put his jacket on. You stood there next to him like a little statue, utterly terrified, and I grabbed you and refused to let you go. In a fury, he snatched up his keys and marched out to the car. I called to him—we both called to him—but he didn't look back, not once. He just climbed into the car and started up the engine and shot away up the hill. The car seemed to be gaining speed when the dustcart came lumbering round the corner." Annabel pauses. "Do you remember this?"

"The impact was like an explosion," Ellie says. "It seemed to shake the whole street. You set me down by our gate and told me to stay and you ran to the top of the hill."

"Tom was lying in the narrow strip of road between the parked cars. He'd been thrown through the windscreen. Everything about him looked twisted and smashed, and blood was oozing from his mouth. One of the dustbin men was injured, too. The other dashed off to ring for an ambulance. Tom tried to say something. I knelt down next to him and cushioned his head in my lap. I couldn't bear to see him like that, all broken. 'Tom,' I whispered. 'Tom, whatever you've done, I love you.' He opened his eyes and stared at me, and then suddenly his voice was clear and he said—"

Ellie can hardly breathe. "What? What did my father say?"

"'Ellie,' he said. 'Ellie belongs to me.'"

"How could he have said that? I arrived on the scene within minutes," Ellie says, "and his eyes were blank when I got there. He was—I'm certain he was—already dead. And it was all because of me."

Annabel reaches out and twines a strand of Ellie's hair around her finger. "New penny hair," she says. "So lovely." She takes Ellie's hands in her own. "He was going to carry on hurting you, darling. I couldn't let that happen."

"Mother, what are you saying? I don't understand."

"I worked as a nurse, Ellie. I was strong. I didn't even think about it. It was our only chance. I wrapped both arms around his head and I used my upper body. I twisted. There was a dreadful crunching sound, that was all and then it was over."

"Oh, my God, Mother. You killed him. But if that's what happened, why, oh why, did you blame me for his death?"

"What do you mean, blame you?" There's puzzlement in Annabel's eyes.

"I can remember your precise tone, the expression on your face. You accused me of killing him. I came running up the hill, and you lifted your head, and you looked at me and you flung it out: '*Oh, God,*' you said. '*What have you done?*' "

Suddenly, the penny drops. "Do you mean to tell me, Mother . . ."

Annabel bows her head. "Yes, Ellie. That's right. I was in anguish. I hardly knew you were there. When I cried out '*What have you done?*' my pet, I was referring to myself."

CHAPTER 100

Ellie sits in silence after Annabel's extraordinary revelation. Trying to absorb it. Trying to recalibrate her life to match the pattern of the new information.

Annabel, however, is far from subdued. She begins to talk, her words hurried and headlong, as if a gag has been ripped away, telling Ellie things that Ellie has never heard before. About the honeymoon. About Tom Porter's brooding silences. About the mysterious gaps in his account of his early life. These things have been closeted away in the back of Annabel's mind for twenty-two years; she's never discussed them with anyone, least of all Ellie, before.

Ellie doesn't want to hear. She sits with her elbows on the table, and her head in her hands. There is a ceaseless noise inside her mind, halfway between a rackety clamor and a keening wail, that blanks out every other sound.

Ellie can't hear, but she's not stopped thinking. She's thinking about what her mother has told her. Thinking about how her mother twisted her father's neck as he lay helpless. She snapped his spinal cord. Murdered him in cold blood. Ellie can hardly bear to think about it. She doesn't even know whether to believe it, or at least she didn't know at first; it seemed so fantastical. But as her mother's words spilled out, faster and faster, one memory chasing another, Ellie could finally tell from the relief on Annabel's face that every word of it was true.

She's thinking also about the wasted years. All those years when she thought her father's death was down to her. All those years, when her mother knew the truth. Could have told her. Could have set her free.

Loose ends. Ellie rises from the table and busies herself with preparations for the grading. Annabel chatters on. Ellie transfers her gi from the washer to the dryer. She scrubs at a spot of grease on her belt. *Out, out damned spot.* She searches for clean white knickers and a bra. She has a cursory shower and brushes her teeth. She dresses.

When she returns to the kitchen table, Annabel has stopped talking at last. Her mother is sitting quietly, eyeing her. "You're going to the grading?" she says.

Ellie nods. "Yes. I'm going. I may fail—quite likely will, and I'll deserve it, too, for neglecting my training. But I'll have a go."

"Are you sure you're up to it?"

Ellie reaches out and touches the empty plastic dome of Odysseus's cage. It feels cold and slightly greasy. "Not sure," she says, shrugging. "But nothing happens if you don't try, does it? Anyway, the important thing is, I'm a grown-up now. I was a child way back then, and my choices were impossible, not choices at all. But I'm not a child any longer. I'm not a victim." Not guilty, either, she thinks. And my mother—

Ellie sets the meager contents of her first aid box down on the table in front of Annabel. "Will you clean my scalp wound?" she says.

Annabel parts the hair and has a closer look. "It's likely to hurt. Can you bear it?"

"You're a nurse," Ellie says. "I'm certain you can make it better if you try."

CHAPTER 101

There's only—what?—only an hour left to get to the grading after her mother finally leaves. Ellie opens the front door just as the cab throbs into the street. She swings her gym bag inside, clambers in after it, and collapses, eyes closed, against the leather seats. She opens them seconds later to a clean but faded interior that smells faintly of citrus, like her mother.

"Where you wanna go?" the driver asks. He checks her out in the rearview mirror and turns up the volume on his CD player. "Canary Wharf?" The music is Arabic, Turkish maybe, and he clicks the fingers of his left hand in time to the rhythm.

"Stratford. The big leisure center there," Ellie says, handing him a sheet of paper with a blurry map printed on. "You know it?"

The driver shrugs. "Ya ya," he says, waving aside the map and returning to his clicking.

As Ellie enters the low-ceilinged lobby of the leisure center, she can feel the beginnings of a headache. Fluorescent lights that flicker and spit. Carpet tiles grubby with the dirt from summer sandals. An odor of frying onions. It's all too hideously familiar, all too reminiscent of other gradings, other anxious times. She doesn't linger in the changing room, where the air is hot and bright with tension. Her stomach already has more knots than a fisherman's net, and the presence of a dozen anxious candidates—their awkward conversation, their inappropriate laughter, the general air of hysteria—doesn't help. The headache builds. The butterflies swarm. Ellie gets out as quickly as she can.

She threads her way down the corridor to the caf. Should she—could she?—eat something? Could she keep a glass of juice down? She sees Tony Mannix chatting to a couple of black belts over a toasted sandwich. He catches sight of her and waves her over, but the angle of his arm leads her gaze to something behind him. It's a man. It's Carl Hewitt, who turns at that moment and looks directly at her. He wants something. She can tell. She can almost hear him calling—*Eleanor!*—as he did outside her door the other evening, as he has been calling all her life.

Ellie spins on her heel and heads back down the corridor. All the feelings of helplessness sweep over her again. What's he doing here? What does he want from her? What *more* does he want?

"Ellie?" Vikesh appears at her shoulder. "The grading starts soon," he says. "Where are you going?"

"I need a few minutes, Vik. Just a little time on my own. I'll be back, I promise."

There's a swimming pool adjoining the leisure center. Inside, at the top of the spectactors' section, it's quiet and shadowy. The screams of the Saturday children splashing in the wave pool seem a long way off. Ellie hooks her bare heels over the edge of the bench and rests her chin on her knees.

She can't go back in there, not now. Not with Hewitt around. Whatever made her think she could? She's always been weak. She let her father use her. Didn't stand up to him. Was afraid to challenge him, afraid of losing his love.

She was the ideal prey for someone like Will. Compliant. Needy. No sense of self-worth. And no wonder he rejected her in the end. She's pathetic.

Hewitt's presence reminds her of all this, but she can see now that her child's-eye view of Hewitt was wrong. Hewitt acted like a coward; he didn't follow through on his intention to help her. But he had meant well. And he was only a teenager himself. How many people—how many adults—would have the courage to intervene in a situation like that? He tried. He failed. But he doesn't deserve her contempt.

And Hewitt isn't to blame for her predicament now. For all previous gradings, Ellie trained herself into the ground. She dedicated herself to karate. Not this time. This time, she has been drinking too much, eating too freely, training too little. Carl Hewitt reminds her of her own helplessness, her own victimhood. But she hasn't got a hope in hell of passing this grading, and it won't be Carl Hewitt's fault, it will be her own.

A cry reaches out from the swimming pool. Ellie raises her head and sees a knot of children sitting on a float. A child has just tumbled off. A shivering little body, armbands around the thin arms, struggles out of the pool, the slump of her shoulders showing that she's weeping. Before she's reached the top step, a man appears and scoops her up and swaddles her in a towel. Ellie sits up to watch as the father strides off toward the kiosk with the little girl in his arms. She's left with an image of Hewitt, a younger Hewitt, staring solemnly at Mr. Tinkle and with a thought so simple that it is almost shocking.

Mr. Tinkle belonged to a little girl a long time ago, but Ellie Porter is not that girl. Ellie Porter is not the child her father misused. Not even the woman Will abandoned—not any longer. Ellie Porter is the woman who confronted Carl Hewitt. The woman who rescued Jessica Barnes. Ellie Porter didn't down that thug, Tull, with a great deal of style, but she did it decisively. *Toute seule*, Ellie laughs, and clambers up onto the bench.

Tekki Shodan, she urges. *Come on, Ellie, come on: run through the kata in your head*. But her mind flips back again to those astonishing slow movements in Gankaku. She watches the flickering shadows from the pool playing on the ceiling, and imagines herself sinking slowly on one leg, and hooking her left foot behind the other knee. Making a perfect snap kick to the side. Changing direction, giving a spirit shout precisely on target. She shouts *"KIAI"* aloud, and doesn't even mind when the echo bounces off the walls and swimmers turn to stare.

Ready, she thinks, and strides toward the leisure center. As she goes, she dabs the sweat from her forehead with a spit-dampened tissue. She ties her hair back and smooths her uniform. She moves down the corridor in a mimicry of confidence so convincing that she almost believes in it herself.

She steps onto the shiny wooden floor of the massive dojo. Candidates are milling about; the youngest candidates are staging mock fights, and the more mature are fiddling with their uniforms, or pacing the perimeter of the room. Black belts in club blazers and flannels come and go, arranging tables for the examiners and grouping candidates. High up on the end wall, the spectators' gallery is filling up with supporters who've come to watch the display.

Ellie allows herself a glance at the table where the crisp new brown belts have been laid out. Wearing the brown belt shows that you have what it takes to be an expert. That's why the grading is so rigorous. Why the corridor today is filled with anxious fathers putting their sons and daughters through their paces. Why the examiners will not hesitate to turn down any candidate who does not have superlative technique, self-control, and confidence in action. For a moment, Ellie allows herself the fantasy of what it might feel like to loop one of the long humus-colored coils around her waist. Then Fukuyama Sensei— the sixth dan black belt who will lead the examination—arrives. There is a signal, and Ellie moves across the dojo and takes up her position on the floor, sitting cross-legged among a line of candidates near the perimeter wall. Within seconds, the line is complete, and another row forms in front. *No turning back.*

She hears a voice she recognizes. Striker is moving down the rows, collecting a license from each candidate in turn. She rises to her feet and stands with eyes cast down. "Good luck," he says in an undertone. *"Uss,"* Ellie replies. "I'll do my best." There's a pause. Striker seems to be waiting for something. He reaches out as if he's going to straighten her jacket, and then snatches his hand back. Ellie looks up and flashes him a kindly smile, before he turns away and marches on.

Much of the grading goes by in a blur. The warm up: the incredible relief of moving at last, of circling her arms and pumping her legs and flexing her hips. *All grown up now, Ellie,* she chants under her breath. The examination of the basics: there's a hitch here as the order comes to perform Ushiro Geri and her mind goes blank. The Japanese words mean nothing to her. Two seconds of sheer panic and then suddenly, miraculously, she has it—*Not a child anymore*—and she turns through 180 degrees and lifts her right leg and kicks back hard from the hip. Then, the group kumite. Ellie and others approach the examiners' table. The air is a tumult of fists and feet as they punch and block and kick at high speed, without an instant to think between moves. For the first time in this grading, Ellie's not nervous. She's excited. She's focused. It's the way she should be.

A pause that's taut with strain and ragged breathing chasing through the room as candidates brace themselves for the examination of individual pairs. Ellie searches the acne-scarred planes of Fukuyama Sensei's face to get a measure of his mood. Will he be generous in his judgments? Or will he sense, will he know, that she's flying by the seat of her pants? Grading, the masters say, is not about achievement, it's about character. Will Fukuyama Sensei see the empty place in Ellie where there should be determination, self-control, and concentration? *Oh, if only she'd practiced more. If only William De-Quoyne hadn't distracted and confused her. If only she hadn't let Carl Hewitt get in the way.*

It's the part of the examination that Ellie's been dreading. She's desperate to get it over with, but Ellie and her opponent are placed near the end of the line. They'll have to wait. The first pair are put through their paces. They run into trouble. The instructor makes them do it again—and again—while the clock on the far wall ticks off the minutes. Time crawls as one pair is examined, and another and another. Ellie's jaw is sore from being clenched. She tries to swallow, but her mouth is painfully dry. Her lower back begins to ache. If she doesn't relax, her joints will stiffen and she won't be able to fight at all. To distract herself, she conjures up the cottage on the downs where her grandmother used to live. The springy turf and the smell of grasses. The flames from the fire licking the bottom of her wineglass and Jonathan, laughing.

Then comes the signal. Her turn at last. Ellie faces her opponent and exchanges bows. He is not much bigger than her; but there's something swaggeringly assertive about the way he moves. Ellie presses back an uprising of panic. She readies herself. She stands in Yoi position, her feet turned inward like those of a pigeon, poised to leap to either side to avoid a blow. Her fists are positioned to protect her groin. At the command—Kihon Ippon—a swell of adrenaline sweeps her into the kumite. Her opponent attacks with a right-hand punch to the face. Ellie steps back sharply and throws her weight onto her back leg. She knocks his punch out of the way with the side of her left hand before striking knife hand to the neck with her right.

Her opponent parts his teeth, and Ellie can see the hint of a sneer. His lips move. There's no sound, but she can catch the meaning. *Not a chance, bitch.* Ellie tries to escape from his confrontational stare. Her gaze slides to the spectators' gallery where Carl Hewitt is pushing to the front. Leaning his forearms on the rail. Staring at her. Will he never stop calling? Will he never go away?

The punch is on her before she sees it. She intercepts the blow before it reaches her head, but she loses her balance and goes rigid with alarm. *She's screwing up!* Somehow, it is exactly what she expects. It's what she deserves. To be beaten. To fail.

No! It's over! Ellie's heart is thundering in her chest. *Carl Hewitt is nothing to her now. She's not a child anymore. All grown up now.* She has to say it twice—muttering, so that her opponent scowls with confusion—before it takes root. *All grown up now. Not a child. Not a victim anymore. Not, for God's sake, guilty.* She glances again at the gallery, and in that flick of an instant before her eyes lock on to her opponent, Hewitt turns and retreats, pushing his way back out of the crowd.

Suddenly her head clears. All she sees is her adversary, his lip curled. Her mind empties of everything but the minute tightening of a muscle in his thigh, the barely perceptible lifting of his hip. Mind like water. This time, she's ready. This time Carl Hewitt stays where he should be, completely outside her train of thought.

Her opponent throws another punch, twisting his wrist so the knuckles are uppermost at the point of impact. Ellie steps back. She deflects his blow with an upper-rising block, then delivers a powerful roundhouse kick—Mawashi Geri—just as she'd imagined herself doing at the swimming pool. *No chance, eh?* She sees his face tighten in astonishment as she follows with a raking bottom fist punch to the stomach. Ellie—*not a child, not a victim*—laughs, and holds his arm to drag him into the punch.

Not guilty anymore.

CHAPTER 102

The grading kata comes after the kumite, and Ellie finds it a breeze. She's struggled her way to the top of the rise. This is the exhilarating downhill ride. *All grown up,* Ellie sings to herself, as she draws her right arm up to form a high block. *Not a victim,* she chants. She sweeps the left foot up to the right thigh and then drives around with the right arm. She pulls her fists back to the hip, punches hard out to the right, draws her feet together and returns to Yoi.

Fukuyama Sensei makes them do the kata again, but he is pleased with their performance. "Good level," he says, when they're gathered together after the examination. "Keep up with your training." They bow—"*Uss*"—and there are smiles of relief all round. For Ellie, the best moment by far is when she draws her new brown belt from its cellophane package and coils it round her waist. She tries to look cool and unconcerned, but her elation must show in her features. Even a whispered "Ellie" from the gallery doesn't faze her; calmly, she raises her head, prepared to outstare Carl Hewitt if need be, prepared to show by her manner how little he concerns her now. But instead of Hewitt, she sees Vikesh, his thumbs up in a gesture of triumph, and behind him the blue eyes and big smile of Jonathan Roberts.

Jonathan is waiting outside the changing room. He reaches for her gym bag. "Tell me, is the belt in here?"

Ellie nods. "What did you think of the grading?"

"Not bad," he says, "for a night lawyer." He takes her arm and begins to steer her along the corridor.

Oh. Ellie stops. "Jonathan, I'm sorry. I haven't had a chance to tell you."

"Tell me what?"

"Only, I sent a letter to Clive a couple of days ago. A letter of resignation, you know. I've quit. I don't work for the *Chronicle* anymore." As she says this, Ellie is cooling, cooling, her sense of triumph seeping away. She used the grading as a reason for not thinking about the future. Now that she's won her brown belt, she's going to have to confront the mess that is her life.

"Oh, is that all?" Jonathan begins walking again, circling past groups of kids who are roughhousing outside the caf.

"All?" Ellie is indignant. "It's my job, Jonathan. Not much, I grant you, but the closest I come to a career. Not to mention my only source of income. I've got nothing now."

"On the contrary, Miss Porter. You've got a brown belt. Oh, and you've got a message from Clive. He said to tell you that there've been problems with postal deliveries during the last few days. He said to tell you that he never got your letter."

"Clive said—?"

"Precisely. You're the night lawyer, Miss Porter. *Toute seule*. That's what he said."

And there—right there in the shabby, fried-onion-smelling foyer— Ellie is suddenly caught by the sound of a buoyant melody coming through the sound system, and she can't resist. She rises up on her toes and begins to sway. She takes three light steps past the reception desk, quite oblivious of the astonished looks from passersby. She twirls round, with her arms outstretched, until Jonathan joins in, and they dance all the way to the parking lot.

CHAPTER 103

Carl Hewitt is furious by the time he arrives at the leisure center in Stratford. He should have been here for the start of the grading. He wanted to see it all. Wanted to see how Eleanor Porter would perform. Whether she had enough guts, and enough sense of herself, to make it to brown belt. Carl knows how much it takes to get that far. If she could do that, maybe he could rest a little easier about her. Maybe he could conclude that she was a stronger person, a more to-gether person, than her damaged childhood might suggest. He hopes so. He really hopes so, for her sake. And for his own. If Eleanor

Porter can make it to brown belt, then maybe Carl Hewitt doesn't have to feel quite so much like a shit.

The gallery is packed with spectators. They're crowded along the railing, where the clearest view is to be had. Carl's not going to miss this. He threads his way through the spectators, and takes his place at the railing as the crowd closes in again behind. He scans the roomful of candidates and picks Ellie out straightaway.

He's just in the nick of time. The grading of the kumite is underway and Eleanor and her opponent are up next. She starts well, her stance correct, her movements sharp and clean. She's good, he decides, with a curious kind of pride. Then something happens. There's a showdown of some kind—a staring match—and she lets her attention wander. Her gaze sweeps over the spectators' gallery. She sees him. She freezes. She almost takes a punch to the head.

Carl's mobile begins to beep. He fishes it out of his pocket, trying to keep his eye on the grading at the same time. There's a message from Denise. *Carlie, come home ASAP. Can't wait to see you.* She doesn't say what it's about.

Two or three seconds longer—just long enough for Eleanor Porter to recover her concentration again—and Carl turns and tunnels his way back through the crowd. An old thrill runs through him, the kind he used to get from Denise's phone calls early on in their marriage; but then he suppresses the tempting thought. Not a chance. Denise doesn't want him. How could she—how could anybody—want a hopeless coward like Carl?

Cars are parked along the verge on Kingfield Street by the time Carl arrives home. He bends over to retrieve the key from under the bush, and the pain in his groin is barely noticeable. No permanent damage, then. That's one thing that's gone right. Inside the house he stops short. Another mini-meet. He can see them through the arched doorway to the sitting room. He can hear their twitterings, their laughter, the soft to and fro of their conversation. He can see Stephanie, and Mrs. Padfield, and a lady with crutches, crowded up together on the sofa opposite the door.

He can't take this, not now. Not today. He turns to beat a retreat, fumbling for the doorknob, but before he even opens the door, Denise is on him.

"Carlie! Where do you think you're going?" She tugs at his arm. He pulls back. He hasn't taken his shoes off yet. "Never mind that, sweets," she says. "The girls are dying to welcome the hero. I haven't said a thing. They want to hear all about it from the horse's mouth. From you!"

Carl stands gawping at Denise. Hero? Him?

"Oh, Carlie. Have you forgotten? That awful man. That killer. Kevin Tull, they say his name is. You saw him with the tourist's camera, and you notified the police. Well, it was on the local news. They've arrested him. And it's all down to you. You're a real hero, Carl!"

They take a step through the arched entrance, Denise leading Carl by the hand, and as they move forward, there's a cheer and all the girls put their mugs down and begin to clap. "Bringing law and order to the Isle of Dogs!" one of them calls out, playfully. "Will there be a reward?" asks another. "Come on, Carl, tell us all about it."

But Carl doesn't hear their comments, because Denise has put her soft plump arms around him and kissed him with an eager loving kiss the way she used to. "Aniseed balls," she whispers in his ear, and Carl forgets the ache in his groin, and his failure with Eleanor Porter, and he throws back his head and laughs.

ABOUT THE AUTHOR

MICHELLE SPRING abandoned her career as a social scientist and adopted crime writing after becoming the target of a stalker. Her first novel, *Every Breath You Take,* marked the debut of private investigator Laura Principal and was nominated for both an Anthony Award and an Arthur Ellis Award. Spring's subsequent novels include *Running for Shelter, Standing in the Shadows* (another Arthur Ellis Award nominee), *Nights in White Satin,* and *In the Midnight Hour* (which won the Arthur Ellis Award as Best Crime Novel of the Year). Spring is currently a Royal Literary Fund Fellow at Newnham College, Cambridge, where she holds writing tutorials with undergraduate and postgraduate students. She lives in Cambridge, England. Visit Michelle Spring's website at www.unusualsuspects.co.uk.

ABOUT THE TYPE

This book was set in Sabon, a typeface designed by the well-known German typographer Jan Tschichold (1902–74). Sabon's design is based upon the original letter forms of Claude Garamond and was created specifically to be used for three sources: foundry type for hand composition, Linotype, and Monotype. Tschichold named his typeface for the famous Frankfurt typefounder Jacques Sabon, who died in 1580.